THE DEVIL'S ADVOCATE

MORRIS WEST was born in Australia, where he served a six-year novitiate with the Christian Brothers but left before taking his final vows. He became a teacher and joined the army in 1940. After the war he moved to Europe, where he now lives with his family, and began writing: his sixteen books have been translated into twenty-seven languages. His most recent novel is *Proteus*.

Morris West has always been renowned for the authenticity of his facts and settings, whether connected with diplomacy, religion, international business or science, and each of his books was written after extensive travel and research in countries throughout the world.

MORRIS WEST

The Devil's Advocate

FONTANA BOOKS
by agreement with
HEINEMANN

First published in Great Britain in 1959
by William Heinemann Ltd
First published in Fontana Books 1977
Seventh Impression August 1983

© by Morris L. West 1962

Made and printed in Great Britain by
William Collins Sons & Co. Ltd, Glasgow

Of the inspiration for The Devil's Advocate, *Morris West records:*

It was my literary agent, Paul Reynolds, who first gave me the idea for *The Devil's Advocate*. The title had always interested him—the office and the function represented a startling paradox: the application of human legality and the rules of evidence to the intervention of God in the affairs of men. Somewhere, he told me, there must be a book in it.

For me, the impact of the thought was immediate. It brought into dramatic focus a whole complex of ideas which had troubled me since my life in Naples had first revealed to me the contrast between the human and the divine elements in Christian beliefs.

CHAPTER ONE

IT WAS his profession to prepare other men for death; it shocked him to be so unready for his own.

He was a reasonable man and reason told him that a man's death sentence is written on his palm the day he is born; he was a cold man, little troubled by passion, irked not at all by discipline, yet his first impulse had been a wild clinging to the illusion of immortality.

It was part of the decency of Death that he should come unheralded with face covered and hands concealed, at the hour when he was least expected. He should come slowly, softly, like his brother Sleep—or swiftly and violently like the consummation of the act of love, so that the moment of surrender would be a stillness and a satiety instead of a wrenching separation of spirit and flesh.

The decency of Death. It was the thing men hoped for vaguely, prayed for if they were disposed to pray, regretted bitterly when they knew it would be denied them. Blaise Meredith was regretting it now, as he sat in the thin spring sunshine, watching the slow, processional swans on the Serpentine, the courting couples on the grass, the leashed poodles trotting fastidiously along the paths at the flirting skirts of their owners.

In the midst of all this life—the thrusting grass, the trees bursting with new sap, the nodding of crocus and daffodil, the languid love-play of youth, the vigour of the elderly strollers—he alone, it seemed, had been marked to die. There was no mistaking the urgency or the finality of the mandate. It was written, for all to read, not in the lines of his palm, but in the square sheet of photographic negative where a small grey blur spelt out his sentence.

"Carcinoma!" The blunt finger of the surgeon had lingered a moment on the centre of the grey blur, then moved outwards

7

tracing the diffusion of the tumour. "Slow-growing but well established. I've seen too many to be mistaken in this one."

As he watched the small translucent screen, and the spatulate finger moving across it, Blaise Meredith had been struck by the irony of the situation. All his life had been spent confronting others with the truth about themselves, the guilts that harried them, the lusts that debased them, the follies that diminished them. Now he was looking into his own guts where a small malignancy was growing like a mandrake root towards the day when it would destroy him.

He asked calmly enough.

"Is it operable?"

The surgeon switched off the light behind the viewing screen so that the small grey death faded into opacity; then he sat down, adjusting the desk lamp so that his own face was in shadow and that of his patient was lit like a marble head in a museum.

Blaise Meredith noted the small contrivance and understood it. They were both professionals. Each in his own calling dealt with human animals. Each must preserve a clinical detachment, lest he spend too much of himself and be left as weak and fearful as his patients.

The surgeon leaned back in his chair, picked up a paper-knife and held it poised as delicately as a scalpel. He waited a moment, gathering the words, choosing this one, discarding that, then laying them down in a pattern of meticulous accuracy.

"I can operate, yes. If I do, you'll be dead in three months."

"If you don't?"

"You'll live a little longer and die a little more painfully."

"How much longer?"

"Six months. Twelve at the outside."

"It's a grim choice."

"You must make it yourself."

"I understand that."

The surgeon relaxed in his chair. The worst was over now. He had not been mistaken in his man. He was intelligent, ascetic, self-contained. He would survive the shock and accommodate himself to the inevitable. When the agony began he would wear it with a certain dignity. His Church would guarantee him against want and bury him with honour when he died; and, if there were none to mourn him, this too might be counted the final reward for celibacy, to slip out of life without regret for its pleasures or fear of its unfulfilled obligations.

Blaise Meredith's calm, dry voice cut across his thought:

"I'll think about what you've told me. In case I should decide not to have an operation—go back to my work—would you be good enough to write me a report to my local doctor? A full prognosis, a prescription, perhaps?"

"With pleasure, Monsignor Meredith. You work in Rome, I believe? Unfortunately I don't write Italian."

Blaise Meredith permitted himself a small wintry smile.

"I'll translate it myself. It should make an interesting exercise."

"I admire your courage, Monsignor. I don't subscribe to the Roman faith, or to any faith for that matter, but I imagine you find it a great consolation at a time like this."

"I hope I may, Doctor," said Blaise Meredith simply, "but I've been a priest too long to expect it."

Now he was sitting on a park bench in the sun, with the air full of spring and the future a brief, empty prospect spilling over into eternity. Once, in his student days, he had heard an old missioner preach on the raising of Lazarus from the dead: how Christ had stood before the sealed vault and ordered it to be opened, so that the smell of corruption issued on the still, dry air of summer; how Lazarus at the summons had come out, stumbling in the cerecloths, to stand blinking in the sun. What had he felt at that moment, the old man asked? What price had he paid for this return to the world of the living? Did he go maimed ever afterwards, so that every rose smelled of decay and every golden girl was a shambling skeleton? Or did he walk in a dazzle of wonder at the newness of things, his heart tender with pity and love for the human family?

The speculation had interested Meredith for years. Once he had toyed with the idea of writing a novel about it. Now, at last, he had the answer. Nothing was so sweet to man as life;

nothing was more precious than time; nothing more reassuring than the touch of earth and grass, the whisper of moving air, the smell of new blossoms, the sound of voices and traffic and high bird-songs.

This was the thing that troubled him. He had been twenty years a priest, vowed to the affirmation that life was a transient imperfection, the earth a pale symbol of its maker, the soul an immortal in mortal clay, beating itself weary for release into the ambient arms of the Almighty. Now that his own release was promised, the date of it set, why could he not accept it—if not with joy, at least with confidence?

What did he cling to that he had not long since rejected? A woman? A child? A family? There was no one living who belonged to him. Possessions? They were few enough—a small apartment near the Porta Angelica, a few ornaments, a roomful of books, a modest stipend from the Congregation of Rites, an annuity left to him by his mother. Nothing there to tempt a man back from the threshold of the great revelation. Career? Something in that maybe—Auditor to the Sacred Congregation of Rites, personal assistant to the Prefect himself, Eugenio Cardinal Marotta. It was a position of influence, of flattering confidence. One sat in the shadow of the Pontiff. One watched the intricate, subtle workings of a great theocracy. One lived in simple comfort. One had time to study, liberty to act freely within the limits of policy and discretion. Something in that ... but not enough—not half enough for a man who hungered for the Perfect Union which he preached.

Perhaps that was the core of it. He had never been hungry for anything. He had always had everything he wanted, and he had never wanted more than was available to him. He had accepted the discipline of the Church, and the Church had given him security, comfort and scope for his talents. More than most men he had achieved contentment—and if he had never asked for happiness it was because he had never been unhappy. Until now ... until this bleak moment in the sun, the first of spring, the last spring ever for Blaise Meredith.

The last spring, the last summer. The butt end of life chewed and sucked dry like a sugar stick, then tossed on to the rubbish heap. There was the bitterness, the sour taste of failure and disillusion. What of merit could he tally and take with him to the judgment? What would he leave behind for which men would want to remember him?

He had never fathered a child nor planted a tree, nor set one stone on another for house or monument. He had spent no anger, dispensed no charity. His work would moulder anonymously in the archives of the Vatican. Whatever virtue had flowered out of his ministry was sacramental and not personal. No poor would bless him for their bread, no sick for their courage, no sinners for their salvation. He had done everything that was demanded of him, yet he would die empty and within a month his name would be a blown dust on the desert of the centuries.

Suddenly he was terrified. A cold sweat broke out on his body. His hands began to tremble and a group of children bouncing a ball near a bench edged away from the gaunt, grey-faced cleric who sat staring with blind eyes across the shimmering water of the pond.

The rigors passed slowly. The terror abated and he was calm again. Reason took hold of him and he began to think how he should order his life for the time left to him.

When he had become ill in Rome, when the Italian physicians had made their first, tentative diagnosis, his instinctive decision had been to return to London. If he must be condemned, he preferred to have the sentence read in his own tongue. If his time must be shortened, then he wanted to spend the last of it in the soft air of England, to walk the downs and the beechwoods and hear the elegiac song of the nightingales in the shadow of old churches, where Death was more familiar and more friendly because the English had spent centuries teaching him politeness.

In Italy, death was harsh, dramatic—a grand-opera exit, with wailing chorus and tossing plumes and black baroque hearses trundling past stucco palaces to the marble vaults of the Campo Santo. Here in England it had a gentler aspect—the obits murmured discreetly in a Norman nave, the grave opened in mown grass among weathered headstones, the libations

11

poured in the oak-beamed pub which stood opposite the lych-gate.

Now this, too, was proved an illusion, a pathetic fallacy, no armour at all against the grey insidious enemy entrenched in his own belly. He could not escape it, any more than he could flee the conviction of his own failure as a priest and as a man.

What then? Submit to the knife? Cut short the agony, truncate the fear and the loneliness to a manageable limit? Would not this be a new failure, a kind of suicide that the moralists might justify, but conscience could never quite condone? He had enough debts already to bring to the reckoning; this last might make him altogether bankrupt.

Go back to work? Sit at the old desk under the coffered ceiling in the Palace of Congregations in Rome. Open up the vast folios where the lives and works and writings of long-dead candidates for canonisation were recorded in the script of a thousand clerks. Examine them, dissect them, analyse and notate. Call their virtues in question and cast new doubts on the wonders attributed to them. Make new notes in a new script. To what end? That one more candidate for canonical honours might be rejected because he had been less than heroic, or less than wise in his virtues; or that half a century hence, two centuries maybe, a new Pope might proclaim in St Peter's that a new saint had been added to the Calendar.

Did they care, these dead ones, what he wrote of them? Did they care whether a new statue were permitted to wear an aureole, or whether the printers circulated a million little cards with their faces on the front and their virtues listed on the back? Did they smile on their bland biographers or frown on their official detractors? They had died and been judged long since, as he must die and soon be judged. The rest was all addendum, postscript and dispensable. A new cultus, a new pilgrimage, a new mass in the liturgy would touch them not at all. Blaise Meredith, priest, philosopher, canonist, might work twelve months or twelve years on their records without adding a jot to their felicity, or a single pain to their damnation.

Yet this was his work and he must do it, because it lay ready to his hand—and because he was too tired and too ill to begin any other. He would say Mass each day, work out his daily stint at the Palace of Congregations, preach occasionally in the English Church, hear confessions for a colleague on vacation, go back each night to his small apartment at the Porta Angelica, read a little, say his office, then struggle through the restless nights to the sour morning. For twelve months. Then he would be dead. For a week they would name him in the Masses . . . 'our brother Blaise Meredith'; then he would join the anonymous and the forgotten in the general remembrance . . . 'all the faithful departed'.

It was cold in the park now. The lovers were brushing the grass off their coats and the girls were smoothing down their skirts. The children were dragging listlessly down the paths in the wake of scolding parents. The swans were ruffling back to the shelter of the islets, to the peak-hour drone of London traffic.

Time to go. Time for Monsignor Blaise Meredith to pack his troubled thoughts and compose his thin features into a courteous smile for the Administrator's tea at Westminster. The English were a civil and tolerant people. They expected a man to work out his salvation soberly or damn himself with discretion, to hold his liquor like a gentleman and keep his troubles to himself. They were suspicious of saints and chary of mystics, and they more than half believed that God Almighty felt the same way. Even in the hour of his private Gethsemane, Meredith was glad of the convention that would force him to forget himself and attend to the chatter of his colleagues.

He got up stiffly from the bench, stood a long moment as if unsure of his own tenancy in the body, then walked steadily down towards Brompton Road.

Doctor Aldo Meyer had his own preoccupations this mild Mediterranean evening. He was trying to get drunk—as quickly and painlessly as possible.

All the odds were against him. The place where he drank was a low stone room with an earthen floor that stank of stale wine. His company was a brutish peasant proprietor and a stocky mountain girl with the neck and buttocks of an ox and melon breasts straining out of a greasy black dress. The drink was a fiery *grappa*, guaranteed to drown the stubbornest sorrow—but Aldo Meyer was too temperate and too intelligent to enjoy it.

He sat hunched forward over the rough bench, with a guttering candle beside him, staring into his cup and tracing monotonous patterns in the spilt liquor that flowed sluggishly in the wake of his finger. The *padrone* leaned on the bar, picking his teeth with a twig and sucking the remnants of his supper noisily through the gaps. The girl sat in the shadows waiting to fill the cup as soon as the doctor had emptied it. He had drunk swiftly at first, gulping on each mouthful, then more slowly as the raw spirit took hold of him. For the last ten minutes he had not drunk at all. It was as if he were waiting for something to happen before making the final surrender to forgetfulness.

He was a year short of fifty, but he looked like an old man. His hair was white, the skin of his fine Jewish face was drawn tight and spare over the bones. His hands were long and supple, but horned like a labourer's. He wore a townsman's suit of unfashionable cut, with frayed cuffs and shiny lapels, but his shoes were polished and his linen clean, save for the fresh stains where the *grappa* had splashed. There was an air of faded distinction about him which matched oddly with the crudeness of his surroundings and the coarse vitality of the girl and the *padrone*.

Gemello Minore was a long way from Rome, longer still from London. The dingy wine shop bore no resemblance at all to the Palace of Congregations. Yet Doctor Aldo Meyer was concerned with death like Blaise Meredith and, sceptic though he was, he too found himself embroiled with Beatitude.

Late in the afternoon he had been called to the house of Pietro Rossi, whose wife had been in labour for ten hours. The midwife was in despair and the room was full of women chattering like hens, while Maria Rossi groaned and writhed in the spasms, then relapsed into weak moaning when they left her. Outside the hovel the men were grouped, talking in low voices and passing a wine bottle from hand to hand.

14

When he came they fell silent, watching him with oblique, speculative eyes, while Pietro Rossi led him inside. He had lived among them for twenty years, yet he was still a foreigner; in these moments of their tribal life he might be necessary to them, but he was never welcome.

In the room with the women, it was the same story: silence, suspicion, hostility. When he bent over the great brass bed, palpating and probing the swollen body, the midwife and the girl's mother stood close beside him, and when a new spasm came, there was a shocked murmur, as if he were the cause of it.

Within three minutes he knew there was no hope of normal birth. He would have to do a Cæsarean. He was not unduly perturbed at the prospect. He had done them before, by candlelight and lamplight, on kitchen tables and plank benches. Given boiling water and anaesthetic and the tough bodies of the mountain women, the odds were loaded in the patient's favour.

He expected protests. These people were thick-headed as mules and twice as panicky—but he was unprepared for an outburst. It was the girl's mother who began it—a stout, muscular shrew, with lank hair and gapped teeth and black snake eyes. She rounded on him, yelling in thick dialect:

"I'll have no knives in my girl's belly. I want live grandchildren, not dead ones! You doctors are all the same. If you can't cure people you cut 'em up and bury 'em. Not my daughter! Give her time and she'll pop this one out like a pea. I've had twelve of 'em. I ought to know. Not all of 'em were easy, but I had 'em—and I didn't need a horse-butcher to gouge 'em out either!"

A burst of shrill laughter drowned the moaning of the girl. Aldo Meyer stood watching her, ignoring the women. He said simply:

"If I don't operate, she'll be dead by midnight."

It had worked before—the bald professional pronouncement, the contempt for their ignorance—but this time it failed utterly. The woman laughed in his face.

"Not this time, Jew-man! Do you know why?" She

15

plunged her hand inside her dress and brought up a small object wrapped in faded red silk. Her fingers closed over it and she thrust it under his nose. "You know what that is? You wouldn't, of course—you being an infidel and Christ-killer. We've got a saint of our own now. A real one! They're fixing to have him canonised in Rome any minute. That's a piece of his shirt. A real live relic, stained with his blood. He's worked miracles too. Real ones. They're all written down. They've been sent on to the Pope. Do you think you can do more than he can? Do you? Which do we choose, folks? Our own Saint Giacomo Nerone—or this fellow!"

The girl on the bed screamed in sudden agony and the women fell silent, while the mother bent over the bed, making little soothing noises and rubbing the dingy relic round and round on the swollen belly under the coverlets. Aldo Meyer waited a moment, searching for the right words. Then, when the girl was quiet again, he told them soberly:

"Even an infidel knows that to expect miracles without trying to help ourselves is a sin. You can't throw away medicines and expect the saints to cure you. Besides, this Giacomo Nerone isn't a saint yet. It will be a long time before they even start to discuss his case in Rome. Pray to him if you want, but ask him to give me a steady hand, and the girl a strong heart. Now stop being silly and get me boiling water and clean linen. I haven't much time."

No one moved. The mother barred his way to the bed. The women stood ranged in a tight semi-circle, shepherding him in the direction of the door, where Pietro Rossi stood, blank-faced, watching the drama. Meyer swung round to challenge him.

"You, Pietro! Do you want a child? Do you want your wife? Then for God's sake listen to me. Unless I operate quickly, she will die and the child will die with her. You know what I can do—there are twenty people in the village to tell you. But you don't know what this Giacomo Nerone can do—even if he is a saint . . . which I very much doubt."

Pietro Rossi shook his head stubbornly.

" 'Tisn't natural to rip out a child like a sheep's gut. Be-

16

sides, this isn't an ordinary saint. He's ours. He belongs to us. He'll look after us. You'd better go, Doctor."

"If I do, your wife won't see out the night."

The matt peasant face was blank as a wall. Meyer looked round at them, the dark secret people of the South, and thought despairingly how little he knew of them, how little power he had over them. He made a shrugging gesture of resignation, picked up his bag and walked towards the door. At the threshold he stopped and turned to face them.

"You'd better call Father Anselmo. She hasn't much time."

The mother spat contemptuously on the floor, then bent down again to rub the little silk bundle on the twitching belly of the girl, mumbling prayers in dialect. The other women watched him, stony-faced and silent. When he walked out and down the cobbled road, he felt the eyes of the men like knives at his back. It was then that he decided to get drunk.

For Aldo Meyer, the old liberal, the man who believed in man, it was the final gesture of defeat. There was no hope for these people. They were rapacious as hawks. They would eat your heart out and let you rot in a ditch. He had suffered for them, fought for them, lived with them and tried to educate them, but they took everything and learned nothing. They made a mockery of the most elementary knowledge, yet lapped up legends and superstitions as greedily as children.

Only the Church could control them, though it could not better them. It plagued them with demons, obsessed them with saints, cajoled them with weeping madonnas and fat-bottomed bambini. It could bleed them white for a new candelabrum, but it could not—or would not—bring them to a clinic for typhoid injections. Their mothers wasted away with TB and their bambini had swollen spleens from recurrent malaria. Yet they would as soon put a devil in their mouths as an Atabrine tablet—even though the doctor paid for it himself.

They lived in hovels where a good farmer would not house his cattle. They ate olives and pasta and bread dipped in oil, and goat meat on feast days, if they could get it. Their hills were bare of trees and their terraces held a niggardly soil, from which the nourishment leached out with the first rains

17

and was lost on the stony slopes. Their wine was thin and their corn was meagre and they moved with the sluggish gait of folk who eat too little and work too hard.

Their landlords exploited them, yet they clung to their coat-tails like children. Their priests lapsed often into liquor and concubinage, yet they fed them out of their poverty and treated them with tolerant contempt. If the summer was late or the winter was harsh, the frost burned the olives and there was hunger in the hills. They had no schools for their children, and what the State would not supply they would not make for themselves. They would not sacrifice their idle hours to build a school-house. They could not pay a teacher, yet they would dig into their tiny hoards of lire to finance the canonisation of a new saint for a Calendar that was already overloaded with them.

Aldo Meyer stared into the dark lees of his *grappa* to read futility, disillusion and despair. He lifted the cup and tossed off the dregs at a gulp. They were bitter as wormwood and there was no warmth in them at all.

He had come here first as an exile, when the Fascisti had rounded up the Semites and the left-wing intellectuals and the too vocal liberals, and presented them the curt alternative of rustication in Calabria or hard labour on Lipari. They had given him the ironic title of Medical Officer, but no salary, no drugs and no anaesthetics. He had arrived with the clothes he stood up in, a bag of instruments, a bottle of aspirin tablets and a medical compendium. For six years he battled and intrigued, cajoled and blackmailed to build up a sketchy medical service in an area of constant malnutrition, endemic malaria and epidemic typhoid.

He lived in a crumbling farmhouse which he restored with his own hands. He farmed a stony two acres, with the help of a cretinous labourer. His hospital was one room in his house. His theatre was his kitchen. The peasants paid him in kind, when they paid at all, and he exacted from the local officials a tribute in drugs and surgical instruments, and protection from a hostile Government. It had been a bitter servitude, but there had been moments of triumph, days when he seemed at last to be entering into the closed circle of the primitive mountain life.

When the Allies straddled the straits of Messina and began their slow bloody progress up the peninsula, he had fled and joined the Partisans, and after the armistice he had spent a brief while in Rome. But he had been away too long. Old friends were dead. New ones were hard to make, and the small triumphs of the locust years challenged him to greater ones. With freedom and money, and the impetus to reform, a man of good will might work miracles in the South.

So he had come back—to the old house, in the old town, with a new dream and a sense of renewed youth in himself. He would become a teacher as well as a doctor. He would lay down a prototype organisation for co-operative effort, an organisation that would attract development money from Rome and aid money from overseas foundations. He would teach them hygiene and the conservation of soil and water. He would train young men who would carry his message to outlying districts. He would be a missioner of progress in a land where progress had stopped three centuries before.

It had been a fine, fresh dream twelve years ago. He knew it now for a bleak illusion. He had fallen into the error of all liberals: the belief that men are prepared to reform themselves, that good will attracts good will, that truth has a leavening virtue of its own. His plans had made shipwreck on the venality of officials, the conservatism of a feudal Church, the rapacity and mistrust of a primitive, ignorant people.

Even through the thick fumes of the liquor he saw all too clearly. They had beaten him. He had beaten himself. And now it was too late to mend.

From the dusk outside came a long, wailing cry of women's voices. The girl and the *padrone* looked at each other and crossed themselves. The doctor stood up and walked unsteadily to the door to stand looking out into the cool spring twilight.

"She's dead," said the *padrone* in his thick, husky voice.

"Tell the saint about it," said Aldo Meyer. "I'm going to bed."

As he lurched out into the roadway the girl put out her tongue at him and made the sign against the evil eye.

The dirge-cry rose and fell, whining like a wind over the sleeping mountain. It followed him down the cobbled street and into his house. It battered on his door and searched at his shutters and haunted him through the night of restless, muttering sleep.

In the fall of the same spring dusk, Eugenio Cardinal Marotta walked in the garden of his villa on Parioli. Far below him the city was wakening from the torpor of afternoon and settling back to business with screaming horns and clattering motor scooters and chaffering shopkeepers. The tourists were trudging remorsefully back from St Peter's and St John Lateran and the Coliseum. The flower sellers were spraying their blooms for the last assault on the lovers of the Spanish Steps. The sunset spilled over the hills and down on to the roof-tops, but down in the alleys the dust haze hung thickly, and the walls of the buildings were grey and tired.

Up on Parioli, however, the air was clear and the avenues were quiet, and His Eminence walked under drooping palms to the scent of jasmine flowers. There were high walls about him and grilled gates to keep him private, and armorial bronzes on the lintels to remind the visitor of the rank and titles of Eugenio Cardinal Marotta, Archbishop of Acropolis, Titular of St Clement, Prefect of the Sacred Congregation of Rites, Pro-prefect of the Supreme Tribunal of the Apostolic Signature, Commissioner for the Interpretation of Canon Law, Protector of the Sons of St Joseph and the Daughters of Mary Immaculate and twenty other religious bodies great and small in the Holy Roman Church.

The titles were ample, the power that lay behind them was ample too; but His Eminence wore it with a bland good humour that masked a subtle intelligence and a dominating will.

He was a short, round man, with small hands and feet and a dewlapped face, and a high domed head, bald as an egg under the scarlet skullcap. His grey eyes twinkled with benevolence and his mouth was small and scarlet as a woman's against the matt olive of his complexion. He was sixty-three years of age, which is young for a man to reach the red hat. He worked hard, though without apparent effort, and still had energy left for the devious diplomacies and manipulations of power inside the closed City of the Vatican.

There were those who favoured him for election to the papacy itself, but there were others, more numerous, who held that the next Pontiff should be a more saintly man, less concerned with diplomacy than with the reform of morals among clergy and laity alike. Eugenio Marotta was content to wait on the outcome, knowing that he who goes into the conclave a Pope is likely to leave it a Cardinal. Besides, the Pontiff might be old, but he was still a long way from dead, and he looked with small favour on those who coveted his shoes.

So His Eminence walked in his villa garden on Parioli, watching the sun decline over the Alban hills and pondering the day's questions in the relaxed attitude of a man who knew he would answer them all in the end.

He could afford to relax. He had come by steady progression to the high plateau of preferment from which neither malice nor disfavour could unseat him. He would remain a Cardinal till the day he died, a Prince by protocol, a Bishop by irrevocable consecration, citizen of the smallest and least vulnerable State in the world. It was much for a man in his vigorous sixties. It was much more, because he was untrammelled by a wife, unplagued by sons and daughters, set far beyond the pricks of passion. He had come as far as talent and ambition could drive him.

The next step was the Chair of Peter; but this was a high leap, half way out of the world and into a vestibule of divinity. The man who wore the Fisherman's ring and the triple tiara carried also the sins of the world like a leaden cope on his shoulders. He stood on a windy pinnacle, alone, with the spread carpet of the nations below him, and above, the naked face of the Almighty. Only a fool would envy him the power and the glory and the terror of such a principality. And Eugenio Cardinal Marotta was very far from being a fool.

In this hour of dusk and jasmine he had problems enough of his own.

Two days before, a letter had been laid on his desk from the Bishop of Valenta, a small diocese in a run-down area of Calabria. The Bishop was known to him vaguely as a rigid reformer with a taste for politics. He had caused a stir two years previously by unfrocking a couple of country curates for concubinage and pensioning off some of his elderly pastors on the grounds of incompetence. The election figures from his diocese had shown a marked swing towards the Christian Democrats, and this had earned him a Pontifical letter of commendation. It was only the more subtle observers like Marotta who had noted that the increase had come from the Monarchist Party and not from the Communists, who had also registered a slight gain. The Bishop's letter was simple and explicit—too simple to be guileless and too explicit not to rouse suspicion in a seasoned campaigner like Eugenio Cardinal Marotta.

It began with salutations, florid and deferential, from a humble bishop to a princely one. It went on to say that a petition had been received from the parish priest and the faithful of the villages of Gemelli dei Monti for the introduction of the Cause for Beatification of the Servant of God, Giacomo Nerone.

This Giacomo Nerone had been murdered by Communist Partisans in circumstances which might well be called martyrdom. Since his death, spontaneous veneration had been paid to him in the villages and the surrounding countryside, and several cures of a miraculous nature were attributed to his influence. Preliminary investigations had confirmed the reputation for sanctity and the apparently miraculous nature of the cures, and the Bishop was disposed to grant the petition and admit the case to juridical investigation. Before doing so, however, he sought counsel of His Eminence, as Prefect of the Congregation of Rites, and his assistance in appointing, from Rome itself, two wise and godly men—one as the Postulator of the Cause, to organise the investigation and carry it forward, the other as the Promoter of the Faith, or Devil's Advocate, to submit the evidence and the witnesses to the severest

22

scrutiny in accordance with the appropriate provisions of canon law.

There was more, much more, but this was the core of the apple. The Bishop might have a saint in his territory—a convenient saint, too, martyred by the Communists. The only way he could prove the sanctity was by a judicial investigation, first in his own diocese and then in Rome, under the authority of the Congregation of Rites. But the first investigation would be made in his own See and under his own authority, with officials appointed by himself. Local bishops were normally jealous of their autonomy. Why then this deferential appeal to Rome?

Eugenio Cardinal Marotta walked the trim lawns of his villa garden and pondered the proposition.

Gemelli dei Monti lay deep in Midday Italy, where cults proliferate and die as quickly, where the Faith is overlaid with a thick patina of superstition, where the peasants make with the same hand the sign of the Cross and the sign against the evil eye, where the picture of the Bambino is hung over the bed and the pagan horns are nailed over the barn door. The Bishop was a canny man who wanted a saint for the good of his diocese, but declined to put his own reputation on trial with that of the Servant of God.

If the investigation went well, he would have not only a *beato*, but a rod to beat the Communists. If it went ill, the wise and godly men from Rome could bear some of the blame. His Eminence chuckled at the subtlety of it. Scratch a Southerner and you found a fox, who smelled out traps a mile away, and trotted around them to the chicken run.

But there was more at stake than the reputation of a provincial bishop. There was politics involved, and Italian elections were only twelve months away. Public opinion was sensitive to the influence of the Vatican in civil affairs. The anti-clericals would welcome a chance to discredit the Church, and they had enough weapons without putting another into their hands.

There were deeper issues yet, matters less relevant to time than to eternity. To name a man Blessed was to declare him a

23

heroic servant of God, to hold him up as an exemplar and an intercessor for the faithful. To accept his miracles was to admit beyond all doubt the divine power working through him to suspend or cancel the laws of nature. Error in such a matter was unthinkable. The whole massive machinery of the Congregation of Rites was designed to prevent it. But premature action, a botched investigation, could cause grave scandal and weaken the faith of millions in an infallible Church which claimed the direct guidance of the Holy Ghost.

His Eminence shivered as the first chill darkness came down on Parioli. He was a man hardened by power and sceptical of devotion, but he too carried on his shoulders the burden of belief and in his heart the fear of the noonday devil.

He could afford less than others the luxury of error. Much more depended on him. The penalty of failure would be so much more rigorous. In spite of the pomp of his title and the secular dignity which attended it, his prime mission was spiritual. It related to souls—their salvation and damnation. The curse of the millstones could fall equally upon an erring Cardinal and a faithless curate. So he walked and pondered soberly while the faint harmony of bells drifted up from the city and the crickets in the garden began their shrill chorus.

He would grant the Bishop of Valenta his small triumph. He would find the men for him—a Postulator to build the case and present it, a Devil's Advocate to destroy it if he could. Of the two, the Devil's Advocate was the more important. His official title described him accurately: Promoter of the Faith. The man who kept the Faith pure at any cost of broken lives and broken hearts. He must be learned, meticulous, passionless. He must be cold in judgment, ruthless in condemnation. He might lack charity or piety, but he could not lack precision. Such men were rare, and those at his disposal were already occupied on other causes.

Then he remembered Blaise Meredith, the spare, sober man with the greyness of death on him. He had the qualities. He was English, which would remove the taint of political involvement. But whether he had the will or the time left to him was

24

another matter. If the medical verdict were unfavourable he might not feel disposed to accept so heavy an assignment.

Still, it was the beginning of an answer. His Eminence was not unsatisfied. He made one more leisurely circuit of the darkened garden, then walked back to the villa to say vespers with his household.

CHAPTER TWO

TWO DAYS later Eugenio Cardinal Marotta sat in his study chair behind the great buhl desk and talked with Monsignor Blaise Meredith. His Eminence had slept well and breakfasted lightly and his round, good humoured face was fresh and shining from the razor. In the lofty room, with its coffered ceiling and its Aubusson carpets and its noble portraits in gilded frames, he was invested with the unconscious dignity of possession.

By contrast, the Englishman seemed small and grey and shrunken. His soutane hung loosely on his thin body and the scarlet piping only emphasised the unhealthy pallor of his face. His eyes were clouded with fatigue and there were deep furrows of pain at the corners of his mouth. Even in the brisk, Romanesque Italian his voice was flat and expressionless.

"There it is, Eminence. I have at best, twelve months. Half of that, perhaps, for active work."

The Cardinal waited a few moments, watching him with detached pity. Then he said gently:

"I grieve for you, my friend. It comes to all of us, of course; but it is always a shock."

"Yet we of all people should be prepared for it." The drooping mouth twitched upward into a wry smile.

"No!" Marotta's small hands fluttered in deprecation. "We mustn't overrate ourselves. We are men like all the others. We are priests by choice and calling. We are celibates by canonical legislation. It is a career, a profession. The powers we exercise, the grace we dispense, are independent of our own worthiness. It is better for us to be saints than sinners—but like our brothers outside the ministry we are generally something in between."

"Small comfort, Eminence, when one stands in the shadow of the judgment seat."

"It is still the truth." The Cardinal reminded him coolly

26

"I've been in the Church a long time, my friend. The higher one climbs the more one sees—and the more clearly. It's a pious legend that the priesthood sanctifies a man, or that celibacy ennobles him. If a priest can keep his hands out of his pockets and his legs out of a woman's bed till he's forty-five, he stands a reasonable chance of doing it till he dies. There are plenty of professional bachelors in the world too. But we are all still subject to pride, ambition, sloth, negligence, avarice. Often it's harder for us to save our souls than it is for others. A man with a family must make sacrifices, impose a discipline on his desires, practise love and patience. We may sin less, yet have less merit in us at the end."

"I am very empty," said Blaise Meredith. "There is no evil that I repent and no good that I count. I have had nothing to fight. I cannot show even scars."

The Cardinal leaned back in his chair, toying with the big yellow stone on his episcopal ring. The only sound in the room was the soft ticking of an ormolu clock on the marble mantel. After a while he said thoughtfully:

"I can release you now if you wish, I can provide you with a pension from the funds of the Congregation. You could live quietly. . . ."

Blaise Meredith shook his head.

"It's a great kindness, Eminence, but I have no talent for contemplation. I should prefer to go on working."

"You will have to stop one day. After that?"

"I shall go into hospital. I understand I shall suffer a good deal. Then . . ." He spread his hands in a gesture of defeat. "*Finita la commedia.* If it were not too much to ask, I should like to be buried in Your Eminence's church."

In spite of himself Marotta was touched by the bleak courage of the man. He was tired and sick. The worst of his Calvary was yet to come, yet he was walking towards it with a desolate dignity that was typically English. Before the Cardinal had time to comment, Meredith went on.

"In all this, of course, I assume that Your Eminence wants to use me. I . . . I'm afraid I can't guarantee the best of service."

27

"You have always done better than you knew, my friend," said Marotta gently, "you have always given more than you promised. Besides there is a matter in which you can help me greatly—and perhaps——" he paused as if struck by an odd afterthought—"perhaps help yourself too."

Then, without waiting for an answer, he told him of the petition of the Bishop of Valenta, and his need of a Devil's Advocate in the cause of Giacomo Nerone.

Meredith listened, intent as a lawyer on the details of a new brief. A new life seemed to take possession of him. His eyes brightened, he straightened in his chair and a small tinge of colour crept into his faded cheeks. Eugenio Marotta noted it but made no comment. When he had finished his outline of the situation he asked:

"Well, what do you think of it?"

"An indiscretion," said Meredith precisely. "It's a political move and I distrust it."

"Everything in the Church is political," Marotta reminded him mildly. "Man is a political animal who has an immortal soul. You cannot divide him—any more than you can divide the Church into separate and unrelated functions. Everything the Church does is designed to give a spiritual character to a material development. We name a saint as patron of television. What does it mean? A new symbol of an old truth: that every lawful activity is conducive to good or can be perverted to evil."

"Too many symbols can cloud the face of reality," said Blaise Meredith dryly. "Too many saints can bring sanctity into disrepute. I've always thought that was our function at the Congregation of Rites—not to put them into the Calendar, but to keep them out of it."

The Cardinal nodded soberly.

"In a sense that's true. But, in this as in all cases, the first motion doesn't come from us. The Bishop begins it in his own diocese. Only afterwards the papers are forwarded to us. We have no direct authority to forbid the investigation."

"We might counsel against it."

"On what grounds?"

28

"Discretion. The timing is bad. We are on the eve of elections. Giacomo Nerone was murdered by Communist Partisans in the last year of the war. What do we want to do? Use him to win a provincial seat—or as an example of heroic charity?"

The Cardinal's red lips twitched into a small ironic smile.

"I imagine our brother Bishop would like to have it both ways. And up to a point he's likely to get it. Miracles have been claimed. An apparently spontaneous cult has sprung up among the people. Both must be judicially investigated. The first investigation has been made and the verdict leans towards approval. The next stage follows almost automatically . . . the introduction of the Cause for Beatifications to the Bishop's own court."

"Once that happens, every newspaper in Italy will run the story. The travel agencies will start organising unofficial tours. The local merchants will start shouting from the housetops. You can't avoid it."

"But we may be able to control it. That's why I've decided to give His Lordship what he wants. That's why I'd like you to become the Devil's Advocate."

Blaise Meredith pursed his thin, bloodless lips, considering the offer. Then after a moment he shook his head.

"I'm a sick man, Eminence. I could not do you justice."

"You must let me judge that." Marotta reproved him coolly. "Besides, as I said, I believe it may help you too."

"I don't understand."

The Cardinal pushed back his high, carved chair and stood up. He walked across the room to the window and drew back the thick curtains so that the morning sun flooded into the room, lighting the scarlet and the gilt, making the rich patterns on the carpet leap into life like flowers. Blaise Meredith blinked at the raw brilliance and shaded his eyes with his hand. The Cardinal stood looking out into the garden. His face was hidden from Meredith, but when he spoke his voice was touched with a rare compassion.

"What I have to say to you, Monsignor, is probably a presumption. I am not your confessor. I cannot look into your

29

conscience; but I believe you have reached a crisis. You, like many of us here in Rome, are a professional priest—a career churchman. There is no stigma in that. It is much already to be a good professional. There are many who fall far short even of this limited perfection. Suddenly you have discovered it is not enough. You are puzzled, afraid. Yet you do not know what you should do to restore the lack. Part of the problem is that you and I and others like us have been removed too long from pastoral duty. We have lost touch with the people who keep us in touch with God. We have reduced the Faith to an intellectual conception, an arid assent of the will, because we have not seen it working in the lives of common folk. We have lost pity and fear and love. We are the guardians of mysteries, but we have lost the awe of them. We work by canon, not by charity. Like all administrators we believe that the world would topple into chaos without us, that we carry even the Church of God on our backs. It is not true, but some of us believe it till the day we die. You are fortunate that even at this late hour you have been touched with dissatisfaction . . . yes, even doubt, because I believe that you are now in the desert of temptation. . . . That is why I believe this investigation may help you. It will take you out of Rome, to one of the most depressed areas of Italy. You will rebuild the life of a dead man from the evidence of those who lived with him—the poor, the ignorant, the dispossessed. Be he sinner or saint, it makes no difference in the end. You will live and talk with simple people. Among them perhaps you will find the cure for your own sickness of spirit."

"What is my sickness, Eminence?" The pathetic weariness of the voice, the desolate puzzlement of the question, touched the old churchman to pity. He turned back from the window to see Meredith slumped forward in his chair, his face buried in his hands. He waited a moment, weighing his answer; then he gave it, gravely.

"There is no passion in your life, my son. You have never loved a woman, nor hated a man, nor pitied a child. You have withdrawn yourself too long and you are a stranger in the human family. You have asked nothing and given nothing.

30

You have never known the dignity of need nor gratitude for a suffering shared. This is your sickness. This is the cross you have fashioned for your own shoulders. This is where your doubts begin and your fears too—because a man who cannot love his fellows cannot love God either."

"How does one begin to love?"

"From need," said Marotta firmly. "From the need of the flesh and the need of the spirit. A man hungers for his first kiss, and his first real prayer is made when he hungers for the lost Paradise."

"I am so very tired," said Blaise Meredith.

"Go home and rest," said the Cardinal briskly. "In the morning you can leave for Calabria. Present your credentials to the Bishop of Valenta and begin work."

"You are a hard man, Eminence."

"Men die every day," Eugenio Marotta told him bluntly. "Some are damned, some achieve salvation; but the work of the Church continues. Go, my son—in peace and in the name of God!"

At eleven o'clock the following morning Blaise Meredith left Rome for Calabria. His luggage was one small suitcase of clothes, a briefcase containing his breviary and his notebooks, and a letter of authority from the Prefect of the Congregation of Rites to His Lordship the Bishop of Valenta. There was a ten-hour journey ahead of him and the *rapido* was hot, dusty and crowded with Calabresi returning from an organised pilgrimage to the Holy City.

The poorer folk were herded like cattle into the second-class coaches, while their betters spilled over into first-class and spread themselves and their belongings over the seats and the luggage racks. Meredith found himself anchored firmly between a stout matron in a silk frock and a swarthy-faced cleric chewing noisily through a packet of peppermints. The seat opposite was occupied by a country man and his wife and four children who squalled like cicadas and tangled themselves in everyone's feet. All the windows were closed and the air was sour and stifling.

He took out his breviary and settled down with grim concentration to read his office. Ten minutes out of Rome Central he gave up in disgust. The foul air nauseated him and his head throbbed with the chatter of the train and the shrilling of the children. He tried to doze, but the stout woman shifted uneasily in her tight dress and the noisy mastications of the priest fretted him to screaming point. Defeated and dyspeptic, he struggled out of the seat and into the corridor, where he stood, propped against the panelling, looking out on the countryside.

It was green now, with the first flush of spring. The scars of erosion and tillage were covered with new grass, the stucco of the house-fronts had been washed clean by the rains and bleached by the sun, and even the ruins of the aqueducts and the old Roman villas were flecked with fresh moss and weeds that sprouted out of their weathered stones. The cyclic miracle of rebirth was more vivid here than in any other country of the world. Here was a tired land, raped ruinously for centuries, its hills eroded, its trees cut down, its rivers dry, its soil bled into dust; yet somehow every year it made this brief, brave show of leaf and grass and flower. Even in the mountains, on the ragged tufa slopes, too poor for goat-cropping, there was still a faint dapple of green for a reminder of past fruitfulness.

If one could leave the land a while, thought Meredith, if one could empty it of its proliferating tribes for half a century, it might come into heart again. But it would never happen. They would breed and breed while the land died under their feet—slowly indeed, yet too fast for the technicians and agronomists to restore it.

The moving sunlit vistas began to weary his eyes, and he looked up and down the corridor at the others who had been driven out of the compartments by cigar smoke and stale salami and garlic and the smell of unbathed bodies. There was a Neapolitan business man with stovepipe trousers and short-tailed coat and a flashing zircon on one pudgy finger, a German tourist with thick shoes and an expensive Leica, a pair of flat-chested Frenchwomen, an American student with cropped hair and a freckled face, and a pair of provincial lovers holding hands near the toilet.

It was the lovers who held Meredith's attention. The youth was a nuggety peasant from the South, dark as an Arab, with flashing eyes and voluble hands. His thin cotton trousers were moulded over his flanks and his sweat-shirt clung to his chest so that the whole, compact maleness of him was suggestively visible. The girl was short and as dark as he was, thick of waist and ankle, but her breasts were full and firm and they strained against the low-cut bodice of her dress. They stood facing one another across the narrow corridor, their locked hands a barrier against intrusion, their eyes blind to all but themselves, their bodies relaxed and swaying to the rhythm of the train. Their passion was plain, yet it gave no impression of urgency. The boy was preened like a cock, yet confident of his possession. The girl was content with him and with herself, in the small private eternity of new love.

Looking at them, Blaise Meredith was touched with a vague nostalgia for a past that had never belonged to him. What did he know of love but a theological definition and a muttered guilt in the confessional? What meaning had his counsel in the face of this frank, erotic communion, which by divine dispensation was the beginning of life and the guarantee of the human continuum? Soon, this very night perhaps, these two would lie together in the little death out of which a new life would spring —a new body, a new soul. But Blaise Meredith would sleep solitary, with all the mysteries of the universe reduced to a scholastic syllogism inside his skull-case. Who was right—he or they? Who came nearer to the perfection of the divine design? There was only one answer. Eugenio Marotta was right. He had withdrawn himself from the human family. These two were thrusting forward to renew it and perpetuate it.

His feet began to burn. His back ached. The small nagging pain started again in the pit of his belly. He would have to sit down and rest awhile. As he made his way back to his seat he found the Calabrian cleric launched on a full-scale sermon:

". . . A wonderful man, the Holy Father. A saint in his own right. I was very near him in St Peter's. I could have stretched out my hand to touch him. One could feel the power going out from him. Wonderful . . . wonderful . . .! We should thank

God all the days of our lives for the privilege we have enjoyed on this pilgrimage."

A wave of peppermint wafted through the compartment. Blaise Meredith closed his eyes and prayed for a respite, but the thick Calabrese voice droned on and on:

"... To have come to Rome, to have trodden in the footprints of the martyrs and knelt at the tomb of Peter, what other experience could match this? Here one sees the Church as it really is—an army of priests and monks and nuns preparing themselves to conquer the world for Christ. ..."

If this is the way we conquer it, thought Blaise Meredith irritably, God help the world. This sort of mummery never did anyone any good. The fellow talks like a travelling salesman. If only he would shut up and think a little.

But the Calabrese was well launched now and the presence of a brother cleric only urged him to greater efforts.

"They are right when they call Rome the Holy City. The spirit of the great Pontiff broods over it night and day. Mind you, not all the saints of the Church are in Rome. Oh no! Even in our own small province we have a saint—not an official one yet—but real. Ah yes! Very real!"

Blaise Meredith was instantly alert. His irritation vanished, and he waited intently for the rest of it.

"Already the Cause of his Beatification has been opened. Giacomo Nerone. You have heard of him perhaps? No? A strange and wonderful story. No one knows where he came from, but he appeared one day in the village, like a man sent by God. He built a little hermitage with his own hands and gave himself over to prayer and good works. When the Communists moved in to take over the village after the war they murdered him. He died a martyr in defence of the Faith. And since his death miracle after miracle has been performed at his tomb. The sick have been cured; sinners brought to penance: sure marks of the favour of the Almighty."

Blaise Meredith opened his eyes and asked innocently:
"Did you know him, Father?"

The Calabrese shot him a swift, suspicious glance.

"Know him? Er, well, not personally. Though, of course, I

know a lot about him. I'm from Cosenza myself. The next diocese."

"Thank you," said Blaise Meredith politely, and closed his eyes again. The Calabrian shifted uncomfortably in his seat and then got up to relieve himself in the toilet. Meredith took advantage of his absence to stretch his legs and ease his aching head against the padded back-rest. He felt no compunction for what he had done. More than ever now, this sort of claptrap was distasteful to him. It was a kind of ecclesiastical jargon, a debased rhetoric that explained nothing but brought the truth into disrepute. It begged all the questions and answered none. The massive structure of reason and revelation on which the Church was founded was reduced to a ritual incantation, formless, fruitless and essentially false. Peppermint piety. It deceived no one but the man who peddled it. It satisfied no one but old ladies and girls in green-sickness; yet it flourished most rankly where the Church was most firmly entrenched in the established order. It was the mark of accommodation, compromise, laxity among the clergy, who found it easier to preach devotion than to affront the moral and social problems of their time. It covered fatuity and lack of education. It left the people naked and unarmed in the face of terrifying mysteries: pain, passion, death, the great 'perhaps' of the hereafter.

The swarthy Calabrian came back, fumbling with the buttons of his cassock, and determined to re-establish himself with his audience and with this lean-jowled Monsignor. He sat down, blew his nose noisily and then tapped Meredith confidentially on the knee.

"You are from Rome, Monsignor?"

"From Rome, yes." He was nettled by this intrusion on his rest, and his tone was terse; but the Calabrese was a hard-head, blind to all obstacles.

"But you are not Italian?"

"No. I'm English."

"Ah, a visitor to the Vatican? A pilgrim?"

"I work there," said Meredith coldly.

The Calabrese gave him a fraternal smile that showed a mouth full of carious teeth.

"You are fortunate, Monsignor. You have opportunities denied to us poor country folk. We work the stony acres, while you till the lush pastures of the City of Saints."

"I don't till anything," Meredith told him baldly. "I'm an official of the Congregation of Rites, and Rome isn't the City of Saints any more than Paris or Berlin. It's a place that's kept fairly orderly because the Pope insists on his rights under the Concordat to preserve its sacred character as the centre of Christendom. That's all."

The Calabrese was as canny as a badger. He sidestepped the snub and seized swiftly on the new topic presented to him.

"You interest me very much, Monsignor. You live of course in a bigger world than I. You have much more experience of affairs. But I have always said that the simple country life is much more conducive to sanctity than the worldly bustle of a great city. You work with the Congregation of Rites. You deal, possibly, with the causes of saints and *beati*. Wouldn't you agree?"

He was trapped and he knew it. He would be plagued into conversation in the end. It would save time and energy to submit now—and try to change his seat at Formio or Naples. He answered dryly:

"All my experience is that saints are found in the most unlikely places—at the most unpromising times."

"Exactly! This is what has interested me so much about our own Servant of God, Giacomo Nerone. You know the place where he lived, Gemelli dei Monti?"

"I've never been there."

"But you know what the name means?"

"What it says, I imagine . . . the mountain twins."

"Precisely. Twin villages, set on the horns of a hill in some of the most desolate country in Calabria. Gemello Minore the little town. Gemello Maggiore the greater. They're about sixty kilometres from Valenta, and the road is a nightmare. The villagers are as poor and depressed as any in our province. At least they were, until the fame of the Servant of God began to spread."

"And then?" In spite of himself, Meredith found his interest quickening.

"Ah, then!" One stubby hand was raised in a preacher's gesture. "Then a strange thing happened. Giacomo Nerone had lived and worked in Gemello Minore. It was in this village that he was betrayed and murdered. His body was taken secretly to a grotto near Gemello Maggiore and buried there. Since that time Gemello Minore has sunk deeper and deeper into ruin and poverty, while Gemello Maggiore grows more prosperous every day. There is a new church, a hospital, an inn for tourists and pilgrims. It is as if God were visiting punishment on the betrayers and reward on those who sheltered the body of the Servant of God. Don't you agree?"

"It's a dubious proposition," Meredith told him, with thin irony. "Prosperity isn't always a mark of divine favour. It could be the result of some shrewd promotion by the Mayor and the citizens—even the parish priest. These things have happened."

The Calabrese flushed angrily at the imputation and burst into an impassioned rebuttal.

"You presume too much, Monsignor. Wise and godly men have looked into this matter—men who understand our people. Do you set yourself in opposition to them?"

"I'm not in opposition to anyone," said Meredith mildly. "I simply disapprove of rash judgment and doubtful doctrine. Saints are not made by popular verdict but by canonical decision. That's why I'm going to Calabria now, to act as Promoter of the Faith in the cause of Giacomo Nerone. If you have any firsthand evidence to offer, I'll be happy to receive it, in the proper form."

The priest gaped at him a moment; then his confidence collapsed in mumbled apologies, cut mercifully short by their arrival at Formio.

They had twenty minutes to wait for the south-bound train, which gave Blaise Meredith the opportunity to stretch his legs —and the grace to be ashamed of himself.

What had he gained by this cheap, dialectic victory over a country cleric? The Calabrese was a bore—and, worse, a pious

37

bore—but Blaise Meredith was a dyspeptic intellectual with no charity in him at all. He had gained nothing and given nothing —and he had missed the first opportunity of learning a little about the man whose life he was charged to investigate.

As he paced the sunlit platform, watching the peasant travellers pressing about the drink vendor, he asked himself for the hundredth time what was the lack that cut him off from free communication with his fellows. Other priests, he knew, found an intense pleasure in the raw, salty dialect of peasant conversation. They picked up pearls of wisdom and experience over a farmhouse table or a cup of wine in a workman's kitchen. They talked with equal familiarity to the rough-tongued whores of Trastevere and the polished *signori* of Parioli. They enjoyed the ribald humour of the fish market as much as the wit of a Cardinal's dinner table. They were good priests, too, and they did much for their people, with a singular satisfaction to themselves.

What was the difference between him and them? Passion, Marotta had told him. The capacity to love and to desire, to feel with another's pain, to share another's joy. Christ ate and drank wine with touts and tavern girls, but Monsignor Meredith, his professional follower, had lived alone amid dusty tomes in the library of the Palace of Congregations. And now, in this last year of his life, he was still alone, with a small grey death growing in his belly—and no soul in the world to bear him company.

The guard blew his whistle and Meredith climbed aboard again, to sweat out the long, humid voyage—Naples, Nocera, Salerno, Eboli, Cassano, Cosenza and, in the late evening, Valenta, where the Bishop was waiting to welcome him.

Aurelio, Bishop of Valenta, was a surprise, in more ways than one. He was a tall, spare man, still in his vigorous forties. His iron-grey hair was meticulously brushed and his fine aquiline features were bright with intelligence and humour. He was a Trentino, which seemed an odd choice for a Southern diocese, and before his translation he had been an auxiliary in the Patriarchate of Venice. He was waiting at the station with his own car and instead of driving into the town he took Meredith a dozen kilometres into the country to a handsome villa, set in acres of oranges and olives, and looking down into a valley where a narrow stream glowed faintly under the moon.

"An experiment," he explained in clear metallic English. "An experiment in practical education. These people imagine that the clergy are born in cassocks, and that their only talent is for Paters and Aves and swinging censers in the cathedral. I was born in the North. My people were mountain farmers—good ones. I bought this place from a local landowner who was up to his eyes in debt, and I'm farming it with half a dozen lads, to whom I'm trying to teach the rudiments of modern agriculture. It's a battle; but I think I'm winning. I've also made it my official residence. The old one was hopelessly antiquated . . . right in the middle of the town, next to the cathedral. I've handed it over to my Vicar General. He's one of the old school—loves it!"

Meredith chuckled, caught by the infectious good humour of the man. The Bishop shot him a quick, shrewd look.

"You are surprised, Monsignor?"

"Pleasantly," said Blaise Meredith. "I expected something quite different."

"Bourbon baroque? Velvet and brocade and gilt cherubs with the paint peeling off their backsides?"

"Something like that, yes."

The Bishop brought the car to a stop in front of the stuccoed portico of the villa and sat a moment behind the wheel, looking over the fall of the land, where the moonlight touched the treetops with silver. He said quietly:

"You will find more than enough of it here in the South . . . formalism, feudalism, reaction, old men following old ways because the old ways seem safer, and they are unprepared for the new. They see poverty and ignorance as crosses to be borne and not injustices to be remedied. They believe that the more priests and monks and nuns there are, the better for the world. I'd like to see fewer and better ones. I'd prefer to have fewer churches and more people going to them."

"Fewer saints too?" asked Meredith blandly.

The Bishop looked up sharply, then burst out laughing.

"Thank God for the English! A little tramontane scepticism would do us all a lot of good at this moment. You wonder why a man like me should take up the cause of Giacomo Nerone?"

"Frankly, yes."

"Let's keep it for the fruit and the cheese," said His Lordship without malice.

A servant in a white coat opened the car door and ushered them into the house.

"Dinner in thirty minutes," said His Lordship. "I hope you'll find your room comfortable. In the morning you can look right down over the valley and see what we've done."

He took his leave, and the servant led Meredith upstairs to a large guest-room with french doors that opened on to a narrow balcony. Meredith was struck by the clean, modern lines of the furniture, the ascetic strength of the wooden crucifix over the prie-dieu in the corner. There was a shelf of new books in French, Italian and English, and a copy of the *Imitation of Christ* on the bedside table. A door opened from the bedroom into a freshly tiled bathroom, with a toilet and a shower recess. His Lordship had the instincts of a builder and the good taste of an artist. He also had a sense of humour, a virtue all too rare in the Italian Church.

As he bathed and changed, Meredith felt the weariness and frustration of the journey falling away from him like a sloughed skin. Even the nagging pain of his illness seemed to subside, and he found himself looking forward with pleasure and curiosity to dinner with His Lordship. It was a simple meal—*antipasto*, *zuppa di verdura*, a roast of chicken, local fruit and a sharp country cheese—but it was cooked with distinction and meticulously served, and the wine was a full-bodied Barolo from the vineyards of the North. The talk that went with it was much more subtle; a fencing match between experts, with the Bishop making the first probing thrusts.

"Until you came, my dear Meredith, I was beginning to feel I had made a mistake."

"A mistake?"

"In appealing to Rome for assistance. It involved a concession, you see—a certain sacrifice of my autonomy."

"Did it cost Your Lordship so much?"

The Bishop nodded gravely.

"It could have, yes. Modernisers and reformers are always suspect, especially here in the South. If they succeed they become a reproach to their more conservative colleagues. If they fail, they become an example. They have tried to do too much, too fast. So I've always found it wiser to go my own way and keep my affairs to myself—and leave the critics to make the first move."

"Do you have many critics?"

"Some, yes. The landowners don't like me—and they have strong voices in Rome. The clergy find me too rigid in matters of morals, and too indifferent to local ritual and tradition. My metropolitan is a Monarchist. I'm a moderate socialiser. The politicos mistrust me, because I preach that the party is less important than the individual who represents it. They make promises. I like to see that they are kept. When they're not, I protest."

"Do you find support in Rome?"

His Lordship's thin mouth relaxed into a smile.

"You know Rome better than I do, my friend. They wait for the results—and the results of a policy like mine in an area like this may not be seen for ten years. If I succeed, well and good. If I fail—or make the wrong mistake at the wrong time —they'll nod their heads wisely and say they've been expecting it for years. So I prefer to keep them guessing. The less they know, the freer I am."

"Then why did you write to Cardinal Marotta? Why did you ask for Roman priests as Postulator and Promoter of the Faith?"

His Lordship toyed with his wineglass, twirling the stem between his long, sensitive fingers, watching the light refract through the red liquid on to the snowy tablecloth. He said carefully:

"Because this is new ground to me. I understand goodness, but I am unfamiliar with sanctity. I believe in mysticism, but

I've had no experience of mystics. I'm a northerner, a pragmatist by nature and education. I believe in miracles, but I've never expected to find them performed on my own doorstep. That's why I applied to the Congregation of Rites." He smiled disarmingly. "You are the experts in these matters."

"Was this the only reason?"

"You talk like an inquisitor," said His Lordship, with wry good humour. "What other reason should there be?"

"Politics," said Meredith flatly. "Election politics."

To his surprise, the Bishop threw back his head and laughed heartily.

"So that's it. I wondered why His Eminence was so cooperative. I wondered why he'd sent an Englishman instead of an Italian—and a secular priest instead of a long-faced Barnabite. Clever of him! But I'm afraid he's wrong." The laugh died suddenly on his lips and he was as serious again. He set down his wineglass and spread his hands in an eloquent gesture of explanation. "He's quite wrong, Meredith. That's what happens in Rome. The stupid get stupider still and the clever fellows like Marotta get too clever for everyone else's good. There are two reasons why I'm interested in this case. The first is simple and official. It's an unauthorised cultus. I have to investigate it, for approval or condemnation. The second isn't half so simple—and the officials wouldn't understand it."

"Marotta might," said Meredith quietly. "I might too."

"Why should you two be different?"

"Because Marotta's a wise old humanist—and because I'm due to die of a carcinoma in twelve months."

Aurelio, Bishop of Valenta, leaned back in his chair and studied the pale, drawn face of his visitor. After a long moment he said softly:

"I've been wondering about you. Now I begin to understand. Very well, I'll try to explain. A man in the shadow of death should be beyond scandal, even from a bishop. I believe that the Church in this country is in drastic need of reform. I think we have too many saints and not enough sanctity, too many cults and not enough catechism, too many medals and

42

not enough medicine, too many churches and not enough schools. We have three million workless men and three million women living by prostitution. We control the State through the Christian Democratic Party and the Vatican Bank; yet we countenance a dichotomy which gives prosperity to half the country and lets the other half rot in penury. Our clergy are under-educated and insecure and yet we rail against anti-clericals and Communists. A tree is known by its fruits—and I believe that it's better to proclaim a new deal in social justice than a new attribute of the Blessed Virgin. The first is a necessary application of a moral principle, the second is simply a definition of a traditional belief. We clergy are more jealous of our rights under the Concordat than the rights of our people under the natural and divine law. . . . Do I shock you, Monsignor?"

"You encourage me," said Blaise Meredith. "But why do you want a new saint?"

"I don't," said the Bishop, with surprising emphasis. "I'm committed to the case, but I hope, with all my heart, it fails. The Mayor of Gemello Maggiore has collected fifteen million lire to advance the cause, but I can't get a thousand out of him for a diocesan orphanage. If Giacomo Nerone is beatified, they'll want a new church to house him—and I want nursing nuns and an agricultural adviser and twenty thousand fruit trees from California."

"Then why did you ask His Eminence for help?"

"It's a principle in Rome, my dear Meredith. You always get the opposite of what you ask for."

Blaise Meredith did not smile. A new and disturbing thought was shaping itself in his mind. He paused a little, trying to find words to frame it.

"But if the case is proved? If Giacomo Nerone is really a saint and a wonder-worker?"

"I'm a pragmatist, as I told you," said His Lordship with side-long humour. "I'll wait on the facts. When would you like to begin work?"

"Immediately," said Meredith. "I'm living on borrowed time. I'd like to spend a few days studying the documents.

Then I'll move out to Gemelli dei Monti to begin taking depositions."

"I'll have the records delivered to your room in the morning. I hope you will regard this house as your home and myself as your friend."

"I am grateful to Your Lordship, more grateful than I can say."

"There is nothing to be grateful for." The Bishop smiled in deprecation. "I shall be glad of your company. I feel we have much in common. Oh . . . there is a small counsel I would give you."

"Yes?"

"It's my private opinion that you will not find the truth about Giacomo Nerone in Gemello Maggiore. They venerate him there. They make profit from his memory. In Gemello Minore, it's quite another story—provided you can get them to tell it. So far none of my people has succeeded."

"Is there any reason?"

"Better you ask the reasons for yourself, my friend. As you see, I'm rather prejudiced." He pushed back his chair and stood up. "It's late and you must be tired. I suggest you rest late in the morning. I'll have breakfast sent to your room."

Blaise Meredith was touched by the patrician politeness of the man. He was chary of confidences, jealous of his own privacy, but he said very humbly:

"I am a sick man, Your Lordship. I am suddenly very lonely. You have made me feel at home. Thank you."

"We are brothers in a big family," said the Bishop gently. "But being bachelors we grow selfish and singular. I'm glad to be of service. Goodnight—and golden dreams."

Alone in the big guest-room with the moonlight streaming through the open casements, Blaise Meredith prepared himself for another night. Its course was familiar to him now, but none the less frightening. He would lie wakeful till midnight, then sleep would come, shallow and restless. Before the cocks began to screech at the false dawn he would start up, his belly cramped with pain, his mouth full of the sour taste of bile and blood. He would struggle to the toilet, weak and retching, then cram himself with opiate and go back to bed. Just before sunrise he would sleep again—one hour, two at most—not enough to refresh him, but enough to keep the sluggish, diminishing life-stream flowing in his arteries.

It was a strange compound of terrors: the fear of death, the shame of slow dissolution, the eerie solitude of the believer in the presence of a faceless God whom he acknowledged unseen but must soon meet unveiled and splendid in judgment. He could not escape them into sleep and he could not exorcise them by prayer, since prayer had become an arid act of the will which could neither stifle pain nor set a balm to it.

So tonight, in spite of his fatigue, he tried to defer the purgatory. He undressed, put on pyjamas, slippers and dressing gown and walked out on the balcony.

The moon was high over the valley—a ship of antique silver, placid on a luminous sea. The orange groves glowed coldly and the olive leaves were bright as dagger tips out of a twisted mass of shadows. Below them the water lay flat and full of stars, behind a barricade of logs and piled rubble, while the arms of the mountains encircled it all like ramparts, shutting out the chaos of the centuries.

Blaise Meredith looked at it and found it good. Good in itself, good in the man who had made it. Man did not live by bread alone—but he could not live without it. The old monks had had the same idea. They planted the Cross in the middle of a desert—and then planted corn and fruit trees, so that the barren symbol flowered into a green reality. They knew, better than most, that man was a creature of flesh and spirit; but that the spirit could not function except in and through the flesh. When the body was sick, the moral responsibility of man was reduced. Man was a thinking reed, but the reed must be anchored firmly in black earth, watered at the roots, warmed by the sun.

Aurelio, Bishop of Valenta, was a pragmatist, but a Christian pragmatist. He was the inheritor of the oldest and most orthodox tradition in the Church: that earth and grass and tree and

45

animal were the issue of the same creative act that produced a man. They were good in themselves, perfect in their nature and in the laws that governed their growth and decay. Only Man's misuse could debase them to instruments of evil. To plant a tree was therefore a godly act. To make barren earth flourish was to share in the act of creation. To teach other men these things was to make them, too, participate in a divine plan. . . . Yet Aurelio, Bishop of Valenta, was suspect to many of his own colleagues.

This was the mystery of the Church: that it should hold in organic unity humanists like Marotta and formalists like Blaise Meredith and fools like the Calabrian, reformers, rebels and puritan conformists, political Popes, and nursing nuns, worldly priests and devout anti-clericals. It demanded an unwavering assent to defined doctrine and permitted an extraordinary divergence of discipline.

It imposed poverty on its religious, yet played the stock markets of the world through the Vatican Bank. It preached detachment from the world, yet collected real estate like any public company. It forgave adulterers and excommunicated heretics. It was harsh with its own reformers, yet signed concordats with those who wanted to destroy it. It was the hardest community in the world to live in—yet all its members wanted to die in it, and Pope, Cardinal or washerwoman, they would take their viaticum with gratitude from the lowest country priest.

It was a mystery and a paradox, yet Blaise Meredith was further from understanding it, further from accepting it than he had been for twenty years. This was what troubled him. When he had been well, his mind had bent naturally to accept the idea of a divine intervention in human affairs. Now that the life was bleeding out of him, slowly, he found himself clinging desperately to the simplest manifestation of physical continuity —a tree, a flower, lake water quiet under an eternal moonlight.

A faint breeze stirred along the valley, rattling the crisp leaves, ruffling the stars in the water. Meredith shivered in the sudden chill and went inside, closing the french door behind

46

him. He knelt down on the prie-dieu under the wooden figure of the Christus and began to pray . . .

"*Pater Noster qui es in Coelis . . .*"

But heaven, if heaven there were, was shut blank against him, and there was no answer from the faceless Father to his dying son.

CHAPTER THREE

Doctor Aldo Meyer stood at the doorway of his house and watched the village wake sluggishly to a new day.

First, old Nonna Patucci opened her door, peered up and down the cobbled street, then tottered across the road and emptied her chamber pot over the wall and on to the vine terrace below. Then she went inside, furtive as a witch, and closed the door with a resounding slam. As if at a signal, Felici the cobbler came out, in singlet and trousers and wooden pattens, to stand yawning and scratching his armpits and watch the sun light up the roof of the new hospital in Gemello Maggiore, two miles across the valley. After a minute of contemplation, he hawked noisily, spat on the ground and proceeded to unbolt his shutters.

Then the door of the priest's house opened and Rosa Benzoni waddled out, fat and shapeless in a black dress, to draw water from the cistern. As soon as she had gone the upstairs window opened and Father Anselmo's tousled grey head appeared, tentative as a tortoise making its first cautious exploration of the day.

Martino the smith came next, squat, barrel-chested, brown as a nut, to open the door of his shed and start the bellows working. By the time the first strokes of his hammer began to sound on the anvil, the whole village was stirring—women emptying slop pails, barelegged girls wandering down to the cistern with great green bottles on their heads, half-naked children piddling against the road wall, the first labourers moving off to the terraces and the garden patches, with ragged coats slung over their shoulders and their bread and olives wrapped in cotton handkerchiefs.

Aldo Meyer watched it all, without curiosity, without resentment, even when they passed him with averted heads or made the sign of the evil eye in the direction of his door. It was the measure of his disillusionment that he could ignore their hostility and yet cling like an animal to familiar sights and sounds: the rhythmic clang of the hammer, the trundle of a donkey cart on the stones, the shrill cries of children, the scolding of housewives; the vines and the olive groves, climbing down the hillside towards the valley fields, the straggle of crumbling houses up the road towards the big villa that crowned the hilltop, the gleam of sunrise on the prosperous town on the farther hill where the saint worked wonders for the tourists while Maria Rossi died in child-bed with his relic on her swollen body.

Each day he promised himself that tomorrow he would pack and go—to a new place with a new future—and leave this graceless tribe to its folly. But each night the resolution drained out of him and he sat down to drink himself into bed. The comfortless truth was that he had no place to go and no future to build. The best of himself was here—faith, hope and charity poured out to exhaustion, sucked up and wasted in a barren earth, trodden by a thankless, ignorant people.

From far down in the valley he heard the muted clatter of a motor-cycle and, when he turned towards it, he saw a small Vespa with a pillion passenger jolting up the track in a cloud of grey dust. The spectacle was banal enough but it moved Aldo Meyer to wintry amusement. The Vespa and the Contessa's automobile were the only motor vehicles in Gemello Minore. The Vespa had caused a minor riot and a gaping wonder that went on for weeks. Its rider was an oddity, too—an English painter, house-guest of the Contessa who lived in the villa on the hilltop and who owned all of the farmland and most of Gemello Minore as well. The painter's name was Nicholas Black, his pillion passenger was a local youth, Paolo Sanduzzi, who had attached himself to Black as guide, baggage animal and instructor in local dialect and customs.

To the villagers, the Englishman was *matto*—a crazy fellow who ambled about with a sketch book or sat for hours in the sun painting olive trees and tumbled rocks and angles of ruinous buildings. His dress was as crazy as his habits, a bright red shirt, faded denims, rope sandals and a battered straw hat, under whose brim a faun-like face grinned crookedly at the

49

world about him. He had not even the excuse of youth—he was past thirty—and when the girls gave up sighing after him, the elders began to make crude gossip about his association with the Contessa, who lived in solitary splendour behind the grilled gates of the villa.

Aldo Meyer heard the rumours and discounted them. He knew too much about the Contessa, and in his Roman days he had met too many artists, and quite enough Englishmen like Nicholas Black. He wondered more about Paolo Sanduzzi, with his slim, Arab body and his smooth face and his bright, shrewd eyes and his tyranny over his eccentric master. He wondered the more because he had seen the boy into the world and he knew that his father was Giacomo Nerone, whom folk were beginning to call the Saint . . .

At the lower end of the village the Vespa stopped, the youth got off and Meyer watched him scrambling down the hillside towards his mother's house, a rough stone hut set in the middle of a small garden patch and sheltered by a clump of ilex. The Vespa started off again with a clatter and a few moments later came to a halt outside Meyer's cottage. The painter eased himself stiffly out of the saddle and threw out his arm in a theatrical salutation:

"*Comé va, Dottore?* How goes it this morning? I'd like some coffee if you've got any."

"There's always coffee," said Meyer, with a grin. "How else would I face the sunrise?"

"Hangover?" asked the painter with malicious innocence.

Meyer shrugged wryly and led the way through the house and out into a small walled garden, where an old grey fig tree made a canopy against the sun. A rough table was covered with a checked cloth and set with cups and dishes of Calabrese pottery. A woman was bending over it, laying out new bread, a cut of white cheese and a bowl of the small local fruit.

Her legs and feet were bare in the peasant fashion, and she wore a black cotton dress and a black head-scarf, both meticulously clean. Her back was straight, her breasts deep and firm, and her face was pure Greek, as if some ancient colonist from

50

the coast had wandered into the mountains and mated with a woman of the tribes, to begin this new hybrid strain. She was perhaps thirty-six years of age. She had borne a child, yet she had not coarsened like the mountain women, and her mouth and eyes were curiously serene. When she saw the visitor, she gave a small start of surprise and looked inquiringly at Meyer. He said nothing, but made a cautionary gesture of dismissal. As she walked back into the house the painter's eyes followed her and he grinned like a knowing goat.

"You surprise me, Doctor. Where did you find her? I've never seen her before."

"She belongs here," said Meyer coolly. "She has a house of her own and she keeps pretty much to herself. She comes up each day to clean and cook for me."

"I'd like to paint her."

"I don't advise it," Meyer told him curtly.

"Why not?"

"She's the mother of Paolo Sanduzzi."

"Oh." Black flushed and let the subject drop. They sat down at the table and Meyer poured the coffee. There was silence for a few moments; then Black began to talk, volubly and dramatically.

"Big news from Valenta, Dottore! I was down there yesterday to pick up canvases and paints. The place is humming with it."

"What sort of news?"

"This saint of yours, Giacomo Nerone. They're going to beatify him, it seems."

Meyer shrugged indifferently and sipped his coffee.

"That's not news. They've been talking about it for twelve months."

"Ah, but it is!" The sharp faun's face lit up with sardonic amusement. "They've stopped talking and started an official process. They're circulating the notices now—tacking them up in all the churches, and calling for any person who has evidence to give. The Bishop's got a house-guest, a Monsignor from Rome who has been appointed to open the case. He'll be coming up here within a few days."

"The devil he will!" Meyer set down his cup with a clatter. "Are you sure of that?"

"Certain of it. It's all over town. I saw the fellow myself driving in His Lordship's car—grey and pinched like a Vatican mouse. He's English, it seems, so I took it on myself to offer an invitation from the Contessa to lodge him. She's a godly woman and lonely, as you know." He chuckled and reached out to pour himself another cup of coffee. "This place will be famous, Dottore. You'll be famous too."

"That's what I'm afraid of," said Meyer sombrely.

"Afraid?" The painter's eyes brightened with interest. "Why should you be afraid? You're not even a Catholic. It's no concern of yours."

"You don't understand," Meyer told him irritably. "You don't understand anything."

"On the contrary, my dear fellow!" The long artist's hands gestured emphatically. "On the contrary I understand everything. I understand what you have tried to do here and why you have failed. I know what the Church is trying to do, and why it will succeed, at least for a while. What I don't know—and what I'm dying to see—is what will happen when they start digging up the real truth about Giacomo Nerone. I'd intended to leave next week; but now I think I'll stay. It should be quite a comedy."

"Why did you come here in the first place?" There was an edge of anger in Meyer's voice and Nicholas Black was quick to notice it. He grinned and fluttered an airy hand.

"It's very simple. I had an exhibition in Rome—quite successful, too, even though it was on the fringe of the season. The Contessa was one of my clients. She bought three canvases. Then she invited me to come down here and paint for a while. I'm hoping she'll finance another show in the near future. It's as simple as that."

"Nothing is ever as simple as that," said the doctor mildly. "And the Contessa is not a simple person. Neither are you. What you see as a provincial comedy may well turn into a grand tragedy. I advise you not to become involved in it."

52

The Englishman threw back his head and laughed.

"But I am involved, my dear Doctor. I'm an artist, an observer and recorder of the beauty and the folly of mankind. Imagine what Goya could have made out of a situation like this one. Fortunately he's been dead a long time, so now it's my turn. There's a whole gallery of pictures here—and the title's ready made: 'Beatification', by Nicholas Black! A one-man show on a single theme. A village saint, the village sinners and all the clergy, right up to the Bishop himself. What do you think of that?"

Aldo Meyer looked down at the backs of his hands, studying the brown liver spots and the rough slack skin that told him more clearly than words how old he was getting. Without lifting his eyes, he said quietly:

"I think you are a very unhappy man, Nicholas Black. You are looking for something you will never find. I think you should go away immediately. Leave the Contessa. Leave Paolo Sanduzzi. Leave us all to deal with our problems in our own way. You don't belong here. You speak our language, but you don't understand us."

"But I do, Doctor!" The handsome, epicene face was lit with malice. "I do indeed. I know that you've all been hiding something for fifteen years, and now it's going to be dug up. The Church wants a saint and you want to keep a secret that discredits you. That's true, isn't it?"

"It's half a truth; which is always more than half a lie."

"You knew Giacomo Nerone, didn't you?"

"I knew him, yes."

"Was he a saint?"

"I know nothing about saints," said Aldo Meyer gravely. "I only know men."

"And Nerone . . .?"

". . . was a man."

"What about his miracles?"

"I have never seen a miracle."

"Do you believe in them?"

"No."

The bright sardonic eyes were fixed on his drawn face.

"Then why, my dear Doctor, are you afraid of this investigation?"

Aldo Meyer pushed back his chair and stood up. The shadow of the fig tree fell across his face, deepening the hollows of his cheeks, hiding the stark pain in his eyes. After a moment he answered:

"Have you ever been ashamed of yourself, my friend?"

"Never," said the painter cheerfully. "Never in my life."

"That's what I mean," said the doctor softly. "You will never understand. But I tell you again, you should go—and go quickly."

His only answer was a smile of rueful mockery as Black stood up to take his leave. They did not shake hands and Meyer made no attempt to accompany him out of the garden. Half way to the house, the painter stopped and turned back.

"I'd almost forgotten. There's a message for you from the Contessa. She would like you to dine with her tomorrow evening."

"My thanks to the Contessa," said Meyer dryly. "I'll be happy to come. Good day, my friend."

"*Ci vedremo*," said Nicholas Black casually. "We'll see each other again—quite soon."

Then he was gone, a slim, faintly clownish figure, too jaunty for the years that were beginning to show themselves in his intelligent, unhappy face. Aldo Meyer sat down again at the table and stared unseeingly at the broken crusts and the brown, muddy dregs in the coffee cups. After a while the woman came out of the house and stood looking down at him, with gentleness and pity in her calm eyes. When he looked up and saw her standing there, he said curtly:

"You can clear the table, Nina."

She made no move to obey him, but asked:

"What did he want, that one who looks like a goat?"

"He brought me news," said Meyer, lapsing into dialect to match the woman's. "They are starting a new investigation into the life of Giacomo Nerone. A priest has come down from Rome to assist the Bishop's court. He will be coming here shortly."

"He will ask questions, like the others?"

"More than the others, Nina."

"Then he will get the same answer—nothing!"

Meyer shook his head slowly.

"Not this time, Nina. It has gone too far. Rome is interested. The press will be interested. Better they get the truth this time."

She stared at him in shocked surprise.

"You say that? You!"

Meyer shrugged defeatedly and quoted an old country proverb.

"Who can fight the wind? Who can drown the shouting they make on the other side of the valley? Even in Rome they have heard it—and this is the result. Let's tell them what they want and be done with it. Maybe then they will leave us in peace."

"But why do they want it?" There was anger now in her eyes and in her voice. "What difference does it make? They called him all sorts of names in his life—now they want to call him a *beato*. It's just another name. It doesn't change what he was—a good man, my man."

"They don't want a man, Nina," said Meyer wearily. "They want a plaster saint with a gold plate on top of his head. The Church wants it because it gives them another hold on the people—a new cult, a new promise of miracles to make them forget their bellyaches. The people want it because they can get down on their knees and beg for favours instead of rolling up their sleeves and working for them—or fighting for them. It's the way of the Church—sugar for old sour wine."

"Then why do you want me to help them?"

"Because if we tell them the truth, they'll drop the case. They'll have to. Giacomo was a remarkable man, but he was no more a saint than I am."

"Is that what you believe?"

"Don't you, Nina?"

Her answer shocked him like a blow in the face.

"I know he was a saint," she told him softly. "I know he did miracles, because I saw them."

Meyer gaped at her; then he shouted:

"God Almighty, woman! Even you? He slept in your bed. He gave you a bastard child, but never married you. And you can stand there and tell me he was a saint who did miracles. Why didn't you tell the priests that the first time? Why didn't you join our friend across the way and go shouting to have him beatified?"

"Because he would never have wanted it," said Nina Sanduzzi calmly. "Because it was the one thing he asked—that I should never tell what I knew about him."

He was beaten and he knew it, but there was one more weapon left and he struck with its viciously.

"What will you answer, Nina, when they point to your boy and say, 'There is a saint's son, and he makes himself a *feminella* for the Englishman'?"

There was no hint of shame in the calm, classic face as she replied:

"What do I say when they point to me in the street and whisper: 'There is the one who was a saint's whore'? Nothing, nothing at all! Do you know why, Dottore? Because before Giacomo died, he made me a promise, in return for mine. 'No matter what happens, *cara*, I shall look after you and the boy. They can kill me, but they can't stop me caring for you from now to eternity!' I believed him then, I believe him now. The boy is foolish but he is not lost yet."

"Then he damned soon will be," said Meyer brutally. "Go home now, for God's sake, and leave me in peace."

But even after she was gone there was no peace; and he knew there never would be until the inquisitors came and dragged the truth out into the daylight.

No hint of morning had yet entered the high, baroque room in the villa where the Countess Anne Louise de Sanctis slept behind velvet curtains. No premonition of trouble could penetrate the barbituric haze beyond which she dreamed.

Later, much later, a servant would come in and open the curtains to let the sun flow over the worn carpet and the rusted velvet and the dull patina of the carved walnut. It would not reach as far as the bed, which was a kindness, because the Contessa in the morning was an unpleasing spectacle.

Later still, she would wake, dry-mouthed, grey, puffy-eyed and discontented with the advent of a new day exactly like the old. She would wake, and doze, then wake again and thrust the first cigarette of the day into her pale, down-drawn lips. The cigarette finished, she would pull the bell-cord and the servant would return, smiling in anxious good humour and carrying a breakfast tray. Since the Contessa disliked eating alone at any time, the servant would remain in the room, folding the scattered clothes, laying out fresh ones, bustling back and forth to the bathroom, while her mistress kept up a flow of waspish comment on the household and its shortcomings.

Breakfast finished, the servant would take away the tray, the Contessa would smoke one more cigarette before beginning the small intimate ritual of the toilet. It was the one important ceremony of her unimportant day, and she performed it in rigid secrecy.

She stubbed out her cigarette in the silver ashtray, then got out of bed, walked to the door and locked it. Next she made a circuit of the room, standing at each of the windows and looking out on the terraces and over the gardens to make sure that no one was near. Once an inquisitive gardener had stood staring through the casements, and he had been instantly dismissed for this sacrilegious intrusion into the mysteries.

Assured at last of her privacy the Contessa went to the bathroom, undressed and stepped into the great marble bath with its gilt taps and its array of soaps and sponges and bottles of bath salts. There was no pleasure now to be compared with this first solitary immersion in steaming water that soaked away the effusions of a drugged sleep and brought back the illusion of youth to an ageing body. Unlike other pleasures this one could be renewed at will, prolonged to satiation. It demanded no partner, involved neither dependence nor surrender; and the Contessa clung to it with the passion of a devotee.

As she lay back in the steaming water, she surveyed herself: the lines of the flanks, still slim and youthful, the belly fat and unmarked by childbearing, the waist, thickening a little, but not too much, the breasts massaged to firmness, small but round and still youthful. If there were lines about her neck, there was no mirror yet to tell her, and the telltale creases at mouth and eyes could still be massaged into subjection. Youth had not yet dried out of her and age could be held a little longer at bay with a weekly consignment of compounds from a discreet salon on the Via Veneto.

But the bath was only the beginning. There was the drying with soft warm towels, the rubbing with rough ones, the perfuming with sharp, astringent lotion, the powder dusted on and whisked gently away, the first combing of the hair—no grey in it yet, though the gold was fading—the ribbon to tie it back from the scrubbed and shining cheeks. Finally, she was ready for the processional climax of the ritual.

Naked and glowing from the new illusion, she walked back into the bedroom, crossed to the dressing table and took from the top drawer the photograph of a man in the uniform of a colonel of Alpini and set it up facing the room. Then, self-conscious as a mannequin, she began to dress herself in front of it, carefully, coquettishly, as if to charm him out of the frame and into her expectant arms.

When she was clothed, she laid the photograph back in the drawer, closed it, locked it, then, quite calmly, sat down in front of the mirror and began to make up her face.

Twenty minutes later, dressed in a modish summer frock, she walked out of the bedroom, down the stairs and into the bright garden, where Nicholas Black, stripped to the waist, was working on a new canvas.

He turned at her footfall and came to greet her with theatrical pleasure, kissing her hands and then spinning her round to display her frock, while he chattered like a happy parrot:

"Magnificent, *cara*! I don't know how you do it! Every morning is like a new revelation. In Rome you were beautiful but rather terrifying. Here you're a country beauty reserved for my private admiration. I must paint you in that frock. Here, sit down and let me look at you."

She bridled happily at the compliments and let him lead her to a small stone seat shaded by a blossoming almond tree. He made a great show of settling her to his satisfaction, fanning out her frock along the bench, tilting her head upward to the flowers and settling her hands in her lap. Then he snatched up a sketch block and, with swift, bravura strokes, began to draw, talking all the time.

"I had coffee with our doctor friend this morning. He had his usual hangover, but he brightened up when I told him of your invitation to dinner. I had the idea he's more than half in love with you. . . . No, no! don't talk, you'll spoil the pose. I don't suppose the poor fellow can help it. He's lived so long among the peasants, you must seem like the fairy princess up here in your castle. . . . Oh, and another thing: the Bishop of Valenta is starting a full-scale investigation into the life and virtues of Giacomo Nerone. He's imported an English Monsignor from Rome to act as Devil's Advocate. He'll be coming up here in a few days. I took the liberty of telling His Lordship you'd be happy to have him as a guest."

"No!" It was a panic cry. All her composure fell away and she stared at him, angry and afraid.

"But, *cara*!" He was instantly penitent. He put down the sketch block and went to her, with solicitous hands and voice. "I thought that's what you'd want me to do. I couldn't consult you, but I knew you were friendly with the Bishop and I knew there was really no other place for the visitor to lodge. He couldn't sleep with the peasants, now could he? Or under the counter in the wine shop? Besides, he's a countryman of yours—and mine. I thought it would give you pleasure. If I've offended you, I'll never forgive myself."

He went down on his knees beside her and buried his face in her lap, like a penitent child.

It was an old, old trick to charm the dowagers, and it worked again. She ran her fingers caressingly through his hair and said gently:

"Of course you haven't offended me, Nicki. It was surprise, that's all. I . . . I'm not prepared for them now as I used to be. Of course you did right. I'll be happy to have this Monsignor."

"I knew you would be!" Instantly he was gay again. "His

59

Lordship was grateful—and I don't think our visitor will be too stuffy. Besides . . ." A small smiling malice shone again in his eyes. "We'll be able to follow the investigation from the inside, won't we?"

"I suppose so." Her face clouded again and she began to pluck nervously at the folds of her frock. "But what will he do here?"

Nicholas Black gestured airily.

"What they all do. Ask questions, take notes, examine witnesses. Come to think of it, you'll probably be one yourself. You knew Nerone, didn't you?"

She shifted uneasily and refused to meet his eyes.

"Only slightly. I . . . I couldn't tell anything worth knowing."

"Then what are you worrying about, *cara*? You'll have a box seat at a village comedy—and some Roman gossip as well. Come on now, settle yourself again and let me get this sketch done."

But for all his care, he could not charm the fear out of her, and when he came to draw her face, every stroke was a lie. But all women were fools. They saw only what they wanted to see —and Nicholas Black had been making a profit from their follies for the best part of his life.

When the sketch was done, he handed it to her with a flourish and grinned inwardly at her expression of relief and pleasure. Then with calculated casualness he kissed her hand and dismissed her:

"You disturb me, darling. You're a beautiful nuisance. Go and pick me some flowers for the bedroom and let me finish my picture."

As he watched her walking uncertainly across the lawn he chuckled to himself. She had been kind to him, and he bore her no personal malice. But he too had his secret pleasures, and the most subtle of all was to humble by intrigue what he could never subdue by possession—the hungry, hateful flesh of womankind.

For Anne Louise de Sanctis the moment had far other meanings. She was neither stupid nor vicious, though she consented equally to the follies of middle age and the vices that a still lively body imposed on her. When she submitted herself to the small tyrannies of the painter, it was because they piqued her vanity, and because she knew that she still held the balance of power. He wanted her to finance a new exhibition in Rome. She could do it—or she could send him packing tomorrow, back to the catchpenny life of a mediocre artist, and the sedulous pursuit of complaisant dowagers.

It pleased her to see that he, too, was getting old, and that each new conquest was a little more difficult. His malice was like the malice of a child, hurtful sometimes, but always joined with an unacknowledged need of her. And it was a long time since she had been needed by anyone. She had her own needs, too, but though he understood them and played on them, he was powerless to use them against her. He played on her fears and her loneliness, but the real terror he had not yet discovered.

It was this terror that walked with her now in the dappled garden on the hilltop, where wealth and cheap labour had planted an oasis in the raw, parched land of Calabria. The earth for the lawns and flower beds had been brought up the hill in baskets on the shoulders of village women. The stone had been hacked out of the hillside by local masons, the olives and the pines and the orange groves planted by tenant farmers as their tribute to the family that had held them in fee for centuries. Neapolitan artists had painted the walls and the coffered ceilings, and a dozen connoisseurs had bid for the pictures and the statuary and the porcelain demanded by Count Gabriele de Sanctis for his English bride.

The circling wall had been built, and the crested gates forged, to give her privacy. The staff had been chosen by the Count himself to serve her solicitously. The house and the land and everything in it were his wedding gift to her; a provincial retreat after the hectic season of Rome, where Gabriele de Sanctis was rising high in the service of the Duce. For the daughter of a minor diplomat, fresh from her first season in London, it was like an Arabian night's enchantment, but the terror had come in with her at the gates and it had stayed with her all the years since.

Gabriele de Sanctis had begun it—but he was dead long ago, a discredited suicide in the Libyan desert. A dozen other men had come and gone in the intervening years, but none of them had been able to rid her of it.

Then there was Giacomo Nerone. In this same garden, on a morning such as this, she had humbled herself and begged him to exorcise her, but he had refused. She had revenged herself in the end, but the revenge had brought new furies to torment her—nightmares in the big baroque bed, ghosts haunting the olive groves and grinning like satyrs through the orange blossom. Lately they had plagued her less. There were drugs to bring sleep, and Nicholas Black to divert her in the daytime.

But now a new man was coming: a grey-faced cleric from Rome commissioned to dig into the past, to tally old debts and record buried guilts, no matter what pain might follow the revelation. He would lodge in her house and eat at her table. He would pry and probe and even the locked door of her bedroom would keep no secrets from him.

Suddenly the life she had drawn in from the morning bath seemed to drain out of her, leaving her slack and tired. She made her way with slow, dragging steps to a small arbour on the fringe of the olive plantation where a small statue of a dancing faun was poised on a weathered stone pedestal. In front of the faun was a rustic bench over which honeysuckle drooped, languid and cloying. She sat down, lit a cigarette and inhaled greedily, drawing the smoke down into her lungs and feeling the tension in her relax slowly.

She understood now. She had been running too long. There was no escape from the fear which she carried like a tenant in her own body. There must be an end to it, else she would topple over into the black madness that threatens all women who come to the climacteric unhappy and unprepared. But how to end it? Break down all doors, humble herself to the inquisitors, submit to a confessional purging? She had tried it before, and it had failed utterly.

There was one alternative, bleak, perhaps, but sure: the small bottle full of gelatine capsules that seduced her nightly into sleep. The little more—the so little more—and it would be finished, once for all. In a sense it would be the completion of her revenge on Giacomo Nerone, and a revenge on the body which had betrayed her to him, and him to her.

But not yet. There was still a little time. Let the priest come, and if he did not press her too hard it would be a favourable omen—a promise of other solutions. If he did . . . why, then it would be simple, ironic and final; and when they found her she would still be beautiful as she was each morning from the perfumed bath.

CHAPTER FOUR

FOR BLAISE MEREDITH, the days he spent in the Bishop's house were the happiest of his life. A cold man by nature, he had begun to understand the meaning of fellowship. Withdrawn and self-sufficient, he saw, for the first time, the dignity of dependence, the grace of a shared confidence. Aurelio, Bishop of Valenta, was a man with a gift of understanding and a rare talent for friendship. The loneliness and the wintry courage of his guest had touched him deeply, and with tact and sympathy he set about establishing an intimacy between them.

Early the first morning he came to Meredith's room carrying the bulky volume of records on the first investigation of Giacomo Nerone. He found the priest, pale and fatigued, sitting in bed with the breakfast tray on his knees. He put the volume down on the table and then came, solicitously, to sit on the edge of the bed.

"A bad night, my friend?"

Meredith nodded wanly.

"A little worse than usual. The travel perhaps, and the excitement. I must apologise. I had hoped to serve Your Lordship's mass."

The Bishop shook his head, smiling.

"No, Monsignor. Now you are under my jurisdiction. You are forbidden all but the Sunday Mass. You will sleep late and retire early, and if I find you working too hard, I may have to withdraw you from the case. You're in the country now. Take time for yourself. Smell the earth and the orange blossom. Get the dust of the libraries out of your lungs."

"Your Lordship is kind," said Meredith gravely, "but there is all too little time."

"All the more reason to spend some of it on yourself," the Bishop told him. "And a little on me as well. I'm a stranger here too, remember. My colleagues are good men, most of them, but very dull company. There are things I should like to show you, talk I should like to hear from you. As for this"—he pointed to the bulky, leather-bound volume—"you can read it in the garden. Half of it is repetition and rhetoric. The rest you can digest in a couple of days. The people you want to see are only an hour away by car . . . and mine is at your disposal at any time, with a driver to look after you!"

A slow, puzzled smile dawned on Meredith's pallid face.

"You are kind to me and I find it strange. I wonder why?"

A youthful grin brightened the face of the Bishop.

"You have lived too long in Rome, my friend. You have forgotten that the Church is a family of the faithful, not simply a bureaucracy of believers. It's a sign of the times—one of the less hopeful signs. This is the century of the machine and the Church has conceded too much to it. They have time clocks in the Vatican now and adding machines and ticker tape to tally the stock market."

In spite of his weariness, Meredith threw back his head and laughed heartily. The Bishop nodded approvingly.

"That's better. A little honest laughter would do us all good. We need a satirist or two to give us back a sense of proportion."

"We'd probably prosecute them for libel," said Meredith wryly, "or indict them for heresy."

"*Inter faeces et urinam nascimur,*" the Bishop quoted quietly. "It was a Saint who said it—and it applies equally to Popes and priests and the prostitutes of Reggio di Calabria. A little more laughter at our comic estate, a few honest tears for the pity of things—and we'd all be better Christians. Now finish your breakfast and then take a walk in the garden. I've spent a lot of time on it; and I'd hate an Englishman to ignore it!"

An hour later, bathed, shaved and refreshed, he walked out into the garden, taking with him the volume of depositions on Giacomo Nerone. It had rained during the night and the sky was clear, while the air was full of the smell of damp earth and washed leaves and new blossom. The bees were bumbling round the orange flowers and the scarlet hibiscus, and the yellow gillyflowers stood straight and strident round the stone borders of the paths. Again Meredith was touched with hunger for a permanence on this thrusting earth whose beauty he was seeing for the first time. If only he could stay with it longer, root himself like a tree, to be weathered and blown, but still survive for the rain and the sun and the renewal of spring. But no. He had lived in the dust of the libraries too long and when the time came they would bury him in it. No flowers would grow out of his mouth as they did from the mouths of humbler men, no roots would twine themselves round the mould of his heart and his loins. They would screw him down in a leaden box and carry him to a vault in the Cardinal's church, where he would moulder, barren as he had lived, until Judgment Day.

Round the trunks of the olive trees the grass was green and the air was warm and still. He took off his cassock and his stock and opened his shirt to let the warmth fall on his thin chest; then he sat down, leaning against the bole of a tree, opened the big leather volume, and began to read:

'Preliminary depositions on the life, virtues and alleged miracles of the Servant of God, Giacomo Nerone. Collected at the instance and under the authority of His Lordship, Aurelio, Titular of Valenta in the Province of Calabria, by Geronimo Battista and Luigi Saltarello, priests of the same Diocese.'

Then followed the careful disclaimer:

'The following depositions and information are of a non-judicial character, since to this date no court has been set up and no authorities promulgated to examine officially the cause of the Servant of God. Though every effort has been made to arrive at the truth, witnesses were not sworn, nor placed under canonical sanction to reveal any matters known to them. None of the processes of a diocesan court have been observed either as to secrecy or the method of recording. Witnesses have, however, been warned that they may be called to give evidence under oath at such a court, when and if constituted.'

Blaise Meredith nodded and pursed his thin lips with satisfaction. So far so good. This was the bureaucracy of the

Church in action—Roman legality applied to the affairs of the spirit. The sceptics might sneer at it, believers might chuckle at its excesses, but in essence it was sound. It was the same genius that had given to the West the civilising code under which, in part at least, it still lived. He turned the page and read on:

'*De non cultu*. (*Decree of Urban VIII, 1634*)

'In view of the reports about the visits of pilgrims and the veneration paid by certain members of the faithful at the resting place of the Servant of God, we deemed it our first duty to inquire whether the decrees of the Pontiff Urban VIII prohibiting public cultus have been observed. We found that many members of the faithful, both visitors and local people, do visit the tomb of Giacomo Nerone and pray there. Some of them claim spiritual and temporal favours through his intercession. The civil authorities and, in particular, the Mayor of Gemello Maggiore have organised certain press publicity and improved transport facilities to encourage the flow of visitors. While this may constitute an indiscretion, it does not contravene the canons. No public worship is permitted in the canonical sense. The Servant of God is not invoked in liturgical ceremonies. No pictures or images are exposed for public veneration and, apart from garbled press accounts, no books or leaflets containing accounts of miracles have so far been circulated. Certain relics of the Servant of God are in private circulation among the faithful but no public veneration has been permitted to be paid to them. It is our view therefore that the canons prohibiting public cultus have been observed. . . .'

Blaise Meredith drowsed lightly over the formal phrases. This was old ground to him—familiar but reassuring. It was the function of the Church not merely to impose belief, but to limit it as well, to encourage piety but discourage pietists. The laws were there, however much they were obscured by ignorance, and their cool reason was a curb on the excesses of devotees and the harsh demands of the puritans. But he was still a long way from the heart of the problem—the life and virtues and alleged miracles of Giacomo Nerone. The next paragraph brought him no closer. It was headed:

'De scriptis

'No writings of any kind attributable to the Servant of God have been found. Certain references, noted later in the depositions, point to the possible existence of a body of manuscript which has been either lost, destroyed or is being deliberately concealed by interested persons. Until a judicial process has begun and it is possible to bring moral pressure to bear on witnesses, we are unlikely to get further information on this important point.'

Blaise Meredith frowned with dissatisfaction. No writings. A pity. From a judicial point of view the things a man wrote were the only sure indication of his beliefs and intentions, and, in the rigorous logic of Rome, these were even more important than his acts. A man might murder his wife or seduce his daughter and still remain a member of the Church; but let him reject one jot of defined truth and he set himself immediately outside it. He might spend himself in lifelong charities, yet have no merit in him at the end. The moral value of an act depended on the intention with which it was performed. But when a man was dead, who was to speak the secrets of his heart?

It was a discouraging beginning and what followed was even less reassuring:

'Biographical Summary

'*Name:* Giacomo Nerone. There is reason—noted later in the depositions—to assume that this was a pseudonym.

'*Date of Birth:* Unknown. Physical descriptions by witnesses vary considerably, but there is general agreement that he was from 30 to 35 years of age.

'*Place of Birth:* Unknown.

'*Nationality:* Unknown. There is evidence that Giacomo Nerone was at first accepted as an Italian, but that, later, doubts were cast on his identity. He was described as tall, dark and brown-skinned. He spoke Italian fluently and correctly though with a Northern accent. He did not at first speak dialect, but later learned it and spoke it constantly. During the period covered by his life in Gemelli dei Monti, there were units of German, American, British and Canadian troops operating in the province of Calabria. Various guesses have been made at his nationality, but the evidence advanced in support of them is, in our view, inconclusive.

'We are of the opinion, however, for reasons not yet clear that he did make a deliberate effort to conceal his true identity. We are also of the opinion that certain persons knew his identity and are still attempting to hide it.

'*Date of Arrival in Gemelli dei Monti:* The exact date is uncertain, but there is general agreement that it was towards the end of August, 1943. This date corresponds roughly with the Allied conquest of Sicily and the operations of the British Eighth Army in the Calabrian Province.

'*Period of Residence in Gemelli dei Monti:* August, 1943, to 30th June, 1944. The whole of the testimony refers to this period of less than twelve months and any claims to heroic sanctity must be judged on the available records of this unusually short time.

'*Date of Death:* June 30th, 1944. 3 pm. Giacomo Nerone was executed by a firing squad of Partisans under the leadership of a man known as Il Lupo, the Wolf. Both the date and the time are specific and confirmed by eye-witnesses. The circumstances are also confirmed by unanimous testimony.

'*Burial:* The burial took place at 10.30 pm on June 30th. The body of Giacomo Nerone was removed from the place of execution by six persons and buried in the place known as Grotta del Fauno, where it now lies. Both the identification of the body and the circumstances of the burial are confirmed by the unanimous testimony of those who took part in the interment.'

Blaise Meredith closed the thick volume and laid it down on the grass beside him. He leaned his head back against the rough bole of the olive tree and thought about what he had just read. True, it was only a beginning, but from the point of view of the Devil's Advocate it was a dubious one.

There were too many unknowns and the imputation of deliberate secrecy was disturbing. All that was known and covered by testimony was a period of eleven months, out of a lifetime thirty to thirty-five years. There were no writings available for scrutiny. None of these things precluded sanctity, but they might well preclude proven sanctity, which was the matter of Meredith's investigation and the judicial process of the Bishop's court.

Always, in cases like this, one was forced back to the cool logic of the theologians.

It began with the premise of a personal God, self-continuing, self-sufficient, omnipotent. Man was the issue of a creative act of the divine will. The relationship between the Creator and His creature was defined first by the natural law, whose workings were visible and apprehensible by human reason, then by a series of divine revelations, culminating in the Incarnation, the Teaching, Death and Resurrection of God-made-Man, Jesus Christ.

The perfection of man and his ultimate union with the Creator depended on his conformity to the relationship between them, his salvation depended on his being in a state of conformity at the moment of death. He was aided to this conformity by divine help, called grace, which was always available to him in sufficient measure to guarantee salvation, provided he co-operated with it by the use of free will. Salvation implied perfection, but a limited perfection.

But sanctity, heroic sanctity, implied a special call to a greater perfection, through the use of special graces—to none of which a man could attain by his own power. Every age has produced its crop of saints, not all of them were known, and not all known were officially proclaimed.

Official proclamation involved something else again: the implication that the Divinity wished to make known the virtues of the saint by calling attention to them through miracles—acts beyond human power—divine suspensions of the laws of nature.

It was this implication that troubled Meredith at the outset of the case of Giacomo Nerone. It was a simple axiom of every theologian that an omnipotent Being could not, of his nature, lend himself either to triviality or to trivial secrecy.

There was nothing trivial in the birth of a man, since it involved the projection of a new soul into the dimensions of the flesh. There was nothing trivial in the progression of his life,

70

since every act conditioned him for the last moment of it. And his death was the moment when the spirit was thrust out of the body in the irrevocable attitude of conformity or rejection.

So, whatever the gaps in the personal history of Giacomo Nerone, they must be filled in. If facts were concealed, Blaise Meredith must ferret them out, because he, too, must soon be called to judgment.

But what a man must do and what his strength permits him are often two different things. The air was warm, the bourdon of the insects was deceptively soothing and the weariness of a sleepless night crept back insidiously. Blaise Meredith surrendered himself to it and slept on the soft grass until lunchtime.

His Lordship chuckled delightedly when Meredith made rueful confession of his morning's slackness.

"Good! Good! We'll make a countryman of you yet. Did you dream pleasantly?"

"I didn't dream," said Meredith with dry good humour. "And that was as big a mercy as sleep. But I didn't get much work done. I glanced through a few of the testimonies just before lunch, but I'm afraid I find them rather unsatisfactory."

"How?"

"It's hard to define. They're in the normal form. They're obviously the result of careful cross-examination. But—how shall I put it?—they give no clear picture either of Giacomo Nerone, or of the witnesses themselves. And for our purposes both are important. The picture may grow, of course, as I go further, but just now there are no clear outlines."

The Bishop nodded agreement.

"It was my own impression, too. It is one of the reasons for my doubts about the matter. The depositions are all of one piece. There are no elements of conflict or controversy. And saints are generally very controversial people."

"But there are elements of secrecy." Meredith put it to him quietly.

"Precisely." The Bishop sipped his wine and considered his explanation. "It is almost as if one section of the population had convinced itself that this man was a saint and wanted to prove it at all costs."

"And the other section?"

"Was determined to have nothing to say—either for or against."

"It's too early for me to judge that," said Meredith carefully. "I haven't read enough or studied enough. But the tone of the statements I have read so far is stilted and strangely unreal, as if the witnesses were speaking a new language."

"They are!" said the Bishop with sharp interest. "Oddly enough, my friend, you have put your finger on a problem that has exercised me for a long time: the difficulty of accurate communication between the clergy and the laity. It is a difficulty which grows greater, instead of less, and which inhibits even the healing intimacy of the confessional. The root of it, I think, is this: the Church is a theocracy, ruled by a priestly caste, of which you and I are members. We have a language of our own —a hieratic language if you like—formal, stylised, admirably adapted to legal and theological definition. Unfortunately we have also a rhetoric of our own, which, like the rhetoric of the politician, says much and conveys little. But we are not politicians. We are teachers—teachers of a truth which we claim to be essential to man's salvation. Yet how do we preach it? We talk roundly of faith and hope as if we were making a fetishist's incantation. What is faith? A blind leap into the hands of God. An inspired act of will which is our only answer to the terrible mystery of where we came from and where we are going. What is hope? A child's trust in the hand that will lead it out of the terrors that reach from the dark. We preach love and fidelity, as if these were teacup tales—and not bodies writhing on a bed and hot words in dark places, and souls tormented by loneliness and driven to the momentary communion of a kiss. We preach charity and compassion but rarely say what they mean —hands dabbling in sickroom messes, wiping infection from syphilitic sores. We talk to the people every Sunday, but our words do not reach them, because we have forgotten our mother tongue. It wasn't always like this. The sermons of St Bernardine of Siena are almost unprintable today, but they reached hearts, because the truth in them was sharp as a sword, and as painful. . . ." He broke off and smiled, as if in deprecation of his own intensity. Then, after a moment, he said gently, "That's the trouble with our witnesses, Monsignor. We don't understand them because they are talking to us as we talk to them. And it means as little either way."

"Then how do I, of all people, come near them?" asked Meredith, with wry humility.

"The mother tongue," said Aurelio, Bishop of Valenta. "You were born, like them, *inter faeces et urinam*, and they will be surprised to know that you have not forgotten it—surprised enough, maybe, to tell you the truth."

Later that afternoon, while the sun blazed outside the closed shutters and the wise folk of the South dozed away the heat, Blaise Meredith lay on his bed and pondered the words of the Bishop. They were true and he knew it. But the habit of years was strong on him; the careful euphemism, the priestly prudery, as though his tongue should be shamed by mention of the body that bore him and the sublime act that gave him being.

And yet Christ himself had dealt in such common coinage. He had talked in the vulgar tongue of vulgar symbols: a woman screaming in labour, the fat eunuchs waddling through the bazaars, the woman whom many husbands could not satisfy and who turned to a man who was not her husband. He had invoked no convention to shield himself from the men He had himself created. He ate with tax farmers and drank with public women, and He did not shrink from the anointing hands that had caressed the bodies of men in the passion of a thousand nights.

And Giacomo Nerone? If he were a saint, he would be like his Master. If he were not, he would still be a man and the truth about him would be told in the simple language of the bedroom and the wine shop.

As the afternoon wore on and the first chill of evening filtered into the room, Blaise Meredith began, slowly, to understand the task that lay ahead of him.

His first problem was a tactical one. Although the notices had been published, and the two major officials appointed, the court itself had not yet been constituted. Since all court testimony would be sworn and secret—and since there was no point in wasting its time with frivolous or unco-operative people—it was necessary to test them first in private and unsworn interviews, in the same fashion as a civil lawyer tests his witnesses before presenting them.

They had already been interviewed once by Battista and Saltarello, whose records were in his hands. But these were local priests, and by presumption impartial—if not actually in favour of the candidate. His own position was vastly different. He was a foreigner, a Vatican official, the crown prosecutor. He was suspect by the very nature of his office, and if worldly interests were involved—as they undoubtedly were—he could count on active and powerful opposition.

Those who were promoting the Cause of the Saint would be careful to steer him clear of any contentious information. If they had given testimony in favour of Giacomo Nerone, they would not change it for the Devil's Advocate—though they might break down if he could find grounds on which to challenge them. It was folly, of course, to make intrigues about the Almighty, but there was as much folly and intrigue inside the Church as there was outside. The Church was a family of men and women, none of them guaranteed impeccable even by the Holy Ghost.

His best chance therefore seemed to lie with those who had refused to give evidence at all. It might not be easy to find out why some people didn't believe in saints and regarded their cults as a noxious superstition. These might well be willing to reveal anything that pointed to clay feet on a popular idol. Some folk believed in saints but wanted no truck with them at all. They found them uncomfortable company, their virtues a perpetual reproach. There was no one so stubborn as a Catholic at odds with his conscience. Finally there might be those who hesitated to reveal facts creditable to the candidate because they were discreditable to themselves.

The next problem was where to find such people. According

74

to the records of Battista and Saltarello, all the positive information came from Gemello Maggiore, the prosperous village, and all the refusals from the depressed twin across the valley. The distinction was too obvious to be ignored and too artificial to be accepted without question. Meredith decided to discuss it with the Bishop at their next meal together.

His Lordship approached the question with more than usual caution.

"For me, too, this has been one of the most puzzling features of the situation. Let me try to put it into perspective for you. Here are two villages, twins by name and twins by nature, perched on the horns of the same mountain. Before the war, what were they? Typical Calabrian hamlets—small depressed places, inhabited by tenant farmers of absentee landlords. In their outward aspect and in their standard of living there was no perceptible difference between them; except that in Gemello Minore there was a resident *padrona*, the Contessa de Sanctis. . . ." The Bishop leaned ironically on the parenthesis. "An interesting woman, the Contessa. I'll be curious to know what you think of her. You'll be her house-guest when you go to Gemello Minore. However, her presence, then as now, made no difference to the state of the local population. . . . Then came the war. The young men were taken for the Army, the old ones and the women were left to farm the land. It is poor land at best, as you will see, and it got poorer and poorer as the years went on. There was a State levy on the crops, and by the time the landlords had taken their share, there was little enough left for the peasants, and often there was real starvation in the mountains. Now . . ." His Lordship's long, sensitive hands gestured emphatically. "Into this situation comes a man, a stranger, who calls himself Giacomo Nerone. What do we know about him?"

"Little enough," said Blaise Meredith. "He arrives from nowhere dressed in peasant rags. He is wounded and sick with malaria. He claims to be a deserter from the fighting in the South. The villagers accept him at face value. They have sons of their own who are far away. They have no sympathy with a lost cause. A young widow named Nina Sanduzzi takes him into her house and cares for him. He enters into a liaison with her which is later broken off . . . right in the middle of her pregnancy."

"And then?" The Bishop prompted him shrewdly.

Blaise Meredith shrugged in puzzled fashion.

"Then I find myself at a loss. The record is unclear. The witnesses are vague. There is talk of a conversion, a turning to God. Nerone leaves the house of Nina Sanduzzi and builds himself a small hut in the most desolate corner of the valley. He plants a garden. He spends hours in solitude and contemplation. He appears in church on Sundays and takes the Sacraments. At the same time—the same time, mark you—he appears to have taken over the leadership of the villages."

"How does he lead them, and to what? I'm quizzing you, Meredith, because I want to see what you, the newcomer, have made of this story. I myself know it by heart, but I am still puzzled by it."

"As I read the evidence," said Meredith carefully, "he began by going from house to house offering his services to anyone who needed them—an old man whose land was getting away from him, a grandmother, feeble and alone, a sick farmer who wanted someone to hoe his tomato patch. From those who could afford it he demanded a payment in kind—goat milk, olives, wine, cheese—which he passed on to those who were in need of these things. Later, when winter came, he organised a pooling of labour and resources, and enforced it rigorously, sometimes violently."

"An unsaintly proceeding, surely?" suggested the Bishop, with a thin smile.

"That was my own feeling," admitted Meredith.

"But even Christ whipped the money-changers out of the temple, did he not? And when you know our Calabresi, you'll agree that they have the hardest heads and the tightest fists in Italy."

Meredith was forced to smile at the trap the Bishop had set for him.

He conceded the point, smiling:

"We mark it then to the credit of Giacomo Nerone. The

next thing is in his favour too. He nurses the sick and appears to have given some kind of rough medical service in collaboration with a certain doctor, Aldo Meyer, a political exile, who curiously enough refuses to give any testimony in the case."

"That point, too, has been much in my mind," the Bishop told him. "It is the more interesting since, before and after the war, Meyer himself had tried to organise these people for their own benefit, but failed completely. He's a man of singular humanity, but handicapped by being a Jew in a Catholic country—perhaps by other things too. You should try to get close to him. You may be surprised. . . . Go on, please."

"Next we find evidence of more religious activity. Nerone prays with the sick, comforts the dying. He makes journeys in the snow to bring the priest with the Last Sacrament. When there is no priest he himself waits out the death watch. Now there's an odd thing . . ." Meredith paused for an uncertain moment. "Two of the witnesses say: 'When Father Anselmo refused to come . . .' What would that mean?"

"What it says, I imagine," His Lordship told him coolly. "There has been much scandal about this man. I have thought often of removing him, but so far I have decided against it."

"You have a reputation for rigid discipline. You have removed others. Why not this one?"

"He is an old man," said the Bishop softly. "Old and, I think, very near to despair. I should hate to think I was the one who drove him into it."

"I'm sorry." Meredith was instantly apologetic.

"Not at all. We're friends. You have a right to ask. But I'm a Bishop, not a bureaucrat. I carry the shepherd's crook and the stray sheep are mine, too. Go on. Read me more of Giacomo Nerone."

Meredith ran a hand through his thinning hair. He was getting tired. It was an effort to keep his thoughts in order.

"Somewhere about March, 1944, the Germans came—a small detachment at first, then a larger one—garrison reinforcements for those fighting against the British Eighth Army, which had crossed the Straits of Messina and was fighting its way up the toe of Calabria. Giacomo Nerone is the one who negotiates with them, successfully, it seems. The peasants will supply a guaranteed minimum of fresh food in return for medicines and winter clothing. The garrison commander will discipline his troops and protect the women whose husbands and brothers are away. The bargain is kept reasonably well, and Nerone establishes himself as a respected mediator. This association with the Germans was later alleged as a reason for his execution by the Partisans. When the Allies broke through and began pushing up towards Naples, they by-passed the villages and left the local Partisans to deal with the scattered and retreating German forces. Giacomo Nerone stayed on . . ."

The Bishop checked him with a slim, up-raised hand.

"Stop there a moment. What do you see, so far?"

"Ignotus!" said Meredith calmly. "The unknown. The man from nowhere. The lost one, who suddenly becomes the godly one. He has a sense of gratitude, a touch of compassion, a talent, and perhaps a taste, for leadership. But who is he? Where does he come from, or why does he act as he does?"

"You see no saint in him?"

Meredith shook his head.

"Not yet. Godliness perhaps, but not sanctity. I have not yet examined the evidence for the alleged miracles, so I leave this out of consideration. But I make one point. There is a pattern in sanctity, a great reasonableness. As yet I see no reason here, only secrecy and mystery."

"Perhaps there is no mystery—just ignorance and misunderstanding. Tell me, my friend, what do you know of conditions here in the South at that time?"

"Little enough," Meredith admitted frankly. "For all of the war I was locked inside Vatican City. I only knew what I heard and read—and that was garbled enough, God knows."

"Then let me explain them to you." He got up and walked to the window, to stand looking out on the garden, where the wind stirred faintly through the shrubbery and the shadows were deep because there was still no moon over the hilltops. When he spoke his voice was tinged with an old sadness. "I am an Italian, and I understand this story better than most though I do not yet understand the people in it. First you must realise that a defeated people has no loyalties. Their leaders have failed them. Their sons have died in a lost cause. They believe in no one—not even in themselves. When our conquerors came in, shouting democracy and freedom, we did not believe them either. We looked only at the loaf of bread in their hands and calculated exactly the price they would ask us to pay for it. Hungry people don't even believe in the loaf until it is safely swallowed and they can feel it aching in their unaccustomed stomachs. That's the way it was here in the South. The people were defeated, leaderless, hungry. Worse than that, they were forgotten; and they knew it."

"But Nerone hadn't forgotten them," Meredith objected. "He was still with them. He was still a leader."

"Not any more. There were new barons in the land. Men with new guns and full bandoliers and a rough rescript of authority from the conquerors to clean out the mountains and hold them tidy until a new and amenable Government was established. Their names and their faces were familiar— Michele, Gabriele, Luigi, Beppi. They had bread to bargain with and meat in tin cans and bars of chocolate, and old scores to settle as well: political scores and personal ones. They saluted with the clenched fist of comradeship, and with the same fist beat the faces of those who dared to differ from them. They were many and they were strong, because your Mr Churchill had said that he would do business with anybody who could help him to clean up the mess in Italy and let him get on with the invasion of France. What could Giacomo Nerone do against them—your Ignotus from nowhere?"

"What did he try to do? That's what interests me. Why did some folk cling to him as the holy one and others reject him and betray him to the executioners? Why were the Partisans against him in the first place?"

"It's in the record," said His Lordship with a tired smile. "They called him a collaborator. They accused him of profitable commerce with the Germans."

Meredith rejected the suggestion emphatically.

"It's not enough! It's not enough to explain the hate and the violence and the division and why one village prospers and

79

the other lapses deeper into depression. It's not enough for us either. The people claim a martyrdom—death in defence of the Faith and moral principles. All you've shown me is a political execution—unjust and cruel maybe—but still only that. We're not concerned with politics, but with sanctity, the direct relationship of a man with the God who made him."

"Perhaps that's all it was—a good man caught up in politics."

"Does Your Lordship believe that?"

"Does it matter what I believe, Monsignor?"

The shrewd patrician face was turned towards him. The thin lips smiled in irony.

Then, quite suddenly, the truth hit him like cold water in the face. This man too had a cross to bear. Bishop he might be, but there were still doubts to plague him and fears to harry him on the high peak of temptation. A rare compassion stirred in the dry heart of Blaise Meredith and he answered quietly:

"Does it matter? I think it matters much."

"Why, Monsignor?" The deep, wise eyes challenged him.

"Because I think that you, like me, are afraid of the finger of God."

CHAPTER FIVE

NICHOLAS BLACK, the painter, was making a new picture.

It was a simple composition but oddly dramatic: a tumble of bare rocks, pitted and weathered, stained by fungus and mottled like the sloughed skin of a snake; out of the rocks grew a solitary olive tree, dead and bare of leaves, whose naked arms were out-flung like a cross against the clear blue of the sky.

He had been working on it for an hour now, in the bright solitude of a small plateau behind the shoulder of the hill, with the chequerboard valley below him, and above, the heave of the tufted mountain, splashed with noon sun.

The sun was warm on his brown, stringy torso. The air was languid and dry but noisy with cicadas, and Paolo Sanduzzi dozed a yard from his feet, relaxed as a lizard on a grey rock.

Nicholas Black was a stranger to contentment, and full satisfaction came to him rarely; but in this quiet place and hour, in the company of the sleeping boy, with a picture growing strongly under his hand, he was as close to it as he had ever been.

He painted steadily, contentedly, his thoughts turned outwards on the canvas and on the grey, writhing tree, which was like a gallows on a miniature Golgotha. There was a strength in it that appealed to him—a sinew in the wood, muscle and bone under the rough, grey bark, as if one day it might split asunder and a man emerge shining and new to a kind of resurrection in the dawn.

He admired strength—the more because there was so little in himself—yet he was rarely able to translate it into his works. The critics had noted the lack long ago. They admired the charm of his pictures, the bravura, the dramatic brilliance, but deplored the soft bone and the pale blood beneath their sleek skin. Later they called him *raté*—the man who would never quite make it, because of some fundamental weakness in his own personality. After that, of course, they were kind to him, in the condescending style they reserve for amiable mediocrities and hardy perennials. They always noticed his shows. They gave him praise enough to keep the dowagers buying and the smaller dealers mildly interested. But they never took him seriously.

Now and again one of the young bloods sharpened his teeth on a Nicholas Black exhibition, and it was one of these who had written the brutal epitaph that set London laughing for a week and drove Black across the Channel to Rome and Anne Louise de Sanctis.

"One of the eunuchs of the profession," said the clever young critic. "Doomed to live forever in the contemplation of beauty, but never, never to possess it."

In the Bag O' Nails and the Stag and the BBC Club they chuckled into their beer. In the Georgian sitting-rooms of Knightsbridge they giggled over the cocktails. Under the mansards of Chelsea they made a bawdy lyric about it; and the one who shared his flat and more than half his love chanted it to his face at the end of a quarrelsome evening.

It was the bitterest moment of his life, and even now, two thousand miles and six months away from it, the memory was vivid and shameful. It was a special terror, this one; a very particular hell reserved for those poor devils who, by oversight or irony of the Creator, come into the world defective in those attributes which define a man. Their more normal fellows disdain them, as poetasters disdain a parody which points to the pomposities of their own work, as honest wives disdain a prostitute who sells for money what they refuse for love. So they make a kingdom among themselves, a half world of lost lovers, of furtive encounters and strange marriages. There is loyalty in the half world, but not enough of it for armour against the intriguers inside and the mockers at the flimsy gates. And when a man like Nicholas Black leaves it he becomes the lone pilgrim of a secret cult, whose symbols are the *graffiti* on toilet walls, the phallic gesture and the brushing touch in an assembly of strangers.

But now he had come to an oasis on the pilgrim road. He

was painting a tree as strong and alive as a man. And a boy, berry-brown and languid, was sleeping at his feet in the sun. He made one last careful stroke, then laid down his brush and palette and stood looking down at Paolo Sanduzzi.

He was lying on his back, one knee drawn up, one arm pillowed under his head, the other lying slack on the warm grey rock. His only clothing was a pair of stained shorts and worn leather sandals. In the dry, warm air his skin shone like oiled wood and his smooth boyish face wore, in repose, an air of curious innocence.

Nicholas Black had long been a stranger to innocence. He had joined too often in the mockery and seduction of it. But he could still recognise it, still be jealous of it—and here, remote from the mockery, he could still regret the loss of it.

He sat down on the warm rock a few paces from the boy and smoked a pensive cigarette, caught in the rare syncope of contentment between the accusing past and the dubious future.

Suddenly the boy sat up and looked at him with shrewd, speculative eyes.

"Why do you always look at me like that?"

Black smiled calmly and said:

"You are beautiful, Paolino. Like the Young David whom Michelangelo carved out of a piece of marble. I am an artist—a lover of beauty. So I like to look at you."

"I want to piss," said the boy, grinning.

He leapt up, and walked to the edge of the plateau and stood straddle-legged, easing himself in full view of Nicholas Black, who saw the mockery in it but made no protest. The boy came lounging back and squatted down beside him. He was still smiling, but there was a sidelong calculation in his dark eyes. He asked bluntly:

"Will you take me to Rome when you go?"

Black shrugged in the manner of the South.

"Who knows? Rome is a long way and expensive. I can get plenty of servants here. But a friend—that might be different."

"But you told me I was your friend!" The eagerness was so bright and childish that it might have deceived him, but the truth was in the boy's eyes, dark as onyx.

"A friend must prove himself," said the painter, with careful indifference. "There's time yet. We'll see."

"But I'm a good friend. A true one," Paolo pleaded childishly. "Look, I'll show you!"

He flung his arms round Black's neck, embraced him quickly, and then leapt away, shy as an animal, out of reach. The painter wiped his mouth with the back of his hand and then got up slowly, with the salt taste of disillusion on his tongue. He did not look at the boy who stood, arms akimbo, on a rock ledge ten feet away. He walked to the easel, picked up his brush and palette and said over his shoulder:

"Take off your clothes!"

The boy stared at him.

Black yelled at him harshly.

"Go on! Take them off. I want to use you as a model. That's what you're paid for, among other things."

After a moment's uneasy pause, the boy obeyed, and Black smiled with sardonic satisfaction when he saw how the boldness and the challenge was stripped from him with the tattered breeches. He was just a child now—scared, uncertain, in the presence of a temperamental employer.

"Stretch out your arms. Like this."

The boy raised his arms slowly to the level of his shoulders.

"Now hold them there."

With swift sure strokes Nicholas Black began to paint a crucified figure on the writhing shape of the olive tree: no tormented Christus, but a youth in full puberty with the face and body of Paolo Sanduzzi, nailed to the tree bark through hands and feet, with a red spear thrust in his breast, but smiling even while the life bled out of him.

The boy was weary long before it was finished, but he kept him standing there and cursed him whenever he dropped his arms. Then when it was done he called him over and showed him the picture. The effect was startling. The boy's face crumpled into a mask of terror, his mouth dropped open and he stood shivering and gibbering and pointing at the canvas.

"What's the matter? What are you trying to tell me?"

Black's voice was high and harsh but it made no impression

84

on Paolo Sanduzzi. He was like someone at the beginning of an epileptic fit. Black walked up to him and slapped him sharply on both cheeks. The boy cried out in pain and then began to weep, squatting on the ground and covering his face with his hands, while Black knelt beside him trying to soothe him. After a while he asked him again:

"What's the matter? What frightened you?"

The boy's voice was almost a whisper.

"The picture!"

"What's the matter with it?"

"That's my father's tree!"

The painter gaped at him.

"What do you mean?"

"That's how they killed my father. On that same tree. They stretched him out on it, like on a cross, tied him up—and then shot him."

"O God!" Nicholas Black swore softly. "Sweet angels, what a story! What a sweet, sweet story."

Then after a while he began to laugh, and the boy slunk away, frightened and subdued, carrying his trousers and sandals in his hand.

The same noontide saw Doctor Aldo Meyer restored to temporary favour in Gemello Minore.

Martino the smith had suffered a stroke while working at the anvil. He had fallen against the forge and been badly burned on the breast and face. They had carried him down the road to Meyer's cottage and the doctor was working on him now, assisted by Nina Sanduzzi, while Martino's wife watched nervously from the corner of the room and the villagers crowded outside the cottage chattering like starlings over this crumb of drama.

The thick barrel body of the smith was wrapped in blankets and laid on the plank table in Meyer's kitchen. One side of him was completely paralysed—the leg and arm useless, the face wrenched sideways into a rictus of surprise and fear. His eyes were closed and his breathing was shallow and noisy. As Meyer probed and swabbed the burns on his cheeks, a low,

85

mumbling cry issued from his twisted mouth. When they had finished dressing the face, they unrolled the blankets and Meyer gave a low, thoughtful whistle as he saw the extent and the depth of the body burns. Nina Sanduzzi stood impassive as a statue, holding the bowl of boiling water and the swabs. When Martino's wife started forward, she laid down the bowl quite calmly and led her back to the corner, soothing and chiding her in a low confident voice. Then she came back to Meyer and, attentive as any nurse, helped him to pick the charcoal from the burns, cleanse them and dab them with gentian violet and the last small stock of Merthiolate.

When the dressings were done, Meyer made another auscultation and a pulse count, wrapped the blankets back again, and turned to talk to the weeping woman in the corner. He told her gently:

"You'd better leave him here for a couple of hours. Then I'll have him taken home to you."

She pleaded with him, plaintive as an animal.

"He won't die, will he, Doctor? You won't let him die?"

"He's as strong as an ox," said Meyer calmly. "He won't die."

She caught at his hands, kissing them and calling on the saints to bless the good doctor. Meyer disengaged himself brusquely.

"Go home now, like a good woman, and get your children fed. I'll send for you, if I want you—and later you'll get your husband home."

Nina Sanduzzi took her by the arm and led her out of the room, and when he turned back to his patient he heard her at the door, shouting at the bystanders and urging them off about their business. When she came back she asked him bluntly:

"Did you mean what you told her? He will live?"

"He'll live," Meyer told her, shrugging. "But he'll never be any good to himself or to her."

"He's got six children."

"Too many," said Meyer with thin humour.

"But he has them," she persisted stubbornly. "Who is to feed them now that he cannot work?"

Meyer shrugged.

"There's public relief. They won't starve."

"Public relief!" She flung it back at him scornfully. "A dozen interviews and a hundred printed forms for a kilo of pasta! What sort of answer is that?"

"It's the only one I know these days," Meyer told her with cool bitterness. "I used to have lots of others, but no one would listen. They wanted to go on in the old way. Well . . . this is the old way!"

Nina Sanduzzi stared at him. There were pity and contempt in her dark, intelligent eyes.

"You know what Giacomo would have done, don't you? He'd have gone into the forge himself and worked. He'd have knocked on every door and begged or bullied people into helping. He'd have gone up to the villa and talked to the Contessa for money and work for Martino's wife. He'd have prised some poor-box money out of Father Anselmo. He understood this sort of thing. He knew how scared people get. He could never bear to hear a child crying . . ."

"He was a remarkable man, your Giacomo," said Meyer tersely. "That's why they killed him. Martino, as I remember, was one of those who fired the volley."

"And you signed a paper saying that he had been legally executed after a proper trial." There was no anger in her voice, only a quiet recollection of familiar facts. "But none of you ever told the true reason why he was killed."

"What was it, then?" he challenged her harshly.

"There was not one reason. There were twenty. There was Martino's reason and the Contessa's and Father Anselmo's and Battista's and Lupo's and yours, too, *dottore mio*. But you couldn't admit them, even to one another, so you found one that suited you all—Giacomo was a collaborator, a lover of Fascists and Germans! You were the liberators, the friends of freedom, the little brothers of all the world. You brought us democracy. All Giacomo ever brought was a crust of bread and a bowl of soup and a pair of hands to work when the man of the house was sick."

Her calm indictment goaded him and he blazed back:

"That's the whole damn trouble with this country. That's why we're still fifty years behind the rest of Europe. We won't organise, we won't discipline ourselves. We won't co-operate. You can't build a better world on a bowl of pasta and a bucket of holy water."

"You can't build it on bullets, either, Dottore. You got what you wanted. You killed Giacomo. Now what's to show for it? Martino can't work any more. Who's to feed his wife and six children?"

There was no answer to this brutal logic and he turned away, shamed and impotent, and walked to the door that gave on to the hot, bright garden. After a moment Nina Sanduzzi followed him and laid a tentative hand on his sleeve.

"You think I hate you, Dottore. I don't. Giacomo didn't hate you either. Before he died, he came to see me. He knew what was going to happen. He knew you were concerned in it. But do you know what he said to me? 'This is a good man, Nina. He has tried to do too much, but he is unhappy because he has never really understood what it is to love and to be loved. He wants to organise and reform, but he does not see that these are barren things without loving. I'm lucky, because I had you to teach me in the beginning. He has been alone too long. When I am dead, go to him and he will be kind to you. If a time should come when you find that a man is necessary to you again—this would be one who would be good to you and to the boy.' He wrote a letter to you and put it among his papers. I was to deliver it to you, after he died."

Meyer swung round to stare at her.

"A letter! Where is it, woman? Where, for God's sake?"

Nina Sanduzzi spread her hands in despair.

"I had all his papers in my cupboard. When Paolo was little, one day he got to them and jumbled them together. Some he tore, others he crumpled, and when I gathered them up again, I could not tell one from the other. . . ." She blushed as if at a shameful revelation. "I—I've never learned to read!"

His hands reached out and grasped her roughly by the shoulders.

"I must see the papers, Nina. I must see them. You don't know how important it is."

"Six children are important," said Nina Sanduzzi quietly. "And a woman whose man cannot work any more."

"If I help them, you'll show me the papers?"

She shook her head in outright refusal.

"That was something else Giacomo said: 'One should never bargain with people's bodies.' If you want to help them you will do it, without asking to be paid. Later we can talk about the papers."

He was beaten and he knew it. There was a granite strength in this woman who could not read, an inviolable reserve of wisdom which he, the lifetime student, could not match. What puzzled him was that there were no roots for it in her peasant origins and he would not admit she had acquired it from Giacomo Nerone. Yet she, like Nerone, held the key to a mystery that had eluded Aldo Meyer for twenty years: why some men with talent, good will and compassion never achieve full human contact and raise only contention and ridicule among those they try to help; and why others, with no apparent effort, walk straight into intimacy and are remembered with love long after their death.

In Nerone's papers he might read the answer which he lacked the courage to ask from Nina Sanduzzi. But he could only get them on her terms. So he shrugged in resignation and told her:

"I'm dining tonight with the Contessa. I'll tell her about Martino and see what we can do."

A smile lightened her calm, classic face. With an impulsive gesture, she caught up his hand and kissed it.

"You are a good man, Dottore. I'll tell Martino's wife. No one should be left afraid too long."

"You can tell me something too, Nina."

"Yes, Dottore?"

"What would you say if I asked you to marry me?"

Her dark, deep eyes showed neither surprise nor pleasure.

"I would tell you what I told you the first time, Dottore. Better you didn't ask."

Then she left him quickly and Aldo Meyer returned to his patient to feel the fluttering, uncertain pulse and hear the hardy peasant heart battling for life inside the scarred breast.

Paolo Sanduzzi stood on the edge of the stream, bouncing pebbles off the water and watching them skip into the bushes on the opposite side. The stream had one name and three faces. Its name was Torrente del Fauno—the torrent of the faun—because in the old days, long before Christ came down from Rome with St Peter, the fauns used to play here, chuckling goat boys, chasing the tree girls who were called dryads. After the church was built, they all went away; which was rather a pity, because the valley was dull without them. But the name persisted and sometimes the boys and girls of the village met here secretly to play the old pagan games.

The face of the stream changed with the seasons. In winter it was dark, cold and sinister, fringed sometimes with the white rime of frost and piled snow. In spring it was brown and boisterous, roaring so loud with thaw water that one could hear it right up in the village. By summer it had dwindled to a thin, clear runnel singing softly over the stones, lying in quiet pools under the overhang of the banks. Before autumn came, it was dry again—a parched bed full of bleached stones. Now it wore its gentle face, and Paolo Sanduzzi, who was like a faun himself, was glad to be here away from the dead gallows tree and the Englishman whose laughter was like water bubbling in a black pot.

He had never been so frightened in his life; and he was still frightened. It was as if the painter held the key to his life: to the past which shamed him and to the future which he could see only dimly as a vision of Rome with its churches and palaces, its streets full of shiny automobiles and its pavements crowded with girls who dressed like princesses.

The vision laid a spell on him—half-pleasant, half-sinister—like the charms old Nonna Patucci gave to the girls to draw their lovers to them. He could feel it working now, an itch under his skin, an oppressive image behind his eyeballs. Sooner or later it would draw him back to the Englishman, whose mocking smile sometimes made him feel awkward as a child and sometimes woke strange, disturbing passions in him, without even a word or a hand's touch.

He tossed a last negligent stone into the water, thrust his hands into his pockets and began to walk downstream. As he rounded a bend in the bank, a shrill voice hailed him.

"Eh, Paoluccio!"

He looked up and saw Rosetta, the daughter of Martino the smith, sitting on a rock and dangling her legs in the water. She was a thin, elfin child, a year younger than himself, with lank hair and a small, pert face and budding breasts under the faded cotton shift which was her only clothing. In the village he ignored her studiously, but now he was glad to see her. He waved an indifferent hand.

"Eh, Rosetta!"

Then he went and sat beside her on the rock.

"My father's sick. He fell down in a fit and burned himself on the forge. He's in the doctor's house."

"Is he dying?"

"No. The doctor says he'll live. Mother's crying. She gave us all bread and cheese and sent us out to play. Want some?"

She held up a hunk of rough bread and a cut of goat cheese.

"I'm hungry," said Paolo.

She broke the bread and the cheese carefully into equal pieces and handed him his share. They sat there munching silently in the sun, cooling their feet in the water. After a while she asked him:

"Where have you been, Paoluccio?"

"With the Englishman."

"What doing?"

He shrugged indifferently, as a man does with inquisitive women.

"Working."

"What sort of work?"

"I carry his things. When he paints, I watch. Sometimes he asks me to model for him."

"What's model?"

"I just stand there and he paints me."

91

"Teresina says there are girls in Naples who take off their clothes for men to paint them."

"I know." He nodded wisely.

"Do you take your clothes off, too?"

The question caught him unawares and he answered it roughly.

"That's my business."

"But you do, don't you? If you're a model, that is."

"It's a secret, Rosetta," he told her seriously. "Don't tell anyone; they wouldn't understand."

"I won't tell. I promise." She put her thin arm round him and leaned her head on his bare shoulder. The gesture embarrassed him, but pleased him, too. He let her stay there and because he was pleased, he said:

"The Englishman says I'm beautiful, like the statue that Michelangelo carved out of marble."

"That's silly. Only women are beautiful. Boys are nice or nasty. Not beautiful."

"That's what he said anyway," he answered defensively. "He said I was beautiful and he loved beauty and liked to look at me!"

In her odd elfin way she was angry with him. She took her arm away from him and slewed round to face him.

"Now I know you're making it up. Men don't say things like that. Only women!"

She put her arms round his neck and pressed her lips on his, and when he tried to resist, she held him more tightly; and when he felt her breasts against him through the shift, he decided that it was pleasant after all. And he began to kiss her, too.

Later she took his face in her small hands and said gravely:

"I love you, Paoluccio. I love you really. Not like a statue."

"I love you, too, Rosetta!"

"I'm glad." She leaped up and stood holding her hand out to him. "Now take me for a walk!"

"Why?"

"Because we love each other, silly, and that's what lovers do. Besides, I've got a secret."

"What secret?"

"Take me for a walk and I'll show you."

In spite of himself, he reached up his hand to her. She caught it and dragged him to his feet, and they walked upstream, through the clear water and under the green bushes, to share the old secrets that the dryads told to the dancing fauns.

From his high, plateau eyrie behind the shoulder of the mountain, Nicholas Black looked down on the spread pattern of his past. For the first time in his life, its form was clear to him—and how the future grew out of it, inevitable and identical, as the new shoots on a tree.

From the beginning, he had been cheated: the hidden foetal beginning when the determinant elements were doled out by whatever power decided that, out of the blind coupling of man and wife, there should grow a parody of a man.

He had been born a twin—identical in face and form with the brother who preceded him by an hour out of the womb. He had been born a Catholic, to one of the old Fenland families who had kept the Faith whole from the time of the first Elizabeth to that of the last George. He had been baptized with his brother and blessed with the same blessing, in the manor chapel from whose steps the lawns flowed down broad and green to the reed fringe and the grey fen water.

But here the identity ended and the slow division began. The first-born grew swart and strong, the second was wan and sickly. They were like Esau and Jacob—but Esau enjoyed the birthright: the field sports, the fishing, the long rides in the dappled summer; while Jacob clung to the shelter of the house and the same harbour of the sewing-room and the library. At school he lagged behind, was a year late at Oxford; and while his twin went off with a gunnery commission in the Western Desert, he was confined to a hospital bed with rheumatic fever. All the strength was in the one; all the weakness in the other. All the maleness belonged to the first-born, and in Nicholas Black there was only an epicene beauty, the soft subtlety of a mind turned back too long upon itself.

While his brother lived, there was a hope for him that he

93

might borrow strength and find dignity in affection. Afterwards, when the word came through, "Missing, believed killed", the last hope died and the hidden bitterness began to grow. He had been cheated: by God, by life, by his dead twin, by his father, who after a hushed scandal in London had warned him out of the house and given him a small annuity to keep him away from it.

He had been solitary ever since. His belief had been shipwrecked on the most difficult mystery of all: that a just God can make monsters and still expect them to live like men. His heart had been hardened by the brief loves of the half-world. And now, suddenly, power was put in his hands—power to make another what he had failed to make himself: a man, noble in nature, talent and execution. In the making he might reframe his own life—to dignity, to understanding, to a purer love than any he had yet experienced.

He was getting old. Passion woke more slowly and was easier to control, except when it was piqued by vanity and competition. With the boy as his ward, he would achieve a kind of paternity, which would give to his own life a discipline and a direction it had always lacked.

It was a dizzy moment, a god-like elevation.

This youth was the son of a reputed saint, begotten on the body of a village whore. His life was as predictable as that of a million others in the workless villages of Midday Italy. He would mature in idleness, marry too young and breed too often and live aimlessly on the extreme margin of poverty. Whatever talent he had would be stifled by the brute struggle for existence. The Church would censure him while he lived and absolve him before he died. The State would be saddled with a dozen reproductions of him, fecund and hungry as rabbits, eating out the last green of an impoverished land.

But take him out of the village, give him opportunity and education, and he might well grow to greatness, justifying himself and his teacher as well. Where his father had failed, and the Church had failed, Nicholas Black might yet succeed—and his success would be a splendid negation of the beliefs he had long rejected.

94

To the critics, Nicholas Black was a mediocre artist. If out of this peasant clay he could mould a perfect man, it would be a triumph beyond cavil, a masterwork beyond the reach of malice.

It was a strange ambition, and yet, in its own idiom, no stranger than the triumphs and revenges that other men dreamed for themselves—financial empires strong enough to crush all opposition, power in the press to make men or bury them in obscurity, woman dreams and opium dreams and the dream of standing one day at the dispatch box to hear one's enemies say . . . 'The Right Honourable the Prime Minister . . .'

Each man to his own damnation, and nobler men have dreamed more basely in their nightshirts than Nicholas Black on his sunlit plateau in Calabria.

It was late and he had not eaten, but he was drunk on the heady wine of anticipation and he did not care. The village would be settling down to siesta. The Contessa would be locked in her baroque room and he could bring his picture into the villa without exciting too much attention.

He was counting much on this canvas. He wondered how Anne Louise de Sanctis would react to it—and Aldo Meyer, and the grey cleric who was coming to research into the past of Giacomo Nerone. He smiled as he pictured them gaping at it for the first time, their secrets written in their eyes and on their faces.

He cast about for a title, and found one almost immediately —'The Sign of Contradiction'. The more he thought of it, the more he liked it. It reminded him of the old *graffito* in which an ass is crucified to represent the Christus, a bawdy joke by a bumpkin comedian. But for Nicholas Black the symbol had a new significance: youth nailed to the cross of ignorance, superstition and poverty, half-dead and damned already, but smiling still, a drugged, ecstatic victim of time and its tyrannies.

CHAPTER SIX

MONSIGNOR BLAISE MEREDITH and Aurelio, Bishop of Valenta, were concerned with another contradiction: the alleged miracles of Giacomo Nerone.

They were standing on the broad, flagged terrace of the villa looking down into the valley, where workmen were moving slowly up and down the plantation, spraying the young trees from new shoulderpacks of American pattern. On the wall of the small dam others were working to install new sluice gates that would control the flow of water to farms outside the Bishop's domain. Beyond the spillway, on a grey, untilled hillside, women with baskets on their backs were carrying stones to build new vine terraces, and earth to pack behind them.

They were like ants, small and industrious, and Meredith was moved to the ironic reflection that this was as great a miracle as any in his leather folio: barren land being built back slowly to fruitfulness by the creative will of one man. He said as much to the Bishop, whose lean, intelligent face puckered into a smile.

"It's bad theology, my friend; but a pleasant compliment. To these people, it is a kind of miracle. Suddenly there is work and bread on the table and an extra litre of oil for the cookpot. They cannot understand how it has happened, and, even now, they have a shrewd suspicion that there's a catch in it somewhere. Those sprays for instance . . ." He pointed to the humped figures threading their way between the orange trees. "I had to buy them with my own money, but they were worth every lira. It is only a year or two since these people were washing their trees from a spit bucket—a pail of water set in the middle of the floor, into which the men of the house spat tobacco juice as they smoked or chewed. Some of the old ones still refuse to see that my method is better than theirs. The only thing that will convince them is when I get three oranges to their one, and sell them for twice the price because they are full of juice. But we'll show them in the end."

"You puzzle me," said Meredith frankly.

"Why?"

"What have oranges got to do with the human soul?"

"Everything," said the Bishop flatly. "You can't cut a man in two and polish up his soul while you throw his body on the rubbish heap. If the Almighty had designed him in that way, he would have made him a biped who carried his soul in a bag round his neck. If reason and revelation mean anything they mean that a man works out his salvation in the body by the use of material things. A neglected tree, a second-rate fruit, are defects in the divine scheme of things. Unnecessary misery is an even greater defect because it is an impediment to salvation. When you don't know where your next meal is coming from, how can you think or care about the state of your soul? Hunger has no morals, my friend."

Meredith nodded thoughtfully.

"I've often wondered why missionaries are usually better priests than their brothers in the centres of Christendom."

His Lordship shrugged and gestured with expressive hands.

"Paul was a tentmaker and he worked at his trade so as not to be a burden on his people. Christ himself was a carpenter in Galilee of the Gentiles—I imagine he was a good one. When I am dead, I should like to be remembered as a good priest and a good farmer."

"It is enough," said Meredith gravely. "Enough for you, enough for me. I imagine the Almighty Himself would hardly quarrel with it. But is it enough for everybody?"

"What do you mean?"

"There are miracles all around us: the miracle of an orange tree, the miracle of design that holds the fidget wheels of the universe spinning on their axes. But still people want a sign— a new sign. If they don't get it from the Almighty they turn to palmists and astrologers and table-rappers. What does all this mean"—he tapped the heavy volume of depositions—"but that folk demand wonders in the sky and miracles on earth?"

"And get them sometimes," the Bishop reminded him tartly.

"And sometimes make them for themselves," said Blaise Meredith.

"You're not satisfied with the miracles of Giacomo Nerone?"

"I'm the Devil's Advocate. It's my business to be dissatisfied." He smiled ruefully. "It's a curious assignment, when you come to think of it. To test by reason the alleged operations of Omnipotence, to apply the code of canon law to the Lawgiver who framed the universe."

His Lordship nodded a grave assent and said quietly:

"It may be less disturbing to think about Giacomo Nerone."

Blaise Meredith put on again his prim, pedant's manner.

"It's the problem with all new Causes—to apply to alleged miracles the medico-legal methods of the twentieth century. In the case of Lourdes, for example, it's fairly easy. A medical bureau has been established and a series of tests laid down which conform to both medical knowledge and the rigid demands of the Church. A sufferer arrives with a complete medical history. The bureau examines the patient in the approved fashion—X-rays, clinical and pathological tests. All diseases of neurological or hysterical origin are discounted as grounds for a miraculous claim. Only deep-seated organic disorders whose prognoses are familiar are accepted. If a cure is claimed, the bureau examines the patient again and makes an interim certification of the cure. But it is not finally certified until two years afterwards, and then on new medical evidence.

"So far as it goes, it is a sound method. It enables us to say that, in the present state of medical knowledge, this cure has taken place in defiance of, or by a suspension of, the known laws of nature. Now . . . in the case of a new thaumaturge, in a new place, these tests cannot be applied. At best we have eye-witness accounts, a garbled medical history, with perhaps a certification from a local doctor. It may well be a miracle. But in the legal sense, demanded by canon law, we find it very hard to prove. We may accept it on the sheer weight of non-expert evidence, but generally we don't."

"And the evidence in the case of Giacomo Nerone?"

"Of the forty-three depositions I have read, only three show any conformity to the canonical demands. One is the cure of

98

an elderly woman certified as suffering from multiple sclerosis, the second is that of the Mayor of Gemello Maggiore, who claims to have been cured of a spinal injury incurred during the war, and the third is that of a child in the last stages of meningitis who recovered after an application of a relic of Giacomo Nerone. But even these . . ." He paused and went on in his emphatic advocate's voice. "Even these will require a much more rigid examination before we go half way to accepting them."

To his surprise the Bishop smiled, as if at some private joke. Meredith was nettled.

"Have I said something amusing to Your Lordship?"

"I was asking myself what happened in the old days when medical knowledge was limited and the rules of evidence were less stringent. Is it not possible that many miracles then accepted were not miracles at all?"

"Very probable, I should say."

"And that certain saints are venerated whose records are so obscure that their very existence is doubtful?"

"That's true. But I don't see where Your Lordship is leading me."

"I've been reading recently," said His Lordship coolly, "that certain theologians are again advancing the opinion that the canonisation of a saint constitutes an infallible declaration by the Pope, binding on all the faithful. In my view it's a dubious proposition. Canonisation is generally based on biography and the historical record of miracles. Both are open to error—and the Pope is only infallible in the interpretation of the deposit of Faith. He can't add to it. And every new saint is an addition to the Calendar."

"I agree with Your Lordship," said Meredith with a puzzled frown. "But I don't see that a minority theological opinion matters very much."

"It's not the opinion that worries me, Meredith. It's the tendency: the tendency to elaborate so much by commentary, glossary and hypothesis that the rigid simplicity of the essential Faith is obscured, not only for the faithful but for honest inquirers outside it. I deplore this. I deplore it greatly because

I find it raises barriers between the pastor and the souls he is trying to reach."

"Do you believe in saints, Your Lordship?"

"I believe in saints as I believe in sanctity. I believe in miracles as I believe in God, who can suspend the laws of His own making. But I believe, too, that the hand of God writes plainly and simply, for all men of good will to read. I am doubtful of His presence in confusion and conflicting voices."

"As I am doubtful of the miracles of Giacomo Nerone?"

The Bishop did not answer him immediately, but walked away from him to stand looking out across the peace of the valley, at the grey olives and the green orange trees and the flat water where the men were working on the sluices, stripped to the waist in the sun. His face was clouded as if he were absorbed in an inner struggle. Meredith watched him with puzzlement and anxiety, afraid of having offended him. After a while the Bishop came back. His face was still sombre, but his eyes were full of a grave gentleness. He said slowly:

"I have thought much these last days, Meredith. I have prayed too. You have come into my life at a moment of crisis. I am a Bishop of the Church, yet I find myself in opposition to much that is currently being said and done by my colleagues in Rome, not in matters of faith, but in discipline, policy, attitude. I believe that I am right, but I know there is danger that in following my own path I may tumble into pride and ruin all I hope to do. You were right when you told me that I am afraid of the finger of God. I am . . . I sit on a high pinnacle. I am subject only to the Pontiff. I am lonely and often puzzled . . . as I am by this matter of Giacomo Nerone. I told you I do not want a saint. But what if God wants him? This is only one thing. There are many others. Now you come, a man in the shadow of death. You too are puzzled and afraid of the finger of God. I find in you a brother, whom I have come to love and trust with my heart. Both of us at this moment are looking for a sign . . . a light in the darkness that besets us."

"I lie awake at night," said Meredith. "I feel the life slipping out of me. When the pain comes, I cry out, but there is no prayer in it, only fear. I kneel and recite my Office and the

Rosary but the words are empty—dry gourds rattling in the silence. The dark is terrible and I feel so alone. I see no signs but the symbols of contradiction. I try to dispose myself to faith, hope and charity, but my will is a blown reed in the winds of despair . . . I am glad that Your Lordship prays for me."

"I pray for both of us," said Aurelio, Bishop of Valenta. "And, out of the prayer, I have come to a decision. We should ask for a sign."

"What sign?"

The Bishop paused, and then, very solemnly, he told him.

"We should make this prayer, both of us. 'If it is your will, O God, to show the virtue of your servant Giacomo Nerone, show it in the body of Blaise Meredith. Restore him to health and hold him longer from the hands of death, through Jesus Christ our Lord!'"

"No!" The word was wrung from Meredith like a cry. "I can't do it! I daren't!"

"If not for yourself, then for me!"

"No! No! No!" The desperation of the man was pitiful, but the Bishop pressed him brutally.

"Why not? Do you deny omnipotence?"

"I believe in it!"

"And mercy?"

"That too!"

"But not for yourself?"

"I've done nothing to earn it."

"Mercy is given, not earned! Bestowed on beggars, not bought with virtue!"

"I dare not ask for it." His voice rose higher in fear. "I dare not!"

"You will ask for it," the Bishop told him gently. "Not for yourself, but for me and all poor devils like me. You will say the words even if they mean nothing, because I, your friend, ask you."

"And if they fail. . . ." Meredith lifted a ravaged face at last. "If they fail, I am in greater darkness yet, not knowing whether I have presumed too much or believed too little. Your Lordship lays a new cross on my back."

"It is a strong back, my friend—stronger than you know. And you may yet carry Christ on it across the river."

But Meredith stood like a stone man, staring out across the sunlit land, and after a while the Bishop left him, to talk with the gardeners who were spraying the orange trees.

It was the moment he had long dreaded, but never quite understood: the moment when the harsh consequences of belief became finally clear.

For a man born into the Church there is a singular comfort in the close-knit logic of the Faith. Its axioms are easy of acceptance. Its syllogisms are piled one on top of the other, firm as the bricks in a well built house. Its disciplines are rigid, but one moves freely inside them, as one does in the confines of a well-bred family. Its promises are reassuring: that if one submits to the logic and the discipline, one walks naturally in the way of salvation. The complex, terrifying relationship of Creator and Creature is reduced to a formula of faith and a code of manners.

For priests and monks and nuns, the logic is more meticulous, the disciplines more rigid, but the security of body and spirit is commensurately greater. So that if a man can surrender himself completely to the Will of the Creator, as expressed by the Will of the Church, he can live and die in peace —either a cabbage or a saint!

Blaise Meredith was by temperament a conformist. He had kept the rules all his life; all the rules—except one: that sooner or later he must step beyond the forms and the conventions and enter into a direct, personal relationship with his fellows and with his God. A relationship of charity—which is a debased Latin word for love. And love in all its forms and degrees is a surrender of bodies in the small death of the bed, the surrender of the spirit in the great death which is the moment of union between God and Man.

Never in his life had Blaise Meredith surrendered himself to anyone. He had asked favours of none—because to ask a favour is to surrender one's pride and independence. Now, no matter what name he put to it, he could not bring himself to ask a favour of the Almighty, in whom he professed belief, to whom, according to the same belief, he stood in the relationship of son and father.

And this was the reason for his terror. If he did not come to submission he would remain for ever what he was now: lonely, barren, friendless, to eternity.

Aurelio, the Bishop, sat in his cool, austere study, writing letters. It was an activity he distrusted, even when his office forced it upon him. He had been bred a farmer, and he would rather watch a tree grow than write a treatise on it. He had been trained to diplomacy and he knew that a thing, once written, is beyond recantation. Many a hapless fellow has been damned for heresy simply because he was weak in grammar or discretion.

So, when he wrote officially, over the seal of his bishopric, he kept to the conventions for his clergy, a blunt message thinly coated with Southern rhetoric; for Rome, a studied circumlocution, a careful qualification, a slightly florid style. Those who knew him well chuckled at his shrewdness. Those who knew him little—even acute fellows like Marotta—were apt to be misled by it. They regarded him as a somewhat stuffy provincial who would be very good for the locals, but a bumbling nuisance in Rome. Which was precisely the Bishop's intention. Too many new men had been abruptly translated to Rome, just when they were getting things done in their own diocese. It was the Vatican's way of kicking them upstairs: a bishop in his own See is a power to be reckoned with; in the city of the Popes he is very small beer indeed.

But this afternoon's letters were private ones, and His Lordship composed them with more than usual care. To Anne Louise de Sanctis he wrote:

... I am more grateful than I can say for your offer to receive Monsignor Meredith as a house-guest during his stay in Gemello Minore. We clerics are often a burden to our flock—and sometimes an embarrassment; but I am sure you will find in Monsignor Meredith an agreeable and witty compatriot. He is a sick man who is marked, unfortunately, for

103

an early death; and whatever you can do for him I shall count as a personal favour.

You are much in my mind these days. I am not unaware of the loneliness which afflicts you as the châteleine of a poor and primitive community. It is my hope that you will find in Monsignor Meredith, a confidant for your problems and a counsellor in the affairs of your conscience.

> Believe me, my dear Contessa,
> Yours affectionately in Christ Jesus
>
> Aurelio +
> Bishop of Valenta

He signed his name with a flourish and sat awhile scanning the letter, wondering whether he should have said less or more —and whether there were words to touch the heart of a woman like this one.

Women were the perennial problem of the priesthood. More women than men knelt at the Judas-window of the confessional. Their outpourings were franker and more disturbing to the celibate who sat behind it. Often they tried to use him as the replacement for an unresponsive husband and what they dared not whisper in the marriage-bed they talked freely and often grossly in the coffin-box at the side of the church. The men could be reached through the women—the children too. But often the old Adam who slept under the cassock was wakened dangerously by the murmured confidences of an adolescent girl or a dissatisfied matron.

Aurelio, Bishop of Valenta, was very much a man, and he was quick to see the passion that stirred behind the polished gentility of the Contessa de Sanctis. She, too, was one of his sheep, but discretion put her beyond the reach of his shepherd's crook and he asked himself whether Blaise Meredith, the cold, suffering man, might come any closer to her.

To Doctor Aldo Meyer he wrote in far different terms:

. . . Monsignor Blaise Meredith is a sensitive and liberal man whom I have come to cherish as a brother.

His commission to investigate the life of Giacomo Nerone is a difficult one, and I have hopes that you may be willing to place your considerable local knowledge at his disposal. You

104

may feel, however, that, as a non-Catholic, you prefer not to embroil yourself in this delicate affair. Let me assure you then that neither Monsignor Meredith nor I would wish to embarrass you with inquiries.

I have, however, a personal favour to ask you. Monsignor Meredith is a very ill man. He is suffering from carcinoma of the stomach and, in the normal course of events, will die very soon. He is reserved, as the English are, but he has considerable courage, and I am concerned lest he overwork himself and endure more pain than is necessary.

It would please me greatly, therefore, if you would consent to act as his medical adviser during his stay in Gemello Minore, and do your best to look after him. I shall make it my business to procure for you whatever drugs you may need and I shall be personally responsible for all the expenses of consultation and treatment.

I commend him most warmly to your charity and your professional care. . . .

Basta! thought his Lordship. Enough. One does not make homilies to the Sephardim. They understand us as well as we understand them. They are theocrats as we are—absolutists as we are. They know the meaning of charity and fraternity; and often they practise them better than we do. They have been persecuted as we have. They have had their Pharisees as we—God help us—have ours, even in the highest places. Meredith my brother will be in good hands.

The third letter was the most difficult of all, and His Lordship pondered it a long time before he wrote, in a fine cursive hand, the superscription:

The Very Reverend Don Anselmo Benincasa,
Pastor of the Church of the Madonna of the Seven Dolours,
Gemello Minore,
Diocese of Valenta.

Dear Reverend Father,
We write to inform you of the arrival in your Parish of the Right Reverend Monsignor Blaise Meredith, Auditor of the Sacred Congregation of Rites, who has been appointed Promoter of the Faith in the Ordinary Cause for the Beatification

of the Servant of God, Giacomo Nerone. We beg that you will extend to him a fraternal hospitality and render him every assistance to carry out his canonical commission.

We are aware of your poverty and the straitness of your accommodation and we have, therefore, accepted an invitation from the Contessa de Sanctis to lodge him during his stay in the parish. We know, however, that you will not deem yourself dispensed on this account from the courtesies owed to a brother priest, who is also a commissioner of the Diocesan Court.

We have been long exercised, Reverend Father, by reports reaching us of the low state of spiritual affairs in your parish, and of certain scandals touching your own private life. Not the least of these scandals is your long association with the widow Rosa Benzoni, who acts as your housekeeper.

Normally such an association would have caused us to institute a canonical process against you, but we have refrained from this drastic step in the hope that God may give you grace to see your error and reform it, so that the last years of your priesthood may be spent in penitence and dignity and the proper service of your flock.

It may well be—God grant it so!—that because of your advanced years, this association may have lost its carnal character and that we may be disposed to permit you to retain this woman in your employment in discharge of the debts you have contracted towards her. But such lenience on our part would not dispense you from the moral duty of repairing the scandal and of devoting yourself with renewed vigour to the interests of your people.

We suggest that the presence of a visiting priest in your parish may give you the opportunity of taking counsel with him and setting your conscience in order without too much embarrassment.

Our patience has been long and we have great care for you as our son in Christ, but we cannot ignore the sorry state of the souls in your charge. One cannot tempt God too long. You are already old and time grows dangerously short.

We remember you daily in our prayers and we commend you to the patron of your church, the Madonna of the Dolours.

Yours fraternally in Christ,
Aurelio +
Bishop of Valenta

He laid down the pen and sat a long time staring at the thick crested notepaper and the script that flowed across it in urgent disciplined lines.

The case of Father Anselmo was a symbol of all the ills of the Mediterranean Church. It was not an isolated case. It was common enough to have become a cliché in the depressed area of the South—and it was none too rare in the North either. In its local context, it was a small scandal—the Church was founded on the idea of sin, and its oldest maxim was that the habit did not make a monk, nor the tonsure a religious man. But in the context of a national Church, of a country in which Catholicism was the dominating influence, it pointed to grave defects, to a singular need of reform.

A man like Anselmo Benincasa was the product of a seminary ill-staffed and dispensing an outdated system of education. He came to ordination half-educated, half-disciplined, and with his vocation wholly untested. He emerged another priest in a country where there were too many priests and not enough priestliness—and immediately he became a charge on another depressed community. His stipend from the diocese was purely nominal. With the swift debasement of modern currency, it would not buy him a loaf of bread. And the Hierarchy still clung to the comfortable fiction that those who preached the gospel should live by the gospel—without caring to define too clearly how they were to do it. He had no pension, and there was no institution to receive him when he lapsed into senility: so that he was plagued by the constant fear of age, and the constant temptation of avarice.

When he came to a village like Gemello Minore, he represented another mouth to feed. And if he opened his mouth too wide, he was liable to go hungry. So he was forced to accommodate himself: to submit to the patronage of the local landowner, or make an unhappy compromise with his depressed flock. In many Calabrian communities there was a shortage of men. Pre-war emigration and war-time levies had denuded them, and women lived for years separated from their husbands, while marriageable girls were forced to take temporary lovers, or husbands years older than themselves. But the priest was there. The priest was poor and dependent on the poor to get his washing done and his food cooked and his house cleaned and his collection plate full enough to buy next week's pasta.

Small wonder that he lapsed often and that his bishop preferred to deplore the lapse as fornication, rather than haul him to court for the canonical scandal of public concubinage.

It was the system that was to blame as much as the man, and reformers like Aurelio, Bishop of Valenta, were hard put to change it, saddled as they were with the historic sins of a feudal Church. The answer was fewer priests and better ones, money to provide at least a basic living independent of the contributions of the faithful, pensions for old age and sickness, better seminary training, more rigid screening of aspirants to Holy Orders. But money was short and prejudice was strong and men like Anselmo Benincasa took a long time to die, and the youths who grew up in the villages were uneducated and unsuitable.

A bishopric like Valenta was poor and obscure. Rome was rich, remote and preoccupied—and requests for special funds to make tendentious reforms were greeted coldly by the Cardinals who were the stewards of the Patrimony of Peter.

So Anselmo Benincasa stayed on in Gemello Minore and His Lordship of Valenta was left with the problem of what to do with him, and how, at least, to salvage his immortal soul.

He folded the letters, put them in envelopes, sealed them with red wax and the arms of his bishopric, then rang for a messenger to arrange their immediate delivery, by motor-cycle, to Gemello Minore. He had no illusions about their importance. He had been a long time in the priesthood and he understood that the truth can lie barren for a hundred years until it strikes root in the heart of a man.

On the eve of his departure for Gemello Minore, Blaise Meredith was lonelier than he had ever been in his life.

The brief, brotherly communion between himself and the Bishop was about to be broken. He must go out among strangers, a sedulous inquisitor digging up unpopular facts. His night-time terrors he must bear alone. He could give no more confidences, only try to worm them out of others. He must exchange the trim privacy of the Bishop's domain for the poverty and depression of a mountain village, where there was little privacy even for birth, death and the act of love.

He would be the house guest of a woman—and, unlike many of his colleagues, he had small talent for dealing with the opposite sex. He was a celibate by profession and a bachelor by disposition; and he resented the effort he would have to make for small-talk over the coffee cups. His strength was running out swiftly and he could not bear to waste it on the trivia of domestic intercourse.

So, while the labourers slept under the olive trees and His Lordship wrote in his study, he surrendered himself to the final indulgence of a walk round the plantations. He took off his cassock and stock, rolled up his sleeves to let the sun shine on his thin, pale arms, and then headed down the narrow path that led to the dam and the outer fringe of the domain.

Under the trees the air was cool and the path was dappled with sunshine, but when he broke out into the valley, where the dam lay shining between the grey walls of the hill, the heat hit him like an oven blast. When he looked about him he could see it rising in shimmering waves from the tufa rock. He hesitated a moment, regretting the shelter of the plantations, but then, ashamed of his weakness, walked steadily forward round the fringe of the dam and towards the retaining wall.

On the slope above the path the labourers were sleeping, heads pillowed on their jackets, in the shadow of jutting rocks. Their short brown bodies were sprawled, slack as rag dolls, and Meredith, who had long been a stranger to sleep, was moved to envy of their good fortune.

They were poor, but not so poor as many. They had work with a benevolent master. Their clothes were stained and dusty and they wore wooden sandals instead of shoes, but they could sleep quietly and walk home with dignity, because they had work, and pasta for the table and wine and oil to go with it. In a poor land with three million workless it was very much indeed.

At the edge of the spillway the path forked into two goat

tracks, one leading down to the bed of the stream, the other heading up towards the saddle of the hill. Meredith chose the upward path, hoping vaguely that from the top he might get a view of the surrounding countryside. The track was rough and covered with sharp stones, but he trudged on with dull determination, as if to defy the weakness·of his wasting body and affirm that he was still a man.

Half way up, he found himself on a small plateau, invisible from the valley, where the rock walls folded back into a shallow re-entrant like a cave. There was a shadow here and he sat down gratefully to rest a few moments. As his eyes rested themselves from the glare, he saw near the base of the wall a few courses of rough stonework, reticulated in the old Roman manner, and above them the toolmarks on the walls where other courses had once been keyed to the natural stone. He stood up and began to examine them more closely, and followed the lines of the stonework back towards the rear of the re-entrant.

The shadows were deeper here, and it was a moment or two before he noticed a small shelf cut back into the rock on which lay a few withered marigolds and crumbling vine leaves. Behind the offerings was a piece of marble, so old and weathered and stained that at first he could not make out what it was. Then he saw that it was part of the base of an old statue, roughly cubic in shape, out of which jutted the crude shape of a phallus.

In antique days, when the hills were covered with forests before the hungry tribes had denuded them for fuel and building, this cave must have been the shrine of a wood god. Now all that was left of him was the symbol of fertility; but the flowers were of the twentieth century—the first offering of spring to an old discredited god.

Meredith had heard, often enough, of the superstitions that still persisted among the mountain people—of charms and spells and love philtres and odd rites—but this was the first time he had seen the evidence with his own eyes. The marble block was stained and discoloured, but the phallus was white and polished as if by frequent contact. Did the women come here, as they used to in old times, for an assurance against barrenness? Did the males still worship the symbol of their dominance? Was there yet in these mountain folk a half conscious hope that Pan might do what the new god had not done: make the raped land virgin again and fruitful with grass and trees?

The worship of the male principle was rooted deep among these people. The young men stood arrogant as preened cockerels while the girls came in at least putative virginity to present themselves for inspection and admiration. When they were married they bred their women into exhaustion and coddled their sons to precocious maleness while they beat their daughters into chastity. In a barren land they were the last symbols of fruitfulness and the first symbols of joy to a woman whose end would be a joyless servitude in a tumbling hovel in the hills.

Perhaps this was why the correlative Christian symbol was not the agonised Christus, but the fruitful Madonna with the Bambino suckling at her peasant breast.

Blaise Meredith found himself curiously fascinated by the crude stone symbol and its active survival not half a mile from the Bishop's domain. Perhaps this was the explanation of much of the anomaly of the Mediterranean Church: the strong belief in the supernatural, the thick overlay of superstition, the fierce zeal of the Latin saints and the equally fierce rejection of the Communists and the anti-clericals. Perhaps this was the reason why cool liberals and urbane sceptics made so little impact on these people; why an exalted mysticism was the only answer to the Bacchic frenzy that woke in their brown, undernourished bodies. Was this the real explanation of the death of Giacomo Nerone, that he had been trampled under the hoofs of the goat-god?

And how could Blaise Meredith, the legalist from Rome, enter into the mind of this secret people who were old when Rome was young, and who had once made alliance with the black, fiery god of Hannibal's Carthage?

In spite of the heat he felt suddenly cold. He turned away from the obscene little image and walked out into the sunlight.

111

An old woman, bent almost in two under a load of twigs and driftwood from the stream, was struggling up the path, towards the saddle. When she came abreast of him he raised his hand and called a greeting in his precise Roman Italian. She turned her head and stared at him with blank rheumy eyes, then passed by without a word.

Blaise Meredith stood a moment looking after her, then turned his face towards the valley. He felt old and tired and strangely afraid of going to Gemello Minore.

CHAPTER SEVEN

ANNE LOUISE DE SANCTIS woke from her siesta in a mood of black depression. When she remembered that Aldo Meyer was coming to dinner her mood became blacker still; and when His Lordship's letter was delivered into her hands by the messenger, her temper was frayed to screaming point. It was all too much. She could not cope with these intrusions on her privacy. Even boredom was preferable to the effort she would have to make to be agreeable.

When they met for tea in the afternoon, Nicholas Black was quick to notice her ill-temper, and subtle enough to suggest an immediate remedy.

"You're tired, *cara*," he told her solicitously. "It's the heat —spring fever. Why not let me charm it out of you?"

"I wish you could, Nicki."

"Will you let me?"

"How? I still have to cope with Meyer. And tomorrow this cleric arrives." Her voice took on the petulant tone of a child's. "I wish they'd leave me alone."

"You have me, *cara*," he said gently. "I'll keep them amused. I shan't let them bother you. Now, why don't you let me give you a face massage and do your hair for dinner?"

She brightened immediately.

"I'd love that, Nicki. It's the thing I miss most here. I feel I'm getting to be an old hag."

"Never, *cara*! But a new hat and a new hair-do are the best cures for the megrims. Where shall we do it?"

She hesitated a moment, then answered with affected casualness:

"I suppose the bedroom's the best place. I've got everything there."

"Come on, then! Let's start. Give me an hour and I'll have you ravishing as any Roman beauty."

He took her hand with stagey gallantry and led her upstairs to the baroque bedroom, chuckling inwardly at the easy victory. If there were secrets to be learned about the Contessa he would find them here, given time, patience and the sedulous skill of his own soft hands.

When the door closed behind them he made a sexless little ceremony of helping her off with her dress and wrapping the negligée about her and settling her in a brocaded chair opposite the dressing table with its rows of toiletries in crystal jars. She bridled dutifully and made coquettish remarks intended to underline the intimacy of the occasion. The painter smiled and flourished his towels and let her prattle contentedly. He had a chameleon talent for identifying himself with every situation even while his thoughts and plans ran contrariwise. Now he was the *parrucchiere*—my lady's confidant, witness of things denied even to lovers, teller of scabrous little tales for which my lady had no need to blush, since valets are impervious to the best pretended virtue.

He laid her head back, cleansed the face of makeup, creamed it carefully and then began to massage with firm but gentle fingers, upward from the slack throat and the corners of the discontented mouth. She was stiff and cautious with him at first, but she surrendered quickly to the rhythmic, hypnotic touch and after a while he could feel the slow sensuality waking in her. It gave him a special satisfaction to coax her while he himself remained unmoved; and, while he worked, he began to talk in the devious idiom of the salon:

"You have beautiful skin, *cara*; supple as a girl's. Some women lose that very quickly. You're one of the fortunate ones . . . like Ninon de L'Enclos, who kept the secret of eternal youth . . . That was a strange story. When she was still the rage of Paris, at sixty, her own son came to pay court to her without knowing who she was. He fell in love with her, and committed suicide when he found out the truth . . ." He chuckled lightly. ". . . You're lucky you have no sons!"

She gave a small complacent sigh.

"I've always wanted children, Nicki. But . . . perhaps it's just as well I didn't have them."

"You could still have them, couldn't you?"

She giggled girlishly.

"I'd need some help, wouldn't I?"

"I've often wondered why you never married again; why an attractive woman chose to bury herself in the wilds of Calabria. You're not poor. You could live anywhere you liked—London, Rome, Paris . . ."

"I've been there, Nicki. I still go regularly to Rome, as you know. But this is my home. I always come back."

"You haven't answered my question, *cara*." His deft hands covered the malice in the query. As he massaged her cheeks and the fine network of lines about her eyes, he could feel the tension gathering in her as she fumbled for an answer.

"I've been married, Nicki. I've been in love. I've had affairs too and I've had proposals. None of them really satisfied me. It's as simple as that."

But it wasn't simple, and he knew it; she was more complex than any other woman he had known—and she was shrewd enough to turn the tables on him immediately.

"You've never married either, darling. Why?"

"I've never needed marriage," he told her lightly. "I've always managed to get what I want outside it."

"You gay bachelors!"

"If there weren't gay bachelors, *cara*, there wouldn't be merry widows—only frustrated dowagers."

"Do you ever get frustrated, Nicki?"

He smiled secretly at the new plaintive note in her voice. Odd, he thought, how the word brings them every time; how they use the Freudian jargon as if it were the answer to the ultimate riddle of the universe. They're never spoilt. They're never hot for a man they can't have. They're never scared of getting too old for a tumble in the hay. They're frustrated. I am too, for that matter, but I'm damned if I'll let her know it.

"With you, *cara*, how could any man be frustrated?"

As if in gratitude for the compliment she reached up and took his hand, still greasy from the cream, and pressed it to her lips. Then, without warning, she drew it down and laid it on the naked curve of her breast under the negligée. The action took him by surprise and he reacted sharply.

"Don't do that!"

Then, surprisingly, she laughed.

"Poor Nicki! Didn't you think I knew?"

"I don't know what you're talking about!" His voice was high with irritation, but Anne Louise de Sanctis was still laughing.

"That you're different, darling. That you don't really care for women at all. That you're head over heels and gone for young Paolo Sanduzzi. It's true, isn't it?"

He was almost weeping with anger as he stood there with the towel in his hands, staring over her head at the gilt *amorini* on the ceiling. Her hand reached out for him again and held him. She stopped laughing and her voice was low, almost caressing.

"You don't have to be angry, Nicki. You don't have to have secrets from me!"

He wrenched away from her fiercely.

"There's no secret, Anne. I like the boy. I think I could do a great deal for him. I'd like to get him out of the village and have him educated and give him a decent start in life. I haven't much money, God knows, but I'd be willing to lay out every penny on that."

"And what would you want in return?" Her voice was still soft, but edged with irony.

He gave the answer with an odd pathetic dignity.

"Nothing. Nothing at all. But I don't expect you to believe that."

For a long moment she stared at him with bright, speculative eyes. Then she told him:

"I do believe you, Nicki. And I think I might help you to get him."

Wondering, he raised his head and looked at her, trying vainly to decipher the thoughts behind her subtle, smiling lips.

"I have my own reasons, Nicki. But I mean what I say. You help me handle this priest and I'll help you with Paolo Sanduzzi. Is that a bargain?"

He bent and kissed her hand in abject gratitude, and she rumpled his hair with the half maternal, half contemptuous gesture she used towards him.

It was an alliance of interest, and each of them knew it. But even enemies smile at one another across the treaty table. So, when Doctor Aldo Meyer arrived for dinner, the Contessa was radiant and Nicholas Black was as deferential as a page in the service of a beloved mistress.

Meyer himself was tired and ill-disposed for society. He had spent the whole afternoon with Martino the smith, waiting for the second, and possibly fatal, seizure which might well follow the first one. It was nearly dark when he decided it was safe to move the patient to his own house, and then he had been forced to listen to the lamentations of the wife who had just become aware of the precarious situation of her family. He had had to give assurances that he was unconfident of fulfilling: that the illness would not last too long, that someone—the Countess perhaps—would see the family fed, that he himself would make arrangements for assistance from the commune, that he would try to find someone who would keep the smithy working and not charge too much.

By the time he made his escape he had mortgaged his soul and his reputation twenty times over, and was more convinced than ever of the hopelessness of reform among this ignorant people, bred for centuries to feudalism, who would kiss the hand of the meanest baron provided it held a loaf of bread and offered them an illusion of safety against acts of God and the politicians.

When he reached his house, he found the Bishop's letter waiting for him, and this was another straw added to the burden of the day's irritations. His Lordship asked nothing but a medical service, better paid than that which he normally performed, but he suggested much more: a courtesy that might grow into a heavy commitment. Aldo Meyer the liberal Jew had a healthy mistrust of the absolutist churchman whose predecessors had harried his people out of Spain and then given them uneasy refuge in the ghettos of the Trastevere. But,

117

willy-nilly, the Englishman would come, and under his Æsculapian oath Meyer would be bound to serve him. He hoped perversely that he would not be seduced into friendship.

There was no friendship in his relations with Anne Louise de Sanctis. He was her physician for want of a better one. He was her guest for want of other educated company to divert her dinner table. Occasionally he was the mouthpiece of the villagers in their pleas to the *padrona*. But beyond these narrow definitions, there was an area of unspoken mistrust and concealed animosity.

Both had known Giacomo Nerone. Each, for an opposite reason, had been involved in his death. Meyer knew only too well the nature of his patient's illness though he never put the diagnosis into words. Anne Louise de Sanctis knew her doctor's failures and she goaded him with them because he knew too much about her own. But, because they saw each other rarely, they rubbed along in reasonable politeness, and in a cross-grained fashion were grateful to each other—Meyer for good wine and a well-cooked meal, the Contessa for the chance to dress and dine with a man who was neither a clod nor a cleric.

But tonight there was something else in the wind. The presence of Nicholas Black and the coming of the Roman emissary lent a new and faintly sinister character to the occasion. As he shaved and dressed by the yellow light of a paraffin lamp, he prepared himself for a disagreeable evening.

At first meeting his fears seemed groundless. The Contessa was well-groomed, relaxed and charming. She seemed genuinely glad to see him. The painter's smile was free of sardonic subtleties, and he talked well and amiably on whatever subject was started.

With the *aperitif* they talked weather and local customs and the decline of the Neapolitan school of painters. By the soup they were up to Rome, and Black was retailing the pleasanter scandals of the Via Margutta and the price the critics were charging for a favourable notice. When the fish was brought they were through the Vatican and out among the politicos, discussing the prospects for the forthcoming election. The wine had loosened the doctor's tongue and he was launched on a lively dissertation:

". . . last time the Christian Democrats came in through the confessional box and the American dollar aid. The Church held damnation over the head of every Catholic who voted Communist, and Washington waved a bundle of dollar bills on the sideline. The people wanted peace and bread at any price, and the Vatican was still the only institution in Italy with stability and moral credit. So between them they carried the polls. But we still have the strongest Communist party outside of Russia, and a singular disunity of aim even among those who voted under the Vatican banner. What's going to happen this time? The Democrats will hold on, of course, but they'll lose votes in a general swing to the left. The Monarchists will gain somewhat in the South, and the Communists will stay about where they are—a hard core of discontent."

"What will cause the losses in the Christian Democrats?" Nicholas Black put the question with sharp interest.

Meyer shrugged expressively.

"The record first. There are no spectacular reforms, no perceptible diminution in the pool of unemployed. There is an equilibrium in industry, held by the infusion of American money and aid from the Vatican Bank. There is a rise in the national income, which is reflected hardly at all in the living standards of vast numbers of the population. But it's enough to keep the financiers reasonably happy and the votes stable for another term. The second reason is that the Vatican itself has lost credit through its identification with a party. It's the trouble with a political Pope. He always wants it both ways— the kingdom of Heaven and the majority in the earthly parliament as well. In Italy he can get it—at a price, and the price is anti-clericalism among his own flock."

"It interests me." Black caught at the tag of the statement. "All over Italy you meet women who communicate every day and men who wear the badges of half a dozen confraternities and they still quote the old phrase: *Tutti i preti sono falsi*—All priests are cheats. It's amusing, but damned illogical."

Meyer laughed and spread his hands in mock despair.

119

"My dear fellow, it's the most logical thing in the world. The more priests you get, the more their faults show up. Clerical government is like petticoat government—bad for both sides. I don't believe all priests are liars. I've met some damned good ones in my time. But I'm an anti-clerical for all that. The Latin is a logician at heart. He's prepared to admit that the Holy Ghost guides the Pope on matters of faith and morals; but he chokes on the proposition that he fixes the bank rate as well."

"Talking of priests," said Anne Louise de Sanctis, "I wonder what Monsignor Meredith will be like."

It was as bland as butter, but Aldo Meyer understood the malice of it. They had herded him like a sheep from one topic to another—and now they had him penned and they watched him, grinning with subtle mockery, to see what he would do to escape. To hell with them, then. He wouldn't give them any satisfaction. He shrugged off the question.

"You mean our Roman inquisitor? He's no concern of mine. He comes and he goes away. That's all. Just now I have problems of my own—which I wanted to discuss with the *padrona*."

"What sort of problems?" The Contessa frowned at this check to her mockery.

"Martino, the smith, had a stroke today. He's paralysed and incapacitated. The family's going to need help. I wondered if you'd make some money available—and also take a couple of the girls into service here. Teresina and young Rosetta are old enough to begin work."

To his surprise the Contessa took it quite casually.

"Of course. It's the least I can do. I've been thinking quite a lot lately about the young people. There's nothing for them here—and even if they try to migrate, they end up on the streets in Reggio or Naples. I thought we should begin to revive some of your plans, Doctor, and create work for them here."

"A good idea," said Meyer cautiously; and wondered where the devil she was leading him. Her next words showed him all too plainly.

"Paolo Sanduzzi, for instance. Nicki tells me the boy is

intelligent and willing. It seems such a waste to have him lounging about so much. I'll bring him here and set him to work with the gardeners. No doubt his mother could use some extra money."

Now he was really trapped. He had accepted a favour and he must take the sour portion that went with it. They sat there, smiling at him over the rims of their glasses, challenging him to protest and make a fool of himself. Instead he nodded and said indifferently:

"If you can use him, why not? You'd have to discuss it with his mother, of course."

"Why?" asked Nicholas Black.

"Because he's under age," said Meyer pointedly. "His mother is still his legal guardian."

The painter flushed and buried his nose in his glass, and Anne Louise permitted herself a small, secret smile at his discomfiture. She said simply:

"You might ask Nina Sanduzzi to call and see me to-morrow, Doctor."

"I'll ask her, certainly. She may not care to come."

"For barefoot peasants, we ride damned high!" Black commented sourly.

"We're an odd people," Meyer told him mildly. "It takes time to understand us."

Anne Louise said nothing, but signalled to the servant to pour more wine and serve the roast. She had made her point. Meyer had taken it—and if Nicki cared to cross swords with the Jew, she might be amused, but she would not be embroiled. Meyer's next words drew her back into the argument.

"I had a letter from the Bishop today. He asks me to act as medical adviser to Monsignor Meredith. Apparently he's dying of carcinoma."

"My God!" Nicholas Black swore softly. "That's a damned nuisance."

"You invited him, Nicki," said the Contessa irritably. "I don't see what you have to complain about."

"I was thinking of you, *cara*. A sick man in the house is a big burden."

121

"There's a room in my place," said Meyer amiably. "It's none too comfortable, but it's adequate."

"I wouldn't hear of it." She reacted sharply. "He'll stay here. There are servants to look after him and you can visit him whenever he needs you."

"I thought you'd say that," said Meyer calmly and there was no hint of irony in his eyes.

The roast was brought and the wine was served and they ate for a while in silence, each totting up the score in the battle of interests that had gone on under the thin politeness of the talk. After a while the Contessa put down her fork and said:

"I've been thinking that, as a courtesy to His Lordship, we should arrange a welcome for this man."

Nicholas Black choked suddenly over the chicken.

"What sort of welcome, *cara*? A procession of the Confraternity of the Dead and the Children of Mary and the Society of the Holy Name? Banners and candles and acolytes, and Father Anselmo trotting behind in a dirty surplice?"

"Nothing of the sort, Nicki!" Her tone was harsh and peremptory. "A quiet dinner party, tomorrow night, with ourselves and the doctor and Father Anselmo. Nothing elaborate, but a simple occasion to meet the people in the village who are best able to help him."

Aldo Meyer kept his eyes studiously fixed on his plate. How could you match a woman like this one? A simple dinner party!—with the *padrona* playing gracious lady to a country doctor and a cloddish priest who would fumble the cutlery and slop his wine and probably fall asleep over the fruit bowl while the Roman Monsignor looked on with tolerant good-humour. And when he came to take the evidence, whom would he lean on, but this same gracious lady, who gave him such courteous house room? A simple party—how very, very simple!

"Well, Doctor, what do you think?"

He looked up, cool and unsmiling.

"It's your house; he's your guest."

"But you'll come?"

"Certainly."

He could see her relax, and he caught the furtive triumph dawning in her eyes. When he looked at Nicholas Black, he too was smiling and Aldo Meyer felt suddenly naked to the daggers of this oddly matched pair of intriguers.

"I wonder what he'll be like?" Black asked the question of no one in particular.

"Who?" queried the Contessa.

"Our Monsignor from Rome. When I saw him in Valenta he looked pinched and grey and rather like a mole."

"He's dying," said Meyer bluntly. "That tends to spoil a man's complexion."

The painter laughed.

"But not his temper, I hope. I hate people who are crotchety at meals. He's English, of course, which should make a difference. Probably dry and brilliant and dull as ditch-water in conversation. I wonder if he'll be stuffy. Some of the Roman clergy are very liberal. Others would like to see creation rearranged to have universal autogenesis. I'm anxious to see what this one makes of the love affair of Giacomo Nerone."

Aldo Meyer turned sharply to face him.

"What do you know about it?"

The painter's smile was a bland insult.

"Not quite as much as you perhaps. But I do employ his son and you've got his mistress doing your housework. Of course that could be useful, too. The recent lists are full of virgins and confessors and beardless boys just out of novitiate. They could use a good penitent like Augustine or Margaret of Cortona. It helps them to cope with the sinners. You know . . . 'There's always a way to come back to God!' They're great opportunists, these clerics. Don't you agree, Doctor?"

"I'm a Jew," said Meyer with tart finality. "I have small taste for Catholicism, but even less for blasphemy. I'd like to change the subject."

The Contessa added her own abrupt warning:

"You're drinking too much, Nicki!"

The painter flushed angrily, pushed back his chair and marched out of the room. At a sign from the Contessa the servant left too, and Anne Louise de Sanctis was alone with her medical adviser.

She took a cigarette, pushed the box across the table to Meyer and waited while he lit up for both of them. Then she leaned forward and blew a cloud of smoke full in his face.

"Now then, *dottore mio*, stop fencing and say what you have to say."

Meyer shook his head.

"You wouldn't thank me, Anne. And you wouldn't believe me."

"Try me. I'm in a receptive mood tonight." She laughed lightly and held out her hand to him across the table. "You're an obstinate fellow, Aldo *mio*, and when you look down that damn Jewish nose at me, you make me obstinate too. Come on now, tell me, and tell me nicely—what's wrong with me, and what's your prescription?"

For a moment he sat silent, staring at the face which had once been beautiful—the fine bones of it, the slack sagging muscles, the crowsfeet round the eyes, the dragging lines of discontent, the tired skin under the careful makeup. Then with clinical bluntness he answered her.

"I'll give you the prescription first. Stop stuffing yourself with barbiturates. Stop collecting oddities like Black who fill you up with dirty stories and give you no joy at the end of it. Sell up this place—or put a steward in—and get yourself a flat in Rome. Then get yourself married to a man who'll keep you happy in bed and make you keep him happy afterwards."

"You've got a dirty mind, Doctor," she told him with a smile.

Aldo Meyer went on, unsmiling:

"It gets dirtier yet. You missed satisfaction in marriage because you were too young and your husband too careless to worry. You've never had it since because, every time you tried, you failed yourself and the man. It's common enough and curable enough, provided you face up to what you want and what you need to prepare yourself to get it. But you've never done that. You've retired into your own private little world, and filled it with a kind of mental pornography that drives you crazy with desire and leaves you still unsatisfied.

124

You're the wrong age for that, my dear. It's dangerous. You end up with gigolos and fellows like Nicholas Black and an overdose of sedatives at the end of it. You can still be a lover. But you may make yourself a bawd—as you're doing with Paolo Sanduzzi."

She ignored the last thrust, and asked him, smiling:

"And how do I get myself a husband, Doctor? Buy one?"

"You might do worse," said Aldo Meyer soberly. "Given the elements, you'll probably do better with an honest bargain than a dishonest love. That's why you like to tyrannise over your painter, because you're under the tyranny of an unsatisfied body."

"Anything else, Doctor?"

"Only one thing," said Meyer calmly. "Get Giacomo Nerone off your mind. Stop trying to strike at him through Nina and the boy. You aren't the first woman who destroyed a man because he rejected her. But if you can't look that one in the face, you'll end by destroying yourself."

"You've forgotten the most important thing, Doctor."

Meyer looked at her with sharp interest.

"What's that?"

"I've always wanted a child, needed one more than you know. My husband couldn't give me one. Giacomo Nerone refused me and bred himself a boy out of a barefoot peasant. I hated him for that. But I don't hate him any more. If you didn't stand between me and his mother, I could do something for the boy . . . give him a good start in life, save him from running to seed like the rest of the lads in the village."

"What would you do with him, Anne?" asked Meyer coldly. "Hand him to your painter?"

Without a word, she picked up a half empty wineglass and dashed the contents in his face. Then she laid her head down on her arms and sobbed convulsively. Aldo Meyer wiped the wine from his thin cheeks, got up from the table and rang for a servant to show him out.

When he reached his house, he was surprised to find the lamp lit and Nina Sanduzzi sitting at the table with a pile of mending in front of her. Her presence at this late hour was sufficiently rare to make him comment on it. Her answer was quite simple.

"I spent the evening with Martino's wife. She's a fool, but kind, and she just begins to see what trouble she is in. When I got the family bedded down and made Martino comfortable, I thought I would wait here and see what news you had from the Contessa."

For a moment he was tempted to vent his feelings in an ironic outburst; then he remembered that she did not understand irony and would only be troubled by it. So he answered her baldly:

"It's good news for Martino. The Contessa will make a gift of money and also take Teresina and Rosetta into service with her. With their wages and the bit of help from public assistance, they won't be too badly off."

"Good!" She gave him one of her rare, calm smiles. "It's a beginning. Later, perhaps, we can improve it. Would you like coffee?"

"Yes, please." Meyer slumped heavily into a chair and began unlacing his shoes. Instantly she was at his feet, helping him. This, too, was new; she had never before assumed the functions of a body servant. Meyer said nothing, but sat watching her thoughtfully as she crossed the room to light the small primus under the coffee pot. He said, without emphasis:

"The Contessa would like to see you tomorrow, too."

"Why would she want to see me?"

"She wants to offer Paolo a job helping the gardeners."

"Is that the only reason?" She was still bending over the primus.

"For you, yes. For Paolo, there could be other reasons!"

Slowly she turned to face him across the shadowy room. She asked:

"What sort of reasons?"

"The English painter has a fondness for him. The Contessa wishes to use him in a way that is not yet clear. Also I think she wants the boy to be there when this priest comes from Valenta to inquire about Giacomo."

126

"They are like dogs rutting on a dung heap," said Nina Sanduzzi softly. "There is no love in anything they do. I won't go. The boy won't go, either."

Meyer nodded agreement.

"I promised only that I would tell you. For the rest, I think you're wise. It's a house with a touch of madness in it."

"They practise on us, as if we were animals." She threw out her arms in an angry gesture. "This is a child—a boy with his first manhood stirring in him—and they want to use him like that."

"I warned you," he reminded her soberly.

"I know." She began to lay out the coffee cups on the table, talking as she moved. "And this is another reason I came here tonight. Paolo told me he had been walking by the Torrente del Fauno, with young Rosetta. I was glad of it. They are both young, and this is a good time for love to begin, provided it begins the right way. I think Paolo was glad too. I know he wanted to talk, but he did not know how to put it into words. I wanted to help, but . . . you understand how it is with a boy. He would never believe his mother might know the words, too. It's hard when there's no man in the house, and I wondered whether—whether you might help him a little."

The coffee pot boiled over, and as she hurried to rescue it Meyer had time to consider his answer. He gave it to her gently and haltingly.

"A boy in his first waking is like a strange country, Nina. There are no maps, no signposts. Even the language is different. I could make mistakes and do him harm. What he feels for the Englishman I don't know. What has happened between them I don't know. But whatever it is there will be a shame in it for the boy; just as there is a shame in his first want for a girl. This is what makes him furtive like a fox, timid like a bird. You understand?"

"I understand, surely. But I understand his need too. It is a strange world for him. His father was someone they call a saint. His mother is someone they call a whore. I will not justify myself or his father to him. But how do I explain the wonderful thing there was between us? And how it should be wonderful for him too?"

"How can I explain it"—Meyer grinned ruefully—"when I didn't understand it myself?"

Her next question shocked him out of his weariness.

"Do you hate the boy?"

"God Almighty, no! What makes you say that?"

"He might have been yours—before Giacomo came."

Meyer's face clouded with old memories.

"That's true. But I never hated the child."

"Do you hate me?"

"No. There was a time when I hated Giacomo and when he died I was glad—but only for a while. Now I am sorry."

"Enough to help his son?"

"And you, too, if I could. Send him to me and I'll try to talk to him."

"I've always known you were a good man."

And that for the moment was all the thanks she gave him. She went to the stove, picked up the coffee pot and brought it back to the table. She poured a cup for him and one for herself, and stood watching him while he sipped tentatively at the bitter scalding liquid. Her own cup she tossed off at a gulp and then crossed to the corner of the room to gather up her wooden sandals and the battered basket which held her day's purchases: a bundle of charcoal, pasta and a few vegetables.

Then she came back to the table and held out to him a thick parcel wrapped in cotton cloth and tied with a faded ribbon.

"Take it," she told him firmly. "I don't want it any more."

"What is it?" His eyes searched her calm face.

"Giacomo's papers. Somewhere in there is his letter to you. They may help you to understand him and me. They may help you to help the boy."

Wondering, he took the soiled package and held it between his hands as he had once held the lolling, lifeless head of Giacomo Nerone. Memories flooded back, vivid and oppressive—old fears, old hates, old loves, small triumphs and monstrous failures. His eyes misted and he felt his stomach knot up and a small nerve begin twitching at the corner of his mouth.

When he raised his eyes at last he saw that Nina Sanduzzi was gone and that he was left alone in the lamplight with the soul of a dead man, held between his own trembling fingers.

Nina Sanduzzi walked back to her house in the peace of spring moonlight. The harsh outlines of the hills were soft, under the stars; the crumbling village was no longer drab but silvered to an antique beauty and down in the valley the torrent ran, a ribbon of grey light through the shadows. The air was crisp and clean and her wooden sandals clattered sharply on the stones above the intermittent voices of the crickets and the distant muted sound of the water.

But Nina Sanduzzi was blind to the beauty and deaf to the night-music. She was a peasant, rooted in the countryside as a tree is rooted, tough, persistent, insentient to the pathetic fallacy which is at best a sentimental diversion for the literate. The landscape was a place in which she lived.

Only the figures in it were important. The beauty she saw—and she saw much of it—was in faces and hands and eyes, smiles and tears and the laughter of children, and the memories treasured like water in a cistern. Spring was a sensation in her own strong body. Summer was a warmth on the skin and dust under her bare feet, and winter was a cold hibernation and a careful husbanding of twigs and charcoal.

She could neither read nor write, yet she understood peace, because she had known conflict, and she was receptive to harmony, because it built slowly but perceptibly out of the dissonances of the life about her.

Tonight she was at peace. She could see the beginning of fulfilment to the promise of Giacomo Nerone, that even after his death there would be care of herself and the boy. They were poor, but poverty was their natural state and Giacomo had never let them want too much or too long. Now in their greater need there was Aldo Meyer, ready to pay, out of his own need, a debt to a dead man.

There was harmony in her life, too—a slow concordance

building between her and the villagers. They needed her. They were grateful, like Martino's wife, for her help in their troubles; and, when they called her the old crude names—'the whore', 'the woman who slept with a saint'—there was no longer much malice in it; only a dim memory of old jealousies. They were a harsh people and they used harsh words, because they had few others. Their symbols were vulgar, because their life was brutish—and belly hunger cannot be satisfied with dreams.

So tonight as she walked home to the small hut among the ilex trees she was grateful, and all her gratitude centred on Giacomo Nerone, dead long since and buried in the Grotto of the Faun, where folk came to pray and went away cured of their infirmities of body and spirit.

Everything else in her life was blotted out by the memory of this man: her parents, who had died of malaria when she was sixteen and left her the hut, a few sticks of furniture and a small dowry chest; her husband, a brown, turbulent boy who had married her in the Church and slept with her for a month and then been taken by the Army to die in the first Libyan campaign. After his death she had lived, as the other women did, alone in her small hut, hiring herself out for farm labour and occasional house service when one of the maids fell sick in the Contessa's villa.

Then, Giacomo Nerone had come . . .

It was a summer's night, hot and heavy with thunder. She was lying naked on the big brass bed, tossing restlessly with the heat and the mosquitoes and the need that woke often in her strong body for a man's arms and the feel of him in the bed beside her. It was long past midnight, and even after a gruelling day on the vine-terraces sleep would not come.

Then she heard the knocking—weak and furtive on the barred door. She sat up in sudden terror, drawing the bed-clothes about her breasts. The knocking came again, and she called out:

"Who is it?"

A man's voice answered her in Italian.

"A friend. I'm sick. Let me in, for the love of God!"

The weak urgency of the voice touched her. She got out of bed, pulled on her dress and went to the door. When she unbarred it and opened it cautiously, he tumbled forward on to the earthen floor—a big, dark man with blood on his face and a glutinous stain seeping into the shoulder of his ragged shirt. His hands were bramble-scratched and his boots were broken and gaping, and when he tried to get up, he crawled two paces and then pitched forward on his face.

It took all her peasant strength to drag him and lever him on to the bed. While he was still unconscious, she bathed the cuts on his face and cut his shirt away from the wound in his shoulder and washed that too. Then she took off his boots and drew the bedclothes over him and let him sleep until the first dawn brightened the eastern sky. He woke in the sudden panic of the hunted, staring about him with wide, scared eyes; but when he saw her he smiled and relaxed again, grimacing ruefully at the pain of his shoulder wound.

She brought him wine and black bread and cheese, and marvelled that he wolfed it so greedily. He drank three cups of wine, but would take no more food because, he said, folk were hungry and he had a right only to the traveller's share. He smiled again, as he said it, a wide, boyish smile that charmed the last fears out of her and brought her to sit on the edge of the bed and ask who he was and what had brought him to Gemello Minore and how he had come by the wound in his shoulder.

His accent was strange to her and he had difficulty in understanding her thick Calabrese dialect, but the lines of his story were clear enough. He was a soldier, he said, a garrison gunner based at Reggio at the tip of the boot of Italy. The Allies had taken Sicily and the British Army had crossed the Straits of Messina and was working its way up the peninsula. Reggio had fallen. His unit had broken and he was on the run. If he rejoined his own army they would patch him up and send him back into the line. If the British got him they would make him a prisoner of war. So he was trying to make his way back to Rome, to his own family. He had been hiding by day and travelling by night, living on what he could steal. Last night he had been flushed by a British patrol and they had fired at him. The bullet was still in his shoulder. It would have to be taken out, or he would die.

Because she was a simple peasant, she accepted his story at face value. Because she liked him and because she was lonely for a man, she was willing to hide him and care for him until his wound was better. Her hut was away from the village and no one ever came there. That was the beginning of it: simple and unimportant as a hundred other wartime tales of lonely widows and soldiers on the run. But the richness that grew out of it and the tragedy that ended it, and the peace that followed it, were her daily wonder and her nightly remembrance . . .

When she reached the house, she found the lamp burning low, and Paolo curled up, apparently asleep, on the rough truckle bed on the opposite side of the room from the big brass *letto matrimonio* in which he had been begotten and born. Until the onset of puberty he had slept with her, in the custom of the South, where whole families sleep in the one great bed, husbands and wives and babes and maturing boys and girls growing into womanhood. But for a lone woman and her son it was a bad thing, so she had bought another bed and each of them slept alone.

She closed the door, barred and bolted it, then put down her basket and kicked off her sandals. The boy on the bed watched her through veiled eyes, feigning sleep. Every detail of the ritual that followed was familiar to him though, for a long time now, he had refused to take part in it.

Nina Sanduzzi crossed the room to the rough dower chest that stood at the head of her bed. From the inside of her dress she unpinned a small key with which she unlocked it. Then she took out a flat parcel wrapped in white paper. She unwrapped it carefully and took out a man's shirt, old and tattered and stained in many places as if with rust. She held it a moment to her lips and then unfolded it and spread it over the back of a chair so that the tatters were seen as old bullet holes and the stains were the marks of blood. Then she knelt down awkwardly, buried her face in her hands on the seat of the chair and began to pray in a low muttering voice.

Try as he might the boy had never been able to catch the words. When he had knelt there with his mother she had told him simply to say Paters and Aves as he did in church, because his father was a saint who had great power with God—like San Giuseppe, who was the foster-father of the Bambino. But she would never admit him to the privacy of her own communion with his father and, in an odd way, he was jealous of it. Now he looked on the whole thing as a piece of woman's nonsense.

Her prayers over, Nina Sanduzzi re-wrapped the parcel and locked it away in the dower chest. Then she came over to her son's bed, bent to kiss him and turned away. Paolo Sanduzzi kept his eyes closed and breathed steadily because, although he wanted often to kiss her and have her hold him as she did in the old days, there was now a revulsion in him that he could not explain. It was the same thing that made him close his eyes and turn away his head when she undressed her thickening body or got up to relieve herself in the night. He was ashamed of her and he was ashamed of himself.

So he lay still until his mother blew out the lamp and climbed into the creaking brass bed. Then he too settled himself and lapsed slowly into sleep. While he slept, he dreamed—of Rosetta standing on the rock ledge by the torrent and calling him to her. He went to her running and scrambling, seeing her lips parted and her eyes laughing and her arms outflung to welcome him. But before the arms closed round him, they changed to the arms of Nicholas Black, and instead of the girl's face there was the pale goat visage of the painter.

Paolo Sanduzzi stirred and groaned and opened his eyes in the half sweet, half shameful moment when the sap of youth runs over, and a boy is not sure whether he sleeps or wakes.

CHAPTER EIGHT

IT WAS Blaise Meredith's last night in Valenta: his last in the company of Aurelio the Bishop. They dined, as they always did, comfortably and well. They talked without nostalgia of a variety of subjects, and, when the meal was over, His Lordship suggested that they take coffee in his study.

It was a big, airy room, lined from floor to ceiling with books but sparsely furnished with a desk, a prie-dieu, a set of steel cabinets and a grouping of leather chairs near a big majolica stove. Yet somehow it reflected accurately the character of the man who worked in it: learned, ascetic, practical, with a taste for modest comfort.

The coffee was brought and with it a bottle of old brandy, dusty from the cellar, with the seals still intact. His Lordship insisted on opening it and pouring it himself.

"A libation," he told Meredith, smiling. "The last cup of the *agape*." He raised his glass. "To friendship! And to you, my friend!"

"To friendship," said Blaise Meredith. "I'm sorry I've come to it so late."

They drank, as good men should, of an old and precious liquor, slowly and with savour.

"I shall miss you, Monsignor," said the Bishop gently. "But you will come back. If you're ill, send me word immediately and I'll have you brought back here."

"I'll do that." Meredith's eyes were fixed studiously on his glass to hide the pain in them. "I hope I may do well for Your Lordship."

"I have a small gift for you, my friend." The Bishop put his hand into his breast pocket and brought out a small box of tooled Florentine leather, which he handed to Meredith. "Go on, open it!"

Meredith pressed the catch and the lid flew open to reveal,

134

bedded in satin, a small *bulla*, a bubble of antique gold, about the size of his thumb-pad, attached to a fine gold chain. He took it out and held it in the palm of his hand.

"Open the *bulla*," said His Lordship.

But Meredith's fingers trembled and the Bishop took the ornament from him, opened the bubble, and held it out to him. Meredith gave a small gasp of surprise and pleasure.

Set inside the curve of the gold was a large amethyst, carved with the most ancient symbol of the Christian Church, the fish, with the loaves on its back, whose name was the anagram of the Christus.

"It is very old," said His Lordship. "Probably early second century. It was found during the excavations in the catacomb of San Callisto and presented to me on the occasion of my consecration. The *bulla* was a common Roman ornament, as you know, and this must have belonged to one of the very early Christians—possibly a martyr, I don't know. I'd like you to have it—for friendship's sake."

Blaise Meredith, the cold man, was moved as he had not been moved for twenty years. Tears pricked at his eyelids and his voice was unsteady.

"What can I say, but 'Thank you'. I shall keep it till I die."

"There's a price on it, I'm afraid. You'll have to listen to a final sermon."

"This will be my charm against boredom," Meredith told him with wry humour.

The Bishop leaned back in his chair and sipped his brandy. His opening gambit seemed curiously irrelevant.

"I've been thinking, Meredith, about the little phallic shrine. What do you think I should do about it?"

"I don't know. . . . Destroy it, I suppose."

"Why?"

Meredith shrugged.

"We-ell . . . it's a link with paganism, a symbol of idolatry, an obscene one at that. Someone obviously pays some sort of homage to it."

"I wonder if that's right," His Lordship queried thoughtfully. "Or is it something very much simpler?"

"What, for instance?"

"A good humoured piece of vulgarity—a genial superstition like throwing coins in the Trevi fountain."

"I'd hardly have thought genial was the word," said Meredith. "Bawdy perhaps. Even sinister."

"All primitive peoples are bawdy, my dear Meredith. They live so familiarly with the grosser natural functions that their humour becomes very earthy indeed. Listen to the chatter and the songs at a village wedding and—if you can translate the dialect and the allusions—you'll blush to your reverend ears. But such people have their own modesties too, which, if they seem less logical, are often more sincere than the false modesties of evolved communities. . . . As for 'sinister'—yes, it could be sinister. Vestigial paganism does exist here. You'll find a woman selling charms and love-philtres in Gemello Minore. . . . But what do I do about it? Make a big song and ceremony? Hold an exorcism and break the marble to bits? They can draw a dirty picture on any wall in town if they really want to—and they would probably put my face on top of it. You see?"

In spite of himself, Meredith laughed heartily and the Bishop smiled approvingly.

"My sermon goes well, Meredith. And you've got the text of it already—'*Piano, Piano!*'—walk softly and talk gently. You're an official, remember, and they mistrust officials— Church officials most of all. You've also got the official point of view. Which is a handicap. Look!" He waved an expressive hand at the book-lined walls. "All the Fathers from Augustine to Aquinas. All the great historians, all the great commentators. All the encyclicals of the last five pontiffs— and a selection of the more important mystics as well. The mind of the Church, inside these four walls. The man who wore that *bulla* had never heard of one of them—yet he was as much a Catholic as you or I. He had the same faith, though much of it was implicit and not explicit as it is now. He was close to the Apostles, who taught what they had learned from the lips of Christ and what they had received from the infusion of the Holy Ghost at Pentecost. The mind of the Church

136

is like the mind of a man, expanding itself to new consequences of old beliefs, to new knowledge flowering out of the old, as leaves spring from a tree. . . . Who among my flock can digest all this? Can you or I? This is the mind of the Church, complex and subtle. But the heart of it is simple, as these people are simple. So when you go to them, you must work with your heart and not your head."

"I know," said Blaise Meredith; and the words sounded very like a sigh. "The trouble is I don't know how to work that way. I confess it frankly, it is only with Your Lordship that I have come to any warmth at all. I'm defective in sympathy, I suppose. I regret it, but I don't see how I can mend it. I don't know the words. The gestures are awkward and theatrical."

"It's a matter of attitude, my friend. If you feel pity and compassion you are not far from love. These things communicate themselves even through the most stumbling words. The way to these people is through their needs and through their children. Try filling your pockets with sweets and strolling down the street. Try taking a gift of oil or a kilo of pasta when you go into the houses of the poor. Find out where the sick are and visit them with a flask of *grappa* on your hip. . . . And that, my friend, is the end of my sermon!"

He leaned forward and poured another dram of brandy into their glasses. Meredith sipped the smooth, fragrant liquor and looked down at the small golden *bulla* in its satin bed. Aurelio the Bishop was a good pastor. Everything he preached he practised himself. And Blaise Meredith had not yet performed the one thing asked of him in friendship. He confessed it gravely:

"I've tried several times to bring myself to pray for this miracle, but I can't do it. I'm sorry."

His Lordship shrugged as if the delay were of no consequence.

"You will come to it in the end. *Piano . . . Piano . . .!* Now I think you should go to bed. Tomorrow will be a long day, and possibly a troubling one for you."

He stood up, and, moved by a sudden impulse, Blaise Meredith knelt to kiss the big Episcopal ring on his finger.

"Will Your Lordship bless me for the journey?"

Aurelio, Bishop of Valenta, raised a slim hand in the ritual gesture.

"*Benedicat te Omnipotens Deus....* May God bless you, my son, and keep you from the noonday devil—and from the terror of the long night ... in the name of the Father and of the Son and of the Holy Ghost ..."

"Amen," said Blaise Meredith.

But the blessing had no virtue against the pain which took him that night: the worst of his illness, a retching agony that drained him of all strength, so that when he left in the morning he looked like a man riding to his own funeral.

From Valenta to Gemello Minore the survey distance is sixty kilometres, but the road is so winding, the surface so poor and rutted, the climb so steep, that it takes two full hours by car.

Immediately after he left the town, Meredith lapsed into an uneasy doze, but soon the jolting and wrenching wakened him, and he began to take a forced interest in the landscape. The hills were not high by alpine standards, but they were steep and scarped and folded one upon the other so that the road seemed to cling precariously to their flanks, now crawling upwards, now plunging downwards out of a hairpin bend towards a rickety bridge that looked as if it would hardly support a mule cart.

The valleys were green where the peasants farmed the silt-wash, but the hills were sparsely grown, hardly fit for goat pasture. It was hard to believe that in the old days the Romans had cut pines here to build their galleys and burned charcoal for the armourers' forges. All that was left now was a rare plantation encircling a villa whose owner or steward was a better farmer than his fellows.

Some of the villages were built on the saddles of the hills, a huddle of rusty buildings round a crumbling church, built perhaps by some old Angevin mercenary who had trailed his pike and his petty title round this roistering, southern kingdom. Others were simply a line of peasant huts lower down in the valleys, where the water was nearer and the soil less sparse. But all of them were poor, shambling and depressed. Their inhabitants had the weathered, used-up look of the mountains themselves. Their children were draggled and spindly as their goats and chickens and cage-ribbed cows.

This was poverty as Meredith had not seen it, even in the baser alleys of Rome. This was what Aurelio the Bishop had meant when he pointed out the folly of coming here with a textbook in one hand and a missioner's cross in the other. These people understood the Cross . . . they had endured their own crucifixion for a long time; but they could not eat ideas, and the Christ of Calabria would need to announce himself with a new miracle of the loaves and fishes, and the old compassion for the maimed and the unclean.

They lived in houses that were no better than cow byres. Some of them were still troglodytes, inhabiting caverns in the rocks, where the damp festered on the walls. They had no gas, no electricity, no sewage, no safe water supply. Their children died of malaria and tubercular infections and pneumonia. Their women died of septicaemia and puerperal fever. Their men were twisted with arthritis before they were forty. Typhoid could wipe out a whole community in a month. Yet somehow they survived. Somehow they clung to a belief in God and the hereafter, in prayer and the ministrations of the Church—clung to it with a fierce logic because in this belief were the roots of human dignity. Without it they would become what they seemed to most of the world, animals in form and habit.

Blaise Meredith's heart sank as they drove farther and farther into the mountain reaches. A deep depression had settled on him after his night's ordeal, and he pictured himself wasting helplessly among these people and begging for death to release him from their company. If he must die out of due time, then at least let him die in dignity, with clean sheets and a clean smell and sunlight coming through the windows. It was a childish thought and he tried to put it away, but the

139

depression stayed with him, until, suddenly, at the top of a steep rise, the driver halted and pointed across the valley:

"*Ecco, Monsignore!* Look! There they are, *Gemelli dei Monti*—the Mountain Twins!"

Meredith got out of the car and walked to the edge of the road to get a better view. Below him the road ran steeply into a valley on the other side of which a single mountain reared itself up against the clear sky. For more than half its height it was a solid mass; then it parted into twin peaks, separated by a broad cleft, about two miles across. On each peak was a village, girt by a crumbling wall, below which the cultivation began and spread itself into the hollow between them. Out of this hollow a stream flowed, tumbling down the solid flank of the mountain into the valley at Meredith's feet.

What struck him most sharply was the difference between the two peaks. One of them was in full sunlight; the other shadowed darkly by its twin. The sunlit village seemed larger, less ruinous; and right in the centre of it, under the campanile of the church, a large white building shone in bright contrast to the burned tiles of the surrounding roofs. The road which forked up to it was black and shining with new bitumen and at the top of it, just outside the walls, a large flat parking space had been made, on which half a dozen cars were standing, their windscreens gleaming in the sun.

"Gemello Maggiore," said the driver at his shoulder. "You see what the saint has done for it. The new building is the hospital for pilgrims."

"He's not a saint yet," said Meredith coolly.

The driver spread his hands in disgust and moved away. One could not reason with a priest who had a belly-ache. Blaise Meredith frowned and turned to look at the darker twin, Gemello Minore.

There were no cars on the dusty goat track that led up to it, only a tiny donkey cart with an old peasant padding beside its wheels. The walls were breached in many places, and on some of the taller buildings he could see the naked roof trees where the tiles had been blown off and never been replaced. The roof line was gapped and ragged in contrast to the compact security of Gemello Maggiore. Meredith knew only too well what it would be like inside the walls—a single main street, a tiny piazza in front of the church, a warren of narrow lanes with washing strung between the walls and filth running over the cobbles and ragged children squalling among the refuse. For a moment his heart failed him and he was half-inclined to head for Gemello Maggiore and make his head-quarters there, in the new hostel or even with the Mayor, who would be happy to welcome an official of the Bishop's court. But he knew that he would never outlive the shame of such a surrender, so he got back into the car and told the driver:

"Gemello Minore. *Subito!*"

The labourers in the lower fields saw him first, as the car lurched over the potholes and skidded in patches of loose gravel. They leaned on their hoes and watched it pass, and some of the younger ones waved derisively, but the old ones simply wiped the sweat from their faces and rubbed their hands on their breeches and began work again. A car or a coach-and-four—or a rocket from the moon—it was all one. You weeded one line and you began another. The women piled the weeds for compost and gleaned the twigs for fuel. And when the last row was weeded there was water to be hauled from the stream and poured avariciously at the roots of the plants. There were stones to be carried too for the storm-breaches in the terraces, and sods to be turned in the fallow. . . . You couldn't make pasta from engine oil, nor get milk from a priest's tit. So to hell with them both—and back to the hoeing!

Paolo and Rosètta saw him as they squatted under a clump of bushes where Paolo swore he had seen quail, and where there was nothing but the droppings of the hare which nibbled the cabbage plants, and an old grey lizard dozing in a patch of sun. Rosetta clapped and shouted and hopped from one leg to another—a brown elf in a ragged frock; but Paolo stood, arms akimbo, staring after the car. The time would come when this fellow would want to talk to him about his father, and he was determined to meet him as a man, not a

141

snot-nosed urchin to be coaxed first and beaten afterwards. Besides, the affair was important to him and if Rosetta was to be his girl she must understand that. And if he was a little afraid of a black ferret rooting into his mother's life and his own, nuzzling the village into an ants' nest of curiosity, this, after all, was his own business, and his girl should be the last one to know it. So, after the car had passed, he took her by the hand and, in spite of all her protests, hurried her through the bushes and down to the secret stretch of the torrent where no one ever came in the daytime.

Aldo Meyer saw him when the car slowed just outside his doorway and began nosing its way slowly through a mob of yelling children. He saw the grey, pinched face and the lips drawn back in a painful smile, and the hand up-raised in a half-hearted greeting to the children. Here, if ever he knew one, was a man with the sign of death on him. He wondered what tortuous reasoning had induced the Bishop to accept an official like this and send him to be harried and badgered by all the conflicting interests in the affair of Giacomo Nerone. He wondered what manner of man he was and what the pain and the daily familiarity with death were making of him: what he would make of the Contessa and her dinner guests and how he would react to the tangled stories he must hear. Then he remembered that he would be taking the butt end of this life into his own hands, and he was ashamed that he had not even saluted the visitor as he passed.

By the time the car had reached the piazza the whole village was out. Even old Father Anselmo had stood peering furtively through his shutters, with the Contessa's summons in his hand, wondering vaguely how he was to show the 'courtesies to a brother priest' which the Bishop demanded of him. His most urgent problem, however, was what to wear to dinner at the villa; and, as soon as the car had passed, he waddled into the kitchen, shouting for old Rosa Benzoni to wash him a collar and sponge the sauce stains off his best soutane.

Only Nina Sanduzzi refused to make herself a spectator of this inauspicious arrival. She was sitting on the bed in the house of Martino the smith, spooning broth into the big man's twisted mouth, and when they beckoned her to the door she would not come. She had her own dignity, and if the priest wanted to see her he would come and she would know what to answer him.

As for Blaise Meredith, he saw them all, yet saw none of them. They were a blur of faces and a clamour of alien voices and a pervasive smell of dust and bodies and refuse rotting in the sun. He was glad when the car pulled out of the village and roared up the last steep incline to the villa, where the porter stood at the great iron gates to let him in and the Contessa was waiting to greet him, fresh as a flower on the cropped lawn.

"My dear Monsignor Meredith! So nice to see you!"

The smile was warm; the eyes unclouded; the hand soft but firm in greeting. After the clatter of village dialect, Meredith was comforted by the sound of an English voice. His pinched face brightened into a smile.

"My dear Contessa! Thank you for having me here!"

"Did you have a good journey?"

"Fair enough. The roads are rough and I'm not a good traveller these days. But I'm here in one piece."

"You poor man! You must be quite exhausted. I'll have Pietro show you your room, then you can wash and rest a little before lunch."

"I'd like that," said Meredith. And he thought gratefully: Thank God for the English. They understand these things better than anyone else in the world! They don't fuss and they know that when a man is tired his first need is privacy and hot water!

At a sign from the Contessa the servant picked up the bags and led Meredith into the house. The Contessa stood on the edge of the lawn watching his stooped, retreating back until the shadow of the doorway swallowed him up.

A moment later, Nicholas Black walked out from the shrubbery and joined her. He was grinning all over his lean satyr's face.

"Well, well, well! So that's what we're in for! He looks like a seedy edition of John Henry Newman. Oxford, I'd say.

Magdalen probably, with a dash of the English College—and a Vatican veneer to top it off. . . . You did it beautifully, *cara*. Not too little, not too much. The charming châtelaine welcoming the Church, the expatriate *Inglesa* doing the honours to a fellow-countryman. You're quite an actress!"

She ignored his irony and said thoughtfully:

"He looks very ill."

"Prayer and fasting will do that too, darling. I wonder if he wears a hair shirt."

"Oh, for God's sake, Nicki!"

He shrugged irritably and demanded:

"What do you expect me to do? Kiss his clerical backside and ask him to bless my medals? What's happening to you, anyway? Don't tell me you're in the full flush of conversion!"

She rounded on him with low, fierce invective.

"Listen, Nicki! You're a nice enough little man and a middling good painter. You're doing very well out of me and I'm helping you to get some things you want very badly. But I've got my own problems with this priest and I'm not having you make bigger ones just to show how clever you are. If you're not prepared to behave, you can pack your bags and I'll have Pietro drive you down to Valenta to catch the next train to Rome! I hope that's clear."

He wanted to scream at her and strike her in the face and call her all the bawdy names he could think of; but, as always, he was afraid. So he caught at her hand and kissed it and said in his penitent boyish fashion:

"I always do it, *cara*, don't I? I'm sorry. I don't know what gets into me. I'll behave. I promise! Please, please forgive me."

Anne Louise de Sanctis smiled. She had made her point. She had tasted again the sour pleasure of flagellation and she could afford to be generous. She rumpled his thin hair and patted his cheek and said:

"All right, darling. We'll forget it this time. But be a good boy in future."

Then she made him take her arm and walk her around the

garden, gossiping about Roman scandals. But, clever as she was, she never quite understood how much he hated her.

Alone in his high room, with the shutters drawn against the noonday heat, Blaise Meredith washed and changed and lay down on the big walnut bed.

Once again, it seemed, he had reason for gratitude. His lodging was comfortable; his hostess was charming; the servants were attentive. Whatever the squalor of the village he could come back here and forget it. Whatever his problems, he could count on the good will of the Contessa to help him unravel them. When he was ill he would not be alone, and, with a full staff, he would not be too much of a burden.

He reminded himself that he should write to the Bishop and tell him of his satisfaction with the arrangements made for him. Then, relaxed and resting, he thought about his work and how he should go about it.

A talk with the Contessa first, he decided: a survey of the village and its characters, an indication of the most likely sources of information on Giacomo Nerone. She would know much. She would have a certain valuable authority. As a feudal châtelaine she would stand *in loco parentis* with the peasants, and a word from her might loosen many tongues.

Then he should call on the parish priest to present his letter of authority and request his official co-operation. Whatever the reputation of the pastor, he still had canonical status in the matter. He had also a long and apparently contentious acquaintance with Nerone. There was a problem here, of course. If he had been, even for a while, Nerone's confessor, he could not be called on for evidence. Even if his penitent had released him from the seal, his evidence could not be admitted in the court. It was a wise provision of the law; but it was also a useful bolt-hole for a man who had something to conceal. He could sit pat and refuse even to indicate sources of information and the canonists would uphold his discretion. On all counts it looked as if Father Anselmo might prove a problem to the Devil's Advocate.

Who next? The doctor, perhaps, Aldo Meyer, who was a

145

Jew and a disappointed liberal. There were problems here too. He would know too much. His evidence was admissible, since even infidels and heretics might give testimony for or against the Cause. But he could not be forced to give it, as a Catholic could, by moral sanctions. One could only depend on his good will. For the present, at least, Doctor Aldo Meyer must be put down as doubtful.

Then there was Nina Sanduzzi, who had been the mistress of Giacomo Nerone and had borne his child. According to the records of Battista and Saltarello, she had refused to give any information at all. It seemed unlikely that a foreign priest would have any greater success with her. But even if he had, the inquiry promised to be most distasteful of all. It would entail a confessional probing into the deepest intimacies of their relationship: their mutual confidences, their moral attitudes, the reasons for their separation, even the nature of their sexual commerce. And all this between a priest who spoke only Roman Italian and a woman whose tongue was the bastard dialect of Calabria with its polyglot elements of Greek, Phoenician, Levantine Arab and Angevin French. . . .

Blaise Meredith was still wrestling with this problem when a servant entered and announced that luncheon was served and that the Contessa was waiting for him downstairs.

Luncheon began well: a pleasant conversation piece between people of taste and breeding, oddly met in a strange land. The Contessa steered the talk carefully. Nicholas Black seemed to enjoy his role as the urbane cosmopolite, and Blaise Meredith, relaxed after his rest, talked with a rare charm and considerable knowledge of books and music and the politics of Europe and the Church.

By the time they came to the cheese and the fruit, the Contessa had begun to feel comfortable again. This was a man she could understand. She had met many like him, in the old days in London and Rome. He had polish and discretion and, what was more important, he understood the English idiom of allusion and understatement. With a little care she could bring him to lean on her to interpret the provincial crudities. Provided Nicki continued to behave himself, there would be no trouble at all. She felt confident enough to put the first probing questions to Meredith.

"You must forgive my ignorance, Monsignor; but how do you usually begin work in a case like this?"

Meredith made a small, rueful gesture.

"I'm afraid there aren't any rules at all. It's a question of talking to as many people as possible and then collating and comparing their information. Later, when the Bishop's court is set up, one can question and cross-examine them under oath—and in secrecy, of course."

"And where do you think you'll start now?"

"I had hoped that you might be able to help me first. You've lived here a long time. You're the *padrona*. Your knowledge of local conditions would be a very good preparation for me."

Nicholas Black shot a swift, ironic glance at the Contessa, but she was smiling calmly.

"I'm happy to do anything I can, of course, but I think there's a danger in referring to me. I'm the *padrona*, as you say, and I'm English as well. I live a different life. I think differently from these people. I could be quite wrong in my ideas. I've been proved so many times. But I do want to help, for your sake and for the Bishop's. He's an old friend of mine, as you know."

"Of course." Meredith nodded and did not press the point.

The Contessa went on:

"After His Lordship wrote to me, I thought that the most helpful thing would be to have you meet the doctor and the parish priest. They both know much more about the village than I do. I've asked them both to come to dinner tonight. Then we can all four of us exchange views. I'll feel more confident then, that you are getting a balanced opinion. Nicki agrees with me, don't you, Nicki?"

"Of course, *cara*. This is a strange country. Quite different from Rome. I'm sure your idea is the right one. Don't you agree, Monsignor?"

"You're the experts," said Meredith deprecatingly. "I appreciate the trouble you're taking for me."

The Contessa pushed back her chair.

"I don't usually take coffee in the afternoon. I find it spoils my siesta. Pietro will serve yours on the terrace, and afterwards Nicki will show you the gardens. Will you excuse me, Monsignor? A woman's beauty sleep, you know. . . ."

The two men stood up as she left the table, and when she was gone, Nicholas Black led the way out on to the terrace, where the coffee service was laid under the shade of a striped awning. The painter offered Meredith a cigarette from a slim gold case.

"Smoke?"

"No, thank you. It's a luxury I've had to give up since my illness."

"The Contessa tells me you've been very ill."

"Very," said Meredith flatly. He was feeling warm and at ease and he did not want to be reminded of death.

The servant came out and poured the coffee and Black smoked a few moments in silence, pondering his next gambit. For all his charm, this fellow was acute and intelligent. A mistake with him might be irreparable. After a while he said, casually:

"While you are here, Monsignor, I hope you will let me paint you. You have an interesting face and expressive hands."

Meredith shrugged disarmingly.

"You must have twenty better subjects than I, Mr Black."

"Let's say you provide the contrast," said the painter with a grin. "The courtly Roman among the provincials. Besides, I'm hoping to make a pictorial record of the whole case of Giacomo Nerone. It could be a wonderful basis for a one-man show. I've thought of calling it 'Beatification'."

"It may never come to beatification," said Meredith carefully. "Even if it does, it may take years."

"From an artistic point of view that hardly matters. It's the characters that count—and there's a fantastic gallery of them here. I'm wondering what you'll make of them, Monsignor."

"I'm wondering, too," Meredith told him frankly.

"The thing that interests me, of course, is the love affair.

I don't really understand how one could possibly consider beatifying a man who seduces a village girl, gives her a bastard boy and then leaves her. He was here long enough to marry her."

Meredith nodded thoughtfully.

"It raises problems, of course—problems of fact and motive. But it doesn't necessarily put the case out of court. There's the classic example of Augustine of Hippo, who lived with many women and had, himself, an illegitimate son. Yet he became in the end a great Servant of God."

"After a much longer life than Nerone's."

"That's true, too. I'll admit candidly the circumstances are puzzling. I'm hoping to find out the full story while I'm here. But, in strict theology, one cannot ignore the possibility of sudden and miraculous conversion."

"If one believes in miracles, of course," said the painter dryly.

"If one believes in God, one believes necessarily in miracles."

"I don't believe in God," said Nicholas Black.

"It's a pointless world without Him," said Blaise Meredith. "And it's rough enough with Him. But . . . one can't argue a man into faith. So let's agree to differ, shall we?"

But the painter was not to be put off so easily. He was too anxious to see what sort of man lay under the black soutane. He returned to the argument.

"I'd like to believe. But there's so much professional mumbo-jumbo. So many mysteries."

"There are always mysteries, my dear fellow. If there were none, there would be no need of faith."

"But you're not taking Giacomo Nerone on faith," said Black pointedly. "You're investigating him legally."

"That's a matter of fact and not of faith," said Meredith.

The painter chuckled happily.

"But you'll still find lots of mysteries, Monsignor. More than you bargain for, I think. And the biggest mystery of all is why nobody in Gemello Minore wants to talk about him . . . not even the Contessa."

"Did she know him, then?" A new interest quickened in Meredith's voice.

"Of course she knew him. She's trying to get his son to come and work for her. She was here when he was alive. She was here when he died. All the others were too. They're not all amnesiacs. But they're as close as oysters just the same. You'll see, at dinner tonight."

"And what's your interest in the case?" There was an undertone of irritation in the question.

"A village comedy," said Black blandly. "And a one-man show growing out of it. It's really quite simple. Anyway, you're involved in the case. I'm not. I'm just giving you a friendly tip. . . . If you're finished with your coffee, I'll show you the garden."

"I'll sit awhile if you don't mind. Then I may take a siesta."

"Just as you like. I'm a painter. I don't like wasting light. I'll see you at dinner, Monsignor."

Meredith sat and watched him go, a tall, slim figure lounging across the lawn and into the shrubbery. He had met men like this before, some few of them, even in the cloth. He wondered what was the root of the malice he bore towards the Contessa and why she continued to give him house room. He wondered also why the Contessa had fobbed off his own request for help with the promise of a country dinner party.

Doctor Aldo Meyer sat in his kitchen and watched while Nina Sanduzzi polished his shoes and pressed his shirt and sponged the lapels of his last respectable suit. He, too, was preoccupied with the Contessa's dinner party. After the scene of the night before, he had been tempted to cut it altogether, but the more he thought, the more sure he was that he should go. It was as if a battle had been joined, and he could not afford to surrender a single advantage to the Contessa and her intriguing cavalier, Nicholas Black.

The real difficulty was that he could not be sure what he was fighting for—unless it were the interests of Nina and Paolo Sanduzzi. But this was too limited a goal to explain his anxiety to meet the English priest, and his complete involvement in the affair of Giacomo Nerone.

He was looking for a key to the mystery of his own failure, and for a signpost in the waste of his future. He had the curious conviction that Blaise Meredith might supply him with both. Part of his answer lay in the papers of Giacomo Nerone, which were still in the drawer of his bureau, but so far he had not found courage to open them.

Several times he had held them in his hands and fumbled with the wrappings; but each time he had drawn back, afraid of the hurt and the shame they might hold for him. They were like the letters of a rejected lover, which, once reopened, would remind him of the times when he had been less than a man. Sooner or later he would have to face the revelation: but not now, not yet.

Nina Sanduzzi looked up from her ironing and said calmly:

"I've been thinking about Paolo. I've decided he should work for the Contessa after all."

Meyer stared at her open-mouthed.

"Good God, woman! Why?"

"First, because Rosetta will be there, and I think she is good for him. She is near to being a woman, and she will fight for what she wants. Also she will talk and I will know what is going on at the villa. Once she starts to work, Paolo will have nothing to do but idle and wander the hills—and the painter will get him anyway."

"The Contessa will be there, too," Meyer cautioned her gravely. "And she is a woman also—older and cleverer than Rosetta."

"I've thought of that," she admitted quietly. "But I have thought also that there will be the priest in the house. He will come to see me, like the others did, and I will tell him what goes on there. I will ask him to look after Paolo."

"He might not believe you."

"If I tell him all the other things—about Giacomo—I think he will believe me."

Meyer looked at her with puzzled, brooding eyes.

"Yesterday you were decided to tell him nothing at all.

151

What made you change your mind? What about your promise to Giacomo?"

"The boy is more important than a promise. And besides" —there was a strange conviction in her voice—"I prayed last night as I always do, to Giacomo. I don't see him, I don't hear him—there is just the shirt he wore when he was killed, with the bullet holes round his heart. But I know what he wants, and this is what I shall do."

"I didn't think people changed their minds when they were dead," said Meyer with wintry humour, but there was no answering smile on the calm face of the woman. She said simply:

"It is not changing his mind. It is just that the time was not right before—and now it is right. The priest will come to me when he is ready. Then I shall tell him."

Meyer shrugged and spread his arms in a small despair.

"Whatever I say, you will do what you want. But before the boy goes to the villa have him talk with me."

"I'll do that. Have you read Giacomo's papers yet?"

"Not yet."

"You should not be afraid," she told him, with singular gentleness. "He did not hate you, even at the end. Why should he shame you now?"

"I'm ashamed of myself," said Aldo Meyer curtly, and he walked out into the garden, where the cicadas were shrilling in the blaze of the afternoon, and the dust clung to the green leaves of the fig trees.

CHAPTER NINE

WHEN MEREDITH came down to dinner that night, he found the Contessa and her guests already assembled, taking drinks in the salon.

The contrast between them was startling. The Contessa was groomed as if for a Roman evening and Nicholas Black was immaculate in a black dinner jacket. Meyer was dressed in a shabby lounge suit, much cleaned and shiny with long wear. His shirt was clean and newly pressed, but the collar and the cuffs were beginning to fray, and his tie was faded and old-fashioned. Yet he carried himself with dignity and his worn, intelligent face was calm. Meredith was drawn to him immediately and his greeting was less reserved than usual.

"I'm happy to meet my medical adviser. I'm going to be in good hands."

"Better reserve judgment, Monsignor," said Meyer, with cool humour. "I have a bad reputation."

And there they left it, while the Contessa drew Father Anselmo out of his corner and presented him to his Roman colleague.

He was a short man, on the wrong side of sixty. His face was lined and weathered like that of a peasant and his lank grey hair was long and brushed down over his collar. The shoulders of his soutane were speckled with dandruff and the front of it was spotted with old wine stains and sauce droppings. His hands were knotted with arthritis and he kept twining and untwining them as he talked. When he greeted Meredith his Italian had the thick, coarse accent of the province.

"I'm glad to see you, Monsignor. We don't get many Romans down this way. Too far and too rough for 'em, I suppose."

Meredith smiled uneasily and murmured a banal remark, but the old man was garrulous and would not be put off.

"That's a trouble we have in this part of the world. The

Vatican doesn't even know what's going on. They've got more money than you could poke a stick at, but we never get a smell of it. I remember when I was in Rome . . ."

He would have gone on talking for an hour, had not the Contessa signalled to the servant, who put a glass of sherry into his hands and edged him gently away from the visitor. Meredith was embarrassed. Seedy clerics were distasteful to him at the best of times, but the prospect of a longish association with this one was daunting in the extreme. Then he remembered Aurelio, Bishop of Valenta, and his care for the lost one of his flock, and he was instantly ashamed of himself. Ignoring the shepherding servant, he moved back to the old man and said in a friendly fashion:

"His Lordship sends you his greeting and hopes that I won't be too much trouble to you. But I'm afraid I'll have to lean on your judgment a good deal."

Father Anselmo took a long swallow of sherry and fixed him with a rheumy eye. He shook his head and said querulously:

"His Lordship sends his greetings! Nice of him! I'm a flea in his ear and he'd like to get rid of me. But he can't do it without a court case. That's the way it is. We might as well understand each other."

Like most polite people, Meredith had no armour against the grossness of others. It pained him, but he lacked the brutality to administer a frank snub. He said, genially enough:

"I'm the visitor, I'm not up on local politics. There's no reason why we shouldn't get along."

Then he turned back to make small talk with Anne Louise de Sanctis.

Aldo Meyer had been quick to notice the brusque little exchange and mark it as a credit to Blaise Meredith. The man had breeding and discretion. There was hope that later he might reveal a heart as well.

Nicholas Black had noticed it too, and he grinned slyly at the Contessa, whose answering eyebrow lift told him plainer than words: This goes as I planned it—crookedly and well. And because his interest was common with hers in this moment, he was prepared to co-operate and forget his hatred of her. While Meredith talked with his hostess and Father Anselmo stood a little apart, with one eye on the sherry and one ear on the talk, he drew Meyer aside and said, grinning:

"Well, *dottore mio*, what do you think of our Devil's Advocate?"

"I'm sorry for him. He has the mark of death on him. Already he must be suffering a good deal."

The painter shivered involuntarily, as if a goose had walked over his grave. He answered plaintively:

"Let's not have death at the dinner table, my dear chap. I was thinking of something else. How do you think he'll work? Pleasantly or . . .?"

He let the question hang, a suspended chord of irony; but Meyer made no move to resolve it.

"Why should we care, you and I?"

"Why indeed," said Nicholas Black tartly, and dropped the subject.

Meyer sipped his sherry and watched Meredith's face as he talked to the Contessa and Father Anselmo. He noted the leanness of it, the sallow transparency of the skin, the lines of pain etched deeper and deeper round the mouth, the tired, injected eyes that slept too little and saw too much of the tears of things. Men reacted variously to pain and fear. This one seemed to be bearing both with courage, but it was too early to see what else was happening to him.

A few moments later dinner was announced and they filed into the dining-room. The Contessa took the head of the table, with Meredith on her right, Meyer on her left and Father Anselmo and Nicholas Black in the lower places. Before they were seated, she turned to Meredith.

"Will you give us a grace, please, Monsignor?"

As he stood with bowed head through the brief Latin formula, the painter chuckled to himself. What an actress the woman was! Not one piece of business forgotten! He was so absorbed in his amusement that, without thinking, he made the Sign of the Cross after the grace and spent an uncomfortable five minutes wondering whether Meredith had noticed it. As a confirmed atheist, the priest would leave him to the mercy of God; but as a lapsed Catholic he would probably come fishing for his soul, which could be an embarrassment in his plans for Paolo Sanduzzi.

As if on cue, the Contessa repeated the name to Aldo Meyer. "About young Paolo, Doctor? Is he coming to work for me?"

"I believe so," said Meyer cautiously. "His mother will probably come to see you tomorrow."

"I'm glad." She bent to explain it to Meredith. "This will probably interest you, Monsignor. Young Paolo Sanduzzi is, of course, the son of Giacomo Nerone. He was baptized with his mother's name. He's rather wild, but we—that is, Doctor Meyer and I—thought it would do him good to begin work. I've offered him a job as assistant gardener."

"That seems a kind thought," said Meredith casually. "How does his mother live?"

"She works for me," Meyer told him.

"Oh."

"She used to be a very pretty woman," said Father Anselmo, with his mouth full of fish. "She's thickened up now, of course. I remember her when she made her First Communion. Lovely child!"

He washed the fish down with a draught of wine and wiped his lips with a crumpled napkin. Then, as nobody answered, he bent over his plate again. Meredith turned to Meyer.

"You knew Giacomo Nerone, I believe, Doctor?"

"Yes, I knew him," Meyer answered with easy frankness. "I was the first person who saw him after Nina Sanduzzi. She called me in to pick a bullet out of his shoulder."

"She must have trusted you, Doctor," said Nicholas Black blandly.

Meyer shrugged the thrust aside.

"There was no reason why she shouldn't. I was a political exile. My sympathies were known to be against the Administration."

The painter grinned and waited for the next question. His face clouded with disappointment when Meredith said simply:

"You're probably aware, Doctor, that in a Cause for Beati-

156

fication even the evidence of non-Catholics is admitted, provided they're willing to give it. I'd like to talk to you about that, at your convenience."

"Any time, Monsignor."

And he thought gratefully: He measures bigger than I thought. They won't snare him too easily.

Anne Louise de Sanctis cut quickly into the small following silence.

"Father Anselmo can probably help you a good deal too, Monsignor. He's very close to all our people. You knew Nerone too, didn't you, Father?"

Anselmo put down his fork with a clatter and took another draught of wine. His voice was thickening noticeably and his accent was broader than ever.

"I never thought much of the man. He interfered too much. Anyone would have thought he was a priest himself. Used to come battering on my door as soon as anyone had a belly-ache. Wanted me to come racing out with the Sacraments. One night he nearly had me shot by the Germans. After that I wouldn't go out after curfew."

"I'd forgotten," said Meredith easily. "You had the Germans here, of course. That must have been uncomfortable."

"They took over the villa," said the Contessa quickly. "I was under open arrest most of the time. It was terrible. I've never been so afraid in my life."

Nicholas Black wiped his thin lips and smiled behind the napkin. He pictured her walking the lawns with the conquerors, making her coquetries on the arm of a blond captain, bedding with him in the big baroque room behind the velvet curtains, while the peasantry starved outside the iron gates and the stone wall. House arrest? There might be other names for it. A little patience and he would have the whole story of Anne Louise de Sanctis.

Blaise Meredith seemed unconscious of the irony and went on:

"The first evidence seemed to indicate that Giacomo Nerone acted as a kind of mediator between the peasants and the occupying troops. What would you think of that, Contessa?"

"I think that's probably an exaggeration. Most if not all of the mediation was done by myself. When relations became strained in the village my servants would tell me, and I would approach the commander.... On a very official basis, of course. Usually he was co-operative. I think perhaps Nerone exaggerated his influence to build up his credit with the people."

At that moment the servants began moving round the table clearing the dishes and laying out the next course. Meredith seemed in no hurry to pursue the question. Nicholas Black took advantage of the lull to pose his own barbed query:

"Has anyone ever established definitely who this man was and where he came from?"

Anne Louise de Sanctis was busy with the manservant. Meyer was quizzically silent. Father Anselmo was busy with another glass of wine and, after a moment's awkward pause, Meredith answered him:

"It's never been clearly established. At first he was accepted as an Italian. Later, it seemed, there was an opinion that he might have been a member of one of the Allied units in the South—English, perhaps, or Canadian."

"Interesting," said the painter dryly. "There were quite a few thousand deserters in the Italian theatre."

"That's possible too," said Meredith. "It's something I hope to find out more definitely."

"If he were a deserter, he couldn't be a saint, could he?"

"Why not?" asked Meyer with sudden interest.

The painter spread his hands in mock humility.

"I'm no theologian, of course; but every soldier takes an oath of service. To break a lawful oath would be a sin, wouldn't it? And a deserter would be living in a constant state of sin."

"For a non-believer you have a very Christian logic," said Meredith, with mild humour. A small chuckle went round the table and the painter flushed uncomfortably.

"It seems a logical proposition."

"Perfectly logical," said Meredith. "But there may be other facts. A man cannot bind himself by oath to commit sin. If a sin is required of him under an oath of service, he is obliged to refuse it."

"How do you establish the fact, Monsignor? And the motive?"

"We must rely on the sworn testimony of those who knew him intimately. Then the court must examine the value of the testimony." He smiled disarmingly. "It's a long job."

"Trouble with you Romans," said Father Anselmo suddenly, "you don't see the simplest things—even when they stick up under your noses . . ." His voice was so blurred and unsteady that the guests looked at one another in sharp uneasiness and then at the Contessa, sitting rigid at the head of the table. The old man stumbled on . . . "Everybody's talking as though they knew nothing. We all knew who he was. I knew. The doctor knew. The . . ."

"He's drunk," said the Contessa, in a clear hard voice. "I'm sorry for this exhibition, Monsignor, but he should be got home immediately."

"He's old," said Meyer quietly. "His liver's packing up and it takes very little to put him under the table. I'll get him home."

The old man stared hazily round the table, fumbling for the thread of his thought. His grey head nodded and a small runnel of wine dribbled down from his slack lips.

"Pietro can go with you," said the Contessa curtly.

"I'll go," said Nicholas Black.

Meredith pushed back his chair and stood up. There was a new ring in his flat precise voice.

"He's a brother priest. I'll get him home, with the doctor."

"Take my car," said Anne Louise de Sanctis.

"Better he walks," Aldo Meyer told her quietly. "The air will sober him up a little. It isn't far. Give me a hand with him, Monsignor."

Together they got him out of the chair and manoeuvred him past the servant at the door and out on to the gravelled drive.

Nicholas Black and the Contessa sat still at the table, staring at one another. After a while the painter said softly:

"A near thing, *cara*, a very near thing, wasn't it?"

159

"Go to hell!" said the Contessa and left him alone, grinning like a satyr at the wreckage of my lady's dinner party.

As they walked down the rough road towards the village with Father Anselmo hanging from their shoulders, his feet trotting aimlessly in rhythm with their own, Meredith was astonished to feel how light he was. In the salon and at the dinner table he had seemed bloated and gross; now he was just a frail old man with a pot-belly and a lolling, greasy head, who mumbled and dribbled and clung to them, helpless as a sick child.

Meredith, who had rarely come near a drunk and had never seen a drunken priest, was at first disgusted and then touched with a sharp compassion. This was what happened to some men when the terror of life caught up with them. This was what they became when age weakened the faculties and decay crept in among the tissues and the will faltered under the burden of time and memory. Who could love this shambling old wreck? Who now could care whether he lived or died and whether his soul was damned to eternity—if indeed a soul was left after the long wasting of the years?

Meyer cared—enough at least to whisk him quickly away from further indignities, to make dignified apology for him, to lend him a shoulder and walk him home on his two feet. Meyer cared: the shabby Semite with the tarnished reputation, who understood what happens when a man's liver packs up and his prostate fails him and he can't hold his spoon straight because of the arthritis in his joints. And Blaise Meredith? Did he care too? Or was he so preoccupied with his own belly-ache that he could not see that there were meaner ways of dying, and sharper torments than his own?

He was still chewing on this tasteless cud when they came to the door of the priest's house. They eased him off their shoulders and propped him against the wall, and Meyer hammered loudly on the front door. A few moments later they heard shuffling footsteps inside, and then the door was opened by a fat old woman in a shapeless black shift with a soiled nightcap askew on her tousled hair. She peered at them sleepily.

"Well! What's the matter? Can't you let a body sleep? If you want the priest, he's not here, he's . . ."

"He's drunk," said Meyer amiably. "We brought him home. You'd better get him to bed, Rosa."

She turned on him angrily.

"I knew it would happen. I warned him. Why can't they leave him alone? He's not made for hobnobbing with the quality. He's just an old man—and a big baby who doesn't know how to look after himself." She took Anselmo's hand and tried to lead him into the house. "Come on, crazy one. Rosa will get you to bed and look after you . . ."

But the old man lurched and stumbled and would have fallen unless Meyer had caught him. He said curtly:

"Come on, Monsignor. We'd better carry him to bed. The woman's almost as old as he is."

They lifted him head and feet and carried him into the house and up a flight of rickety stairs, with Rosa Benzoni lighting the way ahead with a tallow candle. The house smelt stale and musty as a mousehole, and when they came to the bedroom Meredith saw that it held a large double bed covered with greasy blankets, and that one side of it was already in disorder. They carried the old man over to it and laid him down. Meyer began to loosen his collar and his shoes.

The old woman bustled him away, grumbling.

"Leave him! Leave him for pity's sake! You've done enough damage tonight. I can look after him. I've been doing it long enough."

After a moment's hesitation, Meyer shrugged and walked out of the room. Meredith followed him, feeling his way down the creaking stairs, through the fusty air, and out into the grateful freshness of the moonlight.

Meyer put a cigar between his thin lips, lit it and inhaled deeply. Then he gave Meredith a sidelong speculative look and said coolly:

"Are you shocked, Monsignor?"

"I'm sorry for him," Meredith answered in a low voice. "Deeply sorry."

Meyer shrugged.

"The Church is to blame for half of it, my friend. They send a poor devil like Anselmo out to a place like this, with half an education and no stipend and no security at all—and expect him to stay celibate for forty years. He's just a peasant and not very intelligent at that. He's damned lucky to have found a woman like Rosa Benzoni, to bully him and keep his socks clean."

"I know," said Meredith absently. "That's what touched me most of all. She was like a wife to him. She—she loves him."

"Does that surprise you, Monsignor?"

"It shames me . . ." He shook his head as if to chase away a haunting nightmare. "I've spent all my life in the priesthood and I think . . . I think I've wasted it."

"That makes two of us," said Aldo Meyer softly. "Come down to my place and I'll make you a cup of coffee."

In the low, dimly lit room of Meyer's cottage, with its peasant furniture and its rows of copper vessels, polished by the careful hands of Nina Sanduzzi, Meredith felt the same relaxation and intimacy that he had experienced in the house of Aurelio the Bishop. He was grateful for it, as he had been before, but this time he warmed to it more quickly and less consciously. He knew now how much he needed friendship, and he was prepared to go more than half way to the making of it. As Meyer moved about the room laying out the cups, spooning out coffee, and slicing the last of a loaf to go with the cheese, he asked him bluntly:

"What was the meaning of the dinner party tonight? Everything seemed very pointed; but I couldn't see what it was pointing at."

"It's a long story," Meyer told him. "It will take some time to put it in order for you. The party was the Contessa's idea. She wanted to show you the type of people you'd be dealing with—and how much better it would be to lean on her, and not on a couple of country bumpkins like Anselmo and me."

"I had the idea she was afraid of what might be said."

162

"That too." Meyer nodded. "We've all been afraid, for a long time."

"Of me?" Meredith looked at him in surprise.

"Of ourselves," said Meyer with a crooked grin. "All of us there tonight were involved one way and another with the life and death of Giacomo Nerone. None of us came out of it very creditably."

"Does that include the Englishman—the painter fellow?"

"He's a late involvement. He's an odd one—and he's taken a fancy to young Paolo Sanduzzi. He's enlisted the Contessa's help to seduce him."

Meredith was shocked.

"But that's monstrous!"

"It's human," Meyer told him quietly. "It sounds better if it's a girl and not a boy. But the idea's the same."

"But the Contessa said you had agreed the boy should work at the villa."

"She was lying. She's a very accomplished liar. Which makes it difficult to help her."

He brought the coffee pot to the table and poured the steaming contents into the earthenware cups. Then he sat down opposite Meredith, who looked at him with puzzlement in his eyes.

"You're very frank, Doctor—why?"

"I've learned something, very late in life," said Meyer firmly. "You can never bury the truth so deep that it can't be dug up. We've been trying to bury the truth about Giacomo Nerone, and now it's festering round our feet. You'll get it sooner or later—and it's my view you ought to get it now. Then you can go back to Rome and leave us in peace."

"Does this mean you're prepared to give evidence as well?"

"It does."

"And this is your only motive—truth?"

Meyer looked up quickly and saw, for the first time, the inquisitor who lived in the skin of Blaise Meredith. He said cautiously:

"Does my motive matter, Monsignor?"

163

"It colours the evidence," Meredith told him. "It may obscure the truth—which is the truth about a man's soul."

Meyer nodded gravely. He saw the point. He respected the man who made it. After a pause he answered:

"So far as any man can be honest about his motives, this is mine. I've made a mess of my life. I'm not quite sure why. I had a part, too, in the death of Giacomo Nerone. I was wrong in that. But I don't believe I was wrong in my other estimates of him. I want to talk all this out; have another set it in perspective for me. Otherwise I'm going to end like old Anselmo giving myself cirrhosis of the liver because I can't face my nightmares. . . . That's why I was afraid of you, like the others. If I couldn't trust you I couldn't talk to you."

A gleam of amusement showed in Meredith's eyes. He asked quizzically:

"And what makes you think you can trust me, Doctor?"

"Because you have the grace to be ashamed of yourself," said Meyer baldly. "And that's rare enough in the Church or out of it. . . . Now drink your coffee and we'll talk awhile before I send you to bed!"

But there was no more talk for Meredith that night. The first mouthful of coffee choked him; the pain in his stomach took him again and Meyer led him stumbling out into the garden to void the bile and the blood that choked him. Then, when the spasm had passed, he laid him down on his own bed and began palpating the shrunken belly, pressing down to the hard, deadly mass growing against the wall of it.

"Is it like this often, Monsignor?"

"It's getting more frequent," Meredith told him painfully. "The nights are the worst."

"How long did they give you?"

"Twelve months, possibly less."

"Halve it!" Meyer told him flatly. "Halve it again and you'll be nearer to the truth."

"As soon as that?"

Meyer nodded.

"By rights you should be in hospital now."

"I want to stay on my feet as long as I can."

"I'll try to keep you there," said Meyer with grudging admiration. "But too much of this, and it'll take a miracle!"

"That's what the Bishop wanted me to ask for—a miracle." He said it humorously to make a joke out of the new pain that was coming on him. But Meyer seized on the tag like a terrier.

"Say that again!"

"The Bishop wanted me to ask for a sign—a tangible proof of the sanctity of Giacomo Nerone. Some of the reported cures could be miracles, but I doubt we'll prove any of them judicially . . . so I could be the one provable one."

"And you, Monsignor? What did you say to that?"

"I didn't have the courage to agree."

"You would rather bear the pain you have now—and what is still to come?"

Meredith nodded.

"Are you so afraid of your God, my friend?"

"I'm not sure what I'm afraid of. . . . It's—it's as if I were being asked to make a leap through a paper hoop, on the other side of which is either darkness or a shattering revelation. The only way I can find out, is to leap. And I . . . I haven't the courage to do it. Does that sound strange to you, Doctor?"

"Strange—and yet not so strange," Meyer said thoughtfully. "Strange from a man like you; but for me, easy enough to understand."

He was thinking of the papers of Giacomo Nerone that still lay untouched in his bureau; and he was thinking of the fear that came on him every time he tried to open them.

But Meredith did not ask for explanations. He closed his eyes and lay back, pale and exhausted, on the pillow. Meyer let him doze till midnight and, when he woke again, walked him back to the villa and had the gatekeeper take him up to his bedroom.

At midnight Nicholas Black was wakeful, too. He was sitting up in bed, smoking a cigarette and contemplating with deep satisfaction the picture of Paolo Sanduzzi, which was propped on the easel in front of the drawn curtains. He had chosen the position with some care, so that the light fell on it from the correct angle and the white figure of the boy seemed to thrust itself forward from the dark wood of the gallows tree. The scarlet lips smiled at the man who had painted them, and the eyes were bright in contemplation of the veiled, deceptive future.

Narcissus in his pool saw himself no more beautiful than Nicholas Black in his solitary contemplation of his own creation. Yet even this pleasure could not bind him to the pity of his situation: that this was the nearest he could come to what other men had by natural right—sons of their own to love, cherish and train towards the maturity of manhood. Would there never be an end to the pursuit, the panic grasping, the sour humiliation of defeat?

Sometime, with someone, there must be a term to it. Other rakes married their virgins who bred them children and warmed their slippers, while they repented happily in their Indian summer. Soon, soon, he must come to his own harbour, before the winter winds began to blow and the dead leaves rattle around the garden walks.

Then he remembered the dinner talk and hope began to wake again. Tomorrow, Meyer had said, the boy would come. His mother would speak with Anne Louise de Sanctis and he would be signed into service with the gardeners. Morning and afternoon he would be there—a raw peasant to be drawn towards gentility, a servant to be attracted into sonship. It would need tact and gentleness, firmness, too, sometimes, so that from the first the nature of the relationship should be clearly established. Nicholas Black was shrewdly aware of the attraction he had for the boy, equally aware of the boy's capacity to attract him, to their mutual ruin. The boy must be brought to see that all his hopes lay in a disciplined association, and that any attempt to exploit his patron would wreck them utterly. Still, given time and the casual intimacy of the villa, he felt confident that he could do it.

What troubled him still was that he could see only half the motive of the Contessa in helping him to the conquest. The half he saw was simple enough. She wanted his co-operation in handling the priest. She needed an understanding ally to bolster her courage. But the reasons which she still held back were of much deeper concern to him.

The world of lost lovers is a jungle where it is rutting season all the time. There is no mercy in the desperate, headlong flight from loneliness.

The race is to the swift, possession is for the strong. The wild urge to couple and forget colours the most civilised gestures. The simplest words take on a colour of passion and intrigue.

Nicholas Black had lived a long time in the jungle, and he had no illusions left. If Anne de Sanctis helped him, it would be to compass her own designs in the end. What were they? Passion, perhaps? Every season brought its crop of dowagers who hoisted their skirts and played hot cockles with the boys in the Mediterranean spring. The dowagers paid and the boys acted out the cold comedy with Latin cynicism and went back to marry their girls on the profits. But the Contessa was too experienced to make a fool of herself in her own village. Capri was just round the corner. Rome was distant and more discreet. She had money and freedom to pleasure herself where she chose.

So there must be another reason. Her fear of Meredith pointed to a personal involvement with Giacomo Nerone. Potiphar's wife, perhaps? My lady bountiful turned bitch when Joseph fled from her, leaving his cloak in her hands—and taking his fun with a peasant wench instead of the *padrona* of the villa.

Jealousy took freakish forms at times. Paolo Sanduzzi, the stripling boy, would be a perpetual reproach to her failure as a woman and a lover. To seduce him from his mother would be an oblique revenge on his father . . . and a consummate insult to Nicholas Black.

A slow heat of anger grew in him and he lay back on the pillows staring at the picture of Paolo Sanduzzi, loathing the woman who for house room and the promise of an exhibition had thought to buy him into so brutal a bondage.

Anne Louise de Sanctis lay back in her marble bath and felt the soft water move over her skin like a symbol of absolution.

The perfumed steam rose gratefully, blurring the harsh edges of reality and blending with the euphoric haze of the barbiturates which would soon coax her downwards into forgetfulness.

This narrow room, with its crystal bottles and its misted mirror, was the womb from which she issued, new, each morning, into which she retreated each night from the howling confusion of loneliness. Suspended in the fœtal fluid, within the warm, veined walls of marble, she could float, self-absorbed, self-justified, irresponsible, lapped in an illusion of eternity.

But the illusion became more tenuous each night. The impact of each morning became more brutal. Invading hands reached forward into her privacy: voices challenged her out of the twilight into the bitter day and she knew she could not shut them out much longer.

Meyer was the first of her adversaries: the down-at-heel doctor with the disappointed face and the frayed cuffs, the shoe-string reformer, the penny philosopher, the man who knew everything and did nothing, who was the enemy of illusions because he had none himself. Once she might have commanded his alliance against Giacomo Nerone, but now all his care was for Nina Sanduzzi, who had borne Nerone's child. He had refused even the pity she had pleaded from him, and with one brutal sentence had laid bare her self-deceit.

She wanted a child. There was truth in that. She wanted Paolo Sanduzzi. There was truth in that, too. But she wanted him for herself. He was Nerone's boy, flesh of his flesh, bone of his bone. She had love to spend on him—money, too. Love that Nerone had tossed back in her face. Money to ransom him out of the sordid life to which his father had condemned him. But Meyer stood in her way. Meyer and Nina Sanduzzi, and even the grey cleric from Rome.

She had lived a long time in Italy and she understood the subtle workings of the Church in its southern vineyard. Its princes played politics with Machiavellian skill, but they were rigid in the enforcement of the public moralities, through which they ruled a passionate and recalcitrant people. They did not hesitate to invoke the civil statute as a sanction for the ten commandments. As an ally, Meredith could help her greatly; as an enemy he would be implacable and unconquerable.

So, by twisting roads, she came back to Nicholas Black. She had small faith in his stability; but she needed an ally, and this one was already bought and easy to manage. She did not for a moment believe his protestation of pure affection for the boy. She saw it simply as a calculated gambit of seduction; and her promise of help was equally calculated.

She would give the painter time and opportunity to work on Paolo, tempting him with friendship and the promise of a gentleman's life in Rome. The boy would respond quickly, being touched already with the discontents of adolescence. The small scandal of their association would grow to a larger one. Nina Sanduzzi's maternal control would be called in question. Then . . . then the Contessa would step in, the solicitous *padrona*, the châtelaine careful of the interests of her people. She would offer to remove the boy from an occasion of corruption, to educate him, in Rome first and later in England.

Even the Church would see merit in such a course. If Giacomo Nerone were to be raised to the altars, they would not want his son whoring round the villages like so many other country youths. Let Nicholas Black play to his heart's content the role of petty intriguer, she would still win the game in the end. She would walk down the Via Veneto with Paolo Sanduzzi, proud and complete, as though Nerone had fathered him on her own barren body.

She got out of the bath, dried and perfumed herself and dressed for bed. Then she lay down under the great brocaded canopy and let herself drift into a drugged sleep, dreaming of a dark and smiling youth whose hand was clasped firmly in her own. And when he changed from youth to man, from son to passionate lover, this was, after all, a delusion of the night, with no guilt in it at all. . . .

CHAPTER TEN

EARLY THE following morning, while Nina Sanduzzi swept and polished his cottage, Aldo Meyer sat under the fig tree and talked with Paolo.

The interview began awkwardly. The boy was sullen and withdrawn and Meyer's first fumbling queries did nothing to gain his confidence. He kept his eyes fixed on the table-top, chewed nervously at a twig and gave his answers in a mumbling undertone, so that Meyer was forced to fight down his irritation and keep a proper friendliness in his voice.

"Your mother has spoken to you about working for the Contessa?"

"Yes."

"You know young Rosetta's going to the villa too?"

"Yes."

"How do you feel about it?"

"I s'pose it's all right."

"Do you want to go, or not?"

"I don't mind."

"The pay's not bad. You'll be able to help your mother and still have something for yourself."

"Yes, I know."

"This means you're getting to be a man, Paolo."

The boy shrugged and picked his teeth with the twig. Meyer took a sip of coffee and lit a cigarette. The next gambit was the important one. He hoped he would not spoil it. After a moment he said, as gently as he could:

"The beginning of a man's life is the most important part of it. It's usually a father's job to set his son on the right road. You haven't a father, so . . . I'd like to help instead."

For the first time the boy raised his eyes and looked at him squarely. There was a challenge in the look and a faint hostility. His question was blunt and unfriendly.

"Why should you care?"

"I'll try to tell you," said Meyer equably. "If I don't satisfy you, ask me anything you like. The first thing is that I haven't a son of my own. I'd like to have one. You could have been my son, because once upon a time I was in love with your mother. I'm still very fond of her. However, she chose your father—and that was that. I knew your father. For a while we were friends, then . . . we were enemies. I had a hand in his death. I'm sorry for that now. If I can help you, I'll be paying a debt to him."

"I don't need your help," the boy told him roughly.

"We all need help," said Meyer quietly. "You need it because you're involved with the Englishman and you don't quite know what to do about it."

Paolo Sanduzzi was silent, staring down at the mangled twig in his fingers. Meyer went on:

"I want to explain something to you, Paolo. You know what men are, and women. You know how they come to kiss and caress and what passes between them when they make love. You know what you feel when you look at a girl whose breasts are grown and who begins to walk like a woman. But what you don't understand is how you can feel this for Rosetta, and at the same time feel it when the Englishman touches you."

Again the boy's head jerked up, defensively.

"There is nothing between me and the Englishman. He has never touched me!"

"Good!" said Meyer calmly. "Then there is nothing to shame you. Still, you should know that when a man's heart wakes and his body, too, they can be bent this way or that, as the wind bends a sapling. But after a while the sapling stiffens and grows hard as a tree. Then it cannot be bent any more, but grows to its own shape. The proper way for a man to grow is towards a woman—not towards a *feminella*. That is why you cannot stay with the painter. You see that, don't you?"

"Then why are you sending me to work at the villa? He'll be there all the time. He frightens me. He makes me feel that I don't know what I want."

171

"Which do you want—him or Rosetta?"

"I want to get out of Gemello!" said the boy savagely. "I want to go somewhere else, where people don't know about me or my mother or my father. Do you think I like to be called a saint's bastard—the son of a whore? That's why I want to stay with the Englishman. He can do that much for me. He can take me to Rome, give me a new start. . . ."

"And in Rome they'll put a dirtier label on you—and you'll never shake it off wherever you go! Listen, boy . . ." He pleaded with him in a low, passionate voice. "Try to be patient with me. Try to understand what I'm going to tell you. Your mother is a good woman—ten times better than those who put this name on her. Whatever she did, she did for love—and a whore is one who sells herself for money. Your father was one with a touch of greatness in him . . . and I say that—the man who helped to kill him."

"Then why didn't he marry my mother and give me his name? Was he ashamed of it? Or of us?"

"Have you ever asked your mother that?"

"No—how could I?"

"Then I think we should ask her now," said Aldo Meyer. Without waiting for an answer, he called loudly: "Nina! Come here a moment, please."

Nina Sanduzzi came out of the house and the boy watched her approach with frightened eyes.

"Sit down, Nina."

She sat down between them, looking from one to the other with grave, questioning eyes. Meyer told her soberly:

"There is a question the boy has asked, Nina. I think he has a right to the answer. You are the only one to give it. He wants to know why his father didn't marry you."

"Will you believe me if I tell you, son?"

The boy looked up, troubled and ashamed, and nodded dumbly. Nina Sanduzzi waited a moment, gathering her strength and her words; then, in a steady voice, she told him.

Blaise Meredith too was stirring early on this fine spring morning. After his attack in the doctor's house, he had slept

172

less restlessly than usual, and when the servant came to bring his coffee and draw back the curtains on the new day, he decided to get up and begin work.

He drank his coffee, ate a little of the new bread and the salt country butter, bathed and shaved, and went downstairs to read his Office in the sunshine. With this liturgical duty behind him, he would be free to begin his interviews with the witnesses. Meyer's warning was still vivid in his mind. His time was running out faster than he had hoped and he could not afford to waste a minute of it. He was glad that the Contessa and Black were still in bed so that he would be spared the rituals of greeting and breakfast small talk.

He had finished Matins and was half-way through Lauds when he heard the sounds of footsteps on the gravel path and looked up. A woman and a boy were walking towards the rear of the house. The woman was dressed peasant-fashion in shapeless black, with a bandanna tied round her head. The boy had on a striped shirt and a pair of patched trousers, and his feet were thrust into worn leather sandals.

He walked uncertainly, looking this way and that, as if overcome by the splendour of his surroundings after the barren harshness of the village. The woman walked proudly, head erect, eyes straight ahead of her, as if determined to discharge an uncomfortable duty with dignity. Meredith was struck by the classic serenity of her face, rounding with middle age, but still touched with a youthful beauty.

This would be Nina Sanduzzi, he decided. The boy would be the son of Giacomo Nerone, who, Meyer had told him, was the subject of the conspiracy of seduction between the Contessa and Nicholas Black. They would have a long time to wait before the Contessa was up and ready to see them.

Moved by a sudden impulse, he put down his book and called:

"Signora Sanduzzi!"

They stopped in their tracks and turned to look at him. He called again:

"Can you come here a moment, please?"

They looked at one another uncertainly; then the woman walked across the lawn with the boy a couple of paces behind her. Meredith stood up to greet her.

"I'm Monsignor Meredith, from Rome!"

"I know," said the woman calmly. "You came yesterday. This is my son, Paolo."

"I'm happy to know you, Paolo."

Meredith held out his hand, and after a nudge from his mother the boy took it, limply.

"You know why I'm here, signora?"

"Yes, I know."

"I'd like to have a talk with you as soon as possible."

"You'll find me at the doctor's place—or at home."

"I thought perhaps we could talk a little now."

Nina Sanduzzi shook her head.

"We have to see the Contessa. Paolo begins work today."

Meredith smiled.

"You'll have a long wait. The Contessa isn't up yet."

"We're used to waiting," she told him gravely. "Besides, I will not talk to you here."

"Just as you like."

"But when Paolo is working here you can talk to him. That would be different."

"Of course. May I come and see you today?"

"If you want. In the afternoon I'm at home. Now we must go. Come, Paolo."

Without another word she turned away. The boy followed her, and Meredith watched their retreating backs until they disappeared round the rear corner of the villa.

Brief as their encounter had been, the woman had impressed him deeply. There was an air about her—an air of serenity, containment, wisdom perhaps. She walked and talked like one who knew where she was going and how she intended to get there. She had neither the thrusting impudence of some peasant women, nor the practised humility which centuries of dependence had imposed on others. Her tongue was the roughest dialect in Italy, yet her voice was soft and strangely gentle even in her blunt refusal. If Giacomo Nerone had taught her these things, then he, in his time, must have been a greater man than most.

Meredith found his attention wandering from the Latin cadences of the Psalms to the consideration of two important elements in the sketchy life of Giacomo Nerone.

The first was the element of conflict. It was an axiom in the Church that one of the first marks of sanctity was the opposition it raised, even among good people. Christ himself had been the sign of contradiction. His promise was not peace, but the sword. No saint in the Calendar had ever done good unopposed. None had ever been without detractors and calumniators. The absence of this element from the records of Battista and Saltarello had troubled him. Now he was beginning to be aware of its existence and of its strength and complexity.

The second element was equally important: the tangible good or evil that sprang from the life, works and wonders of a candidate for saintly honours. There was an axiom here too: the Biblical axiom that a tree is known by its fruits. Sanctity in one man leaves its imprint like a seal on the hearts of others. A good work reproduces itself as the seed of one fruit grows into another. A miracle that produces no good in a human heart is a pointless conjuring trick unworthy of omnipotence.

If there was good in Nina Sanduzzi, and if this good had sprung from her association with Giacomo Nerone, then it must be weighed in the meticulous reckoning of the Devil's Advocate.

He bent again to his breviary, his lips moving in the familiar strophes of the poet-king. Then, when he had finished, he closed the book, thrust it into the pocket of his cassock and walked out of the villa to talk with Father Anselmo.

Old Rosa Benzoni met him at the door and, after a grumbling parley, let him into the house, where he found the old priest, in shirtsleeves and braces, shaving awkwardly in front of a cracked mirror tacked to the wall of the kitchen. His eyes were blearier than usual and his knotted hands trembled as he scraped at his stubbled chin. He was using an old blade razor

175

and Meredith marvelled that he had not yet cut his throat with it. His greeting was less than cordial.

"Hullo! What do you want?"

"I'd like to talk to you," said Meredith mildly.

"I'll listen. I don't promise to answer, though."

"Better we were private, don't you think?" suggested Meredith.

The old man chuckled and then swore as he nicked himself.

"You mean Rosa? She's half-deaf and I doubt she'd understand a word when you talk with a Roman grape in your mouth. Besides, she's got a bad temper—and I've got to live with her. Go ahead, man, and say what you've got to say."

Meredith shrugged and went on.

"It's about Giacomo Nerone. I notice from the first reports that you refused to give any evidence about him. Is that because you were his confessor?"

"No. I didn't like the fellows they sent round. Long-nosed humbugs the pair of 'em. Read me a long lecture about doomsday and damnation. I sent 'em off with a flea in the ear. Besides, who the hell cares what I say? I'm the scandal of the diocese."

"I'm not interested in scandals," said Meredith coolly.

The old man put down the razor and daubed at his face with a soiled towel. He said roughly:

"Then you're the first one I've met who isn't. God, how they love 'em! Give 'em a piece of dirt and they'll chew on it like dogs on a ham-bone. I had a letter from the Bishop hoping my association with Rosa had lost its carnal character. . . ." He gave a high, harsh laugh. "How long does he think a man keeps going at that sort of thing? At my age the best you can hope for is to keep warm at night."

"At your age," suggested Meredith gently, "most married couples sleep in separate beds."

"In Rome, maybe," growled Father Anselmo. "But down here we haven't enough money to buy a new bed—let alone two sets of blankets. Look . . ." He flung down the towel with a gesture of impatience. "We're not children, Monsignor. I don't like the position I'm in, any more than the

Bishop. But at my age, how do I get out of it? I can't toss Rosa out into the street. She's an old woman. She's been good to me—when a lot of my damned brothers in the cloth couldn't have cared whether I lived or died. I've got little enough. God knows, but she's entitled to half of it. Does His Lordship have any answer to that one?"

Meredith was moved. The naked dilemma of the man was frightening. For the first time in his priestly life he began to understand the real problem of repentance, which is not the sin itself, but the consequences which proliferate from it, like parasites on a tree. The tree has no remedy but must go on lending its life to the parasite, borrowing beauty from it, but dying slowly all the time, for want of a knowledgeable gardener. It was a stark thought that a man might lapse into despair and damnation because he couldn't afford a pair of blankets. Suddenly the case of Giacomo Nerone seemed small and insignificant beside the case of Father Anselmo. If Giacomo was a saint he was lucky—he had finished with the long fight. All else was glossary and of little moment. A sudden thought struck Meredith but he hesitated to give it voice. After a moment he said carefully:

"His Lordship's a surprising man. He'd like to help you. I think—I'm sure—if you were to move Rosa to another bed in another room, he'd accept that and let the rest of it drop."

The old man shook his head stubbornly.

"Who pays for the bed and bedclothes? You don't seem to understand. We live down to the knucklebone here. It's a matter of eating."

"I'll tell you something," said Meredith with a wry smile. "I'll pay for them. I'll give you and Rosa enough to set yourselves up with some new clothes and I'll put a hundred thousand lire in the Banco di Calabria for you. Would that help?"

Father Anselmo shot him a swift suspicious glance.

"And why should you care so much, Monsignor?"

Meredith shrugged.

"I'm due to die in three months. I can't take it with me."

The rheumy eyes stared at him in unbelief. The rough peasant voice questioned him again.

"What else do I have to do?"

"Nothing. If you want me to confess you, I'll do it gladly. You can't tell me much I don't know already, so it shouldn't be too hard. There's no point in going half way. You've got to set your conscience in order some time."

"The Bishop talked about repairing the scandal." There was still doubt in his voice, but the stubborn harshness had gone out of it.

Meredith gave him one of his rare, humorous smiles.

"The Bishop's a character in his own right. I think he knows that most people make their own scandals. Good Christians keep their mouths shut and pray for their brothers in distress. It'll soon get around the village that you're sleeping apart. The rest will grow out of what you do from then on. . . . Well, what do you say?"

Anselmo rubbed a knotted hand across his badly shaven chin. His slack mouth twisted into a grin.

"I—I suppose it's a way out. I've been worried a long time, but I love the old girl in a way, and I'd hate to hurt her."

"I don't think the loving does any harm. I could use some of it myself just now." The voice seemed to belong to another man, not Blaise Meredith, the cold fellow from the Congregation of Rites.

"All right!" said the old man brusquely. "I'll think about it. I'll talk to Rosa and explain things to her. But you can't do things like that in a rush. Women are sensitive—and when they're old they get stupid as well. . . ." His old eyes gleamed shrewdly. "And when do we see the colour of *your* money, Monsignor?"

Meredith took out his wallet and laid thirty one-thousand lire notes on the table.

"That's the beginning of it. You can buy the blankets and the bed. The rest I'll have to fix in Valenta. Will that do?"

"It'll have to," the old man told him grudgingly. "We'd like something fixed before you die. Once the lawyers get their hands on an estate—finish! All that's left is birdseed! Now, what else did you want?"

"Giacomo Nerone. . . . What can you tell me about him?"

"What happens if I do tell you?"

"I'll make notes and then you'll be examined under oath at the Bishop's court."

"Tell you what, Monsignor. Wait till you hear my confession. Then I'll give you the full story. Will that do?"

"A confessional secret is no good for the court record."

The old man threw back his head and laughed in his high harsh fashion.

"That's what I mean, friend! They've had enough scandals out of me already. Damned if I'm going to give 'em another one."

"Just as you say," said Meredith wearily. "I'll call and see you in a few days."

"And don't forget what you have to do in Valenta."

"I won't forget."

He got up and walked to the door. There was no farewell, no word of thanks, and as he walked down the hill towards the doctor's cottage, he had the uncomfortable feeling that he had made a fool of himself.

Meyer greeted him good-humouredly, led him into the garden and poured him a cup of country wine from an earthenware pitcher, cooling in the sun. Meredith was quick to notice the change in him: his eyes were clear, his drawn face was relaxed, and he had the comfortable air of a man who has come to terms with himself and his situation. Meredith commented on it quizzically.

"You look better this morning, Doctor."

Meyer grinned into his wine cup.

"A good beginning to my day, Monsignor. I've talked to a boy like a father; and heard wise things from his mother."

"Nina Sanduzzi?"

"Yes. Between us I hope we have done something for the boy."

"I saw them at the villa—spoke to them for a few moments.

I'm calling on Nina Sanduzzi this afternoon. She's prepared to talk."

"Good." Meyer nodded with satisfaction. "I'll give you a tip, my friend. Walk gently and you will go a long way with her. She is disposed now to be frank. And she wants you to keep an eye on the boy while he's at the villa."

"I'll do my best. She impressed me deeply."

"And Paolo?"

"Is like any other adolescent."

"Not quite like . . ." Meyer cautioned him. "He is in the dangerous years. He is attracted to the Englishman and he is afraid of him as well. Also he is curious about his mother and his father. Not quite so curious now that Nina and I have spoken to him. But when you're old, you never know how much a young man understands—or what bees he has buzzing in his bonnet. And what now, Monsignor?"

"I'd like to talk with you, Doctor."

"About Nerone?"

"Yes."

Aldo Meyer took a long draught of wine and then wiped his thin lips with the back of his hand. He said with bleak humour:

"Isn't it usual to put on a stole when you hear confessions?"

"I'll take off my shoes instead," said Blaise Meredith.

"It's a long story, Monsignor. When it gets dry, you help yourself to a drink. . . .

. . . It was full summer in a world without men. Hot mornings and blazing noons, and nights when the clouds rolled in, sweating, over the valley and then moved on unspent of rain. Tempers were high, and vitality was low, because the armies were like locusts, eating out the land, and there were no men in the beds—except the old ones, who were a nuisance, and occasional visitors, like the *polizia* and the *carabinieri* and the agricultural inspector and the requisitioning officers from the Army. These were a nuisance, too, because when they were gone there were quarrels in the houses and bloody faces and torn skirts in the fields.

The valley was like a nest of cats, musky and hot and languid for coupling, then breaking suddenly into screams and violence. Meyer lived in it, because he was a Jew and an exile and every second day he must tramp across the valley to Gemello Maggiore to assure the *quaestura* that he was neither sick nor dead. They were indifferent either way, but they cursed him when he came and threatened him if he missed a day—and then gave him wine and cheese and cigarettes if their children were sick or their girls pregnant or they themselves went down with malaria. They made coarse jokes about his being a Jew and circumcised and warned him about polluting the pure blood of the women, who, being good Calabrese, were part Greek, part Phoenician, part French and Spanish and Italian and Levantine Arab—anything and everything but Jew.

Meyer swallowed it all, and digested it in secret and kept his ears open to the rumours that bumbled like bees in and out of the valley. The Allies were in Sicily, there were beachheads in other places. Partisans were arming in the hills, deserters were holing up in caves and friendly beds. The Germans were rushing reinforcements south. Sooner or later the end would come and he wanted to be alive to see it.

He worked his rough acres, made his rounds of the sick, dozed at siesta time and in the night sat late over his books and his bottle.

If he kept himself free of the village women, it was because he was a fastidious man, and also because he did not want to face the dawning future with a village shrew at his coat-tails. He had waited a long time. He could afford to wait a little longer.

It was in the night time, late, that Nina Sanduzzi came to see him. She came barefooted lest the sound of her wooden sandals be heard in the sleeping village; and she climbed the garden wall from the valley side, in case some late busybody saw her knocking on the doctor's door. She was right inside the pool of lamplight before he woke from his reverie and saw her. He was startled and angry.

"Nina! What the devil are you doing here?"

181

She put her finger to her lips to silence him and then explained in low, rattling dialect:

"There's a man in my house. He's a deserter and wounded. There's a bullet hole in his shoulder all red and swollen, and he tosses and mutters as if he had the fever. Will you come and see him, please? I've brought money."

She fished into the neck of her dress and brought up a small bundle of greasy notes. Meyer waved it away impatiently.

"Keep it, for God's sake! Does anyone else know he's there?"

"No one. He came last night. I gave him breakfast and he stayed inside all day. When I got back from work he was like this."

"All right, I'll come."

He closed his book, turned down the lamp and gathered up his bag of instruments and his small stock of antiseptic, and followed her out from the back of the house, over the wall and down to the small hut hidden in the ilexes.

He found his patient delirious on the big brass bed, a long dark fellow with days of stubble on his shrunken cheeks, and staring eyes and a drooling, muttering mouth, from which issued broken words and phrases that he recognised as English. A pretty situation! Deserters were bad enough, but an English soldier was sudden death. He made no comment to the girl, but bent over the bed and began cutting the sodden bandages from the shoulder wound.

When he saw it, he gave a low whistle of surprise. It was pulpy and swollen, and a slow yellow suppuration had already begun. An awkward job and a dirty one. It would hurt like hell without an anæsthetic and the fellow might well die in a matter of days.

He turned back to Nina Sanduzzi.

"Get the fire going. Boil me a pot of hot water. Then you'll have to hold him down for me."

The girl's white teeth showed in a smile.

"It's a long time since I've had a man in my arms, Dottore. It'll be a pleasure."

But the pleasure soon went out of it, even for her. The

bullet had struck the shoulder blade and slanted downward against the bone, and Meyer had to probe for it for twenty minutes, while the sick man shouted vainly against the gag they thrust in his mouth, and Nina Sanduzzi had to use all her strength to hold him.

Then when it was over and the worst of the pain was finished they tucked him into the bed, and Nina and Meyer sat down to drink wine and break a crust together.

"You can't keep him here. You know that, Nina. If anyone finds out, you're as good as dead."

She stared at him in astonishment.

"You want me to throw him out. A sick man like that?"

"Afterwards," said Meyer wearily. "When he's better."

"Let's wait for afterwards, then," said Nina Sanduzzi with a smile.

Looking at her then by lamplight in the low room, he had felt his first real temptation in years. Her face was pure Greek. Her body was slimmer than those of her peasant fellows. Her breasts were full and firm and there was a thrusting animal vitality under her olive skin. She had intelligence, too, and courage. She did not wait and scream like the others. She knew what was needed and she did it, calmly and competently. It amazed him that he had passed her a hundred times and never noticed her.

But he was a cautious fellow and accustomed to continence, so he finished his wine quickly and made to go.

"Understand something, Nina. He's very sick and he could die. Make some soup and see if he can hold it down. When you go to work, lock the door and leave him wine and food. I daren't come here in the daytime, but I'll come again in the night after the village has settled down."

"You're a good one," said Nina Sanduzzi softly. "In a place full of pigs you stand up like a man." She snatched up his hand and kissed it quickly. "Now go, *dottore mio*! I'm not used to men around the place!"

As he trudged up the rocky slope, avoiding the roadway, he wondered whether continence was not, like all his other sacrifices, a pointless waste—and whether this might be a woman with whom he could be happy. It was the thing he had been afraid of all his exile—the thing his enemies wanted him to do —go slack, go native, hit the bottle and the country whores, and forget to wash his shirts and use a knife and fork with his dinner. So far he had managed to avoid it. With Nina Sanduzzi he might still avoid it. . . . But the risk was there— and there were faint trumpets sounding in the hills. Better forget it and go home to sleep.

It took him more than a week to nurse the patient out of danger. The wound was deep and new infections broke out, and he had to keep draining the wound with the primitive means at his disposal. More than one night he sat up, with Nina, watching the fever rise and break, until the false dawn lightened in the east and it was time to go home before the village was astir.

Each night he came, he felt the need of her. Each time he left, he felt a pang of jealousy at leaving her alone with the sick man, who now had begun to eat and talk a little between the fever bouts and the long intervals of restless sleep.

At first he was cautious with them; but when he understood Meyer's position as a political exile, and the risks the girl was taking for him, he relaxed a little, but still refused to tell them anything but the story he had first told Nina Sanduzzi.

"Better you don't know any more than that. If you're questioned, you can answer truthfully. Though I hope to God you won't be. I'm Giacomo Nerone, a gunner from Reggio. I'm trying to get back to Rome to my family. When do you think I'll be strong enough to travel, Doctor?"

Meyer shrugged.

"A fortnight, three weeks, maybe—unless you get another infection. But where do you aim to go? There's talk that the Allies have landed north of here, and that they're advancing up the toe from Reggio. But this place is a pocket in the hills. With our chaps pulling back and the Germans moving down, you'll have trouble getting very far. Your accent doesn't belong to Calabria. Sooner or later someone's going to ask questions . . . unless you're going into hiding again—and then how do you eat?"

Nerone smiled ruefully and they saw how the humour transfigured him, into a boy again.

"What else do you expect? I can't stay here."

"Why not?" demanded Nina Sanduzzi. "There's a house and a bed and food. It's not much, but it's better than dying in a ditch with another bullet in you."

The two men looked at each other. After a pause Meyer nodded dubiously.

"She could be right. Besides . . ." He made the point cautiously. "When things change here, you might be in a position to help."

The dark fellow shook his head.

"Not in the way you think, Doctor."

Meyer frowned, then said bluntly:

"You don't understand me. I heard you talking in your sleep. You have other loyalties, it seems. These might be useful to us later."

Now it was the girl's turn to stare. She demanded sharply:

"What do you mean, other loyalties?"

"I'm English," said Nerone. "And now that it's said, forget it."

"English!" Nina Sanduzzi's eyes widened.

"Forget it!" said Meyer harshly.

"It's forgotten." But she smiled as she said it and then put another proposition which left them momentarily speechless. "If you stay here, there's no reason why you can't work for your living. . . . Don't look so surprised! There are half a dozen lads doing it this very minute. They've given the war away too. Two of them are locals and the others come from God knows where. But we're short of men, and there's a lot to be done before winter—and nobody wants to make a fuss about it. If there's anybody suspicious hanging around, the boys go to cover, but most of the time they work out in the open. . . ." She laughed cheerfully. "And they're never short of a bed! I could get you a job with old Enzo Gozzoli. He's the foreman of my crowd. He's lost two sons in the war and he hates the Fascisti like poison. When you're better, I'll talk to him. . . . If you want to, that is."

"I'll think about it," said Giacomo Nerone. "I'm very grateful but I'll have to think about it."

He lay back on the pillow and closed his eyes, and a few moments later he lapsed into sleep.

The girl poured Meyer another cup of wine, and he drank it, thoughtfully, watching her as she bent over the bed, settling the dark head on the pillow, drawing the bedclothes carefully round the wounded shoulder, standing a moment in silent contemplation of the sleeping guest.

When she came back, Meyer stood up, took her in his arms, and tried to kiss her. She pushed him away, gently.

"No, *dottore mio*. Not now."

"I want you, Nina!"

"You don't want me really, *cara*," she told him softly. "Otherwise you'd have taken me long before now—and I'd have been glad of it. It's summer and you're lonely, and we've spent some evenings together. But I'm not for you and you know it. . . . Afterwards you would hate me. I want a man, God knows! But I want all of him."

Meyer turned away and picked up his bag. He made a quick gesture towards the bed.

"Maybe you've got him!" he said dryly.

"Maybe," said Nina Sanduzzi. Then she walked to the door and held it open for him, and as he walked up the hillside he heard it shut—a dry, sharp sound in the languid air.

. . . "And that was the beginning of it?" asked Blaise Meredith.

"The beginning." Meyer reached for the pitcher of wine. "In three weeks he was out and about, working for Enzo Gozzoli. At night he went back to Nina's house and they were lovers."

"And, beyond the fact that he was English, you still had no idea who he was?"

"No." Meyer took a long swallow of wine and wiped his lips with a soiled handkerchief. "There were three things he might have been: an escaped prisoner, a British agent sent to make contact with the first Partisan groups, a deserter."

"And which did he look like to you?"

"I took them in turn and tried to fit him into the mould. An escaped prisoner? Yes. Except that he showed no inclination to do what such a man should do—try to rejoin his unit. An agent? This too. He spoke good Italian—not the *argot* of the cookhouse and the military brothel. He was an educated man. He was alive to the local colour. But when I threw out hints about joining me in an attempt to contact the Partisans, he refused."

"Did he give any reason?"

"No. He refused politely, but quite definitely."

"A deserter, then?"

Meyer pursed his thin lips thoughtfully.

"It seemed the most likely category. But a deserter is a man who is afraid. He has the fugitive look. He lives with the conviction that one day he must be caught. Nerone had none of that. Once he was well, he walked and talked and laughed like a free man."

"Was he an officer?"

"I thought so. As I say, he was a cultivated man. He had the habit of decision, a talent for getting things done. But he carried no identification at all. I pointed out that if he were caught like this by the Germans or the Italians, he could be shot as a spy. He just laughed and said Giacomo Nerone was a good Italian who saw no reason in the war. . . . More wine, Monsignor?"

Meredith nodded vaguely, and as Meyer filled his glass he asked:

"What estimate did you form of his character at this first period?"

"Part of it, I've already given you," said Meyer. "Courage, good humour, a capacity for getting things done. The rest? I wasn't quite sure. I was jealous of him, you see."

"Because of Nina Sanduzzi?"

"That and other things. I had lived among these people, served them, too, for years. I had never arrived at intimacy with them. Nerone was at home in a week. The men trusted him. The women loved him. He could make them laugh by

187

twitching his black eyebrows. They told him all the scandals and taught him dialect and shared their wine with him. I was still the outsider—the Jew from Rome."

"I know how you felt," said Meredith gently. "I've been like that all my life. Except that I've never served anyone."

Aldo Meyer shot him a quick appraising glance, but Meredith was staring absently at the dark wine in his cup. He went on.

"The thing that irritated me about him was that he seemed to take everything for granted and for permanent. As if the present were the only thing that mattered. For him it was natural enough, I suppose. He had had his war. He was content with the day. I had been waiting so long that I cried for action and for change."

"So you were at odds with each other?"

Meyer shook his head.

"That's the queer part. When I didn't see him, I disliked him. But when we met in passing—or when, later, he used to come to my place in the evening to talk or borrow a book, he charmed me. There was a calm about him—a gentleness. The same sort of thing you find now in Nina Sanduzzi."

"What did you talk about?"

"Everything—except Nerone. He refused any topic that might give me a clue to his identity. What interested him most was the place itself, the people, their history, their customs, their relationships with one another. It was as if he were trying to forget all that had belonged to him and absorb himself into the life of the mountains."

"Was he concerned for them?"

"At first, no. He seemed to regard himself as one of them. But he had no plans as I had. No schemes for their betterment."

"What were his relations with Nina Sanduzzi?"

Meyer grinned wryly and spread his hands in deprecation.

"They were happy together. One saw it in their faces. That was all I knew. More than I wanted to know. For the rest you'll have to talk to Nina."

Meredith nodded.

"I'm sorry to press you like this, Doctor. But you understand what I am commissioned to do."

"I understand. I'm not hedging. I'm trying to keep my evidence first-hand."

"Please go on."

"The next stage begins about the end of October . . . the middle of autumn. Nerone called me in to examine Nina. She was two months' pregnant."

"What was his reaction to that?"

"He was glad of it. They both were. I think I was never more jealous of him than at that moment. He had come from nowhere and he had achieved what had eluded me all my life: acceptance, love, a promise of purpose and continuity."

"Yet he made no move to marry Nina?"

"No."

"Did she want it?"

"I put it to them both," said Meyer carefully, "not because I was concerned—in a country without men, there is no shame in a fatherless child—but because I wanted to see what sort of man this was."

"What did he say?"

"Nothing. It was Nina who answered. She said: 'Time enough for wedding bells, Dottore, when we know what is going to happen.' "

"And Nerone?"

Meyer looked down at the backs of his hands, spread like spiders on the warm wood of the table. He hesitated a moment, then said:

"I remember the next part very well. Just when it seemed I had measured Nerone for what he was—a fly-by-night who would be on his way before the dawn showed—he surprised me again."

"How?"

"He said, quite simply, apropos of nothing at all: 'It's going to be a bad winter, Doctor. You and I had better start preparing for it now!' "

. . . In the old days, before the men were taken, before the war had started to go wrong, when there was still an authority and a purpose in the land, the winter had been bearable—if never a happy time.

There was charcoal in store and wine laid down and oil in the big green bottles. The onions hung in strings from the rafters and the corncobs were piled in the corner and there were potatoes buried in straw. There was cheese to be bought, and salami and smoked ham and lentils, and the millers had flour to sell for the pasta. The food was there, even if you had to scratch a hole in your breeches to find the money to buy it. Before the snows closed in, there was always a traffic of barter between the villages; and when work in the fields slowed down to a dead stop, the commune paid out a small dole to have the roads cleared and gravel spread on the ice patches.

It was a life—not much of a life, to be sure—but if you hung on to it long enough, you would hear the torrent roaring and smell the first warm winds from the south and feel the ice thawing out of your bones with the coming of spring.

But now there were no men and the crops were poor and the Quartermaster's levies took the best of them. The barter was a nothing, because who would take his donkey cart to market and risk the thieves and deserters and patrols on the way? Better to stay at home and live on your own fat as long as you could. Besides, the boys were straggling back, leaderless, disillusioned and belly-hungry—new mouths to feed out of the diminished stores.

There was no government any more. Those officials who had been reasonable fellows stayed on, hoping their pay packets might arrive and, if they didn't, hoping for a small return for their kindness. Those who had been bastards were moving out, tagging themselves on to still active units, or selling themselves and their local knowledge to the German detachments moving south to engage the Allied Eighth Army.

And in Gemelli dei Monti they smelt the wind, and felt the first rain squalls, and counted the first frosts, and said: "It's going to be a bad winter."

Giacomo Nerone said it too, coolly and emphatically. But he added a rider or two of his own.

"You and I are the only people round here with any brains or any influence. We'll have to run the organisation."

Meyer gaped at him, thunderstruck.

"For God's sake, man! You don't know what you're talking about. You're on the run! I'm a political exile. The moment we stick out our necks, they'll drop the axe on them."

"Who's they, Doctor?" Nerone grinned at him.

"The authorities. The police. The *carabinieri*. The Mayor of Gemello Maggiore."

Nerone threw back his head and laughed as heartily as if it were a washerwoman's joke down by the torrent.

"My dear doctor! These fellows are so scared just now, they're only interested in saving their own hides. We haven't seen any of 'em round here for weeks. Besides, this is our business, not theirs. We handle it ourselves."

"Handle what, for God's sake?"

"The elementary problem of survival for three months. We've got to see that everyone gets enough food and fuel to keep alive during the winter. We've got to get you some more medicines and try to find some more blankets. We've got to set up a central store and see that rations are doled out fairly . . ."

"You're mad!" Meyer told him flatly. "You don't understand these people. They're close-fisted at the best of times, but in famine they're like carrion birds. They'll eat out one another's livers before they'll let a crust of bread pass from one house to another. The family's the only thing that counts. The rest can rot in a ditch."

"Then we'll teach 'em the next step," said Nerone calmly. "We'll make 'em a tribe."

"You can't do it."

"I've already started."

"The hell you have!"

"I've got ten families to agree to put a quarter of their food stocks into a common store for the winter. Each of these families is going to try to bring in one more. Then you and I will go round and try to beat some sense into those who are still standing out."

191

"I don't understand how you did it."

Giacomo Nerone smiled and shrugged.

"I talked to them. I pointed out that there are still more levies to come: Italian, German, Allied. When things get tough—as they will in the winter—there'll be house searches for hoarded stocks. No, while the going's good, we'd better co-operate and build up a common store in a secret place. I told them Nina and I would make our own contribution first, as evidence of good faith; and then we'd set up a committee to administer it. You, me, and three others. Two men and a woman. It took a little time, but they agreed in the end."

"I've been here all this time," said Meyer sombrely, "and I've never been able to do anything like that."

"You have to pay a price for it, of course."

Meyer stared at him, puzzled.

"What sort of price?"

"I don't know yet," said Nerone thoughtfully, "but I think it will come very high in the end. . . ."

. . . "Did he explain what he meant?" asked Blaise Meredith.

"No."

"Did you ask him to explain it?"

"Yes." Meyer made a rueful mouth. "But once again it was Nina who answered for him. She was standing behind him, I remember, and she bent down and kissed his hair and then held his face between her hands. Then she said: 'I love this man, *dottore mio*. He's afraid of nothing—and he always pays his debts!'"

"Did that satisfy you?"

Meyer chuckled and thrust himself back in his chair to reach for the wine.

"You miss the point, Monsignor. When you see a man and a woman like that—and when you are in love with the woman yourself—there's only one satisfaction. And you can't have it. I got up and went home. Next day Nerone and I met again and began to prepare for winter."

"And you succeeded?"

"Yes. Before the first snows came, everybody in Gemello Minore had agreed, and we had nearly three tons of supplies sealed up in the Grotta del Fauno."

Recollections stirred sharply behind the thoughtful eyes of Blaise Meredith.

"The Grotto of the Faun. . . . That's where they buried him, wasn't it?"

"That's where they buried him," said Aldo Meyer.

CHAPTER ELEVEN

WHILE BLAISE MEREDITH talked under the fig tree with Doctor
Aldo Meyer, Anne Louise de Sanctis sat in the ornate salon
at the villa and interviewed Nina Sanduzzi.

She had risen late, but less ill-tempered than usual, and
when the servant informed her that Nina Sanduzzi was waiting
to see her with the boy, she had taken a little longer with her
breakfast and her toilet. She had chatted for ten minutes with
Nicholas Black, who was off to the garden with his paint-box;
she had looked over the household accounts and the menu for
the evening meal; then she had settled herself in the salon and
sent a servant to fetch Nina Sanduzzi.

Now they were alone while Paolo scuffed his feet on the
path outside and watched the gardeners moving up and down
the flower beds and the flight of a yellow butterfly, lazy among
the shrubbery.

The Contessa was seated in a high-backed chair, freshly
groomed, faintly triumphant, her hands placid in her lap, her
eyes searching the blank face of the peasant who stood before
her, dusty from the road, feet bare in wooden sandals, but
straight and proud as a tree waiting for the wind to blow.

"You understand," said Anne Louise de Sanctis, "this is a
great opportunity for the boy." She used the familiar *thou* to
indicate the vast gulf that lay between the châtelaine and the
servant.

"It is work," said Nina Sanduzzi calmly. "That is good for
the boy. If he works well, it is good for you, too."

"How does he feel about it? Is he glad to come?"

"Who can say how a boy feels? He is here. He is ready to
start work."

"We haven't yet discussed payment."

Nina Sanduzzi shrugged indifferently.

"The *dottore* said you would pay what was usual."

Anne Louise de Sanctis smiled benevolently.

"We'll do better than that. Signor Black tells me he is intelligent and willing. We'll pay him a man's wage."

"For a man's work—good! So long as it is a man's work!"

The reply was barbed, but the Contessa, being weak in dialect, missed the sharpness of it. She went on, genial and condescending.

"If the boy works well and shows promise, we may be able to do much for him—give him an education, help him to make a career—send him to Rome, perhaps."

Nina Sanduzzi nodded thoughtfully, but her eyes were veiled and expressionless as a bird's. She said simply:

"His father was an educated man. He used to say, one should educate the heart first and the head later."

"Of course," said the Contessa with unnatural brightness. "His father! Giacomo Nerone was your lover, wasn't he?"

"He was the man I loved," said Nina Sanduzzi. "He loved me and he loved the boy."

"Strange that he never married you."

There was no flicker of emotion in the blank eyes and the calm face. The sentence hung suspended in the silence between them. Anne Louise de Sanctis was irritated. She wanted to strike out and see the marks of her fingers rise in weals on the other's olive cheeks. But this was an indulgence she could not afford, being committed to diplomacy and an alliance of smiles and concealment. She said briskly:

"The boy will lodge here, of course. He'll be well fed and comfortable. You can have him home with you on Sundays."

"I've spoken to the Monsignor from Rome," said Nina Sanduzzi quietly. "I've asked him to talk with the boy and help him. These are awkward years in his life."

"You shouldn't have bothered Monsignor Meredith," the Contessa snapped at her. "He's a sick man and busy with important affairs!"

"He is busy with my Giacomo, Signora. And what could be more important than Giacomo's son? Besides, the Monsignor said he would be happy to help."

"You may go," said the Contessa. "Leave the boy here and the gardener will set him to work."

Nina Sanduzzi made no move to go. Instead she stooped and picked up the straw bag she always carried. She fumbled inside it, brought up a small package neatly wrapped in paper and held it out to the Contessa.

"What's this?"

"My boy is coming into your house. He should not come empty-handed. It's a gift."

The simple grace of the gesture embarrassed her. She took the package in her hands and said awkwardly:

"Thank you. May I ask what it is?"

"We are poor people," said Nina Sanduzzi carefully. "We give from our hearts and not from our wealth. One day Giacomo may be made a *beato*, and then this will be precious to you. It is part of what he wore when they killed him. His blood is on it. I would like you to have it—from his son!"

Anne Louise de Sanctis said nothing, but sat there, staring like a hypnotic at the package, her face dead white, her lips moving in a soundless murmur. When, after a long time, she looked up, Nina Sanduzzi was gone, and there was only the sunlight slanting in through dust motes, and a vista of green lawn where a boy walked side by side with a gardener—a boy who might have been her own son.

Aldo Meyer and Monsignor Blaise Meredith had got up from the table and were walking, side by side, up and down the flagged path that ran the full width of the garden. They passed alternately from sunlight into shadow and their shoes made a dry, crisp sound on the stones.

"To this point," said Meredith, in his precise, legal fashion, "what have we? A man in flight, a man in love, a man assuming leadership and responsibility in the community which has given him refuge. His past is a mystery. His future, a doubt in his own mind. His present . . . what you have told me. We have no indication of his religious belief or his moral attitude. On the face of it, he is living in sin. His acts, good in themselves, have no spiritual value. Now . . ." He kicked at a

196

small pebble and watched it bound away towards the rough stone wall. "Now, according to my records, he comes to a crisis, a moment of conversion, in which, or as a result of which, he turns away from this woman and surrenders himself to God. What do you know about this?"

"Less than I should, perhaps," said Meyer deliberately. "Certainly much less than Nina, to whom you will be talking this afternoon. But I do know something. I give it to you for what it's worth. . . ."

. . . The winter was harder than they had ever dreamed possible. The snows came down in blinding blizzards from the high peaks to the west; they piled in drifts along the roads and in the hollows. They choked the mountain tracks and broke the olive branches and heaped themselves against the doors of the houses. They froze hard, and the winds whipped the powder off them, leaving exposed ridges of ice like ripples on a dead white sea. Then came new calms and new downfalls so that a soft layer was laid on the hard rime underneath.

In the south the engaged armies dug themselves in and waited for the thaw. The patrols bivouacking in the hills lost men from exposure and frostbite. The stragglers and deserters hammered on barred doors in the night and, if they were not opened, died in the snow before morning.

Inside the houses, the families clung together for warmth in the big brass beds, rising only to relieve themselves or to seek food and brew coffee, because charcoal stock had to be conserved, and the earthen floors were frozen and the wind searched keenly through the cracked doors and the crazy window frames stuffed with mud and old newspapers. The old ones coughed and grumbled with the rheumatic cold in their joints; the young ones fretted with flushed cheeks and sore throats and congested chests; and when any of them died, as many did, they were carried out into the snow and buried there until the thaw—because who would make coffins in this bleak weather and who could turn a sod in the Campo Santo when the ground was frozen hard as granite?

They lived like hibernating animals, each litter an island in a sea of snow, drawing warmth from each other's bodies, familiar with each other's stench, munching blindly on the common crust, wondering bleakly how long they would last and whether there would ever be another spring.

If a knock came on the door, they ignored it. Who but thieves or crazy men or starving ones would be abroad at this time? If the knock was persistent, they cursed in chorus, until finally it stopped and they heard the crackling footsteps retreat across the frozen snow. There was only one knock they knew and one voice to which they answered—Giacomo Nerone's.

Every day and all day he was about, making the rounds of the houses—a black-jowled, smiling giant, with his boots wrapped in sacking and his body padded in layers of scarecrow garments and his head muffled in a cap made of one of Nina's stockings. On his back he carried an old army knapsack, filled with rations, and his pockets were stuffed with aspirin tablets and a bottle of cod liver oil and odds and ends of medicine.

When he came into a house, he stayed as long as they needed him and no longer. He checked their food stocks, looked at the sick, dosed them when he could, cooked a broth for those who were incapable, cleaned up the accumulated messes and then moved on. But before he went there were always five minutes for news and greetings, and a couple of minutes for a joke to leave them laughing when he trudged out again into the waste. If they needed Meyer, he would bring him back. If they were ready for a priest, he tried to get one—though this was a rather more chancy proceeding since Father Anselmo was old and cold, and disinclined to stir, and the young curate from Gemello Maggiore often had his hands too full with his own dying.

Always his last call of the day was on Aldo Meyer. They would drink a thimbleful of *grappa*, exchange notes, and then Nerone would plunge off down the hill to Nina's hut.

At first he was cheerful, exulting in the challenge to his strength and vitality. Then, as December wore on into January and there was still no break in the weather, he began to get edgy, preoccupied, like a man who slept too little and thought too much. Meyer urged him to rest, give himself a couple of days at home with Nina, but he refused curtly, and afterwards seemed to drive himself even harder.

Then one evening when it was late and bitter with a new wind, he came in, dumped his pack on Meyer's floor, tossed off the *grappa* at one gulp and said abruptly:

"Meyer! I want to talk to you!"

"You always do," said Meyer mildly. "What's so different about tonight?"

Nerone ignored the irony and plunged on.

"I never told you why I came here, did I?"

"It's your own business. You didn't have to tell me."

"I'd like to tell you now."

"Why?"

"I need to."

"It's a good reason," said Meyer with a grin.

"Tell me . . . do you believe in God, Meyer?"

"I was brought up to believe in Him," said Meyer guardedly. "My friends the Fascisti have done their best to persuade me otherwise. Let's say I have an open mind in the matter. Why do you ask?"

"I could be talking nonsense to you."

"It's a man's right to talk nonsense when he has a need."

"All right. You make what you like of it. I'm English, you know that. I'm an officer, which you didn't know."

"I guessed it."

"I'm also a deserter."

"What do you want me to say?" asked Meyer with dry humour. "How much I despise you?"

"Say nothing, for God's sake. Just listen. I was in the advance guard for the assault on Messina. It was the last toehold in Sicily. For us, nothing to it. Your people were beaten. The Germans were pulling out fast. Just a mopping-up operation. My company was assigned to clean out a half-mile square of tenements leading down to the docks. Scattered snipers, a couple of machine-gun posts . . . nothing. There was a blind alley, with windows facing down towards us and a sniper in the top window. He had us pinned down for ten minutes at the mouth of the alley. Then, we thought we might have got him. We moved in. When we got to the house, I followed the usual routine, and shouted a surrender warning. There was another shot—from the lower window this time. It got one of my boys. I pitched a grenade through the window, waited for the burst and then went in. I found the sniper—an old fisherman, with a woman and a nursing child. All dead. The baby had taken the full burst. . . ."

"It happens in war," said Meyer coolly. "It's the human element. It has nothing to do with God."

"I know," said Giacomo Nerone. "But I was the human element. Can you understand that?"

"Yes, I can understand it. So you decided this was the end for you. You had done what you'd been paid to do. You were dispensed from all the rest. Your war was over. Is that right?"

"More or less."

"You went on the run. But where did you expect to go?"

"I didn't know."

"Why did you come here?"

"I don't know that either. Call it an accident if you want."

"Do *you* believe in God, Nerone?"

"I used to. Then for a long time I didn't."

"And now?"

"Don't press me, man! Let me talk it out!"

Meyer shrugged and poured an extravagant measure of *grappa* into Nerone's glass. When Nerone protested, he said with wintry humour:

"*In vino veritas*. Drink it."

Nerone held the glass with two shaky hands and drank it greedily, then wiped his chapped mouth with the back of his hand. He said moodily:

"When I met Nina, she was a refuge. When we fell in love it was more—a kind of absolution. When she became pregnant, I felt as if I was undoing what had been done; putting a new life back in the place of the one I'd destroyed. When we started to do something for these people, it was my kind of reparation to the old fisherman and the dead woman. . . . It wasn't enough. It still isn't enough."

"It never is," said Aldo Meyer. "But where does God come in?"

"If He doesn't, it's all a monstrous folly. The death means nothing, the reparation means less. We're ants on the carcass of the world, spawned out of nothing, going busily nowhere. One of us dies, the others crawl over us to the pickings. This whole valley could freeze to death and it would mean nothing—nothing at all. . . . But if there is a God . . . everything becomes enormously important . . . every life, every death. . . ."

"And the reparation?"

"Means nothing at all," said Nerone sombrely, "unless you give yourself as part of it."

"You're in deep water, my friend," said Aldo Meyer gently.

"I know," Nerone told him in a dead voice. "I'm damn near drowning in it."

He leaned his head on his hands and began running his fingers through his hair. Meyer came and sat on the edge of the table and said good humouredly:

"Let me give a piece of advice, my friend—medical advice. You're running yourself ragged with fatigue and under-nourishment. You've never been quite sure whether you were right or wrong to walk away from your war; and, because you're fatigued, you're beginning to worry about it. You've done a good job for all of us here and you're still doing it. Now, all of a sudden, you're preoccupied with God. If you'll forgive my saying so—half the shoddy mysticism in the world comes from bad digestion, overwork, lack of sleep or lack of sexual satisfaction. If you want a doctor's advice, stay at home and play honeymooners with Nina for a few days. Vote yourselves an extra day's ration and give yourselves a *festa*."

Nerone looked up and his dark, stubbled face relaxed into a grin.

"You know, Meyer, that's where all you liberals make your mistake. That's why there's no place for you any more in the twentieth century. There are only two things you can do about God: affirm Him like the Catholics or deny Him like

201

the Communists. You want to reduce Him to a belly-ache or a hot flush, or a comforting speculation for the coffee and cigars. You're a Jew. You should know better."

"And what are you?" Meyer was nettled.

"I used to be a Catholic."

"That's your trouble," said Meyer definitely. "You might make a good Communist, but you'll never make a good liberal. You're an absolutist at heart. You've got religion like an itch in the crutch, and you'll carry it till the day you die. . . . But my prescription still stands."

"I'll think about it, Doctor. I've got to think about it—very carefully."

. . . Meredith stopped walking and stood a moment in the shade of the fig tree, absently shredding one of the thick, tough leaves and feeling the white sap glutinous on his fingers. After a while, he said:

"This is the first glimmer I've seen of the thing one looks for in every case history: the entry of God into a man's calculations, the beginning of acceptance of the consequence of belief, the start of a personal relationship between Creator and Creature. If this theme continues . . ."

"It recurs," said Meyer slowly. "But there are gaps in my story. You'll have to fill them in from other witnesses, like Nina Sanduzzi."

"If there were writings," said Meredith thoughtfully, "they would help immensely. One might be able to follow a personal attitude that would explain the external relationships."

"There are writings, Monsignor. I have them."

Meredith stared at him in surprise.

"Is there much of them?"

"There's a large packet. I haven't opened it yet. Nina gave them to me."

"Could I see them?"

"If you don't mind waiting a while," Meyer agreed awkwardly. "I haven't read them myself yet. I've been afraid of them—in much the same way as you have been afraid of your request for a miracle. Somewhere in them may be the answer to a lot of questions that have plagued me for a long time. Till now I haven't been sure I wanted the answer. I'd like to read them this afternoon while you're talking to Nina. Then tomorrow I'll hand them over—with the rest of my own evidence. Would that satisfy you?"

"Certainly. Take longer if you want."

"It's enough," said Meyer with a wry smile. "You're a good confessor, Meredith. I'm glad to talk with you."

A grave pleasure dawned in the eyes of Blaise Meredith. He said:

"If only you knew how glad I am to hear that."

Meyer looked at him quizzically.

"Why, Monsignor?"

"For the first time in my life, I think, I am beginning to be close to people. It terrifies me to think how much time I've wasted—and how little there is left."

"Afterwards," said Meyer soberly, "you will be close to God."

"That terrifies me most of all," said Blaise Meredith.

In a far corner of the villa grounds, Paolo Sanduzzi was at work, sawing a fallen olive tree into firewood. The head gardener, a taciturn fellow, himself gnarled and dark as a tree, had left him there with a curt direction to keep his hands out of his pockets and work off his puppy fat, and have the whole tree cut and corded by sundown.

He was glad to be alone. The place was new and strange. This was his first man's work and his hands were clumsy and inexpert. To be laughed at would be an agony, and he needed time to learn the rhythm of the tool he was using, and the idioms of this life among the *signori*.

He had stripped off his shirt because the sun was hot, and after lopping away the twigs with a hatchet, had set to work sawing off the main branches. The wood was dry and easy enough to cut, but he was too eager and the saw jammed and twanged in his hand until, little by little, he fell into the knack of it, and the teeth bit cleanly into the wood while the sawdust spilled on to the leaves at his feet. He liked the sound of it and the smell of it and the salt taste of the sweat trickling down his face to the corners of his mouth.

It would have been pleasant to have Rosetta here to sit and talk with him and admire his skill, but she was not coming till tomorrow and then she would be in the kitchen with the cook, or dusting and polishing about the villa with the other maids. She would sleep in the women's quarters, sharing a bed with one of the young girls, while he would have his own place—a narrow cubbyhole next to the tool shed, with a straw mattress and a chair and a box with a candle on it. But they would meet at meals and walk out on Sundays, and perhaps at siesta time they might steal an hour together. He would feel better when she was there; less raw and less afraid of the Contessa, whom he had not met, and of the Englishman, whom he had met all too often.

Now that his secret was out and shared with the doctor, now that he knew more of his father, he felt safer, more his own man. To be a bastard was no longer a terrifying mystery, and to be attracted by the Englishman was not, it seemed, so strange a thing at all.

Perhaps even a way might be found to do the thing he wanted most of all: shake the dust of the village off his sandals and go to Rome, where the Pope lived and the President, and the streets were full of fountains and everyone had a car and the girls wore smart clothes and shoes and every house had running water and, sometimes, even a bath and a toilet. These were wonders about which the painter had spoken to him often, and their magic was still strong on him. He had made the first step. He had left the village and entered the green, enclosed world of the villa. Rome was so much nearer, so much more possible.

Thinking of Rome, he thought naturally of Nicholas Black, with his mocking eyes and his mouth twisted up in the smile that could make you feel either a man or a child, and could promise all kinds of revelations without a word spoken. The impression was so vivid that when a dry twig cracked behind him, he spun round, startled, expecting to see the Englishman behind him.

Instead it was the Contessa who stood there, bright as a butterfly, in a new spring frock, with a scarlet beach hat shading her face from the sun.

Not knowing what to do or say, he stood gape-mouthed, arms hanging slackly at his sides, feeling the sweat running down his face and chest, yet not daring to move and brush it away. Then she smiled at him and the smile was in her eyes, too.

"Did I startle you, Paolo?"

"A little," he mumbled awkwardly.

The Contessa came closer and looked around at the sawn wood.

"You've been working hard, I see. That's good. If you work well for me, Paolo, you'll never be sorry."

"I'll try, signora."

Her smile gave him confidence, and when she drew her skirts aside to sit down on the fallen trunk of the olive, he acted on a sudden impulse and spread his shirt on the rough bark.

"The tree's dirty, signora. You'd spoil your dress."

"Charming boy!" murmured Anne Louise de Sanctis. "That was the sort of thing your father would do. Did you know I knew your father?"

"Did my father work for you, too, signora?"

"Dear me, no!" She gave a high, tinkling laugh. "Your father was a friend of mine. He used to come here sometimes to visit me. He was a *signore—a gran' signore!*"

He felt a sudden pang of shame that he should be standing here, a servant, where his father had once walked as a guest of the house. Before he had time to answer, the Contessa went on.

"That's why I brought you here, for your father's sake. Mr Black tells me you're bright and learn things quickly. If that's true, we may be able to make you into a gentleman like your father."

There was no mention of his mother, he noticed, and once again he was ashamed of her, with her rough dialect and her coarse clothes and her bare dusty feet. He said quickly:

"I'd like that, signora. I'll work well, I promise." Then, made bold by her approving smile, he told her: "I don't know very much about my father. What was he like?"

"He was English," said the Contessa. "Like me, like Signor Black and the Monsignor from Rome."

"English!" He seemed not to believe the sound of his own voice. "That means I'm half-English too!"

"That's right, Paolo. Didn't your mother ever tell you?"

He shook his head.

"Didn't she ever say how much you were like him?"

"Sometimes. But not very often."

"That's another reason why I want you to do well here. I'll see that you go to school at Valenta, learn to read and write and speak properly, wear the right clothes. Then, perhaps, you can be my friend, too. Would you like that?"

"And could I go to Rome?"

"Of course!" She smiled at him. "You want that very much, don't you?"

"So much, signora!"

"I might ask Signor Black to take you there for a visit." She was still smiling at him but there was an odd warning in her eyes. Without quite knowing why, Paolo said quickly:

"I'd much rather go with you."

As he flung out his arms in the Southern gesture of appeal, she caught his hands and drew him down so that he was half kneeling, half squatting, at her feet. Her perfume was all about him and he could see her breasts rising and falling under the thin frock. She took his face in her hands and tilted it up towards her and said softly:

"Before I could do that, Paolo, I'd have to trust you. You'd have to know how to keep secrets. Not to gossip to the village people—not even to the Monsignor or Signor Black."

"I would, signora. I promise."

"Then we'll think about it, Paolo. But not a word—even to your mother."

"Not a word."

Her hands were soft and perfumed on his cheeks and he had the odd feeling that she wanted to bend down and kiss him;

206

but at the same moment there was the sound of a footfall behind them and the bland voice of Nicholas Black said:

"Really, *cara*! You're quite shameless! The boy hasn't lost his milk teeth and you're trying to seduce him already."

"You're a fine one to talk about seduction, Nicki!"

The words were English and Paolo did not understand them; but when he looked up at the thin satyr's face of the painter and the flushed angry one of the Contessa, he felt trapped— like a mouse in a corner with two cats ready to pounce.

Shortly after noon, Blaise Meredith returned to the villa to wash and rest awhile before luncheon. He was not unpleased with his morning's work. Meyer was a good witness and his recollections were dispassionate but vivid; so that, for the first time since his assignment began, Meredith was beginning to see Giacomo Nerone as a man and not a legend.

He would have preferred to lunch with Meyer, to have gone on talking about the next critical period in Nerone's life. But Meyer had not invited him, and Meredith sensed that he needed time to recover himself and privacy to begin his reading of the papers of the dead man.

As he lay back, resting on the bed, feeling the familiar ache in the pit of his belly, he wondered how he should comport himself at the meal with the Contessa and Nicholas Black. Now that he knew the Contessa for a liar and the pair of them for conspirators, his position was vastly distasteful to him. As a house-guest he was bound by discretion and courtesy. As a priest, he could not make himself, even by silence, a partner in the corruption of a child. As Devil's Advocate he came in search of evidence and he needed co-operation from his witnesses.

Once again, as it had done in the house of Father Anselmo, the case of Giacomo Nerone faded into unimportance. There were souls at stake, and if priesthood meant anything it meant the care of souls. A simple statement but a complex proposi- tion. One solved nothing by waving the commandments like a bludgeon at people's heads. There was no point in shouting damnation at a man who was already walking himself to hell on his own two feet. One had to pray for the Grace of God and then go probing like a good psychologist for the fear that might condition him to repentance or the love that might draw him towards it. Even then one had to wait for the place and the propitious moment—and one could still fail in the end. When one's own body was sick and one's mind preoccupied, the difficulty doubled itself.

When lunchtime came, he got up, combed his hair, put on a light summer cassock and walked down to the terrace under the striped awning. Nicholas Black was already seated alone at the table. He waved an airy greeting and said:

"The Contessa sends her apologies. She has a migraine. She'll lunch in her room. She hopes to see us both at dinner."

Meredith nodded and sat down, and immediately a servant spread his napkin and poured wine and iced water into the glasses before him.

"A good morning, Monsignor?" asked the painter.

"Very good. Very informative. Doctor Meyer's an excellent witness."

"A clever fellow. I'm amazed he hasn't done better for himself."

Meredith shrugged off the insinuation. He had no wish to be drawn into an argument with the *antipasto*. Black dug into his plate and sipped his wine and they ate in silence for a while. Then the painter asked again:

"How is your health, Monsignor?"

"Indifferent, I'm afraid. Meyer gives me a worse prognosis than I expected. Three months, he says."

"Do you have much pain?"

"Quite a lot."

"In three months," said the painter, "you'll hardly finish your case."

Meredith smiled ruefully.

"I'm afraid not. Fortunately the Church doesn't care to hurry these things. A century or two is neither here nor there."

"And yet I have the impression that you are anxious to get through with it."

"The witnesses are available," Meredith told him coolly. "Some of them are co-operative. The more testimony I can collect now the better for everybody. Besides . . ." He wiped a crumb from the corner of his pale mouth. "When your term has been set, you suddenly become aware of the shortness of it. 'The night comes, when no man can work.' "

"Are you afraid of death, Monsignor?"

"Who isn't?"

Black grinned at him sardonically.

"At least you're frank about it. Many of your colleagues aren't, you know."

"Many of them haven't yet had to face the reality," said Meredith tartly. "Have you?"

Black chuckled and took a long swallow of wine, then leaned back in his chair while the servant changed the dishes in front of him. He said in mock apology:

"I'm teasing you, Monsignor. Forgive me."

Meredith bent over his fish and said nothing. A few moments later, Paolo Sanduzzi came out of the shrubbery and walked across the lawn in the direction of the kitchen. The painter watched him, and Meredith watched the painter with a sidelong speculative eye. When the boy had disappeared round the angle of the house, Black turned back to the table and said casually:

"Charming boy. A classic David. Pity to think he'll go to seed in a village like this. I wonder the Church doesn't do something for him. You can't have the son of a *beato* chasing the girls and getting into trouble with the police like any other youth, can you?"

The bland effrontery of the man was too much for Meredith. He put down his knife and fork with a clatter, and said, with cold precision:

"If the boy is corrupted, Mr Black, you will be the one to do it. Why don't you go away and leave him alone?"

To his surprise the painter threw back his head and laughed.

"Meyer must have been a very good witness indeed, Monsignor. What else did he tell you about me?"

"Isn't that enough?" asked Meredith quietly. "You are

doing a detestable thing. Your private vices are a matter between you and the Almighty. But when you set out to corrupt this boy, you are committing a crime against nature. . . ."

The words were hardly out of his mouth before Black cut him short.

"You've judged me already, haven't you, Meredith? You've picked up every shred of filthy gossip round the village and damned me with it, before you've heard a word in my defence."

Meredith flushed. The accusation was uncomfortably close to the truth. He said quietly:

"If I've misjudged you, Mr Black, I'm deeply sorry. I'd be more than happy to hear you deny these—these rumours."

The painter laughed bitterly.

"You want me to defend myself to you? Damned if I'll do it, Monsignor. I'll take you on your own ground instead. Let's say I am what everybody calls me—an unnatural man, a corrupter of youth. What does the Church offer me by way of faith, hope or charity?" He stabbed a lean, accusing finger at the priest. "Let's understand each other, Meredith. You can bluff your penitents and charm your Sunday congregations, but you can't fool me! I've been a Catholic myself and I know the whole shoddy routine. You know why I left the Church? Because it answers every damn question in the book —except the one you need answering. . . . 'Why?' You tell me I'm committing a sin against nature because you think I'm fond of this boy and intend to get him. Let's examine that. If you can give me a satisfactory answer, I'll make you a promise, I'll pack my bags and leave here on the first available transport. Do you agree to that?"

"I can't bargain with you," said Meredith sharply, "I'll listen and I'll try to answer. That's all."

Nicholas Black laughed harshly.

"You're hedging already, you see. But I'll take you all the same. I know your whole argument on the question of the use and misuse of the body. God made it first for the procreation of children and then for the commerce of love between man and woman. That's the end. All its acts must conform to the end and all else is sin. The sin according to nature is an act in excess of the natural instinct ... like sleeping with a girl before you marry her, or lusting after another man's wife. To want a boy, in the same fashion, is a sin against nature. . . ." He grinned sardonically at the pale, intent face of the priest. "Do I surprise you, Meredith? I was stuffed full of Aquinas, too. But there's a catch, and here's what I want you to tell me. What about my nature? I was born the way I am. I was a twin. See my brother before he died and you'd have seen the perfect male—the excessive male, if you want. Me? . . . It wasn't quite clear what I was to be. But I knew soon enough. It was my nature to be drawn more to men than to women. I wasn't seduced in the shower-room or blackmailed in the bar. This is what I am. I can't change it. I didn't ask to be born. I didn't ask to be born like this—God knows I've suffered enough because of it. But who made me? According to you—God! What I want and what I do is according to the nature He gave me. . . ."

In the passion of the argument his attitude had changed from a sardonic insult to a plea for understanding. He himself was unconscious of it, but Meredith was quick to see it, and he was again ashamed of his own obtuseness. Here was the place and the moment made ready for him, but again, it seemed, for lack of wisdom and sympathy he had misused them. The painter plunged on, the words tumbling out of him in a bitter spate.

". . . Look at yourself! You're a priest. You know damn well that if I were setting out to seduce a girl at this moment instead of young Paolo, you'd take an entirely different view. You'd disapprove, certainly! You'd read me a lecture on fornication and all the rest. But you wouldn't be too unhappy. I'd be normal . . . according to nature! But I am not made like that. God didn't make me like that. But do I need love the less? Do I need satisfaction less? Have I less right to live in contentment because somewhere along the line the Almighty slipped a cog in creation? . . . What's your answer to that, Meredith? What's your answer for *me*? Tie a knot in myself and take up badminton and wait till they make me an angel in Heaven, where they don't need this sort of thing any more? . . . I'm lonely! I need love like the next man! My sort of love! Do I live in a padded cell till I die? You're the Church and the Church has all the answers! Give me this one!"

He broke off and sat, waiting, his silence a greater challenge to Meredith than the rush of his invective. Meredith stared down at the small chaos of crumbs on his plate and picked over the words to frame his answer. He tried to make a silent prayer for this soul, naked in front of him—but the prayer, like the argument he gave, seemed strangely arid and impotent. After a moment, he answered gravely:

"You tell me you've been a Catholic. Even if you weren't you'd understand the words and what they mean. To your problem—and to lots of others—there's no answer that doesn't involve a mystery and an Act of Faith. I can't tell you why God made you the way you are any more than I can tell you why he's planted a carcinoma in my stomach to make me die painfully while other men die peacefully in their sleep. The cogs of creation seem to slip all the time. Babies are born with two heads, mothers of families run crazy with carving knives, men die in plague, famine and thunderstorms. Why? Only God knows."

"If there is a God."

"I'll accept the 'if'," said Meredith, with quiet concern. "If there is no God, then the universe is a chaos with no meaning. You live in it as long and as pleasantly as you can, for the best you can get out of it. You take your Paolo and enjoy him—the police and social custom permitting. I can't quarrel with you. But if there is a God—and I believe there is—then . . ."

"Don't tell me the rest of it, Monsignor," said the painter bitterly. "I know it by heart. No matter what a bloody mess Creation gets into, you take it and like it; because that's a cross God lays on your back. If you take it long enough, they'll make you a saint like Giacomo Nerone. That's no answer, Meredith."

"Have you got a better one, Mr Black?"

"I have indeed. You keep your cross and your hair-shirt, Meredith. I'll take the cash in hand and waive the rest!"

He pushed back his chair, got up from the table, and without another word walked into the house. Blaise Meredith wiped his clammy hands on his napkin and took a sip of wine to moisten his dry lips. He was surprised to find it suddenly sour, like vinegar on a sponge.

CHAPTER TWELVE

EARLY THE same afternoon, in the small hut between the
ilexes, Nina Sanduzzi talked with the Monsignor from Rome.
They sat, one on either side of the rough scrubbed table,
half way between the open door and the big brass bed where
Giacomo Nerone had slept and where his son had been born.
After the blaze outside, the room was cool and shadowy
and even the chatter of the cicadas was muted to a half-heard
monotone.

The tramp down the hill had tired Meredith quickly; his
face was grey and his lips bloodless, and a small knot of pain
tightened in the pit of his stomach. Nina Sanduzzi looked at
him with faint pity. She had small experience of priests and
those she knew, like Father Anselmo, had little to recommend
them. But this one was different; he would have understanding and delicacy. He would not trespass too roughly on the
privacy of her past with Giacomo. Still, she was cautious, and
when he began to question her she answered briefly and without embellishment. Meredith for his own part was sedulously
delicate.

"I want you to understand something first: there are questions that must be asked. Some of them may seem strange—
even brutal. I ask them, not because I think ill of Giacomo
Nerone, but because we must try to know everything, good and
bad, about this man. Do you understand that, signora?"

She nodded calmly.

"Better you should call me by my name, Nina. The doctor
does and you are a friend of his."

"Thank you. Now, Nina, my information is that shortly
after his arrival in Gemello you and Giacomo Nerone began to
live together."

"We were lovers," said Nina Sanduzzi. "It's not quite the
same thing."

Meredith, the legalist, smiled, where once he might have frowned. He went on.

"You were a Catholic, Nina. So was Giacomo. Didn't you think this was a sin against God?"

"When you are lonely, Monsignor, when there is fear just outside the door, and the winter is coming and tomorrow you may not be alive, you think of these things and you forget about sin."

"You can never quite forget."

"Not quite. But when these things happen so often—even to priests—they do not look so bad."

Meredith nodded. A week ago, he might have understood less and said more. Now he knew that the heart had deeper reasons than most preachers ever knew. He asked again:

"Your relations with this man—your physical relations— were they normal? Did he ever ask you for what should not be done between men and women?"

She stared at him in momentary puzzlement. Then her head went up proudly.

"We loved each other, Monsignor. We did what lovers do and were glad of each other. What else could there be?"

"Nothing," said Meredith hastily. "But if you loved each other so much, why didn't you marry? You were having a child. Did you owe nothing to him? What did Giacomo think?"

For the first time since he had known her, he saw a smile brighten on her lips and in her eyes. It was like an echo of the old Nina—the one who had wanted a man to hold in her arms and was prepared to face the executioner to get him. She told him in vivid, slangy dialect:

"You all ask the same question—as if it were big and important instead of a wart on a green melon. You don't understand how it was in those days. Only today was certain. Tomorrow the police might come or the Germans or the English. We could all die of the *tifo* or of malaria. A ring on your finger meant nothing. I had a ring, but I had no man to go with it."

"Did Giacomo refuse to marry you?"

"I never asked him. More than once he told me he would marry me if I wanted it."

"And you didn't want it?"

Once again the old fire flickered in her eyes, and the proud Greek smile twitched at the corners of her mouth.

"You still don't see it, Monsignor. I had a husband once. I wanted to hold him and the Army took him away to be killed. Now I had a man. If he wanted to go—he would go and no ring would keep him. If the police took him or the soldiers, he would still be lost to me. Marriage might come later, if ever it were important enough. Besides, there was another thing Giacomo talked about often. . . ."

"What was that?"

"He had it fixed in his head that one day, soon, something would happen to him. He was a deserter and if the English won the war they would take him. The Fascisti were active still and they might take him. Or the Germans. If they did, I would never know whether he was alive or dead. He wanted me to be free to marry again. Free to disown him so that they could not punish me and the child."

"Was that important to you, Nina?"

"To me, no. But to him, yes. If it made him happy to feel that, I was happy too. Nothing else mattered. Have you never been in love, Monsignor?"

"Never, I'm afraid." Meredith's thin lips puckered into a smile. "You'll have to be patient with me. . . . Tell me, when you were living together, what sort of a man was Giacomo? Was he good to you?"

It was almost eerie to see how memory flooded back on her and how her whole body seemed to come alive like a flower in the rain. Even in her voice there was a kind of splendour.

"What sort of man? . . . How do you expect me to answer that, Monsignor? Everything a woman wants was in this man. He was strong in bed and yet gentle as a babe. He could be angry so that you trembled at the silence of him and yet he never lifted his hand or raised his voice. When I served him, he was grateful and thanked me as if I were a princess. When I was afraid, he would make me laugh and when he laughed it was like the sun coming up in the morning. He was afraid of nobody and nothing except that I should be hurt. . . ."

"And yet," said Meredith, with calculated bluntness, "he left you in your pregnancy and never lived with you again."

Her head came up, proud as a marble goddess in the sun.

"We lived in love and we parted in love—and there was never a day afterwards that I did not love him. . . ."

. . . Winter fretted itself out in a long alternation of storms and frozen calms. In the village and in the mountains there was much sickness. Some died and some recovered—but slowly, because of the damp and the foulness of the closed hovels and because food was getting scarcer every day.

Once there was an epidemic in which people came out in spots and had sore eyes and a fever. Nina herself fell sick of it, and she remembered the doctor and Giacomo talking gravely in the corner about something they called *rubella*. But she got better soon and thought no more of it.

Even Giacomo Nerone was showing the strain of the long, cold time. The flesh was being honed off his big frame; his dark, stubbled cheeks were hollow and his eyes were sunken and burning when he trudged home from a day in the hills.

Nina, with the constant nausea and tiredness that comes to some women in early pregnancy, found the monotony of the food revolted her, and as her body thickened slowly, she was even disinclined for the love-making in which formerly she had taken so much and such frank delight. Both these things troubled her. A man was a man and he demanded to be soothed and satisfied, however his woman felt. But Giacomo was different from the men of her own people. He was gentle with her when she was sick. He made, with his own hands, food to tempt her. If she was unready for him, he would not force himself on her, and in the long mourning nights of the storm he would distract her with stories of strange places and people and cities piled like blocks almost to the sky.

She loved him the more for his attentions because she knew he had his own troubles: problems that kept him wakeful at night and preoccupied in the daytime. Sometimes he would talk them out with her, fumbling for the right phrase in dialect to explain his meaning. In this, too, he was different from

her own menfolk, who took their counsel in the wine shop and
not from their wives, because a woman was supposed to know
nothing but the house and the bed and the simpler aspects of
religion. But Giacomo talked freely, so that she felt strong and
wise with him.

"Listen, Nina *mia*, you know how it is sometimes, that a
man does a thing and his woman hates him, because she doesn't
understand why?"

"I know, *caro mia*, but I understand you. So why should you
worry?"

"Whatever I did, you would still love me?"

"Always."

"Then listen now, Nina. Don't stop me talking, because
this is hard to say. When I'm finished tell me if you don't
understand. For a long time now I've been a lost man. I've
been like a Calabrese standing in the middle of Rome and asking everyone: 'Who am I? Where did I come from? Where
am I going?' No one answers him, of course, because they
don't understand him. . . . And even if they did, he wouldn't
understand because he doesn't speak with a Roman tongue. It
wasn't always like this. There was a time when I was like you.
I knew that I came from God and would go back to Him in the
end, that I could talk to Him in the Church and take Him to
myself in Communion. I could do wrong and still be forgiven.
I could stray a little and still come back to the straight road.
. . . Then, suddenly, there was no road. There was darkness
and voices shouting at me: This way! That way! I followed the
voices into a deeper darkness and then there were other voices.
But no road—I was lost. There was no God, no Church, no
place to go in the end. I was your Calabrese shouting in a city
of strangers. . . . When this thing happened to me in Messina I
could not be like other men and say: 'This is war! This is the
price of peace! I will forget about it and go on fighting for
what I believe.' I didn't believe in anything—in war, in peace,
in anything at all! There was just a child, a woman and an old
man whom I had killed for no good reason at all. . . . Then I
began to run, and suddenly, without knowing why or how, I am
here with you—home again. But nothing is quite the same. I

am changed. It is not dark any more but misty, like the valley in the first grey of morning. I see you and I know you and love you, because you are near and you love me, too. But outside the door there is the mist and the strangeness. Even the people are different. They look at me with wondering eyes. For no reason that I know, I am a big fellow to them. They depend on me. I am their Calabrese who has been to the big city and seen it all, who knows the Pope and the President and the way to get things done. I am their man of confidence. I should be proud of this, but I am not, because I am walking in the mist, still uncertain where I came from and where I am going and what I should do. . . . Can you understand me, Nina? Or am I talking like a crazy man?"

"You are talking to me with love, *caro mio*, and my heart understands."

"Will you understand what I am going to ask you?"

"When you hold me like this and I can feel the love in your hands and in your voice, nothing is hard."

"It is hard for me to tell you. . . . When the spring comes and life is easier, I want to leave you—go away for a while."

"No, *caro mio*!"

"Not from the valley. From this house."

"But why, *caro mio*? Why?"

"There are two reasons and the first is mine. I want to find myself a small secret place—build it, if I must, with my own two hands. I want to live there alone with this God whose face I cannot see any more. I want to say to him: 'Look, I am lost. It's my own fault, but I am lost. If You are there, speak to me clearly. Show me who I am, where I come from, where I am going. These people of Yours who know You—why do they turn to me and not to You to help them? Is there a mark on my forehead I cannot read? If there is, tell me what it means. . . .' I must do this, *cara*."

"And what about me and your child?"

"I will be here all the time. I will see you often and if God speaks to me, I will speak to Him for you—because if He knows anything at all, He knows I love you."

"And yet you go away?"

"There is love in this, too, Nina—more love than you know. And there is great reason in it, too. When spring comes the armies will be on the move again. The Germans will come first and there will be fighting south of here. The Partisans will move in to harry the Germans, and the Allies must in the end push them back. Some of these or all of them will come, in their turns, to Gemello. I will come under their notice because of what I am—Giacomo Nerone, the man of confidence, the big, black one. If I am lucky, they will accept me and I can help the people. If I am not, one or other of them will take me—and possibly kill me."

"*Dio!* No!"

"It may happen, Nina. It may be this is what lies behind the mists and that I will see at the one time the face of God and the face of the executioner. I don't know. But, whatever happens, when spring comes we must be separate. You cannot be involved with me, because there is the child. If I am taken, Meyer will look after you. If not, I shall be here to look after you. And if it falls well, I shall marry you and give the boy my name. You are both mine and I love you and I will not let you suffer for me or the people."

"I will suffer anyway, when you are not here."

"Less that way than the other, Nina. There will be so much hate, you will not believe it possible. I've seen it all before and it is very terrible."

"Hold me, *caro mio*! Hold me, I'm afraid."

"Lie on my arm, *carissima*, and hear my heart beating. I'm your man of confidence, too, and you can sleep safe."

"Now, perhaps—but when you are gone?"

"I shall never be wholly gone, Nina *mia*. Never, til eternity. . . ."

. . . The Biblical simplicity of her narrative was more compelling than any rhetoric, and Blaise Meredith, the dry man from the Congregations, found himself hurried along by it like a twig in a torrent. Even through the harsh dialect the dialogue rang like a poet's lines in the mouth of a lover—long cherished and long remembered. Behind them the face of Giacomo

Nerone took shape and hardened into reality—a lean, dark, suffering face, with a tender mouth and deep eyes suffused with gentleness. The face of a searcher—one of those on whom is laid the burden of mysteries and who come sometimes to a great holiness.

But this was not enough for the grey lawyers at the Congregation of Rites, the inquisitors at the Holy Office. They must see more than this, and Blaise Meredith must give it to them. So, more gently, but no less persistently, he questioned Nina Sanduzzi again:

"When did he leave you?"

"After the thaw, when the spring was breaking."

"And up till the time he left, he slept with you—made love to you?"

"Yes. Why?"

"Nothing. It is a question that must be asked." But what he did not say to her was what it proved to him. This was still a man in the dark, a searcher, perhaps, but one who had not yet found his God, nor made the act of abandonment to His will. There was love in him, but it was yet only a defaced symbol of the love which is the beginning of sanctity.

"And when he left, what then?"

"He went up into the neck of the valley where the caves are and began to build his hut. While it was building, he slept in a cave and cooked his own food and in the daytime did what he had done in the winter—travelled the valley, working for those who could not work, looking after the sick, bringing food to those who needed it."

"Did you see him during this time?"

"He came every day, as he promised."

"Was he changed at all?"

"To me? No. Except that he was more gentle and more careful of me."

"Did he make love to you?"

Once again she smiled at him with that faint pity for his clerical ignorance.

"I was big with the child, Monsignor. I was calm and content . . . and he did not ask it."

"Had he changed in himself?"

"Yes. He was thinner than I had ever seen him. His eyes were sunk right back in his head and his skin was stretched tight over the bones of his face. But he was always smiling and much happier than I had known him."

"Did he say why?"

"At first, no. Then one day he took my hands in his and said: 'I'm home, Nina. I'm home again.' He had been over to Gemello Maggiore to make his confession to young Father Mario and on the Sunday he told me he was going to Communion. He asked if I would go to church the same day."

"And did you?"

"No. On the Saturday the Germans arrived and made their headquarters in the villa. . . ."

. . . They came, early in the morning, while the village was still rubbing the sleep out of its eyes. There was an armoured car, with a sergeant driver and a worried-looking captain sitting in the back. There were two truckloads of troops and a fourth vehicle loaded with ammunition and supplies. They churned up the dusty road with engines roaring, checked a little in the narrow street of the village with a clatter of gears and some strange cursing, then headed straight up the last hill to the villa of the Contessa de Sanctis.

Nina Sanduzzi heard them come, but paid small attention. She was still heavy with sleep, wrapped in the remote contemplation of a woman who feels the first life stirring inside her. She did not wake fully until she heard the urgent knocking on the door and Aldo Meyer's voice calling her to open it.

When she let him in, she was surprised to see him dressed for the road, with heavy boots and a sheepskin jacket and a pack hitched on to his shoulders. First he asked her to feed him, and while she bustled to do it talked to her in swift, terse sentences—half fearful, half elated.

"When you see Giacomo tell him I've pulled out. The Germans are here and it won't be long before they hear there's a Jew in the valley. If they catch me, I'll be shipped north to the concentration camps. I'm taking my instruments and some medicines, but I've left a stock for Giacomo in the big box under my bed."

"But where are you going, Dottore?"

"Farther east, into the hills, towards San Bernardino. It's a Partisan hideout and I've been in contact with them for some time. Their leader's a man who calls himself Il Lupo. I think he came from the North especially for this job. He has the look of a trained man. He has guns and ammunition and a good system of communication. If Giacomo wants to get in touch with me, tell him to go out along the San Bernardino road for about ten kilometres, then turn off at the place they call Satan's Rock. That's where the first Partisan sentries are. He's to climb to the top of the rock, sit down and light a cigarette—then take his handkerchief and knot it round his neck. Someone will come out to make contact with him. Have you got that? It's important. If he forgets, he's liable to get shot."

"I won't forget."

She laid coffee and bread and cheese in front of him, and while he ate she made a parcel of food and stuffed it into his knapsack. It was only when she saw the pistol and felt the hard shapes of the ammunition clips that she understood what Giacomo had told her. The war was coming to Gemello Minore and all the hate and killing, too.

With his mouth full of bread and cheese, Meyer said to her:

"I tried to get Giacomo to come with me and bring you too. The Germans won't be much kinder to him than to me. He could be shot as a spy."

"What did Giacomo say to that?"

"Just laughed and told me he knew the Germans better than I did. I hope he's right. What time do you usually see him?"

She shrugged and made a vague gesture with her hands.

"It changes. Sometimes early in the day, sometimes late. But he always comes."

Meyer looked at her quizzically over the rim of his cup.

"Are you happy with this arrangement, Nina?"

"I'm happy with Giacomo. There was never another man like this."

Meyer smiled sourly.

"You could be right at that. Do you know what he does up there in his hut?"

"He prays. He thinks. He works in his garden . . . when he isn't working for someone else or out among the hills. Why do you ask?"

"I went up there the other night to look for him and talk about this thing. I called to him, but there was no answer although his lamp was burning. I went inside and found him kneeling in the middle of the floor with his arms stretched out. His eyes were closed and his head was thrown back and his lips were moving. I spoke to him and he didn't hear me. I went up and shook him, but his body was quite rigid. I couldn't budge him. After a while I went away."

There was no surprise in her dark eyes. She nodded and answered quite casually:

"He told me he prays a lot."

"And doesn't eat very much either," said Meyer with faint irritation.

"That, too. He's got very thin. But he says the praying gives him what strength he needs."

"He should take more care of himself. Lots of people depend on him. They're going to depend more now that the Germans are here. This prayer business is all right in its way —but men go crazy with too much of it."

"Do you think Giacomo's crazy?"

"I didn't say that. He's strange, that's all."

"Perhaps it's because there aren't so many good men around. We've forgotten what they look like."

Meyer chuckled and wiped his lips with the back of his hand.

"You could be right, Nina *mia*." He stood up and hoisted his pack on to his shoulders. "Well, I must be moving. Thanks for the breakfast and the other stuff. Tell Giacomo what I said."

"I'll tell him."

He put his hands on her shoulders and kissed her on the lips. She did not resist because she liked him and he was a man going off to his own private war.

"Good luck, Dottore!"

"Good luck, Nina *mia*. You deserve it!"

She stood at the door and watched him scrambling down the valley. She thought he had never looked so young nor so alive, and she wondered idly what would have happened if Giacomo had not come to Gemello Minore.

But Giacomo was there and his presence filled all her life, and when he came just before lunchtime she clung to him desperately, crying on his shoulder. He held her there until the strain went out of her; then he disengaged her gently and listened while she told him about Aldo Meyer and his message. He listened gravely and then said:

"I tried to talk him out of it. These Germans are nothing—a patrol detachment, nothing more. They won't bother anyone very much. But Meyer's been waiting so long for his own war he can't see what he's in for."

"It will probably be good for him, *caro mio*. I saw him go and he was happy as a boy going to hunt."

Nerone shook his head gravely and his face clouded.

"Meyer is the wrong man for this company. I've heard about Il Lupo and I can guess where he comes from. He's a professional and he's been trained in Russia. He wants more than a victory. He wants a Communist State in Italy. When the Germans are pushed out and the Allies move in, he'll bid for control of the civil administration. On their record, he'll probably get it. Meyer's in the wrong boat. He thinks Il Lupo wants another gun. What he wants is a man to use afterwards. I wonder what will happen when Meyer finds out." He shrugged and smiled and spread his hands palm-downwards on the table. "Anyway, it's done now. We've got our own work to do here."

She brought a big bowl of pasta to the table and stood over him while he ate it, noting how sparing he was, and how little relish he took in the spicy sauce.

"And what are you going to do, Giacomo?"

"What I'm doing now—except that I've had to bring the Germans into my calculations. I went up to see the Contessa a couple of days ago."

It was something he had not told her and she felt a sharp pang of jealousy. It was as if she saw him stepping back into a world he had left—a world where he had been lost and where she could never reach him. But she said nothing and waited for him to tell her the rest of it.

"I told her I was English. I didn't tell her but I let her think I was an agent, moved in here to prepare the way for the Allies. She was glad to see me. She's in an awkward position. I suggested she nominate me steward of her estate so that I can talk on fairly equal terms with the German commander. She's given me a room in the servants' quarters."

"You're going to live at the villa?"

"I have a room there. I'll sleep there when I must. But I'll get a pass from the commander and I'll be free to come and go. I'll need that. The whole villa has been turned into an armed camp."

"Nice for the Contessa!" she told him with sudden viciousness. "She'll be able to have a new man every night."

Nerone's face clouded. He reached out and took her hands and drew her gently towards him.

"Let's not say that, *carissima*. She's a strange, lonely woman, with a fire in the blood that no man has yet been able to put out. That's a torment and not a joke. Why should we cock our fingers at her when we have so much?"

"She eats men, *caro mio*. And I don't want her to eat you."

"She'll get indigestion if she tries it," he told her with a smile.

But when he was gone the fear was still with her, and often she would wake in the night, dreaming that Giacomo had left her and was married to the woman on top of the hill with her flat, childless belly and her pinched mouth and her predatory eyes. . . .

. . . "There is another thing I must ask," said Blaise Meredith, in his dry voice. "During this time, did Giacomo perform any religious duties? Did he go to mass and the Sacraments?"

Nina Sanduzzi nodded.

226

"Whenever he could—except when there were sick in the mountains, or lost men to be hidden away from the Germans. He used to go to the Mass here on Sundays and I would see him, though it was an arrangement that we would not sit together nor greet each other, because some of the Germans were there. They came, it seems, from a part of Germany where there are many Catholics. When he wanted to go to confession he would walk across the valley to young Father Mario."

"But not to Father Anselmo."

She shook her head.

"Father Anselmo didn't like him. Sometimes there were angry words between them, when Father Anselmo refused to go out to the sick, after curfew."

"And what did Giacomo say about Father Anselmo?"

"That he was to be pitied and prayed for—but that the men who sent him here would have a heavy judgment. He used to say that *Gesù* had built the Church like a house for his family to live in, but that some men—even priests—used it like a market and a wine shop. He said they made trade out of it and filled it with quarrels and shouting and even fouled the floor like drunken men do. He said if it were not for the love of *Gesù* and the care of the Holy Spirit, it would fall into ruin in a generation. He said that was what every house needed—much love and little argument. And he was right."

"I know he was," said Meredith. And wondered that his voice sounded so vehement. "Now tell me, what did Giacomo say and feel about the Germans?"

For the first time, the question seemed to give her pause. She thought about it a long moment and then she said:

"This was a thing he talked about often, and sometimes I found it hard to understand him. He would say that countries are like men and women and that people take the character of the country they live in. Each country has its own special sin and its special virtue. The English were a sentimental people, but tough and selfish with it, because they lived on an island and wanted to keep it for themselves as they had always done. They were polite. They had much justice, but little charity.

When they fought, they fought stubbornly and bravely, but they always forgot that many of their wars had sprung from their own selfishness and indifference. The Americans were different. They were sentimental and tough, too, but they were simpler than the English, because they were younger and richer. They liked to possess things, even though they often did not know how to enjoy them. They were, like all young men, inclined to violence. They could easily be deceived by loud voices and magnificence. And they often deceived themselves, because they like the sound of words, even if they did not understand their meaning. The Germans were something else again. They were hard workers, lovers of order and efficiency and very proud. But there was a grossness in them and a violence that was released by liquor and big speeches and the need to assert themselves. Giacomo used to laugh and say that they liked to feel God rumbling in their bellies when a big music played. . . ."

"Was that all?"

"No. Giacomo liked to talk like that. He said you had to skim the grease off the soup or it would go sour. But he always came back to the same thing: no matter what people were like —or countries—they had to live together like a family. This was how God made them; and if a brother waved a gun at his brother, they would end by destroying each other. There were times when each had to swallow his pride and give way—be polite when he felt like spitting in someone's eye. And that was how he tried to live with the Germans here."

"Did he succeed?"

"I think so. We lived in peace. We were not robbed. A girl could walk safely to the cistern and home again. Sometimes there were killings when the Partisans met a German patrol— but that was always away from Gemello. There was a curfew and we stayed inside at night. If there were quarrels, Giacomo talked to the commander and the thing was worked out. After a while, the Germans went away, moving down to the south, and the Partisans followed them, as wolves follow the sheep in the Abruzzi."

"And afterwards?"

"In May we heard the news that Rome had fallen to the Allies, and early in June Paolo was born—and he was born blind. . . ."

. . . The first warnings came late one morning while Giacomo was with her. They were light and uncertain, but Giacomo was so concerned that he insisted on calling Carla Carrese, the midwife, and Serafina Gambinelli and Linda Tesoriero. They came running and clamouring because he was so urgent with them; but when they saw that she was still on her feet and in no trouble at all, they all stood around with their hands on their hips and laughed at him. Nina laughed too, and was surprised to see the cloud of anger that darkened his face. His voice was angry too and he snapped at them.

"You're fools—all of you! Stay with her and don't leave her. I'm going to get Doctor Meyer."

They gaped at him then, and even Nina was amazed, because this business of bearing a child was a woman's affair. Doctors were for sick people and they knew that, if everything went well, childbirth was a simple if noisy business, with a lot of joy to follow it. But before they had time to tell him all this, Giacomo was gone, a lean, ominous figure, thrusting up the track towards the San Bernardino road.

Nina was concerned for him because of the long distance; but the women soon laughed her out of it. The child would arrive before he got back, they told her; and he and the doctor could get drunk together as good friends should when one of them has fathered a bouncing *bambino*.

They were half right at least. The babe was born and washed, wrapped and laid in her arms an hour before Giacomo arrived with Aldo Meyer. But they did not act like other men at a birth. Giacomo kissed her and held her in his arms for a long time. Aldo Meyer kissed her, too, lightly, like a brother. Then Giacomo lifted the child from her arms and carried him over to the table and held the lamp while Meyer sounded the heart and peered into the ears and lifted the tiny eyelids and bent closer and closer to examine them.

The midwife and the women stood in a small group by the

bed, and Nina hoisted herself up on to the pillows to ask fearfully:

"What's the matter with him? What are you looking for?"

"Tell her," said Aldo Meyer.

"He's blind, *cara*," said Giacomo Nerone gently. "He was born with cataracts growing on his eyes. It was the fever you had, the illness with the spots, which is called *rubella*. A woman who gets it the second or third month sometimes bears a blind child or a deaf one."

It was perhaps half a minute before his meaning reached her. Then she screamed like an animal and buried her face in the pillow while the women huddled about her like hens, clucking to comfort her. After a time, Giacomo came to her and put the child in her arms and tried to talk to her, but she turned her face away from him, because she was ashamed to have given a maimed child to the man she loved so much.

Then a long while later the women went away and Giacomo came back to her with Aldo Meyer. She was calmer now and Meyer talked to her soberly.

"This is a sad thing, Nina; but it has happened and, for the present, it cannot be altered. If things were different, I could take you down to the hospital at Valenta and then, maybe, to Naples to see a specialist and find out if anything can be done. But the war is not over yet. There is still fighting and the roads are cluttered with refugees. Broken German units are fighting their way home and the Partisans are out after them. Naples is a shambles and you would be just another peasant with no one to help her. Giacomo is a wanted man and I am committed to my band in the mountains. So, for the present, there is nothing to do but wait. When there is peace again, we shall see what can be done."

"But the boy is blind!" It was all she could think or say.

"The maimed ones need much love," said Aldo Meyer.

Giacomo Nerone said nothing at all; but her heart almost broke at the grief and the pity in his eyes. Meyer went on talking to her in his gentle, professional fashion, showing her the growths on the child's eyes, making some kind of reason out of the first terror. Giacomo poured wine for them all and then set about preparing a meal. The two men ate it at the table, while Nina held the bowl on her lap and talked to them from the bed. When the child whimpered, she put it to the breast, and when the small, blind bundle nuzzled against her, she found herself weeping silently.

Meyer left before midnight to sleep in his own house, safe at last from the threat of the concentration camp. When Giacomo took him to the door, Nina was dozing, but she heard Giacomo's voice say sharply:

"You're a friend of mine, Meyer, and I understand, even if I don't agree. But keep Lupo away from the village. Keep him away from me."

And Meyer's voice in the terse reply:

"This is history, man! You can't stop it. I can't either! Someone's got to start organising . . ."

The rest of it was lost as they moved to the door and into the clear night. A few minutes later Giacomo came back and bolted the door behind him. He said quietly:

"You can't be alone tonight, *cara*. I'll stay with you."

Then all the disappointment welled up like a spring inside her and she clung to him, sobbing as if her heart were broken, as indeed it nearly was.

Then, when she was calm again, Giacomo settled her on the pillows and turned the lamp low, and through half-closed eyes she saw him do a strange thing. Quite unselfconsciously, he knelt down on the earthen floor, closed his eyes and stretched out his arms like the arms of *Gesù* on the cross, while his lips moved in soundless prayer. There was a moment when his whole body seemed to become rigid, like a tree, and when she called out in fright he did not hear her. She lay back watching him until exhaustion overcame her, and she slid into sleep.

When she woke, the room was full of sunlight and the baby was bawling lustily and Giacomo was boiling the coffee pot for breakfast. He came and kissed her and lifted the child in his arms and said gravely:

"I want to tell you something, Nina *mia*."

"Tell me."

"We will name the boy Paolo."

"He's your son, Giacomo. You must name him—but why Paolo?"

"Because Paolo, the Apostle, was a stranger to God, and, like me, found Him on the road to Damascus. Because, like this boy, Paolo was blinded but saw again, through the mercy of God."

She stared at him in disbelief.

"But the doctor said . . ."

"I am telling you, *cara*." His voice was strong and deep as a bell. "The boy will see. The cataracts will disappear in three weeks; when a baby should begin to see the light, our Paolo will see too. You will hold the lamp in front of his eyes and watch how he blinks and begins to follow it. I promise you, in the name of God."

"Don't tell me that just to comfort me, *caro*. I could not bear to hope and be cheated at the end." There was an agony in her voice, but he only smiled at her.

"It's not a hope, Nina *mia*. It's a promise. Believe it."

"But how do you know? How can you be sure?"

All he said was:

"When it happens, Nina, let it appear like news to you, too. Tell nobody about this morning. Will you promise me?"

She nodded dumbly, wondering how she could bear the waiting and hide the doubt she felt.

Three weeks later, to the day and the hour, she took the child from his cradle and wakened him. When he opened his eyes, they were clear and shining like his father's, and when she held him to the light he blinked. She shaded it with her hand and his eyes stared steadily, then blinked again when she took her hand away.

The wonder of the moment was like a revelation. She wanted to shout and sing and go calling down the village street to tell them all that Giacomo's promise had come true.

But Giacomo was already dead and buried. The village folk turned away in shame as she passed. Even Aldo Meyer had gone to Rome, and she thought he would never come back. . . .

. . . "I should go home now," said Monsignor Blaise Meredith. "It's late and you've given me a lot to think about."

"Do you believe what I have told you, Monsignor?"

Her voice and her eyes challenged him, calmly. He looked at her for a long moment, and then he said, with a curious finality:

"Yes, Nina. I don't know what it means yet. But I do believe you."

"Then you will look after Giacomo's boy, and keep him safe?"

"I'll look after him." But even as he said it, his conscience challenged him: How? In God's name, how?

CHAPTER THIRTEEN

FOR DOCTOR ALDO MEYER, evening was closing in on an afternoon of strange calm.

Immediately after luncheon he had sat down to read the papers of Giacomo Nerone. He had come to them hesitant and afraid, as if to a moment of crisis or revelation. But when he opened them and set them in order and began to read the bold cursive hand, it was like hearing the old challenging arguments of Giacomo himself.

There were moments of shame at his own failures, moments of poignant recollection, of nostalgia for a relationship that had begun in conflict, had come at times close to friendship and was soon to end in tragedy. But there was no bitterness in the record—as there had never been bitterness in Giacomo himself. There were passages of childlike simplicity that touched Meyer almost to tears, and phrases of mystical exaltation that left him groping, as Giacomo had often done, for the explanation of his own bankruptcy.

But at the end there was peace and calm and certainty, which communicated itself to the reader even after the lapse of years. And in the last writing of all, the letter to Aldo Meyer, there was a great gentleness and a singular grace of forgiveness. The rest of the papers were in English, but the letter was in Italian and this, too, was a delicacy not to be lightly forgotten:

My dear Aldo,

I am at home and it is late. Nina is asleep at last and the boy is sleeping, too. Before I go in the morning, I shall leave this note with her, among my other papers, and, when it is all over and the first grief has passed, perhaps it will come safely into your hands.

We shall be meeting tomorrow, you and I, but as strangers, each committed to an opposite belief and an opposite practice.

You will sit with my judges and walk with my executioners, and sign the certificate of my death, when it is all done.

I blame you for none of this. Each of us can walk only the path he sees at his own feet. Each of us is subject to the consequences of his own belief—though I think one day you will come to believe differently. If you do, you will hate what has been done, and you may be tempted to hate yourself for your part in it, the more because there will be no one to whom you can say you are sorry.

So I want to tell you now I do not hate you. You have been my friend and a friend of Nina and the child. I hope you will always lean to them and care for them. I know you have loved Nina. I think you still do. And this will be another cross on your back, because you will never be sure whether, in joining yourself to my condemnation, you have done it from belief or jealousy. But I know and I tell you now that I shall die still counting you my friend.

Now there is a service I want to lay on you. When you get this letter, will you go to Father Anselmo and to Anne de Sanctis and tell each of them that I bear them no grudge for what they have done and that, when I come to God, as I hope I may, I shall remember them both.

So, *dottore mio*, I leave you. It is not long till the dawn and I am cold and afraid. I know what must happen and my flesh crawls with terror at the thought of it. I have no strength left and I must pray awhile. It is a thing I have always desired, the grace to die with dignity, but never, till now, have I understood how hard it is.

Goodbye, my friend. God keep us both in the dark time.

Giacomo Nerone

When Meyer read the letter for the third time, he had been moved to rare tears, but when he had walked awhile and pondered it and read it again, the charity of it lay on him like an absolution. If he had failed in all else—and his failures were written large on the calendar of fifteen years—he would not die unloved or unforgiven. And this was the answer to the question that had plagued him so long: why great men die and drop out of creation without a ripple of care for them, and the memory of others is cherished in the secret hearts of the humble.

The thought lingered with him through the fall of the afternoon, and it was still expanding itself when the knock came at the door and he opened it to find Blaise Meredith standing outside.

The priest's appearance shocked him. His face was ashen, his lips bloodless, and small beads of sweat stood out on his forehead and on his upper lip. His hands were shaky and his voice husky and trembling.

"I'm sorry to bother you, Doctor. I wonder if I could rest awhile with you."

"Of course, man! Come in, for God's sake! What's happened to you?"

Meredith smiled wanly.

"Nothing's happened. I'm on my way back from Nina's place. But it's a long scramble before you get to the road, and it was just a little too much. I'll be all right in a minute!"

Meyer led him into the house, made him lie down on the bed and then brought him a stiff pot of *grappa*.

"Drink that. It's foul stuff, but it will put some life into you."

Meredith choked on the raw spirit, but he got it down and after a few moments he began to feel the warmth spreading out and the strength returning to his limbs. Meyer stood looking down at him with grave eyes.

"You worry me, Meredith. This sort of thing can't go on. I'm half inclined to get in touch with the Bishop and have you sent to hospital."

"Give me a few more days, Doctor. After that, it won't matter so much."

"You're a very sick man. Why drive yourself like this?"

"I'll be a long time dead. Better to burn out than rust out."

Meyer shrugged despairingly.

"It's your life, Monsignor. Tell me—how did you get on with Nina?"

"Very well. I'm deeply impressed by what she's told me. But there are a couple of questions I'd like to clear up with you —if you don't mind, that is."

236

"Ask what you like, my friend. I've gone too far to draw back now."

"Thank you. Here's the first one. Was there an outbreak of German measles here in the winter of 1943? And was Paolo Sanduzzi born blind because of it?"

"Yes."

"How long was it before you saw the child again?"

"Three years—no, nearer to four. I went away to Rome, you see."

"When you came back, the boy could see?"

"Yes. The cataracts had disappeared."

"Medically speaking, was this strange?"

"Quite abnormal. I'd never known another case."

"Did you remark on it to Nina Sanduzzi?"

"Yes. I asked her how and when it had happened."

"What did she say?"

"She just shrugged and said, the way the peasants do . . . 'It just happened.' Our relations then weren't as good as they are now. I didn't press the point. But it puzzled me. It still does. Why do you ask, Monsignor?"

"Nina told me that, on the day of the birth, after you had left, Giacomo had prayed all night—and that, in the morning, he had promised her that the baby would see normally, when other children did—three weeks later. According to her that's just what happened. The cataracts were gone. The child could distinguish light and shadow. And afterwards the sight developed as it did in other children. What would be your opinion of that, Doctor?"

But Meyer did not answer him immediately. He seemed lost in a new thought of his own. When he spoke it was as if to himself:

"So that's what she meant when she said Giacomo had done miracles and that she had seen them."

"When did she say that?" Meredith prompted him sharply.

"When we were discussing your arrival, and I was trying to persuade her to talk to you."

"Would you say she was telling the truth?"

"If she said it," Meyer answered him sombrely, "it was the truth. She would not lie to save her life."

"What would be your medical opinion?"

"At first blush I would say it couldn't happen."

"But it did. The boy is seeing today."

Meyer gave him a long, searching look; then smiled and shook his head.

"I know what you want me to say, Meredith, but I can't say it. I don't believe in miracles, only in unexplained facts. All I can admit is that this doesn't normally happen. I might go further and say I've never heard of another case like it, that I don't know of any medical explanation for it. But I'm not prepared to make a leap in the dark and tell you this is a miracle caused by divine intervention."

"I'm not asking you to say that," said Meredith good humouredly. "I'm asking you whether you can explain it medically."

"I can't. Others might."

"If they could, could they explain Giacomo Nerone's fore-knowledge of the cure?"

"Clairvoyance is an established, if unexplained, pheno-menon. But you can't ask anyone to judge a secondhand report of something that happened fifteen years ago."

"But you accept the truth of the report?"

"Yes."

"You would record it as unexplained and, possibly, un-explainable in the present state of medical knowledge?"

". . . Of my medical knowledge," Meyer corrected him, smiling.

"And you would testify in these terms at the Bishop's court?"

"I would."

"That's all," said Meredith with gentle irony. "I'll put it on record in my notes."

"What's your own opinion, Monsignor?" Meyer quizzed him pointedly.

"I've an open mind," said Meredith precisely. "I shall try, and so will my successor, to prove by every possible means

that this is not a miracle, but simply a rare physical pheno-
menon. As it rests only on one witness and your later testimony, we shall probably end by refusing to accept it as a
miracle—though in fact it may be one. Where you and I differ,
my dear Doctor, is that you reject the possibility of miracles
and I accept it. It's a long argument but I suggest my position
is rather more tenable than yours."

"You'd have made a good lawyer, Monsignor." Meyer
tacked away from the supposition. "What's your next question?"

Meredith gave it to him baldly.

"Who was Il Lupo? And why did Nerone tell you to keep
him away from the village?"

Meyer looked at him in swift surprise.

"Who told you that?"

"Nina. She was half asleep but she heard you and Nerone
talking at the door."

"What else did she hear?"

"You said . . . 'This is history! You can't stop it. Neither
can I. Someone's got to start organising . . .'"

"That was all?"

"Yes. I thought you could tell me what it meant."

"It had many meanings, Monsignor. I can only try to give
its meaning for me. . . ."

. . . Their camp was a shallow basin, high up in the spine of
eastern hills. Aeons ago it might have been the crater of a
volcano. The lip of it was jagged as a saw, and the outer slopes
were barren and scree-covered; but inside there was a small
lake into which the water drained, and beside it there were
copses and a stretch of tough, wiry grass. Their tents were
hidden under the bushes, and the goats and the cow they had
levied from the local peasants cropped safely on the inside of
the saucer, while their lookouts swept the countryside from the
shelter of the high saw-teeth.

There was only one way in—the goat track that began at
Satan's Rock, where the first sentry was posted. The watchers
on the rim could see him all day—and if a visitor were admitted

they could keep him in their sights every step of the way. When he reached the lip of the crater he would be met and searched and two men would walk him down through the tussocks to the tent of Il Lupo, who was their leader.

Meyer remembered him vividly—a short, fair man, with clear eyes and a chubby face and a smiling mouth, from which a placid voice spoke, now in the purest Tuscan, now in the roughest provincial dialect. His dress was rough like that of his men, but his hands and teeth were immaculate and he shaved, carefully, every day. He talked little about his past, but Meyer gathered that he had fought in Spain and then gone to Russia and then returned to Italy before the outbreak of war. He had worked in Milan and Turin and later still in Rome, though how or at what was never quite clear. He had admitted to being a party man, and he discussed policy with authority and expertness.

The day Giacomo Nerone was brought in from Satan's Rock, Meyer was in Il Lupo's tent discussing a new patrol operation. The guards gave his name and his business and Il Lupo stood up and held out his hand.

"So you're Nerone! I'm happy to know you. I've heard a great deal about you. I'd like to talk with you."

Nerone returned the greeting but said briskly.

"Could we leave it? My wife's in labour. I'd like the doctor to see her as soon as possible. It's a long walk back."

"She's had *rubella*," Meyer explained hastily. "We're afraid of complications."

The clear eyes clouded with immediate concern. Il Lupo clucked sympathetically.

"A pity. A great pity. That's where a State Medical Service is such a help. One can start inoculations at the first hint of an outbreak. You had no serum, Meyer, of course."

"No. We can only wait and see how the child is born."

"The midwives are with her?"

Nerone nodded.

"Then she's being looked after, at least. Ten minutes won't make any difference one way or the other. Let's have a cup of coffee and talk a while."

"Relax, Giacomo," Meyer told him genially. "Nina's as strong as an ox. We'll make up the time on the downhill walk."

"Very well."

They sat down on torn canvas chairs. Il Lupo offered cigarettes and shouted for coffee, and after a few moments of polite fencing he came to the point.

"Meyer's told me about you, Nerone. I understand you're an English officer."

"That's right."

"And a deserter."

"That's right, too."

Il Lupo shrugged and blew a cloud of smoke up towards the canvas roof.

"It's immaterial to us, of course. The capitalist armies have served their purpose in winning the war. It's our job to establish the peace we want. So your personal history is no disadvantage. On the contrary, it could even help you—with us."

Nerone said nothing, but sat waiting calmly.

Il Lupo went on in his quiet, educated voice.

"Meyer's also told me of the work you've done in Gemello. The confidence you've built up with the people. That's excellent . . . as a temporary measure."

"Why temporary?" asked Nerone quietly.

"Because your own position is temporary—and equivocal. Because when the war ends—as it soon must—this country will need a strong and united Government to organise it and run it."

"That means a Communist Government?"

"Yes. We're the only people who have a clear platform and the strength to carry it into practice."

"You need a charter too, don't you? A mandate?"

Il Lupo nodded amiably.

"We've got it now. The British have made it clear that they'll play ball with anyone who can help them run the country. They've armed us and given us at least a reasonable scope for military operations. The Americans have other ideas, but they're politically immature and we can discount them for a while. That's the first half of the mandate. The second we must win for ourselves."

"How?"

"How does any party win confidence? By showing results. By establishing order out of chaos. By getting rid of dissenting elements and building unity on strength."

"That's what the Fascisti tried to do," Nerone told him evenly.

"Their mistake was to build their dictatorship on one man. Ours will be the dictatorship of the proletariat."

"And you'd like me to join you in that?"

"As Meyer has done," Il Lupo pointed out calmly. "He's a liberal by nature but he's seen the failure of liberalism. It's not enough to hold out promises of work and education and prosperity as the rewards of co-operation. People aren't built like that. They're naturally stupid, naturally selfish. They need the disciplines of strength and fear. Take yourself, for instance. You've done a good job, but where has it led you? You'll be running round with a basket of eggs on your arm playing Lady Bountiful till the day you die. . . . And they'll let you do it. What's the future in that?"

For the first time since his coming, Meyer saw Nerone relax. His lean, dark face split into a grin of genuine amusement.

"There's no future at all. I know that."

"Why do it, then?"

"The world's a grim place without it," said Nerone lightly.

"Agreed," said Il Lupo. "But in the world we build there won't be any need of it."

"That's what I'm afraid of," said Giacomo Nerone. He stood up. "We understand each other, I think."

"I understand you very well," said Il Lupo, without resentment. "I'm not sure if you understand me. We're moving into the villages one by one and setting up our own administration. Gemello is next on the list. What do you propose to do about it?"

Nerone smiled, denying the proposition before he uttered it.

"I could rally the people and fight you."

242

Il Lupo shook his head.

"You're too good a soldier for that. We have the guns, the bullets and the training to use them. We'd cut you up in an afternoon. What's the profit in that?"

"None," Nerone told him calmly. "So I'll pass the word around to the people to wait it out without violence until the first free elections."

A ghost of a grin twitched Il Lupo's thin lips.

"By that time they'll have forgotten the guns. They'll remember only the bread and the pasta and the bars of American chocolate."

"And the boys you've shot in the ditches!" Sudden anger rang in Nerone's voice. "The old men beaten, and the girls with shaven heads! The new tyranny built on the old—the liberty pawned again for an illusion of peace. They'll submit now, because they're lost and afraid. Later they'll rise in judgment and throw you out!"

"Give a man a day's work, a fully belly at night and a woman in his bed, and he'll never think of Judgment Day." Il Lupo stood up. His lean figure seemed to grow in stature, filling the tent. "Another thing, Nerone..."

"Yes?"

"There's no room for two of us in Gemello. You'll have to get out."

Surprisingly, Nerone threw back his head and laughed heartily.

"You want the meat without the mustard. You want me discredited and running like a rabbit while you march in as the Saviour of Italy. You're too greedy, man!"

"If you stay," said Il Lupo with cool deliberation, "I'll have to kill you."

"I know," said Giacomo Nerone.

"You want to make yourself a martyr, is that it?"

"That would be a folly and a presumption," Nerone told him simply. "I don't want to die any more than the next man. But I stand on land that I've tilled with my own hands, in a place where I've found love and hope and belief. I refuse to be hunted out of it to give you a cheap victory."

"Very well," said Il Lupo without resentment. "We know where we stand."

"Do you mind if Meyer comes now?"

"Not at all. If you'll wait outside a second, we'll just tidy up our business."

When he had gone, Il Lupo said, without emphasis:

"He's a zealot. He'll have to go."

Meyer shrugged uneasily.

"He's a good fellow. He does a lot of good and no harm at all. Why not let him be?"

"You're soft, Meyer," said Il Lupo genially. "We'll be taking over Gemello in ten days. You've got that long to talk some sense into him."

"I wash my hands of it," said Meyer tersely.

Il Lupo smiled at him.

"That's Pilate's line, my dear doctor. The Jews have another one—'It is expedient that one man should die for the people.'"

He was still smiling when Meyer turned and went out to join Giacomo Nerone. . . .

. . . Blaise Meredith lay back on the bed, relaxed in body but active in mind, listening to the cool, clinical narration of the doctor. When Meyer paused awhile, he asked:

"It's a personal question, Doctor. Did you actually join the Communist Party?"

"I never held a party ticket. But that's irrelevant. There weren't any tickets in the mountains. The important thing was that I had committed myself to Il Lupo and to what he stood for: the dictatorship of the proletariat, order imposed by strength."

"May I ask why?"

"It's quite simple." Meyer's hands gestured eloquently in exposition. "For me it was the most natural development. I'd seen the breakdown of liberalism. I'd seen the drawbacks of clericalism. I'd been the victim of a one-man dictatorship. I understood the need for equality and order and a redistribution of capital. I'd also seen the stupidity and stubbornness of

244

depressed people. Il Lupo's answer seemed to me the only one."

"And his threat to Giacomo Nerone?"

"Was also logical."

"But you disagreed with it?"

"I disliked it. I didn't disagree."

"Did you talk to Giacomo about it?"

"Yes."

"What did he say?"

"Surprisingly enough, Monsignor, he agreed with Il Lupo." Meyer's face clouded at the recollection of it. "He said quite plainly: 'You can't believe one way and act another. Il Lupo's right. If you want to build a perfect political mechanism, you must toss out the parts that don't work. Il Lupo doesn't believe in God. He believes in man only as a political entity, so he's quite logical. You're the illogical one, Meyer. You want omelettes for breakfast, but you don't want to crack the eggs.'"

"Did you have any answer to that?"

"Not a very good one, I'm afraid. It was too close to the truth. But I did ask him how he squared up his own admission that there was no future in the work with the fact that he was prepared to die for it."

"What did he say?"

"He pointed out that he, too, had his own logic. He believed that God was perfect and man, since the fall, was imperfect, and that there would always be disorder and evil and injustice in the world. You couldn't create a system that would destroy these things, because the men who ran it would be imperfect, too. The only thing that dignified man and held him back from self-destruction was his sonship with God and his brotherhood in the human family. Giacomo's own service was an expression of this relationship. Between him and Il Lupo conflict was inevitable, because their beliefs were opposed and contradictory."

"And Il Lupo, being the man with the guns, must destroy him?"

"That's right."

"Why didn't he go away?"

"I put that to him, too," said Meyer wearily. "I suggested he take Nina and the boy and move out to another place. He refused. He said Nina would come to no harm—and he himself had stopped running long ago."

"So he stayed in Gemello?"

"Yes. I returned to the mountains. The day before Il Lupo was due to move in and set up his administration, I came back. They were going to use my house as headquarters and I had to get it ready. Also, I had been told to have a last talk with Giacomo Nerone to get him to change his mind. . . ."

. . . It was early afternoon, warm with the late spring, noisy with the first cicadas. They walked together in the garden under the fig tree, and talked as soberly as lawyer and client about what would happen when Il Lupo came down with his men. There was no argument between them. Nerone was firm in his refusal to quit, and Meyer's words were a flat recitation of the inevitable.

"Il Lupo's quite clear on what will be done. You're to be discredited first and then executed."

"How does he propose to discredit me?"

"Their arrival is timed for sunrise. You'll be arrested round about nine and brought here for summary trial."

"On what charges?"

"Desertion from the Allied cause and co-operation with the Germans."

Nerone smiled thinly.

"He shouldn't have much difficulty proving those. What then?"

"You'll be sentenced and taken out for immediate and public execution."

"How?"

"The firing squad. This will be a military court. Il Lupo is careful about the formalities."

"And Nina and the boy?"

"Nothing will be done to them at all. Lupo was quite definite on that. He sees no benefit in raising sympathy by punishing a woman and a child."

"He's a clever man. I admire him."

"He asks me to point out that this leaves you nearly eighteen hours to clear out, if you want to. I'm carrying enough money to keep you and Nina and the baby for two months. I'm authorised to give it to you on your assurance that you'll be clear of the area by sunrise."

"I'm staying. Nothing will change that."

"Then there's nothing more to be said, is there?"

"Nothing. I'm grateful to you for trying, Meyer. We've been good friends. I appreciate it."

"There's one thing—I'd almost forgotten it."

"What's that?"

"Where will you be at nine in the morning?"

"I'll save Il Lupo the trouble. I'll come here."

"That wouldn't do, I'm afraid. He wants a public arrest."

"He can't have everything. I'll walk here on my own two feet at nine o'clock."

"I'll tell him what you say."

"Thank you."

Then, because everything was said that needed to be put into words and because neither quite knew how to say goodbye, they walked in silence up and down the flagged path under the big tree until Meyer said, awkwardly:

"I'm sorry it's ending like this. It's not my business any more, but what are you going to do now?"

Nerone answered him quietly and frankly:

"I'm going down to have Father Anselmo hear my confession. I'll call at the hut to collect a few things and hand them to Nina. Then, I'll walk up to the villa to ask the Contessa if she'll have Nina and the boy there till it's all over. She's British by birth and Il Lupo's too clever to fall foul of the people who are giving him his guns. Then . . ." His dark, hollow face broke into a smile. "Then I'm going to say my prayers. I'm lucky to have time to prepare. It isn't every man who knows the time and place of his death." He stopped pacing and held out his hand. "Goodbye, Meyer. Don't blame yourself too much. I'll remember you in eternity."

"Goodbye, Nerone. I'll have a care for Nina and the boy."

247

He wanted to use the old, familiar formula and say 'God keep you'. But he remembered in time that, in Il Lupo's new world, which was now his own, there would be no God any more. The farewell was therefore pointless, and he did not say it. . . .

. . . Blaise Meredith asked:

"What happened with Father Anselmo?"

Meyer made a gesture of indifference.

"Nothing much. The old man didn't like him. They'd quarrelled often, as you know. He refused to hear his confession. I heard about it later in the village."

"And the Contessa?"

"This isn't firsthand. I gathered it from Pietro, the manservant, who's a patient of mine. Giacomo went up to the villa to ask a refuge for Nina and the boy. Also, I gathered, he wanted to sleep there the night, so that Il Lupo would not know where he was and would have to forgo the value of a public arrest. Anne de Sanctis was willing enough, it seems, but she wanted a price for it."

"What price?"

"She's a strange woman," said Meyer, obliquely. "I've known her a long time, but I would not claim to understand her fully. She is passionate by nature and she has great need of a man—a greater one now that she faces the terror of the middle years. Her husband disappointed her. Her other lovers came and went away as soldiers do in war-time. She was always too proud to satisfy herself with a man from the village. Nerone might have matched her, but he was already in love with Nina Sanduzzi. From the beginning she was jealous of that. So her whole emotional life has taken on a colour of perversion. Her price was that Nina sign over the boy as her ward and Giacomo Nerone sleep with her that night."

"A man on the eve of execution?" Meredith was shocked.

"I told you," said Meyer evenly, "everything is coloured for her. That's why this painter fellow has so much influence at the villa. He panders to her. Anyway, as you might expect, Giacomo refused. Apparently she was shrewd enough to guess

248

that he would spend the night at Nina's place. She sent a man down with a message to Il Lupo. Giacomo was arrested two hours after sunrise."

"So that's why she hates his son."

"I don't think she hates the boy," said Meyer, with grim humour. "If anything, she's probably attracted to him. But she is still jealous of Nina and she hates herself, but doesn't know it."

Blaise Meredith swung his legs off the bed and sat up, running his fingers through his thin hair in a pathetic gesture of weariness and puzzlement. In a voice that was very like a sigh, he said:

"It's late. I'd better get back for dinner. Though, God knows, I don't feel like facing them both tonight."

"Why not dine here?" said Meyer impulsively. "You'll eat worse, but at least you won't have to be polite. I'm nearly at the end of my evidence and you might as well get the rest of it tonight. I'll send a lad up to the villa to make your apologies."

"I'd be grateful, I assure you."

"I'm grateful to you," said Meyer with a grin. "And from a Jew to an inquisitor, that's a big compliment."

In the ornate room at the villa, the Contessa and Nicholas Black dined by candlelight, in the uneasy intimacy of conspirators. The Contessa was irritable and snappish. She was beginning to understand how far the situation had passed out of her control—with Nicholas Black holding her to ransom and Meredith picking up God knows what information from Meyer and Nina Sanduzzi and old Anselmo. Very soon now he must come to her with his dry, pedantic questions and his sunken, probing eyes. Whether she answered or remained silent, she stood to be discredited while the painter walked off, grinning, with the prize.

Nicholas Black was edgy, too. Meredith had forced his hand at lunchtime and things had been said which could never be recalled. Now they were in open opposition and, for all his mockery, Black had a healthy respect for the temporal influence of the Church in a Latin country. If Meredith took it into his head to invoke the help of the Bishop, all sorts of influences might be set in motion—influences reaching back to Rome itself—and the end might be a discreet call from the police and the revocation of his sojourn permit. It had happened before. The Christian Democrats were in power and behind them was the Vatican, old and subtle and ruthless.

So he was quick to seize on the Contessa's fear and exploit it to his own advantage.

"The priest's a damn nuisance, I agree, *cara*. I feel it's my fault for bringing him here. You're in a mess. I'd like to help you get out of it."

Her face brightened immediately.

"If you can do that, Nicki . . ."

"I'm sure we can, *cara*." He leaned over and patted her hand in encouragement. "Now listen! The priest is here. We're stuck with him. We can't get rid of him without a discourtesy, and you don't want that."

"I know." She nodded miserably. "There's the Bishop, you see, and . . ."

Black cut in briskly:

"I know about the Bishop, too, *cara*. You've got to live here, so it pays to be friendly. Meredith must stay. We're agreed on that. But there's nothing to stop you going away, is there?"

"I—I don't understand."

"It's simple, *cara*." He waved an eloquent hand. "You haven't been feeling well at all. Meredith himself knows you've been suffering with migraine and God knows what other feminine ills. You need to consult your doctor immediately. So you go to Rome. You've got an apartment there. You need staff to run it. You take your maid, and Pietro—and, as a special favour to Nina Sanduzzi, you take the boy. You want to buy him new clothes. You want him to be trained to service in polite society. You may even want to think about having him educated by the Jesuits. . . ." He chuckled sardonically. "What mother could refuse an opportunity like that? And if she did? The boy's under a contract of service to you. Italian law is such a confounded muddle, I think you'd get away with it, provided the boy consents. The onus would

250

be on his mother to show why she wanted him here and what work she could find for him. You'd cover that, too, by providing a weekly remittance of part of his wages through your major-domo here."

Her eyes lit up at the new, encouraging thought, but immediately clouded again.

"It's a wonderful idea, Nicki. But what about you? Meredith knows what you want. He'd do his best to make trouble."

"I've thought of that, too," said the painter, with his satiric grin. "I stay here—at least for a week. If Meredith asks any questions, you can tell him quite frankly you think I'm a bad influence on the boy. You want to act like a good Christian and get him away from me. Simple, isn't it?"

"Wonderful, Nicki! Wonderful!" Her eyes sparkled and she clapped her hands in delight. "I'll make all the arrangements tomorrow and we'll leave the day after."

"Why not tomorrow?"

"We can't, Nicki. The train for Rome leaves Valenta in the morning. There wouldn't be time to get everything done."

"A pity," said Black irritably. "Still, it's only a day. I think we can keep our Monsignor at bay for that long. You'd better talk to the boy yourself. I mustn't seem to be involved."

"I'll talk to him in the morning." She reached out and filled his wineglass. "Let's drink, darling! Then we'll open another bottle and make a celebration of it. What shall we drink to?"

He raised his glass and smiled at her over the rim.

"To love, *cara!*"

"To love!" said Anne Louise de Sanctis—then choked suddenly on the thought: But who loves me? And who will ever love me?

"I'll be frank with you, Doctor," said Meredith, picking moodily at the last of his dinner. "At this moment, I'm less concerned with Giacomo Nerone than with his son. Nerone's dead; and, we hope, among the blessed. His boy is in a grave moral crisis, in daily danger of seduction. I feel responsible for him. But how do I discharge the responsibility?"

251

"It's a problem," said Meyer, with sober concern. "The boy's more than half a man. He has free will and he's morally responsible—if inexperienced. He's certainly not ignorant of what's involved. Children mature early in the matrimonial beds. I think he's a sound lad; but Black's a very persuasive character."

Meredith was toying absently with a broken crust, crumbling it on his plate and making small patterns of the grey particles.

"Even in the confessional it's hard to reach an adolescent. They're shy as rabbits and much more complex than adults. If I could get at either the Contessa or Black himself I might stand some chance."

"Have you tried?"

"With Black, yes. But the man is fixed in bitterness and resentment. I couldn't find a common term of agreement. I haven't tried the Contessa yet."

Meyer gave him a wintry smile.

"You may find that even harder, Monsignor. There's no logic in women at the best of times and this one has a sickness on her: the sickness of the middle years and an old love turned sour and shameful. There's a cure for one, but the other . . ." He paused a moment, frowning dubiously. ". . . One thing I'm sure of, Meredith. No priest can cure it."

"How will she end, then?"

"Drugs, drink or suicide," said Meyer flatly. "Three words for the same thing."

"And that's the only answer?"

"If you want me to say that God is the answer, Monsignor, I can't do it. There is another one, but it's a dirty word and you mightn't like it."

To his surprise, Meredith lifted his grey face and smiled at him good humouredly.

"You know, Meyer, that's the dilemma of the materialists. I wonder so few of them see it. They cut God out of the dictionary and their only answer to the riddle of the universe is a dirty word."

"Damn you!" said Meyer, with a crooked grin. "Damn you

for a long-nosed inquisitor. Let's have some coffee and talk about Giacomo Nerone. . . ."

... At eight o'clock in the morning they arrested Nerone in Nina's house. They were not too rough with him, but they bloodied his face and tore his shirt, so that it would seem that he had put up a struggle. In fact he did not struggle at all, but stood there, silent, while two of them held his arms and a third battered him, and the others held Nina, who screamed and struggled like a wild thing—and, when they took him away, collapsed moaning on the bed. The child did not scream, but lay quietly in its cot, groping with tiny bunched hands at the folds of the pillow.

They then marched him up the hill and on to the road, and, to make a better spectacle, they twisted his arms behind his back and bent him almost double to walk through the village. The people stood at their doors, silent and staring, and even the children were hushed as he passed. No voice was raised in protest, no hand raised to help him. Il Lupo had calculated exactly. Hunger had no loyalties. These folk had seen too many conquerors come and go. Their allegiance was to the strong and not to the gentle. This was a harsh land with a harsh history. It was not the inheritance of the meek.

When they came to Meyer's house, they thrust him roughly inside and shut the door. The people came running like ants to stand outside, but the guards drove them back, cursing them into their houses. Il Lupo wanted an orderly trial, and no riots to disturb it.

Inside the room, Giacomo Nerone stood a moment flexing his cramped arms and wiping the blood from his face. Then he looked around him. The room was set like a court. Il Lupo and Meyer and three other men sat at the table, and behind them the guards were ranged—dark, stubble-faced men, in leather jackets and cocked berets, with pistols in their belts and automatic rifles held loosely in their hands. Two other guards stood between Nerone and the door, and between him and the table there was a clear space with a single chair.

All the faces were set and serious, as was becoming to men

253

witnessing a historic act. Only Il Lupo was smiling, clear-eyed and polite as a host at a dinner party. He said in his cool voice:

"I'm sorry we had to be rough with you, Nerone. You shouldn't have resisted arrest."

Nerone said nothing.

"You have a right, of course, to know the charges against you." He picked up a paper from the table and read from it in careful Tuscan: "Giacomo Nerone, you are charged before this military court with desertion from the British Army and with active collaboration with German units operating in the area of Gemelli dei Monti." He laid the paper down on the table and went on: "Before you are brought to trial on these charges, you are at liberty to say anything you wish."

Nerone looked at him with calm eyes.

"Will you put my remarks in the record?"

"Certainly."

"On the charge of desertion, this court has no jurisdiction. Only a British Army court martial can try me for that. Your proper procedure is to hold me in custody and hand me over to the nearest British command.

Il Lupo nodded placidly.

"We will note your objection, which seems to me well-founded, in spite of the fact that you have no proof of your identity as a British soldier. You will, however, be brought to trial on the second charge."

"I challenge your jurisdiction on that, too."

"On what grounds?"

"This is not a proper court. Its officials hold no legal commission."

"I disagree with you," said Il Lupo placidly. "Partisan groups are guerrillas operating in support of the Allies. They have a *de facto* identity as military units and a summary jurisdiction in local theatres of war. Their authority derives ultimately from the Allied High Command and from the Occupation Authority in Italy."

"In that case, I have nothing to say."

Il Lupo nodded politely.

"Good. We're anxious, of course, to see that justice is done.

You will be given some time to prepare your defence. I propose to clear the room. You will be given coffee and something to eat. Doctor Meyer here is prepared to act as your defence counsel. As president of the court I am prepared to give full weight to any points you may care to raise with me. Is that clear?"

For the first time since his arrival, Nerone smiled.

"Quite clear. I'd enjoy the coffee."

At a sign from Il Lupo, the guards went out into the garden and the three men were left alone. Meyer said nothing, but went to the stove and began making the coffee. Nerone sat down and Il Lupo offered him a cigarette and lit it for him. Then he sat on the edge of the table and said pleasantly:

"You were foolish to stay, you know."

"It's done," Nerone told him briefly. "Why discuss it?"

"You interest me, that's why. I have a good deal of admiration for you. But I can't see you in the role of a martyr."

"You cast me for it."

"And you accepted it."

"Yes."

"Why?"

"I like the lines," said Nerone, with grave humour. "The last one most of all: *'Consummatum est.'* "

"You—and the work," said Il Lupo.

Nerone shrugged.

"The work isn't important. A million men can do it better. You will probably do it better yourself. The work dies. How many men did Christ cure? And how many of them are alive today? The work is an expression of what a man is, what he feels, what he believes. If it lasts, if it develops, it's not because of the man who began it, but because other men think and feel and believe the same way. Your own party's an example of it. You'll die too, you know. What then?"

"The work will go on," said Il Lupo. The clear eyes lit suddenly as if at a great revelation. "The work will go on. The old systems will perish of their own corruption, and the people will come into their own. It's happened in Russia. It will happen in Asia. America will be isolated. Europe will be forced

255

into line. It will happen. Nerone, I may not be here to see it, but I'm not important."

"That's the difference between us," said Giacomo Nerone softly. "You say you're not important. I say I am. . . . What happens to me is eternally important, because I was from eternity in the mind of God . . . me! The blind, the futile, the fumbling, the failed. I was, I am, I shall be!"

"You believe that, really?" Il Lupo's eyes probed him like a scalpel.

"I do."

"You'll die for it?"

"It seems so."

Il Lupo stubbed out his cigarette and stood up. He said with flat conviction:

"It's a monstrous folly."

"I know," said Giacomo Nerone. "And it's gone on for two thousand years. I wonder whether yours will last so long."

Il Lupo made no answer. He looked at his watch and then said briskly:

"We'll have coffee and then you can rest for the morning. We'll bring the trial on at one o'clock. How do you propose to plead?"

"Does it matter?"

"Not really. The finding's a matter of course. The execution is fixed for three o'clock."

Nerone's face clouded momentarily and he said:

"Why so late? I'd like to get it over."

"I'm sorry," said Il Lupo politely. "I'm not being cruel. It's just a matter of policy. There'll be less time for riots or demonstrations. By the time they get the gossip over and begin to think about it, they'll be ready for supper. You understand, I hope?"

"Perfectly," said Giacomo Nerone.

Meyer brought the coffee and the breakfast things and they sat together at the table eating in silence, like a family. When they had finished, Il Lupo asked him:

"By the way, do you intend to make any speeches before the execution?"

256

Nerone shook his head.

"I've never made a speech in my life. Why?"

"I'm glad," Il Lupo told him genially. "Otherwise I'd have to have you beaten before you went out. The one thing I can't afford is heroics."

"I'm no hero," said Giacomo Nerone.

For the first time since his arrival, Meyer spoke to him. Without raising his eyes from the table-top, he said gruffly:

"If you want to be private for a while, use the other room. No one will disturb you. I'll call you when we're ready to begin."

Nerone looked at him with gratitude in his sombre eyes.

"Thank you, Meyer. You've been a good friend. I'll remember you."

He got up from the table and walked into the other room, closing the door behind him. The two men looked at each other. After a moment, Il Lupo said, not ungently:

"I'll release you from service after the execution, Meyer. If you take my advice you'll cut loose and go away for a while. You're not made for this sort of thing."

"I know," said Aldo Meyer in a dead voice. "I don't believe enough—either way. . . ."

. . . "And the rest of it," asked Blaise Meredith.

Meyer's long hands made a gesture of finality.

"It was quite simple. He was tried and found guilty. They took him up the hill to the old olive tree, tied him to it and shot him. Everyone was there, even the children."

"And Nina?"

"She, too. She went up to him and kissed him and then stood back. Even when they shot him, she didn't say a word: but when all the others left, she stayed there. She was still there when the burial party came that night to take him away."

"Who buried him?"

"Anselmo, the Contessa, two men from the villa, Nina—and myself."

Blaise Meredith frowned in puzzlement.

"I don't understand that."

"Simple enough. All three of us wanted to hate him—but at the end he shamed us into loving him."

"And yet," persisted Meredith, "when I came you were all afraid of him."

"I know," said Meyer gruffly. "Love is the most terrible thing in the world."

It was after eleven when Blaise Meredith left the doctor's house to walk back to the villa. Before he went, Meyer showed him Nerone's last letter and handed him the package containing the rest of the papers. They said goodnight to each other and Meredith began to stroll slowly up the cobbled street in the grey moonlight.

A sense of remoteness and separation took hold of him, as if he were walking out of his own body, in a strange place and another time. There were no doubts any more, no storms, only a great tranquillity. The storms were all about him, roaring and restless, but he lay becalmed in the eye of the cyclone, in a wonder of silence and flat water.

Like Giacomo Nerone, he was near the end of his search. Like Nerone, he saw how his death must come in a flurry of violence, inevitable but brief as sunset. He was afraid of it, yet he walked towards it, on his own two feet, enveloped in the peace of a final decision.

He came to the iron gates of the villa and passed them, pressing onwards up the last steep incline to the place of Nerone's execution—the small plateau where the olive tree stood like a cross, black against the white moon. When he reached it, he laid down the package and leaned against the tree, feeling his heart pounding and the rough touch of the bark against his skin. He raised his arms slowly, so that they lay along the knotted branches and the dead twigs pricked the skin of his hands.

Giacomo Nerone had stood like this, with wrists and ankles bound and eyes covered, in the moment of final surrender. Now it was his turn—Blaise Meredith, the cold priest from the Palace of the Congregations. His body stiffened, his face knotted in the agony of decision as he struggled to gather his will to the act of submission. It seemed an age before the words wrenched themselves out of him, low and agonised:

"... Take me, O God! Make me what you want ... a wonder or a mockery! But give me the boy—for his father's sake!"

It was over—done, finished! A man sold under the hammer to his Maker. Time to go home. To bed, but not to sleep. Time was running out. Before morning came, there were Giacomo Nerone's papers to be read, and a letter to be written to Aurelio, Bishop of Valenta.

CHAPTER FOURTEEN

To Blaise Meredith, the legalist—and even in this time of climax he could not lay aside the mental habit of a lifetime—the writings of Giacomo Nerone were, in many respects, a disappointment. They added nothing, except by inference, to the biography of his past, and little but glossary to the known details of his life, works and death in Gemello Minore.

What Aldo Meyer had found in them—a poignant recollection, a glimpse into the mind of a man once known, once hated, finally loved—presented itself under another aspect to the Devil's Advocate. Blaise Meredith had read the writing of a hundred saints, and all their agonies, all their revelations, all their passionate outpourings had for him the familiarity of old acquaintance.

They conformed to the same belief, to a basic pattern of penance and devotion, to the same progression from purgation to illumination, from illumination to a direct union with the Almighty in the act of prayer. It was the conformity he was looking for now, as each of the examiners and assessors would look for it, in each of the processes that must follow the first presentation of evidence in the Bishop's court.

To the biographer, to the dramatist, to the preacher, the personality of the man was important. His quirks and oddities and individual genius were the things that linked him to the commonalty of men and made them lean to him as patron and exemplar. But to the Church itself, to the delving theologians and inquisitors who represented it, the importance lay in his character as a Christian—his conformity to the prototype which was Christ.

So, in the slow hours of the night, Blaise Meredith bent himself to the scrutiny, coolly and analytically. But even he could not escape the personal impact—the living man thrusting himself out from the yellowed leaves and the strong, masculine handwriting.

The writing was disjointed: the jottings of a man torn between contemplation and action, who still felt the need to clarify his thoughts and make his affirmations clear to himself. Meredith pictured him, sitting late at night in the small stone hut, cold, pinch-bellied, yet oddly content, writing a page or two before the time came to begin the long prayerful vigil which, more and more, became his substitute for sleep.

Yet, in spite of their random character, the writings had a rhythm and a unity of their own. They grew as the man grew. They ended as the man ended, in dignity and calm and a strange content.

... I write because of the common need of man to communicate himself, if only to a blank sheet of paper; because the knowledge of myself is a weight on me and I have no right to lay it all on the woman I love. She is simple and generous. She would bear it all and still be ready for more, but concealment is as much a part of love as surrender. A man must pay for his own sins and he cannot borrow another's absolution. ...

... To be born into the Church—and I can only speak of my own Church, knowing no other—is at once a burden and a comfort. The burden is felt first. The burden of ordinance and prohibition and, later, of belief. The comfort comes afterwards, when one begins to ask questions; and when one is presented with a key to every problem of existence. Make the first conscious act of faith, accept the first premise, and the whole logic falls into place. One may sin, but one sins inside a cosmos. One is constrained to repentance by the sheer order of it. One is free within a system, and the system is secure and consoling, so long as the will is fixed in the first act of faith. ...

... When Catholics become jealous of unbelievers, as they often do, it is because the burden of belief lies heavy and the constraints of the cosmos begin to chafe. They begin to feel cheated, as I did. They ask why an accident of birth should make fornication a sin for one, and a weekend recreation for another. Faced with the consequences of belief, they begin to regret the belief itself. Some of them end by rejecting it, as I did when I came down from Oxford. . . .

. . . To be a Catholic in England is to submit to a narrow conformity instead of a loose, but no less rigid, one. If one belongs to the old families as I did, to the last Elizabethans, the last Stuarts, it is possible to wear the Faith like a historic eccentricity—as some families sport the bar sinister, or a Regency rakehell, or a gambling dowager. But in the clash of conformities this is not enough. Sooner or later one is forced back on the first act of faith. If one rejects this, one is lost. . . .

. . . I was lost a long time, without knowing it. Without the Faith, one is free, and that is a pleasant feeling at first. There are no questions of conscience, no constraints, except the constraints of custom, convention and the law, and these are flexible enough for most purposes. It is only later that the terror comes. One is free—but free in chaos, in an unexplained and unexplainable world. One is free in a desert, from which there is no retreat but inward, towards the hollow core of oneself. There is nothing to build on but the small rock of one's own pride, and this is a nothing, based on nothing . . . I think, therefore I am. But what am I? An accident of disorder, going nowhere. . . .

. . . I have examined myself a long time on the nature of my act of desertion. At the time, it had no moral significance. The oath of service ends with the invocation of the Deity. But for me there was no Deity. If I chose to risk liberty and reputation and suffer the sanctions of the State, this was my business. If I escaped the sanctions, so much the better. But I did not reason like this at the time. My action was instinctive—an unreasoning reaction from something that did violence to my nature. But, by what I then believed, I had nothing that could be called a nature. I was cast in a common form, like a spark out of a furnace, but if one spark sputtered out, what did it matter? I was lost already . . . I could only plunge a little deeper into darkness. . . .

. . . Then there was Nina. I woke to her as one wakes to the first light of morning. The act of love is, like the act of faith, a surrender; and I believe that the one conditions the other. In

y case, at least, it has done so. I cannot regret that I loved
er, because love is independent of its expression—and it was
nly my expression of it that was contrary to the moral law.
This I regret and have confessed and prayed to be forgiven.
But even in sin the act of love—done with love—is shadowed
with divinity. Its conformity may be at fault, but its nature is
not altered, and its nature is creative, communicative, splendid
surrender. . . .

. . . It was in the splendour of my surrender to Nina, and
hers to me, that I first understood how a man might surrender
himself to God—if a God existed. The moment of love is a
moment of union—of body and spirit—and the act of faith is
mutual and implicit. . . .

. . . Nina has a God, but I had none. She was in sin, but
within the cosmos. I was beyond in sin, in chaos. . . . But in
her I saw all that I had rejected, all that I needed, and yet had
thrown away. Our union was flawed because of it, and one day
she would understand and might come to hate me. . . .

. . . How does one come back to belief, out of unbelief? Out
of sin, it is easy; an act of repentance. An errant child returns
to a Father because the Father is still there, the relationship is
unbroken. But in unbelief there is no Father, no relationship.
One comes from nowhere, goes nowhere. One's noblest acts
are robbed of meaning. I tried to serve the people. I did serve
them. But who were the people? Who was I? . . .

. . . I tried to reason myself back to a first cause and first
notion, as a foundling might reason himself back to the existence of his father. He must have existed, all children have
fathers. But who was he? What was his name? What did he
look like? Did he love me—or had he forgotten me for ever?
This was the real terror, and, as I look back on it now, from the
security I have reached, I tremble and sweat and pray desperately: "Hold me close. Never let me go again. Never hide
your face from me. It is terrible in the dark!" . . .

. . . How did I come to Him? He alone knows. I groped for
Him and could not find Him. I prayed to Him unknown and He
did not answer. I wept at night for the loss of Him. Lost tears
and fruitless grief. Then, one day, He was there again. . . .

263

. . . It should be an occasion, I knew. One should be able to say: 'This was the time, the place, the manner of it. This was my conversion to religion. A good man spoke to me and I became good. I saw creation in the face of a child and I believed.' It was not like that at all. He was there. I knew He was there and that He made me and that He still loved me. There are no words to record, no stones scored with a fiery finger, no thunders on Tabor. I had a Father and He knew me and the world was a house He had built for me. I was born a Catholic but I had never understood till this moment the meaning of the words 'the gift of faith'. After that, what else could I do, but say: 'Here am I, lead me, do what you want with me. But please stay with me, always. . . .'

. . . I am fraid for Aldo. There is much merit in his sceptic honesty, but when the others get hold of him, I do not know what will happen. This is the difference between the two absolutes—the Church and Communism. The Church understands doubt and teaches that faith is a gift, not to be acquired by either reason or merit. Communism permits no doubt and says that belief can be implanted like a conditioned reflex. . . To a point, it is right, but the conditioned reflex answers no questions—and the questions are always there—Whence? Where? Why? . . .

. . . The question of reparation worries me greatly at times. I am changed. I have changed. But I cannot change any of the things I have done. The hurts, the injustices, the lies, the fornications, the loves taken and tossed away. These things have changed and are still changing other people's lives. I am sorry for them now, but sorrow is not enough. I am bound to repair them as far as I can. But how? It is winter. The paths are closed before me and behind. I am a prisoner in this small world I have found. I can only say: When the way is clear, I will do what is asked of me. But the way is never clear. There is only the present moment in which one can live with certainty. Why do I fear so much? Because repentance is only the beginning. There is still a debt to pay. I ask for light, pray for submission, but the answer is unclear. I can only go on in the present. . . .

... Meyer laughs at me about good works. He points out that they have no continuity. The sick die and the hungry are hungry tomorrow. Yet Meyer himself does the same things instinctively. Why? Men like Meyer doubt the existence of God and therefore doubt any but a pragmatic relationship between man and man. Yet I have seen Meyer spend himself more freely than I have ever done. The man who does good in doubt must have so much more merit than one who does it in the bright certainty of belief. 'Other sheep I have which are not of this fold. ...' A warning against the smugness of inherited Faith. ...

... Nina tells me I am getting thin. I don't eat enough or sleep enough and pray too long at night. I try to explain how the need for food and sleep seems to get less, when one is absorbed in this new wonder of God. She seems to understand it better when I point out that she does not feel the need of me, physically, because of the child filling her womb. ... I ask myself what must be done about this question of marriage. We are apart in body now, but close in heart and spirit. I have the feeling that things are being prepared for me over which I have no control and that, for this reason, marriage might be a greater injustice than those I have already done. I am ready to do what seems right. I have told her that she has the first claim to decide, but that I believe it wise to wait. ... I have had so much these last months—of love, of happiness, of spiritual consolation. I must pay for it sometime. I do not know how the payment will be asked. I pray and try to make myself ready. ...

... Father Anselmo worries me. I have quarrelled with him and I regret it. There is nothing solved by anger. I must understand that a priest is just a man with sacramental faculties. The faculties are independent of his personal worth. Anselmo is carrying his own cross, the load of one lapse, multiplied by its consequences. But even in the sin there is an element of love, and this, I know, is a goodness not to be despised. Celibacy of the clergy is an ancient discipline, but not an article of faith. One sees its value, but one must not judge too harshly when men stumble under the weight of it. Poverty is a state which some men accept to make themselves holy. It can be for others conducive to damnation. If there were a way to talk to Anselmo, as a friend . . . but this is another problem for a priest. He is trained to direct the faithful, but never to accept counsel from them. This is a defect in the system. . . .

. . . Today I met the man who calls himself Il Lupo. Strange how quickly and easily we understood each other. I believe in God. He believes in no-God. Yet the consequences of each belief are equally rigid and inescapable. He is honest in what he believes. He does not expect me to be less honest in my own faith. He knows that there can be no co-existence between us. One must destroy the other. He is the prince of this world and he has the power of life and death. What power have I against him? 'My kingdom is not of this world.' I could rally the people. I could make them follow me to resist Il Lupo's band. But to what end? Fratricide is not Christianity. Bullets breed no love. . . . Il Lupo would like me to argue and act. I must not argue. I must only accept. But I fear for Meyer. He is too gentle a man for this embroilment. I must try to make him see that I understand. Later, he will have much to suffer. The weight of doubt is heavy on honest men. . . .

. . . I have a son and the boy is blind. Nina's grief is harsh on me. I understand now how faith can stagger on the mystery of pain. I understand how the old Manichees could fall easily into their heresy—since it is hard to see how pain and evil come into a creation of which an omnipotent Goodness is the sole author. A black time for me. It seems I am back in darkness and I pray desperately and cling to the first act of faith and say: 'I cannot understand; but I believe. Help me to hold to it!' . . .

. . . If faith can move mountains, faith can open blind eyes. If God wills it. How do I know what He wills? Speak to me, O God, for Your Son's sake. . . . Amen. . . .

There was more, much more, and Blaise Meredith scanned it meticulously as a good advocate should, but he had found the core of it, and the core was sound and solid. The conformity was there, the conformity of mind and heart and will. And the surrender had been made by which a man cuts loose from every material support to rest in faith, hope and charity, in the hands that framed him.

On the last page of all, Giacomo Nerone had written his own *obit*.

... If there be any, after my death, to read what I have written, let them know this of me:

I was born in the Faith; I lost it; I was led back to it by the hand of God.

What service I have done was prompted by Him. There is no merit in it of my own.

I have loved a woman and begotten a son, and I love them still in God and to all eternity.

Those I have injured, I beg to forgive me.

Those who will kill me, I commend to God, as brothers whom I love.

Those who forget me will do well. Those who remember me, I beg to pray for the soul of

Giacomo Nerone,
Who died in the Faith.

Blaise Meredith laid down the yellowed sheet on the counterpane, leaned back on the pillows and closed his eyes. He knew now with certainty that he had come to the end of his search. He had looked into the life of a man and seen the pattern of it—a long river winding slowly, but with certainty, homeward to the sea. He had looked into the soul of a man and seen it grow, like a tree, from the darkness of the earth, upward into the sun.

He had seen the fruit of the tree: the wisdom and the love of Nina Sanduzzi, the struggling humanity of Aldo Meyer, the reluctant repentance of Father Anselmo. It was good fruit, and in the bloom of it he saw the mark of the nurturing finger of God. But all the fruit was not yet mature. Some of it might wither on the branch, some of it might fall unripe and rot into extinction, because the gardener was careless. And he, Blaise Meredith, was the gardener.

He began to pray, slowly and desperately, for Anne de Sanctis and Paolo Sanduzzi and Nicholas Black, who had chosen the same desert to walk in as Giacomo Nerone. But before the prayer was finished, the old sickness took him, griping and wrenching, so that he cried out in the agony of it, till the blood welled up, hot and choking in his throat.

A long time later, weak and dizzy, he dragged himself to the writing desk and, in a shaky hand, began to write. . . .

My Lord Bishop,

I am very ill, and I believe that I may die before I have time to record fully the results of my investigations here. In spite of all the medical predictions, I feel that I am being hurried out of life and I am oppressed by the thought of the little time left to me. I want Your Lordship to know, however, that I have made my surrender, as you promised I would, and that I rest content, if not courageous, in the outcome.

First, let me tell you what I have found. I believe most firmly, on the evidence of those who knew him and on the writings which I have found, that Giacomo Nerone was a man of God, who died in the Faith and in the attitude of martyrdom. What the Court will decide is another matter—a legality, based on the canonical rules of evidence, and irrelevant, it seems to me, to the fundamental facts, that the finger of God is here and that the leaven of goodness in this man is still working in the lives of his people.

Your Lordship's best witnesses will be Doctor Aldo Meyer and Nina Sanduzzi. This latter has produced evidence of a cure that may well be miraculous, though I doubt seriously whether it will pass the assessors. The writings of Nerone which I shall send you with this letter are authentic and definitive, and, in my view, sound corroboration of his claim to heroic sanctity.

I confess to you, My Lord, in friendship, that I am less concerned at this moment for the Cause of Beatification than for the welfare of certain souls here in Gemello Minore. I have spoken to Father Anselmo and presumed to suggest that if he separates physically from Rosa Benzoni, even while lodging her still in his house, and if he makes a sincere confession, Your Lordship will accept these as evidence of reform. I'm sorry for him. It is a question of money and security for a poverty-stricken and rather ignorant man. I have promised him a lump sum of a hundred thousand lire from my estate as well as money enough to buy bedding and other needs for a separate sleeping room for Rosa Benzoni. It seems now that I may not have time to arrange these things. May I count on Your Lordship to do them for me, and use this letter for a claim on my executors? To fail Anselmo now would be an intolerable thought.

The other matter touches the Contessa de Sanctis, Paolo Sanduzzi, who is the son of Giacomo Nerone, and an English painter, who is house guest at the villa. It is too sordid to detail in this letter; and I fear there is little Your Lordship could do about it. I have commended them all to God and asked Him to accept my surrender as the price of their salvation. I hope tomorrow to be able to plan more active measures; but I am so weak and ill, I dare not count on anything.

I have two favours to ask, which I trust Your Lordship will not find burdensome. The first is that you write to His Eminence, Cardinal Marotta, explaining my position and making my apologies for what I count as a failure in my mission. Give him my greetings and beg him to remember me in his Mass. The second is that you will permit me to be buried here in Gemello Minore. I had once asked to be buried in His Eminence's church, but Rome is very far—and here, for the first time, I have found myself as a man and a priest.

It is very late, my Lord, and I am tired. I can write no more. Forgive me and, in your charity, pray for me.

I am Your Lordship's most obedient servant in Christ,
Blaise Meredith.

He folded the letter, sealed it in an envelope and tossed it on the desk. Then he crawled back to bed and slept till the sun was high over the green lawns of the villa.

Paolo Sanduzzi was working on the rock garden at the back of the villa. The terraces had been breached in places where the mortar had weathered out, and the soil was spilling. When it rained, the soil would be lost and, in this rocky land, it was too precious for that. The old gardener had shown him how to mix lime with the black volcanic sand from the river, and how to work it into the crevices with a trowel, then trim and surface it.

It was a new thing learned, a new skill to be proud of, and he knelt there with the sun shining on his back, whistling contentedly. The lime burned his fingers and made his hands feel rough and sandy, but this was another small pride—his hands were hardening like a man's. The gardener was pleased with him, too. Sometimes he would stop and talk in his gruff chewing fashion, and tell him the names of the plants, and how they grew and why the grubs would eat one and not another.

At mealtimes, in the long flagged kitchen, the old man would protect him from the chaffing of the women, who made jokes about his young maleness and what the girls would do to him when they got hold of him. The only one who did not laugh at him was Agnese the cook, a waddling mountain of a woman, who fed him double portions of pasta and always had a lump of cheese or a piece of fruit to tuck in the pocket of his breeches.

He had no name to put to all this, but he understood that it was a good way to be. He had a place and work to do, and friendly people about him—and at the end of the month there would be lire to rustle in his pocket and take home to his mother. Even Rome was beginning to recede into a dimmer distance. The Contessa had not spoken to him again, and the painter had left him alone, except for a genial word or two in passing. His fear of them had begun to diminish and they wove themselves pleasantly into his daydream of fountains and girls with shoes, and streets full of shining automobiles.

He was dreaming now, to the rhythm of his own whistling and the scrape of his trowel on the grey stone, when suddenly the dream became a reality. The Contessa was standing behind him and saying in her gentlest voice:

"Paolo! I want to talk to you."

He straightened immediately, dropped his trowel and scrambled down from the rockery to stand before her, acutely conscious of his sweating, naked torso and his grimy hands.

"Yes, signora. At your service."

She looked around quickly as if to make sure they were alone. Then she told him:

"Tomorrow, Paolo, I'm going away to Rome. I'm not very well and I must see my doctor. I'm taking Zita and Pietro to look after my apartment and I thought of taking you, too."

He gaped and stammered at the sudden wonder of it and the Contessa gave her high, tinkling laugh.

"Why are you so surprised? I promised you, didn't I? And you have worked well."

"But . . . but . . ."

"But you didn't believe me? Well, it's true. The only thing is, you'll have to ask your mother. You'll tell her that you'll be away for a couple of months and that part of your money will be paid to her here each month. Is that clear?"

"Yes, signora!" It was clear and bright as summer.

"You will tell her that Pietro is going and Zita, too, and that Pietro will be training you all the time."

"Yes, signora. But . . ."

"But what, Paolo?"

He did not know how to say it, but finally he got it out in a swift stumble of words.

"My . . . my mother doesn't like the Englishman, Signor Black. She may not let me go."

Again she laughed and charmed all the fears out of him.

"You tell your mother, Paolo, that Signor Black is staying here to work. And that this is why I am taking you away, because it is better for you not to see him."

"When—when can I tell her?"

"Now, if you like. Then come back and let me know what she says."

"Thanks, signora. Thanks a thousand, thousand times."

He snatched up his shirt, struggled into it so roughly that he tore it, and then went racing away down the gravelled path towards the iron gates. Anne Louise de Sanctis watched him go, smiling at the boyish eagerness of him. It was a good thing to see, a pleasantness to have near one in the house. This must be what other women found in their sons, in the autumn of marriage, when the sap of passion was drying out, and a husband was a companion perhaps, but no longer a youthful lover.

Suddenly, and quite clearly, she understood what she had done—the malice of it, the dirt of it, the stark damnation into which she had walked herself on the arm of Nicholas Black. Her blood ran cold at the thought. She shivered and turned away; and as she rounded the corner of the house, she walked almost into the arms of Blaise Meredith, who was stepping on to the lawn with a folder of papers in his hand.

When he greeted her, quietly, she was shocked by the look of him. His face seemed to have shrunken overnight. His eyes were like red coals set deep in his skull. His skin was the colour of old parchment and his lips were bloodless. His back was stooped as if he walked under a heavy load and his long hands were tremulous against the black fabric of his soutane.

For a moment she forgot her own thoughts and said:

"Monsignor! You're ill!"

"Very ill, I'm afraid," he told her. "I don't think I have much more time. Would you walk with me a little?"

She wanted to refuse outright, to run from him and hide herself in her bedroom within reach of the small bottle of oblivion, but he took her arm gently and she found herself falling into step beside him, listening to his voice and answering him in a voice that seemed not to belong to her.

"I saw young Paolo running down the path. He seemed to be excited about something."

"He was—very excited. I'm taking him to Rome with me tomorrow, if his mother will let him come."

"Is Mr Black going, too?"

"No. He's staying on here."

"But joining you later, is that it?"

"I—I don't know what his plans are."

"You do." The voice was tired but gentle and it held her, hypnotically.

"You do, my dear Contessa, because you made the plans with him. Terrible plans. Terrible for you and him—and the boy. Why did you do it?"

Her feet were fixed to the treadmill rhythm of their pacing. In spite of herself, the words came out:

"I—I don't know."

"Did you still want revenge on Giacomo Nerone?"

"So you know that, too?"

"Yes. I know."

It didn't matter now. Nothing mattered. He could ask what

he liked and she would answer, and when it was finished she would go upstairs and take a bath, and lie down to sleep and never wake again. This was the last terror. It would soon be over.

His next words shocked her back into reality. Meyer might have said them but not this priest with the mark of death on him. In Meyer's mouth, they would have lacked something—an intimacy, a gentleness, a love, perhaps? It was hard to say.

"You know, my dear Contessa, Italy is a bad country for a woman like you. It is a country of the sun, aggressive in its worship of the processes of generation. It is primitive and passionate. The male symbol is paramount. The woman unloved, unbedded, childless, is a sign of mockery to others and of torment to herself. You're a passionate woman. You have a great need of love—a need, too, of the sexual commerce that goes with it. The need has become a frenzy with you—and the frenzy betrays you into viciousness while it inhibits your own satisfaction. You're ashamed of it and you do worse things, because you don't know how to do better. . . . Is that right?"

"Yes."

It was all she said—but she wanted to add: I know all this, know it more terribly than you. But knowing isn't enough. Where do I go? What do I do? How do I find what I need?

Meredith went on, his dry voice warming as he talked.

"I could tell you to pray about this—and that wouldn't be a bad thing, because the hand of God reaches down even into the private hells we make for ourselves. I could tell you to make a general confession—and that would be a better thing, because it would give you a free conscience, and set you in peace with your God and yourself. But it wouldn't be the whole answer. You would still be afraid, still unsatisfied, still lonely."

"What do I do then? Tell me! For God's sake, tell me!"

The plea was wrung out of her at last. Meredith answered her, calmly.

"Leave this place for a while. Go away. Not to Rome, which is a small city and can be a vicious one. Go back to London and establish yourself there for a while. I'll give you a note to a friend of mine at Westminster, who will put you in touch with a specialist who deals with problems like yours—problems of the body and of the mind. Put yourself in his care. Don't expect too much too soon. Go to theatres, make some new friends, find yourself a charity that interests you.... Maybe, too, you will find a man, not to sleep with only, but to marry you and love you. You're still attractive—particularly when you smile."

"But if I don't find him?" There was a note of panic in her voice.

"Let me tell you something very important," said Meredith patiently. "It is no new thing to be lonely. It comes to all of us sooner or later. Friends die, families die. Lovers and husbands, too. We get old, we get sick. And the last and greatest loneliness is death, which I am facing now. There are no pills to cure that. No formulas to charm it away. It's a condition of men that we can't escape. If we try to retreat from it, we end in a darker hell—ourselves. But if we face it, if we remember that there are a million others like us, if we try to reach out to comfort them and not ourselves, we find in the end that we are lonely no longer. We are in a new family, the family of man, whose Father is God Almighty.... Do you mind if we sit down now? I'm—I'm very tired."

Now it was her turn to take his arm and help him to the small stone seat under the honeysuckle. Meredith sat down but she remained standing, looking down at him with slow wonder and a pity she had never felt for any but herself. After a moment, she asked him:

"How do you understand all this? I've never heard a priest talk like that before."

His bloodless mouth twitched into a tired smile.

"People ask too much of us, my dear Contessa. We're human too. Some of us are very stupid, and it takes us a lifetime to learn the simplest lessons."

"You're the first man in my life who's ever helped me."

"You've been meeting the wrong men," said Meredith, with dry irony.

She smiled at him then, and he saw, as if for the first time, how beautiful she had been.

274

"Would you—would you hear my confession, Father?"

Meredith shook his head.

"Not yet. I don't think you're ready for it."

She stared at him, frowning, more than a little afraid. He went on, gravely:

"Confession is not the psychiatrist's couch, a device to encourage self-revelation, to promote well-being by a purge of memory. It is a judicial sacrament, in which pardon is given on an admission of guilt and a promise of repentance and reform. For you the first part is easy—it is already half done. For the second, you must prepare yourself, by prayer and self-discipline—and by beginning to repair the evil you have already done."

She looked at him with troubled eyes.

"You mean Nicki—Mr Black?"

"I mean you, my dear Contessa—your own desires, your jealousy of Nina Sanduzzi and her son. As for Mr Black . . ." He hesitated a moment; then his eyes clouded and his mouth set into a grim line. "I'll talk to him myself. But I'm very much afraid he won't listen."

CHAPTER FIFTEEN

HALF WAY through the village, Paolo Sanduzzi ran, full tilt, into his mother. She was standing outside the smithy, talking to Martino's wife. Rosetta was with them, dressed in her Sunday finery, ready to be taken to the villa for the first time. Nina stared at him in amazement.

"Where do you think you're going? You're supposed to be working. What's all the hurry?"

The words tumbled out of him in a torrent.

"I don't have to work today. The Contessa told me. I'm going to Rome. She said I was to ask you and tell you that Pietro's going and Zita and I'm going to be trained . . ."

"Wait a minute!" Nina Sanduzzi's voice was harsh. "Start again! Who said you're going to Rome?"

"The Contessa. She's going up there to see her doctor. She'll be there for two months."

"And she wants to take you?"

"Yes."

"Why?"

"She needs servants, doesn't she?"

"You're a gardener, son. There are no gardens in Rome."

The boy's mouth dropped sullenly.

"She wants me, anyway. She sent me down to ask you."

The two women looked at each other significantly. Nina Sanduzzi said bluntly:

"Then you can go straight back and tell her you're not going. I know who wants you in Rome and it's not the Contessa."

"But it isn't like that at all! She told me to tell you. The Englishman is staying on here."

"For how long?" Slow anger began to build behind the classic face. "A week—ten days, maybe! And then he'll be packing his bags for the big city—and for you, Paolo *mio*. That trick wouldn't fool a baby." She caught at his arm roughly.

276

"You're not going and that's flat. I'm your mother and I won't allow it."

"Then I'll go anyway."

She lifted her free hand and slapped him hard on the face.

"When you're a man and can pay your own fare, and find your own work—then you can talk like that. If the Contessa asks me, I'll tell her to her face. And if there's any nonsense I'll have the doctor get in touch with the police at Gemello Maggiore. That'll keep your Englishman quiet for a while. Now forget about it, like a good boy!"

"I won't forget about it! I won't! She's asked me and I want to go. She's the *padrona* and you're nobody! You're just —just a saint's whore!"

Then he wrenched away from her and went running down the street, with his shirt-tails flapping over his rump. Nina Sanduzzi stared after him, her face a marble mask. Martino's wife scuffed the ground with her bare feet and said awkwardly:

"He didn't mean it. He's just a boy. They hear things. . . ."

"His father was a saint," said Nina Sanduzzi bitterly. "And his son wants to make himself a *feminella*."

"He doesn't at all," said Rosetta, in her high clear voice. "He's just a baby. He doesn't know what he wants. I'll bring him back and make him say sorry."

Before her mother could protest, she had started away, running swiftly in her Sunday shoes, and the last they saw of her was a flurry of skirts and a pair of brown legs up-ended over the wall that screened the torrent from the road.

In a sunlit corner of the garden, Nicholas Black was putting the final varnish on the picture of Paolo Sanduzzi crucified on the olive tree. At the sound of Meredith's footfall, he looked up and called an ironic greeting.

"Good morning, Meredith. I trust you slept well."

"Indifferently, I'm afraid. I hope I'm not disturbing you?"

"Not at all. I'm just finishing. Would you like to see it? I think it's my best work so far."

"Thank you."

Meredith walked round to the front of the easel and looked at the picture. The painter grinned when he saw the expression on his face.

"Do you like it, Meredith?"

"It's a blasphemy, Mr Black." The priest's voice was cold.

"That depends on the point of view, of course. To me it's a symbol. I've called it 'The Sign of Contradiction'. An apt title, don't you think?"

"Very." Meredith walked a pace or two away from the picture and then said, "I've come to tell you, Mr Black, that neither the Contessa nor Paolo Sanduzzi will be going to Rome. The Contessa would be pleased if you would leave the villa as soon as possible."

The painter flushed angrily.

"She might have had the politeness to tell me herself."

"I offered to do it for her," Meredith told him quietly. "She's an unhappy woman who needs a great deal of help."

"Which the Church is only too ready to give her. She's quite rich, I believe."

"The Church would like to help you, too, Mr Black—and you are very poor indeed."

"To hell with your help, Meredith. I want nothing from you. Now do you mind going? I'm busy."

"I've brought you something that might interest you."

"What is it—a tract from the Catholic Truth Society?"

"Not quite. They're the personal papers of Giacomo Nerone. Would you care to look at them?"

In spite of himself, the painter was interested. He wiped his hands on a scrap of cloth and, without a word, took the folder from Meredith. He turned back the manila cover and scanned a few pages in silence. Then he closed the folder and asked in an odd, strained voice:

"Why do you show me this?"

Meredith was puzzled by the strangeness of him, but he answered simply:

"They make a very moving document—the spiritual record of a man who had lost the Faith, as you have, and then came back to it. I felt they might help you."

Nicholas Black stared at him a moment; then his lips
ew back in a smile that looked more like a grimace of
,ony.

"Help me! You have a wonderful sense of humour, Mere-
th! You know what you've done, don't you? You've had me
rown out of the house. You've robbed me of the last chance
finance an exhibition that might have re-established my
putation as an artist. And you've dirtied the one decent thing
ve ever tried to do in my life."

Meredith gaped at him blankly.

"I don't understand you, Mr Black."

"Then I'll explain it to you, Monsignor," said the painter, in
e same taut voice. "Like everyone else in this damned vil-
ge, you've convinced yourself that my only interest in Paolo
nduzzi is to seduce him. That's true, isn't it?"

Meredith nodded but did not speak. The painter turned
ay and stood for a long time looking out across the sun-
ppled lawns towards the villa. When he spoke at last, it was
th a strange, remote gentleness.

"The irony is, Meredith, that any time in the last fifteen
ars you might have been right. But not now. I'm fond of
s boy—yes. But not in the way you think. I've seen in him
erything that's been lacking in my own nature. I wanted to
e him and educate him and make him what I could never
—a full man, in body, intellect and spirit. If it meant deny-
; every impulse to passion and every need I have for love and
ection, I was prepared to do it. But you'd never believe
t, would you?"

Then, without thinking, Meredith made the most brutal
nark of his life. He said gravely:

'I might believe you, Mr Black, but you could never do it—
t without a singular grace from God. And how could you
it, not believing?"

Nicholas Black said nothing. He was staring at the picture of
olo Sanduzzi, nailed to the dark olive tree. After a while he
ned to Meredith and said, with bleak politeness:

"Will you please go, Monsignor? There is nothing you can
for me."

Blaise Meredith walked slowly back to the house, sick with the consciousness of his own failure.

Luncheon was a dismal meal for him. His head buzzed, his hands were clammy and whenever he breathed deeply he could feel a sharp pain in the region of his ribs. His food had no taste, the wine had a sour edge to it. But he was forced to smile and make conversation with the Contessa, who, now that her fear of him was gone, was disposed to be talkative.

Nicholas Black did not appear at all. He sent a message by the manservant excusing himself and asking that a collation be sent to his room. The Contessa was curious to know what had passed between them, and Meredith was forced to fob her off with the courteous fiction that they had exchanged a few bad tempered words and that Black was probably too embarrassed to join them.

When the meal was over, he went upstairs to rest through the hot hours. The climb up the stairs told him, more plainly than a doctor, how ill he was. Each step was an effort. Perspiration broke out on his face and his body, and the pain in his ribs was like a knife whenever he breathed deeply. He knew enough of medicine to understand that this was what happened to cancer patients. The growth and the haemorrhages weakened them so much that they lapsed into pneumonia, which killed them quickly. But, by all the norms, he was still a long way from this stage. He was still on his feet and he wanted to stay there as long as he could.

When he reached the landing at the top of the stairs, he did not go straight to his own room, but turned down the corridor to the one occupied by Nicholas Black. He could hear the painter moving about inside; but when he knocked there was no reply, and when he tried the handle he found that the door was locked. He knocked again, waited a moment and then went back to his own room.

Alone in his high room, with the sun slanting through the lattices on to the picture of Paolo Sanduzzi, Nicholas Black lapsed quietly into the final blankness of despair. There was no madness in the act, no wild ruin of reason under the impact of unexplainable terrors. It was a simple, final admission that life was a riddle without an answer, a game not worth the candle that guttered over its last, profitless gambits.

Those who won might surrender themselves a little longer to the gambler's illusion; but those who lost, as he had lost, had no recourse but to walk away with as much dignity as possible from the scattered cards and the spilt liquor, and the staling smoke of the last cigars.

He had staked everything on this last play—money, the patronage of the Contessa, the opportunity to re-establish his reputation as an artist, the hope to justify even the maimed and incomplete manhood with which nature had endowed him. But now he knew that he had been playing, as always, against marked cards and with every pack stacked against him. His own nature, society, the law, the Church, all conspired to shut him out from the simplest and most necessary satisfactions of existence. He was stripped clean—bankrupt even of hope. There was no place for him to go but back to the half-world, which had already laughed him out.

The Church would take him back, but it would exact a brutal price: submission of intellect and will, repentance, and a life-long bitter denial. The grey inquisitors like Meredith would purge him relentlessly, then coax him forward with the stale carrots of eternity. He could not face it and he would not. No man should be asked to pay for the freaks and whims of a sardonic Creator.

He got up, walked to the writing desk, pulled a sheet of note-paper towards him, scribbled three hasty lines and signed them. Then he picked up a palette knife, walked to the picture on the easel and began coolly and methodically, to cut the canvas to pieces.

Never in his life had Meredith felt so ashamed of himself. Whatever the past sins of Nicholas Black, whatever the follies of his thwarted nature, he had still been the subject of calumny, and he had revealed in himself a deep and not unnoble impulse to good. Kindness might have nurtured it, gentleness might have bent it to better purpose. Yet his only comment, his only offering as a priest, had been a cloddish and brutal indiscretion. There was no excuse for it. To invent one would be a hypocrisy. The charity he thought to have acquired through Giacomo Nerone was a monstrous sham, which had failed him when he needed it most. He was what he had been at the beginning: an empty man, devoid of humanity and godliness.

The thought haunted his shallow sleep and when he woke in the late cool, it was still with him. There was only one thing to do. He must make an apology for his grossness and try again to make a humane contact with Black, who must be suffering greatly.

He got up, washed and tidied himself and walked back along the corridor to the painter's room. The door was ajar this time, but when he knocked there was no answer. He pushed it open and looked in. There was no one there. The bed was unruffled. But the picture of Paolo Sanduzzi stood on its easel by the window, slashed to ribbons.

Meredith stepped into the room and walked over to look at it. As he passed the writing desk his eye was caught by a single sheet of paper lying on the green baize top. The superscription bore his own name:

My dear Meredith,
  I've taken the Almighty's jokes all my life. Yours is one too many. You'll be able to make the old sermon on me— Galilean, thou hast conquered. All the best preachers use it.
Yours,
  Nicholas Black.

Seconds ticked past unnoticed as he stood there, staring down at the paper in his pale hand. Then the full horror of it burst on him and he hurried from the room, down the stairs, along the gravelled path, shouting for the gatekeeper to open for him. The old man opened the grille, rubbed the sleep out of his eyes and then trotted out into the roadway to watch the crazy Monsignor pounding up the hills with his cassock flapping about his heels.

It was quite late when they were missed and later still when they were found—Nicholas Black swinging aimlessly from a branch of the olive tree and Blaise Meredith prone at the roots of it. At first it seemed they were both dead, but Aldo Meyer heard the faint beating of Meredith's heart and sent for Father Anselmo, while Pietro drove the Contessa's car like a madman to the Bishop's Palace in Valenta.

Now the thing he had feared most of all was come to pass. He was trying to explain himself—not to justify, because he knew that justification was impossible—but just to explain to God how it had happened, and how he had lapsed, without any intention of malice.

But there was no God, there was only a mist and silence and, out of the silence, the echo of his own voice.

"... I was sleeping, you see. I didn't know he was gone. I ran to find him and he was already hanging there. I couldn't get him down; I wasn't strong enough. I thought he might be alive and I tried to pray with him. I said the Acts of Contrition and of Love—of Faith and Charity, hoping he would hear and join me in them. But he didn't hear. After that I don't remember. . . ."

"But God would hear and God would remember."

The voice came to him out of the mist, familiar, but far away.

"I failed him. I wanted to help, but I failed."

"No one can judge failure but the Almighty."

"A man must judge himself first."

"And then commit himself to mercy."

The mists cleared slowly and the voice came nearer; then he saw bending over him the face of Aurelio, Bishop of Valenta. He stretched out one emaciated hand and the Bishop held it between his own.

"I am dying, My Lord."

Aurelio, the Bishop, smiled at him, the old, brotherly ironic smile.

"As a man should, my son. With dignity and among friends."

He looked beyond the Bishop and saw them grouped at the foot of his bed. Anne de Sanctis, Aldo Meyer, Nina Sanduzzi, old Anselmo in his stained cassock with the sacramental stole round his neck. He asked weakly:

"Where is the boy?"

"With Rosetta," said Nina in dialect. "They are friends."

"I'm glad of that," said Blaise Meredith.

"You shouldn't talk too much," said Meyer.

"It's my last chance, Doctor." He rolled his head on the pillow and turned back to the Bishop. "Nicholas Black . . . you'll give him a Christian burial?"

"Who am I to deny him?" said Aurelio, the Bishop.

"I . . . I wrote a letter to Your Lordship."

"I have it. Everything will be done."

"How are the oranges?"

"Ripening well."

"You should . . . send some to His Eminence. . . . They might help him to understand. A present from me."

"I'll do that."

"Will Your Lordship confess me, please? I'm very tired."

Aurelio, the Bishop, took the grubby stole from the neck of Father Anselmo and laid it on his own shoulders; and when the others had gone from the room, he bent forward to hear the last tally of the last sins of Monsignor Blaise Meredith. When he had absolved him, he called the others back and they knelt around the bed holding lighted tapers while old Anselmo gave him the Viaticum, which is the only food for the longest journey in the world.

When he had received it, he lay back with closed eyes and folded hands, while the room filled slowly with the murmur of the old prayers for the departing spirit. A long time after, after they were finished, Meredith opened his eyes and said, quite clearly:

"I was afraid so long. Now, it's so very easy."

A faint rigor shook him and his head lolled slackly on to the white pillow.

"He's dead," said Aldo Meyer.

"He is with God," said Aurelio, the Bishop.

Eugenio Cardinal Marotta sat in his high-backed chair, behind the buhl desk on which his secretary had just laid the day's papers. Beside him was a small box of polished wood, in which were six golden oranges, each nestling in a bed of cotton-wool. In his hands was a letter from His Lordship, the Bishop of Valenta. He was reading it, slowly, for the third time:

... I regret to inform Your Eminence that Monsignor Blaise Meredith died yesterday morning at nine o'clock in the full possession of his faculties and after receiving the full rites of our Holy Mother the Church.

I regret him, as I regret few men. I mourn him as the brother he had become to me. He had great courage, a singular honesty of mind and a humanity of whose richness he was never fully aware. I know he will be a great loss to Your Eminence and to the Church.

Before he died, he charged me to apologise to Your Eminence for what he termed the failure of his mission. It was not a failure. His researches have thrown great light on the life and character of the Servant of God, Giacomo Nerone, and have proved him, in the moral if not the canonical sense, a man of great sanctity. I am still doubtful whether any good will be served by advancing this Cause even as far as the Ordinary Court, but I have no doubt at all of the good that has already been done through the influence of Giacomo Nerone and the late Monsignor Meredith. An erring priest has returned to God, a child has been kept from great moral harm and a lost and unhappy woman has been given light enough to seek remedies for her condition.

In the worldly sense, these are small and insignificant things. In the true sense of our Faith they are very great ones, and in them I, who am normally sceptical, have seen clearly the finger of God.

The oranges which I send you are a last gift from Monsignor Meredith. They are from my own plantation—first fruits of a new strain which we have imported from California. Next year, God willing, we hope to have more of these trees to distribute on a co-operative basis to local growers. Monsignor

Meredith was much interested in this work; and, had he lived, I think he would have liked to take part in it. His request to send this gift was made on his deathbed. He said—and I quote exactly: 'They might help him to understand.' Your Eminence will no doubt understand the allusion.

The body of Monsignor Meredith is now lying in the Church of the Madonna of the Dolours in Gemello Minore, from whence it will be buried tomorrow, in newly consecrated ground, close to the tomb of Giacomo Nerone. I shall myself officiate at the Mass and the interment.

The usual Masses will, of course, be said, and I myself shall make special, permanent remembrance in my own Masses—as Your Eminence will no doubt wish to do in yours.

I understand that Monsignor Meredith once made a request to be buried in Your Eminence's church in Rome. The reason for his change of heart may be of some final interest. In his last letter to me, written on the eve of his death, he says: 'Rome is very far—and here, for the first time, I have found myself as a man and a priest.'

I am humbled by the thought that many of us have lived longer and done much less.

Yours fraternally in Christ Jesus,
Aurelio +
Bishop of Valenta.

His Eminence laid the letter down on his desk and leaned back in his chair, thinking about it. He was getting old, it seemed. Or perhaps he had lived too long in Rome. He could neither read a letter nor judge a man.

The man who had died was not the man he had sent away—a desiccated pedant with the dust of the libraries thick on his heart.

The Bishop who had written the first request for a Devil's Advocate was not this Aurelio, with his trenchant mind and his more than a hint of irony.

Or perhaps they were the same men, and only he was changed—another victim to the insidious temptations of princes: pride, power, blindness and coldness of heart. Christ had made bishops and a Pope—but never a cardinal. Even the name held more than a hint of illusion—*cardo*, a hinge—as if they were the hinges on which the gates of Heaven were hung. Hinges they might be, but the hinges were useless metal, unless anchored firmly into the living fabric of the Church, whose stones were the poor, the humble, the ignorant, the sinning and the loving, the forgotten of the princes, but never the forgotten of God.

It was a disturbing thought and he promised himself to return to it at the time of his evening examination of conscience. He was a methodical man and now he had other things to attend to. He took out of his pocket a small leather notebook and wrote, under the date for the following day, 'Remembrance in Mass . . . Meredith.'

Then he put the notebook back in his pocket, glanced quickly through his correspondence, and rang to have his car brought round to the entrance. The time was a quarter to eleven. It was the second Friday of the month, the day when the Prefect of the Sacred Congregation of Rites waited on His Holiness the Pope to discuss, among other things, the beatification and canonisation of Servants of God.

Fontana Paperbacks

Fontana is a leading paperback publisher of fiction and non-fiction, with authors ranging from Alistair MacLean, Agatha Christie and Desmond Bagley to Solzhenitsyn and Pasternak, from Gerald Durrell and Joy Adamson to the famous Modern Masters series.

In addition to a wide-ranging collection of internationally popular writers of fiction, Fontana also has an outstanding reputation for history, natural history, military history, psychology, psychiatry, politics, economics, religion and the social sciences.

All Fontana books are available at your bookshop or newsagent; or can be ordered direct. Just fill in the form and list the titles you want.

_____

FONTANA BOOKS, Cash Sales Department, G.P.O. Box 29, Douglas, Isle of Man, British Isles. Please send purchase price, plus 8p per book. Customers outside the U.K. send purchase price, plus 10p per book. Cheque, postal or money order. No currency.

NAME (Block letters) _____

ADDRESS _____

_____

_____